UNEXPECTED OBSESSION

Unexpected Love - Book 1

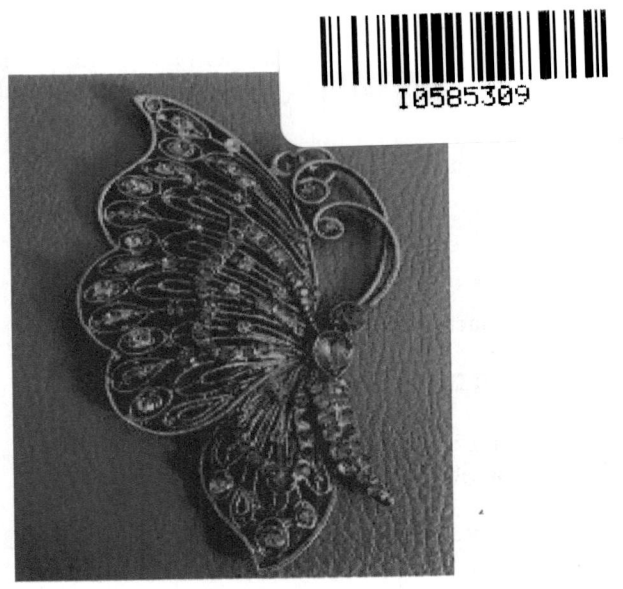

Barbara Strickland

ISBN – BOIHXFVG7Y (eBook)
ISBN – 978-0-6480715-0-1
ISBN – 978-0-6480715-6-3 (IS print)

Brief introduction to Unexpected Passion and Unexpected
Celebration
Copyright © 2021 Barbara Strickland

Cover design and illustration by Christopher Brunton
http://www.cjbrunton.wix.com/brunton-illustration

Author's note: This book was written in Australia and uses
British/Australian spelling conventions such as 'colour' instead of
'color', and 'ise' endings instead of 'ize' on words like 'realize'.
Some words will also have double ll in its spelling e.g., travel will
become travelling.

Disclaimer: This book contains explicit language and sex scenes.

Stories behind the Mask

Dedication

My mother scribbled poetry whenever she could. My father read voraciously. Every Saturday, my library day, my father would ask me to bring back books on all manner of subjects from the Paddington Library. A love of reading and literature came easily. Thank you.

To my dearest friend Gail. I carry the memory of your courage. You are now with someone who will love you and keep you safe forever. I miss you. (You were the first to encourage me in this and I promise we will make it to Norfolk Island. It's on the agenda and I promise to catch you up on everything.)

Acknowledgements

Pat, I couldn't have done this without your help as I am pretty sure the commas might have traumatised me for life. Your willingness to read my work and keep me buoyant, your ability to listen and to look up things has been invaluable. Your friendship is spectacular and not because of those pesky commas.

Tara, you are my soulmate.

Julia, you are a blessing. Alyson, Kay, and Melanie, thank you for your continuing friendship and help. Sue, I am so grateful for your friendship and your encouragement. Rosie and Vanessa, you were there at my fledgling start and Jackie R, I will never forget your generosity. Sean and Kai, you two were the best and always will be in my eyes.

I am also grateful to my children. Every time I see how well you live your lives, I feel a little lighter. I did well despite the fears I would fail you. This time I am hoping not to fail me.

I'd also like to add my special thanks to my cousin, Rita, for keeping my spirits up for the last four years. Thank you to anyone who has put up with me when my head was somewhere else, especially my brother Charles, who thinks I am so much more than I am.

A huge thank you to Luke for never failing to answer any questions and for the support you have given me and so many others on the writing journey. I think it is incredible that you continue to do so. I'm not surprised though because Indie authors are incredibly generous. I would run out of room if I began mentioning all the wonderful people in the Indie Community I have been privileged to come across over the last few years.

That includes you, Ms R, for you are the wise owl on my shoulder and the butterfly wings that keep me afloat, even when I lose hope.

Lastly and most humbly I thank the reader who has picked up my book and is now about to enter this world I have created. Bless you.

Barbara Strickland
October 2021

*To all those
fortunate enough
to find their
soulmate
then be grateful
and
treasure
what you have
always*

Soul-Kissed
(Nico's Lament from Emotions in Eruption)

Awareness so profound
I tremble when you are around.
Adaption so intense
that my intelligence makes no sense.
You live inside my head.
You will live until I am dead.
Chemistry is just a word
to minimise what has occurred.
I bent and kissed your mouth
and to my heart your taste went south.
It fooled me into thinking
love would not cloud my sinking.

I thought I could just stimulate
returning later to manipulate.
Selfishness drove my need
as my ego fought to feed.
What we got was so much more
than I ever dreamed to explore.
I think on reflection we soul kissed.
Fearfully I brutally dismissed.
Then I discovered I was blind
for soul-kissers cannot unbind.

We are forever forged and fused
and those who watch are well amused.
I thought I played a mortal game
with courage then to take the blame.
But when you soul-kiss you become a fool
and fall into that deep and endless pool
where no escape will let you free
where no peace will ever be
for you must pay with deep regret.
Soul-kissing is not something you can forget.

Chapter 1

The scrape of the chair on the cream tiles unnerved her, the noise an intrusion echoing throughout the room. The need to hide the trembling of her limbs uppermost in her mind, she sat down at the dining room table. Uninvited, the act of sitting bolstered her confidence. If the energy she had expended walking through the door, pushing past him hadn't drained her, she might have laughed at the two people battling to deal with her audacity. She might, she thought to herself, have felt embarrassed at her own behaviour.

"What the devil are you doing here? You can't be serious!" Domenico spat the words the way a dragon spouted fire.

His height, the dark eyes intense and glaring, and the tight mouth were enough on their own to make her nervous, without the additional menace in his voice. Angelia looked searchingly at the man in front of her. A stranger in place of the gangly sixteen-year-old she remembered towering over her. With black hair, just short of military precision and a close-shaven face Domenico appeared ready to step onto the red carpet at a Hollywood film premiere. The black suit, the pristine white shirt, and the bold red tie presented as both immaculate and edgy. Certainly, nothing existed of the boy she had once worshipped with her seven-year-old heart. At twenty-eight years of age her height had caught up enough to allow her to meet his eyes if they were standing. From her seated position, he held enough power to have her fear the man he had become, and the chillingly impregnable barriers he projected. *Papa, I know I promised to get our family back. I don't know if I can.*

She swallowed and concentrated on the less than friendly pair. A sharp pain in her chest swayed her stance. *How could Gina, Papa's stepsister, with her embittered features, resemble Papa this much?*

Straightening her shoulders, she reflected on the family history. Nonno had remarried after Nonna Maria, Gina's mother, died. Nonna Enza, his new wife had been a distant relative. She'd had a son, Antonio, Lia's Papa. Enza had refused to name the father of her child causing a scandal, leaving her vulnerable to slurs. Ostracised, she had been eager to enter into a marriage which would offer the means to look after her son in comfort. Gina, bereft of a mother eagerly embraced Enza. A quirk of nature declared Papa and Gina resembled one another. Enchanted by this, Gina had claimed the two-year-old child as her very own live toy. An unpleasant icy tingling slid the length of Lia's spine. *One terrible moment in the past had shattered so many relationships, so many lives.*

"I'm talking to you. What the hell are you doing here?" Domenico's tone did not shy away from intimidation.

"I rang, remember?" Lia met his gaze bravely, aware that flinching would give him the upper hand.

"Domenico, you told her not to come. Why is she here?"

Witnessing Gina clutching her chest as she spoke, and then Domenico move swiftly to prevent his mother's unsteady gait causing a fall, Lia's stomach gave a silent heave. Unsure what to do, a new sound had her spinning her head to her right, revealing a newcomer to the drama. Recognising her Uncle Lucio, Lia braced herself for another emotional outburst. Lucio instead, remained silent, his head at a thoughtful angle. The controlled blandness of expression puzzled Lia. She remembered a different man, one with an expressive face full of warmth, not this quiet man who seemed out of place in his own home. Refusing to let herself be distracted she faced Domenico and his mother.

"You're my family. I have every right to be here."

With a calm belying her racing heart, she tossed the letter she had written to them a scarce few months ago on the table. Returned unopened. Unread like all the other letters her father had sent to his sister over the years. She wondered why it didn't burst into flames under the combined looks garnered from the room's occupants.

"Since a problem exists with the Italian postal service, I thought I'd deliver my letter to you in person. Funny thing though, the mark on the envelope returning it to sender clearly states Catania. Never mind. I have it here now. You know the letter I mean, the one about my father's accident. The one telling you he died."

Lia released the last bit of air she'd been holding in, speculating how long she could have held that same breath. Her determination not to be rattled could become an obsession if the current atmosphere held. The apartment looked familiar, spotless from floor to ceiling. The dining table, a dark, rich mahogany took centre stage. Uncle Lucio had made it himself, and that little bit of knowledge from so long ago gave her confidence against Domenico's looming male presence.

"Is this how people in Australia behave? They walk into someone's home unannounced and uninvited?"

She continued her perusal of the room, stopping to stare at the older man, ignoring the younger one's harsh tone. Shaking hands she could hide behind her back, the fear in her eyes might be another matter.

Standing beside the cream leather lounge where he had placed his mother, the aura he exuded seemed less threatening, a deception. She chose to focus on the lounge, still in excellent condition. Good pieces lasted, she mused. With care they incorporated wear and tear as memories. Yet her aunt had willingly thrown away a lifetime of memories of the only family she had? *Surely people mattered more than things?*

"I told you on the phone we knew, wasn't that enough? Your father is dead..." Domenico stopped short as his mother let out an anguished moan. His face hardened further. "In English, so no misunderstandings prevail – we don't need to know any more about him or you. Naturally, we sympathise but that's as far as it goes. We aren't interested in any letters, and we aren't interested in you."

"Well, isn't that too fucking bad!" Lia narrowed her eyes, daring him to look away and taking the time to enunciate every word slowly and in English. "I'm not going anywhere."

Domenico's mouth tightened, and she smiled. *That should teach you not to fuck with me. Speaking to me in English, like I'm a stranger, an outsider. Not working on this girl, not in this lifetime, dickhead.*

"I thought my aunt," she continued, switching back to Italian, her voice frigid, "might need a sympathetic ear. After all, he was the only family she had left."

"Listen to me, little girl..." Gina's answer came in the form of a snarl.

Pain reverberated in Lia's heart, the heart searching to find the aunt she remembered. Gina, still a pretty woman despite the lines of discord marring her forehead, her uncoloured hair needing a trim, eyed her like something rancid. Lia swallowed back a retort, wondering if bitterness could change someone this much.

"I don't need or want you here. How I feel is my business, so get out. Go home!"

The painful barbs, Gina's obvious lack of regard or affection for her, hurt. Anger rose only to be swiftly replaced by fear as her aunt's face paled further, veins prominent in the shiny, moisture-slick forehead. Laboured breathing hung heavy in the room. A panic attack, Lia hazarded a guess, remaining silent as

Domenico whispered calming words. Despite his mouth pressed to Gina's ear, his dark eyes fierce and piercing, were glued to Lia. His gaze heated her insides, burned a hole in her already overwrought chest.

Nothing is going to plan. This is horrible. The internal dialogue ended abruptly when her peripheral vision noticed her uncle on the move towards Gina, only to halt at the vicious look Domenico threw at his father. Lia swallowed again, bit the inside of her cheek, and willed herself to remain still. *God there's so much happening here! These people! I want to run away but I'll look weak. The letters were supposed to bring a ruptured family to their senses.* Over the years Papa had written his sister hundreds of letters. All of them had been returned. Lia had convinced herself it would be easy to persuade her aunt to read them. Without her father's tangible presence, she stood little chance. The naivety of her plan made her shudder.

"You heard my mother! Get out!"

Domenico's voice, a bombardment to her ears, disheartened her further adding to her already emotional state. She bit down hard on her bottom lip, drawing blood, and flinched. His watchful eyes were daunting. She spun herself around and wiped her mouth.

"And you," Domenico barked in Italian to his father, "go get her medication, or has this one dazzled you with her looks, the way her slut of a mother did."

Lia flinched again but forced herself to turn and face Domenico. He continued the uncomfortable focus on her mouth, satisfaction at Lia's reaction evident in his raised brows and half-smirk. *Arsehole. You miscalculated with that little comment.* He had reasons to say what he did concerning Marissa. His words, unnecessary and taunting in this highly charged moment, had further gouged raw nerves. Purpose and strength flowed into Lia.

She straightened and returned his stare. "I'm staying. I'll sleep on the floor if I have to."

She rose to her feet, pushed all doubts to the side, strode confidently to her luggage and picked up her small backpack. A quick rummage produced a plastic folder. She carried it over to her aunt, halted purposefully in front of her, ignoring Domenico.

"This has every letter my father wrote. I am not leaving until you read them, all of them. He loved you.

He needed you, not your punishment. I know your reasons were good ones, but they belong in the past. It may be too late for him; it's not too late for me to do this for him. You're going to read every word. He deserves to be remembered."

"Who do you think you're dealing with here?" Domenico stepped between Lia and his mother.

The disdain he cast her way, undeserved, only served to strengthen her resolve. "I wasn't talking to you."

With those words, she shrugged as if she hadn't a care in the world, swivelled and retraced her steps to place the bundle in her hand back into her bag. The relief to be away from the unyielding stare nearly buckled her knees.

"You're a rude, arrogant little bitch!" His voice, a low hiss behind her, his tone menacing, the English words as intimidating as the man hovering close.

"It's obvious we're related then," she replied calmly in Italian, fiddling with the zipper of the leather backpack. "Although, arsehole suits you much better. It's more masculine."

She spun back to him then, holding that last word long enough to let him know she wholeheartedly doubted the latter. Smiling inwardly, she acknowledged his tirade as mild compared to the words he might have used in his own language. That was the beauty of the Italian language, she thought, letting herself be distanced from the scene in front of her to recuperate. Swearing and name-calling were extremely creative.

His reply, a supercilious sneer, annoyed Lia further; she didn't censor what came next. "Perhaps, a rude arrogant bastard is more apt? Bastard being the operative word, I'd imagine."

A gasp from her aunt and the morphing of Domenico's features into a terrifying anger effectively silenced her from saying more. His body coiled tight. Lia felt his physical battle to control himself, to consciously relax the tension, finally settling for a dismissive look. Her own body remained tense with shame; nasty, so not her style. She wanted to erase her words, didn't know how, and backing down, not an option. Fortunately, she had an unexpected reprieve from the one other person who might also have taken offence at her words.

"Leave her alone. This is my house and I say she stays."

"Well, of course old man, you would come to her rescue. You fucked her mother in this very home, so what now? The daughter?"

Lia recoiled at the crude words Lucio endured: resolute, not even a blink. Lia found it painful to watch, especially since her aunt seemed unmoved by this interchange. The skin of her face had paled to a grey. Not the steely hue of her thick hair, but a pasty looking imitation.

"Take your mother to her room. She needs her pills and to lie down. Keep your opinions to yourself. I repeat – this is my house."

His quiet voice held an underlying strength. Not surprisingly, Domenico obeyed. Lia reminded herself to breathe.

"Thank you! Uncle Lucio, I'm so sorry. My manners..."

"This is a complicated household. My son took it easy on you. Next time he won't be as pleasant but at least he knows you're a worthy opponent." At her rude badly smothered sound, he laughed. "Believe me, he let you off lightly. He is possessive and protective where his mother is concerned, and he was worried about her. Me, he doesn't care too much for."

The silver flecks in his hair didn't detract from the exceptionally handsome man in front of her. The facial bone structure with its strong jaw line, and the close to perfect oval shape, was reminiscent of statues of Roman gods. Taller than many Italian men, at about half a head under six foot, away from his son's piercing gaze, an air of the old confident Lucio surfaced. Both men had been blessed with looks. The son more so because whilst they shared the same facial structure, Domenico also had a look of Gina around his eyes, eyes dark like the most decadent chocolate, with the long lashes women coveted. Her father's eyes, eyes she shared. Without them she would have been a clone of Marissa, her mother.

"You're different to what I expected. You always seemed so sure of everything. I noticed as young as I was, and I remembered how absurdly good-looking you were. Now, you're..."

"More charming?" He said, arching one eyebrow.

She couldn't help indulging his use of that word with a small laugh. She had been thinking it. He shrugged self-deprecatingly and in that small moment before his eyelids dropped, Lia saw the extent of his sadness.

"Your aunt, my wife, is a hard woman. She lost a child and did considerable damage to her leg. I'm sure you know what happened." He waited for Lia to acknowledge his words. At her nod he continued. "I think it's a lost battle. Her feelings and her ways are ingrained. She doesn't want to change. I am telling you, so you won't be disappointed..."

Lia waited, let her eyes roam his features, noting the mellowness, the approachability and liking the manner in which the edge had been rubbed right off him. Back then his good looks, his surety had frightened her smaller self.

"Disappointed...?"

"Come, I will take you to your room."

"Disappointed? Uncle Lucio, you haven't answered..." She followed as she spoke and entered the spare bedroom.

"When you don't find the woman, the one in your memories. But try anyway to find her. Certainly, Domenico won't make it easy. Ignore him. You are welcome to stay. I think you will be comfortable here. There is plenty of space for your things."

"Thank you."

"I meant what I said. This is my house. However, you will be sharing a bathroom with Domenico."

Lucio's raised eyebrows made her smile. "Is he still a clean freak?"

Lucio laughed quietly in reply. "Definitely. Everything must have a place, usually where he puts it. Remember..."

"Don't leave a wet sink."

He laughed at her interjection, and it warmed her heart.

"You'll find paper towels to wipe the basin down. Can you cope?"

"You're enjoying this, aren't you?" She smiled, a wry reaction to the twinkle in his eyes.

"It might be what this family needs." The twinkle disappeared, replaced with a more sombre look. "Angelia, Domenico is harsh, survives by following rules, his rules, but he is a good person. High expectations and little tolerance and yet for all that, he has never shirked family responsibility, including where I am concerned, when we all know I failed him."

"No."

"Yes. I didn't understand him and let it show. Even as a little girl, you comprehended in ways I never could." He paused, reconsidered his next words, and opted to be the host. "I think it's time I made you a coffee instead of all this serious talking."

"Yes, please." Lia could love this man in front of her. "Uncle Lucio, will she be alright? She didn't look well."

"She gets emotional and needs medication for her heart. Your aunt...your aunt is stronger than she thinks, and stubborn. She didn't believe you'd come. Gina hates confrontations, and to be honest she has hung on to her bitterness for so long she doesn't know anything else. Seeing you is...conflicting. She loved you so much. We all did."

He headed for the kitchen. Lia watched, frowned, nibbling at her lip, torn by the gravity of the situation.

"Are you sure about this?"

Halting, the swift intake of air loud in the room, he kept his back to Lia. "Why don't you settle into your room? Stop thinking so hard. We have time for that."

His words made her feel safe yet unbearably sad. Pulling the bedspread away, she realised she would need sheets and her bags. She blinked and Lucio had returned with her suitcase, sheets, and towels. She blinked again and he had vanished, moving gracefully, a trait he shared with his son. Lia sat on the bed, wondering what she had got herself into. Reality existed outside this room and all of it uncomfortable. Eating, sleeping, sharing a bathroom in a house where two of the occupants wanted her gone, terrified her.

Lucio appeared with the coffee, and a thoughtfully prepared tray containing biscuits, cheese, and olives. Unobtrusively, he lowered the things he carried onto the small bedside table respecting her need to assimilate with her surroundings.

"I've brought you a spare set of keys." Pausing, he raised his head. "They will fight you. Ignore them and treat this as your home. Eat when we eat. Gina will feed you. It is her way, and it might provide an avenue for discussion, or not." He shrugged, looking self-conscious at Lia's intent stare. "She cooks for me, washes and irons my clothes despite the fact we haven't shared much else for twenty years, and she will do the same for you and hate you just as much. She's like that."

"Why? Why are you allowing this?

"I owe Antonio. He was a good man, one of the best, my friend not only my brother-in-law. The past is a heavy burden. Maybe you are the key to change. I am so tired of the cold. Today for the first time I felt warmth. You've brought the sun. I want it to stay."

"Solare," she whispered to his slightly bent retreat. That had been his word for her back then, teasing her, calling Lia his little bit of sunshine. She sat for a long time after he left. Dinner that evening wasn't pleasant, but she stayed, refusing to be baited by either mother or son.

Chapter 2

Gina would play old records on an antiquated record player as she did the housework. Sometimes she would sing, her voice soft and sweet and unexpected from someone who had seemingly forgotten how to smile. Lia would join in and though Gina ignored her, she felt seen in those brief moments. A fortnight of being ignored except in the evenings when Lucio returned from work hit hard. The ignoring did have its merits she thought, recalling the encounter with Domenico which had come close to sending her home.

"Don't you know to knock?" Lia frowned as *Domenico barged into the room Lucio had given her.*

"This is my home, not yours, remember?"

"What do you want?"

"To give you a friendly word of warning, my dear sweet little cousin."

"Step-cousin more like it, and the little bit of blood we share is about two generations removed, thank you very much. Not that it makes a difference. Either way I'm pretty sure your family welcome would still be underwhelming." Lia fought to restrain her smirk.

"I'm watching you. I'm not my father to be swayed by looks."

Lia pulled back on her thoughts, checking on her aunt only to find herself ignored as usual. Eyes fixed, Lia stared at the computer screen needing her attention. Her mind refused to cooperate preferring to return to the memory of that day.

Insolently, Nico had contemplated her body from the pale pink polished toenails and bare feet, stopping only when he reached her mouth. Uneasy she had fought biting down on her lip, her nature not one to give an opponent the upper hand.

"My mother has been through too much in her life. Hurt her in any fashion and I'll make you sorry in ways you can't possibly imagine. I won't let a 'stronza' like you contaminate the air around her."

"So, you can use the Italian language when it suits you. Domenico, seriously, what is your problem? You don't know me. How am I a bitch? How can you judge someone you don't know? I'm not here to hurt anyone."

"Forgive my foolish assumption. It couldn't be because your behaviour in forcing yourself on us suggests no morals or manners."

"Thanks for the little chat. I think the only 'stronzo' here is you. I've been trying so hard to be polite, to avoid arguments. Enough. It's time for you to put a sock in it."

His jaw tightened in disdainful and dismissive amusement. "A sock? Is this some clever Australianism you are imparting on my poor, ignorant brain?"

"Yes, I said sock. To be exact I said put a sock in it. It seems you're not familiar with this expression. I'm surprised, as I've been quite impressed at your command of English."

Domenico lifted an eyebrow and waited, complete distaste for her evident in his inspection.

"How can I explain?"

She'd reached saturation point. Words eluded her. If he wasn't making nasty comments, he acted as if she didn't exist and spoke around her. Domenico presumed and accused, and continually taunted. Remaining friendly, non-combative and searching constantly for the warmth and affection of the past exhausted and disappointed daily. Furious with him for taking such obvious pleasure in hurting her, she leaned into her chair to gather momentum and allowed the wheels to carry her directly in front of him.

"I said, put a sock in it, right here." Lia stretched over as she spoke and grabbed his crotch and twisted. "A sock in here will ensure that everyone understands how big a dick you actually are, not have, but are. If as I suspect your dick is as pathetic as your behaviour, then it appears you may have an issue, a small one but an issue."

Her pleasure at having shocked him lived a short life when her wrist found itself imprisoned by a hand with a determined destination. With cold precision he forced her hand to fully envelop him, a 'him', or 'it', bigger and harder than she needed to know. It throbbed. She squirmed. A feeling she couldn't consider caused her hand to flutter against him and he, it, the thing she couldn't give a name to, jerked against her fingers. For a split second she pushed against him slowly, curiously fascinated by the way 'it' seemed to shape itself to her hand, and the way 'it' felt, hard and soft at the same time. Common sense snapped her back to reality and she tried to pull away.

"You think you are so smart! You foolish little girl! You have no idea what you're up against. Don't ever touch me again unless you're invited, or you will get much more than you bargained for."

She heard herself make a small angry sound, struggled not to grimace at both the pain of his hold and the way her face flooded with colour. She tugged harder to escape the pressure of the hand holding her in place, the warmth in her cheeks a powerful incentive. It did nothing except increase the smug look on his face.

"You already seem to have the more. Feels good, doesn't it? Or at least it does to me. I guess my dick doesn't discriminate as well as I do."

He relaxed his hold, caught up in his own cleverness. Taking the opportunity, Lia squeezed and twisted hard enough to hurt, and heard the hitch in Domenico's breathing. He retaliated by tightening his grip on her wrist, forcing her to relinquish her hold. The pain had been worth his surprise at her attack.

Satisfaction bloomed until she caught the blaze of heat in those dark eyes, sending her heartbeat haywire.

"Well, well, well, it seems to me you have snippets of your mother in you, don't you? Like playing with dicks, do we?"

"I don't know about playing, but in your case 'dick' is the point I was trying to make." She redoubled her efforts to free her hand.

He exerted more pressure, keeping her hand in place. "What a clever play on words. You do seem to enjoy the word 'dick'. Afraid to say 'cock'."

The flame of heat in his eyes contrasted sharply with the coldness in his voice. His use of the word cock had shocked her, the inappropriateness distracting. Her hand relaxed, giving him control. Instinctively her fingers spread to cover him, stirring her addled brain further by creating an odd connection to the more intimate parts of her body. Lia felt sick, glaring at the face sculpted in stone but unable to prevent the tremors.

Domenico let her go. She wiped her hand ruthlessly on her jeans. The stone face relaxed, allowed laughter before shutting down into a semblance of cruelty. Lia was smart enough to recognise she was in over her head but had trouble letting the situation go.

"Disgusting, you are disgusting!" she muttered, completely flustered and furious and not at all able to understand a situation Nico had manipulated to his advantage.

"Really? I fucking loved it. Want me to return the favour? It might add a whole new dimension to our relationship."

"Arsehole!"

"Why? Because I won 'this round'? I always win. If you don't like it, leave."

Nico walked out, leaving her shaken and puzzled, and dismayed at the fact that she had referred to him as Nico even if in her mind. Why that small fact fazed her the most, considering the entire situation, she preferred not to think about.

"Hey. I don't like being ignored. Did he teach you the words to these songs?"

The sound of her aunt's voice brought her back to the present. Unprepared for the social interaction, Lia could barely contain her excitement. Looking up from her computer, she opted for casual eye contact, giving herself time to reply.

"Yes. Or sometimes it would be Mama, especially when she was sick. It helped her pass the time."

"Always the old songs, he liked the old songs, especially this one. Ha! *Calabria Mia* of all things!" Gina huffed, ignoring any mention of Lia's mother.

"It's what it represented, Aunt Gina. Sicily, Calabria or anywhere else still meant Italians far from home. Their sadness and isolation. Please read his letters," Lia asked, not ashamed of the pleading note in her voice.

"So determined!" Gina huffed again.

"Yes. You owe it to your brother."

"I don't owe anybody anything. I did nothing. It was done to me, remember?" Gina paused a moment, circling away towards the kitchen. She swivelled glancing slyly at Lia. "Tell me, little girl, if I read one, will you tell me about the nightmares?"

"Why?" It required all of Lia's self-control not to react to the sudden change in atmosphere.

"I'm curious about you. I don't remember you as such a rude child. I can't help but wonder if maybe guilt at your behaviour is manifesting in your dreams. It can't be easy to be where you are so obviously unwanted."

Lia shut down her computer, trying hard not to let the hurt show. Gina's face, hard to read at the best of times, still wore a sly look, one she lost rapidly when she found Lia standing in front of her. Eyes widened at the sudden proximity, but she remained silent, happy to wait Lia out.

"You're so determined to be the wicked, hateful witch, aren't you? Here's your chance to gloat. It's true. The situation is about guilt. Not exactly the way you might imagine but certainly about guilt."

Lia lifted her arms to the back of her dress, unzipped it, revolving slowly to give Gina the full effect. Slowly, she eased the dress aside so that Gina could follow the unsightly-looking pink line winding to the front of her body. On hearing Gina's in-drawn breath, Lia cringed; she didn't want pity. Then again, pity was an honest emotion, and Lia would take whatever she could get.

"You were there? In the car? No one told us."

"Does it matter? It doesn't make my father less dead, does it, or me any less guilty for surviving."

A gasp then a tangible silence as Lia manoeuvred her arms to refasten the blue denim dress. She winced at the touch of soft hands over hers to help the slide of the zip.

"How?"

Lia turned and stared at her aunt, debating the wisdom of revealing so much. *Did Gina need the unpleasant details, the reality of the accident? Would it make her more amiable, more likely to remember the little brother she once adored? What if Lia could reach both the loving aunt and her father's sister?* Hoping her smile didn't reflect the bitterness she felt, she asked the question.

"What do you want to know?"

~

A long-time later, emotionally spent, Lia left the kitchen, and came back to the table to place an envelope in front of the tear-stained face of an old woman. The letter lay untouched an hour later when Lia checked on the silence filling the apartment. The quiet, Lia decided, made the already cold room colder.

She sat down. Accepting her aunt had gone out, Lia's head drooped between her hands, the letter a symbol of defeat in the household's war of nerves. *There's always tomorrow and the next day. It's not like I have to get back to work or Australia. I can work online.*

Honesty and a sense of fair play demanded she accept disappointment. Early days, she told herself. Papa wouldn't want her to give up. His arguments had been sound. *"Families,"* he'd said, *"are important; they sustain you. What happened isn't black or white, the truth isn't black or white. Maybe the facts are, this happened, that happened but the reasons are more complicated, full of grey areas. I learned the hard way, Lia. Grey softens the edges, helps us clarify what is important, and family is important.*

Lia appreciated situations could become painful, but families forgave, didn't they, she asked herself? The affectionate sister, the loving aunt who had wanted a little girl exactly like Angelia, existed, might still exist. Lia sighed. The damage had been done to Gina and despite her only brother's death, Gina couldn't let the past go. Lia wanted the affection back, needed it. Papa had been right to want this for her. Despite the angst, a companionship had begun to develop between them. Gina could deny it all she wanted but Lia felt it. She wanted to stay, wanted the familial love, wanted her superhero. She laughed at herself. *Domenico would not be an easy conquest.*

Lia shrugged. *Time to be more positive.* The teenage boy, annoyed with her persistence in following him around, had given in. The seven-year-old Lia had put her hand in his to cross the road. He had raised those dark brows. She had smiled, not at all rebuffed by his scowl. From that moment, he had indulged her every whim. *That boy, buried under harsh layers, lay waiting to be revived.* She could do it again. *I have patience and the ability to plan strategically.* Her aunt held the key to harmony. Lia needed to do some shopping for the project spinning in her head.

~

The mixture of fabrics now cut into smaller pieces proved interesting enough to encourage interaction. Pinning the squares together to make rows, a slow procedure needing concentration, had Gina fascinated. By the end of the week Gina had ceased resisting the lure of bright colours and joined Lia at the table, quietly observing, never uttering a word, and never picking up the letter waiting there every day. The battle of wills adjusted itself to quiet murmuring of appreciation. Lia hoped offering opinions would come next. The gentle lull grew, expanded to louder grunts, speaking volumes, spoiled only when Domenico came home for lunch. If looks could kill, Lia would have shrivelled up weeks ago.

This morning, an air of expectation dominated the atmosphere. Last night Gina had come in and soothed her nightmares, and then waited until Lia had fallen asleep again. Now, Gina had picked up the pieces of material to touch them, the dressmaker in her taking control. When Gina had replaced the pieces on the table, Lia swallowed, afraid to breathe, at the rustle of paper. She continued sewing, resisted the urge to cast a look across the room until her aunt put down the letter and silently shuffled away.

Lia picked it up and carried it to her room and placed it in the plastic bag. She removed another before returning the bag to the dresser drawer. Neither woman had spoken about the previous night, yet something had changed. Tomorrow, the second letter would be on the table waiting for Gina, and the next time the memories woke Lia, a hand would chase away the darkness.

~

Gina had read a letter a day for ten days, had become vocal about Lia's creation, and smiled occasionally. Gina's stubbornness, a formidable wall, somehow bent enough for companionship to flourish. Early this morning they had baked. Later they had enjoyed the cake with coffee before setting up the sewing machine. When the phone rang, and Gina looked pointedly at Lia to answer, she fought not to roll her eyes at her aunt. Domenico always rang at this time.

"Pronto."

"Where's my mother?" The voice was curt, dismissive, and distinctly annoyed. Lia thought of it as his trifecta tone, three winning ways to piss off Lia. She wondered what he would think of that little piece of Australianism. *Fuck him. Gina could have her performance.*

"Well hello to you. Yes, I'm doing well. Thanks for asking. What can I do for you? Poison in your coffee?" Any conversation they had was conducted in English.

The determination to make her feel distanced from the family, from the whole country, amused Lia.

"Leave Italy but put my mother on the phone first."

Lia held the phone towards Gina.

"Tell him I'm busy and he can talk to you." Lia bit the inside of her cheek at her aunt's little game.

"She can't talk right now. Can I take a message?" Lia smiled, knowing exactly how irate he'd be at Lia's saccharine tone, and his mother's behaviour. Lia and Nico both knew Gina received some kind of perverse pleasure from their confrontations. That the discussions were conducted in a foreign language only appeared to enhance her enjoyment. The result as usual, ended unpleasantly.

"I'll tell her," Lia kept her voice polite but her temper had its own agenda. "Please do enjoy the rest of your day."

"Why, have you packed your bags?"

"Go fuck yourself."

"Such beautiful manners. You know, as a matter of fact, I was about to follow that suggestion, but not on my own."

"You're a pig." With those words she slammed the phone down. She didn't miss the glimpse of humour on the normally dour face of her aunt. "He's not coming home for lunch and won't be home tonight either."

"Probably Francesca again!" Gina puffed her displeasure.

It hadn't taken Lia long to learn Gina only tolerated Francesca for Domenico's sake. Having met her briefly, Lia understood perfectly. A beautiful, egotistical bitch summed it up nicely.

"Intelligent enough when she can get past herself. Not a frequent event. My Nico is foolish, should know better. Still, her father is an important man…"

Gina stopped, Lia surmised, on realising she was making conversation.

"They deserve each other." Lia couldn't resist the opportunity to speak.

An icy chill in the air obliterated the pleasant atmosphere.

"Because I read the letters you think you have rights now, to criticise my son and his choice of partner?"

"No, I'm sorry. I didn't mean to say anything."

"Yes, you did. You don't like my son. I'll admit he isn't nice to you. Coming here with a total disregard for our feelings negated winning a popularity contest, especially since no thought was given to whom you may hurt or impose on, correct?"

Gina didn't wait for a reply. "He may be difficult at times. Don't pull that face. He's my son so you, you need to keep your mouth shut. I don't care what he says to you or about you, but I care what you say *about* him. Not to him, about him, so be careful."

"That isn't fair Aunt Gina. He is..."

"Don't!"

"But..."

"I said, don't! Now let me finish reading and then another coffee and you can tell me more about Sydney."

Lia knew she would lose the little ground she had gained if she persisted. She continued working in silence while her aunt went back to the letter. Daily she slammed up against the sharp, hard planes of a man who left the bathroom spotless and smelling as expensive as he did. And a man who ensured she felt excluded, marginalised in any way he could think of, without saying it directly.

She accepted that he upset her equilibrium, through his refusal to accept her back into the family fold. Their constant bickering shrouded something cavernous, because at odd times Lia celebrated that same rejection. Grateful to have Nico's room distanced from her nightly outbursts, Lia refused to reflect on her complicated reactions.

~

"Fuck!" Nico slammed the phone down on his desk in his office on the other side of the city. Something about her grated. She had walked in like she owned the place, stirring up emotions best forgotten. As if, he thought, his mother hadn't been hurt enough already with the events of the past, they now had a living reminder. In every movement, every look, the way she held her head he saw Marissa come to life. Only the eyes were different. Marissa's had been a sea green and her hair a touch lighter. Even so, the uncanny resemblance pissed him off, but Lia's mouth managed first prize for causing annoyance. The things she came out with, the acidic language despite the innocence of the perfect face.

Like the comments about his being a mamma's boy because he still lived at home. He cringed at her audacity, cringed at the way she pronounced the Italian word for mother – *mama. Was it some an Australian idiosyncrasy?* Consequently, he never missed the opportunity to incite her, taking pleasure in making her miserable, especially since he couldn't forget the way she had confronted him that day.

A part of him had applauded her recklessness. At the same time, he wanted to squash her like a fly. She had touched his dick, attacked perhaps the better phrase. He had never felt such anger or such a heated response. How he had managed to stay in control of both his temper and his body, he would never know. Her defiance had aroused him, had unleashed a heat he had not thought possible. It stilled burned. *That one moment...her hand shaping...fuck her.* Why couldn't she take the hints and go back to Australia? He gave them out often enough.

Of course, the old man rushed in to defend her at every opportunity, eating up the attention. Who knew what went on in his mind, fawning all over her and her sweet little ways? Why was his mother being so quiet about it all? After the initial outbursts she had become mute. Nico adored his mother. She'd always made him feel safe, and powerful. Not once had she complained when he needed his room a certain way, his things arranged in a predetermined order.

"Mamma, they have to go back exactly like this."

His father on the other hand understood nothing. Nico knew the old man resented finding himself having to marry Gina and Nico did understand this. Those feelings were logical. Being made to take on a wife and child for propriety couldn't have been easy. But that Lucio couldn't accept Domenico's inability to fit the image in Lucio's mind of what a *son* should be...unforgivable. Now Lia had brought the whole situation to the forefront again, simply by existing. She had thrown out his whole routine in his own home.

"I don't get it." He paced around the room as he spoke and then came back, standing directly in front of his mother. *"Has she become your little pet?"*

"Domenico, Nico, that's not exactly a kind way to refer to the girl," she replied, not hiding her amusement at his rant.

"Well, now you're reading the letters, letting her play with your sewing machine, and having cosy little meetings at the kitchen table. What the hell Ma?"

"She entertains me. Such a determined little thing, and she has some right on her side."

"What's the matter Ma? And don't shake that head at me!"

"She's made me realise how limited my life is..."

"That's it, she has to go."

"No, you don't understand. There has to be more to life..."

"I'm not enough? Do I take a heavy toll with my ways?"

"Nico, I enjoy doing things for you. You know that."

"No, I ask too much of you. The bitch is right. I should have my own place."

"Nico, stop! She had better not say that in my hearing." She stopped to pour him another coffee. "Nico. I'll admit you can be challenging," she said with a wink. "As for her...it's hard to explain, but she fills a void. In some ways she isn't so different to you, you know. She likes things clean and tidy, and she helps me willingly. I like it...I..."

"It's an ingratiating act. Come on, Ma. She has an agenda, a twisted one that justifies forcing herself on us."

"Can you let me talk?"

He nodded, looking like a small boy, a sulky one. Gina smiled before speaking. "She is a sharer, of her heart and maybe of her soul, she has...I can't explain but she brings the sun. Solare, you father would say when she was little. Don't pout, my son. It's not like we have to admit any of this to her."

"No. She's Marissa's daughter. I don't trust her. I don't want her here, and if she hurts you in any way...."

"You and I, Nico, have never needed anybody else. Maybe that's not right. We do need others. Leave her alone. I'm not asking you to be nice to her."

"I love you, Mamma. I will do whatever makes you happy. I don't like it though and I don't like her!"

"You did once."

"She was a child then, sweet, not this bitch with letter issues."

"Domenico, he was my brother, my family. Leave her alone, for me."

"Fuck!" he growled back in the present. "Did you lock the door after Ivana left? Good girl," he said, tracing a finger from Francesca's cheek to the full red lips when she nodded. He inserted his finger, and she was quick to suck on it. His dick jerked in response. "And what else did you do?"

In reply she dangled a black lace thong. Taking it, he tossed the piece of silk to the floor. Tangling his hands in the back of her long thick hair, he pushed her face down on his desk to hover a breath away from the solid timber.

"Do you see all my files, my pens, how nicely they are laid out?" He pulled on her hair, and she nodded. "Good. I don't want any disruption to my desk. I have work to finish."

He placed her hands flat above her head over the files he was working on. "Now don't move" he ordered.

He hitched up her skirt, shoving his knee between her legs, pushing her thighs apart without any finesse. She whimpered and thrust her behind higher. Presumptuous bitch, he thought, tugging her hair. Indulging her wasn't a hardship on the odd occasion it suited him. Today, foreplay would be limited. She wouldn't protest, in the same way she never complained when he refused to kiss her. Francesca never knew when and what he would allow, at least about certain things; it kept her eager. He initiated. She followed.

He tugged her hair harder, enjoying the pained response. He smiled when she widened her stance, lifting the smooth tanned skin in a way that made it obvious what she wanted, what she always wanted, him inside that hot, tight bottom. Her slit glistened, begging him to play. He pushed her dress higher. She groaned; he grinned.

"Is this where you want me?"

Accepting his thrusting fingers, she moaned, shaking her head. He taunted her some more before unzipping his pants, sheathing himself, impatient to be done. He thrust his fingers back inside, used the moisture on his fingers around the opening of her anus. Her whole body trembled, and his cock leaped, responding to her excitement. One long finger was replaced by two. She panted, whimpered. He gave her more, feeling the muscles coiling in anticipation. Releasing her, he reached for the little bottle on his desk. Generosity with the lubrication didn't mean he would give warning. Grabbing her hips, he pushed in, let the head sit halfway to its target, enjoying the moment as Francesca arched and cried out in a pleasure pain combination. He moved slowly, testing her patience.

"Yes, yes. More. Give me more."

He froze. She had failed the test. "Do you want me to stop?" His voice roughened by desire encompassed a harsh edge he knew she both relished and feared. "Answer me."

"God no," she shoved against him, impatient in her desires and careless in her reply.

"Then don't tell me how I should fuck you."

He pulled out and walked around to the front of the desk. A statue, she had become a statue and it amused him. He slid his hand over his long, hard length. She salivated, licked her lips but remained quiet. He waited, stroking in unison to her panting. She needed to fully comprehended her mistake.

Nico smiled to himself. He hadn't intended a serious relationship with her. Surprisingly, they suited each other well. Francesca's pride or perhaps ego kept her faithful. She might like her sex specific and rough, but she didn't bed hop. Francesca, a confessed snob, one whose need to protect her reputation constantly conflicted with her greedy, sexual, and often perverse personality, suited him along with her fastidiousness nature. In public, she used her cultured voice and well-dressed body to advantage. Her intelligence and her ability to act as a hostess carried an aristocratic touch of bygone ages. Nico enjoyed the fact and it amused him to know her father was grooming her to take over the family business. The man sincerely believed his daughter only shit gold nuggets, and Francesca employed great lengths to ensure her father kept that belief.

Time to speed things up. He walked up behind her, happy to indulge her for a few moments but his mind had shifted to the waiting files. Nico reached for her breast, pulling on the piercing so that she bucked against him. Her breathing, wild, ragged, and frustrated, pleased him. He, and he alone controlled her release. Increasing his thrusts to pounding, he leaned in whispering in her ear, "Now." She screamed, the sound echoing as he let himself go. *Fuck, it felt good.*

He wasted no time pulling out of her, removed the condom, tied it up and put it into one of the small bags he kept for that purpose. He watched her, noting the smile on her face as she put on her panties. Francesca wasn't at all nonplussed by the clinical coldness of his withdrawal. Her total absorption in her own pleasure, read his behaviour as an appetiser in the 'to be continued next time game'. Nico didn't believe in the perfect partner but as much as possible, he and Francesca were happy together, a neat little package of timed performances. Functioning for him depended on a controlled environment, and she liked being controlled. It worked perfectly.

He walked to the bathroom and washed his hands, smelling his fingers to ensure no remnant remained of Francesca's essence. He washed them again and looked up in the mirror as he rinsed. *That mouth, that delicious annoying mouth with those full lips that pouted so delightfully at his jibes*, he said to his image in the oval mirror, *was going to get her into so much trouble.* He shook himself in annoyance as he realised where his thoughts had led him. They had nothing to do with Francesca.

Chapter 3

"**Is** this what you bought at the markets? It's so plain."

"I want it to contrast against the pattern. Can I use the sewing machine again?"

Lia never knew if she should say more when Gina instigated these moments of conversation. Short and sweet worked best. Gina gave a nod and went back to the letter; the one Papa had sent three months into Mama's remission. Lia knew every word by heart. *I pray every night that she is finally free of this disease,* he had written. Her parents had been reconciled at this point, and Lia knew she would struggle to cope if Gina made any cutting comments.

Fragments of the woman Lia remembered did surface at times. The thawing process in the cold war meandered, the pace infuriatingly slow. Lia no longer hoped for a truce for Papa's sake; she wanted it for herself. Caught up in her musings she almost missed the moment Gina spoke.

"She suffered a great deal, didn't she?"

Lia nodded and blindly picked up a piece of material. Her insides ached. Bile rose in her mouth. She forced it down, concentrating fiercely on remaining silent and still.

"They loved each other?"

Another one of those moments. Should I interrupt by speaking? Today Gina sounded like she cared, the timbre neither stilted nor harsh.

"Yes," Lia finally whispered. "She said the last year of her life was the happiest."

"This is difficult for you, isn't it? Despite the bravado you insist on whipping us with." When Lia didn't reply, her aunt continued. "You know everything, don't you, all the dirty bits and pieces of that awful day? What is it you want? Because it's not about these letters. And you and Lucio, such an inordinate amount of time spent talking so cosily…"

"I like him. I want to bury the past and so does he. I want a family. They, my mother, my father and Lucio, paid a huge price for what they did…"

"And I didn't?"

"Aunt Gina, I know you did but it's been twenty years. Lucio is still here. I know he's done some stupid things over the years, but you shut him out completely, brainwashed his son against him, and he's still here."

"He talks too much. And brainwashed is harsh."

Exasperated Lia fought for control. "Aunt Gina! Please. He doesn't tell me these things. I'm not blind, I see the way things are. My mother paid; her illness made sure of it. Papa paid; he lost her, he lost you. When does it end?"

Gina got up and left the room, but not before Lia had seen tears. Bitterness, loss, and anger, all three had glided across her face and yet a vestige of the real Gina had also made an appearance, the old Gina. The normal severity etched on that forehead had eased into regret. Lia wondered how people could keep feelings so bottled up inside, letting them twist their lives for so long. Her aunt needed time to think. *Hell, I need time to think.*

"Lia?"

"Uncle Lucio, I didn't hear you come in."

"I didn't want to interrupt. You're so determined, like my son. When you want something, you don't let anything get in the way."

Lia winced.

"I don't mean to upset you. I've watched you. Your kindness, gentleness, your patience. You love her. I see it. You tolerate my son who goes out of his way to make life difficult." He sighed, weighing his words, understanding her wariness. "I wanted to tell you…"

"Please don't say you're sorry. I'm so sick of sorry. I want to forget, to move on."

"I know that. I wanted to, not explain maybe but…" He sighed again. "I know you have details, memories. I can't excuse what happened, what we did. I don't want forgiveness. I do want you to understand."

He stopped talking, his face twisted, searching for words. Out of the corner of her eye Lia noticed Gina coming back down the hallway.

"Uncle Lucio, stop, it doesn't matter. There's…"

Afraid Lucio might say something to ruin the precarious relationship between herself and her aunt,

Lia thought desperately about what to say. To her surprise, Gina shook her head and put a finger to her lips.

"You value closure," he said. "You're right. Your mother and I, we never had closure. Gina's pregnancy demanded priority. The passion we had for each other wasn't resolved. Now, I know it wouldn't have lasted. Then, your mother and I weren't given the option to find out. It became the ultimate fantasy of *what ifs*. After living with a fantasy for so long, we couldn't resist finding out if it had a basis. We, your mother, and I, selfishly believed we had to find out if it meant something. We were wrong, and in the process, we destroyed a family. I know it doesn't excuse us." He gave a hollow laugh, a tiny, pitiful expulsion of breath. "I like it, you being here. I'm so tired of all this drama. I want to switch it off like we do the television. But mostly, I don't want you to hate me."

"God," she said, her voice quivering despite a great effort to maintain neutrality. Lia couldn't dismiss the woman listening to the man in front of her bare his soul. "I forced my way into your home, and you have made me welcome. I don't hate you. I hate what you did that day. I understand the reasoning if not the deed. Mama explained the same thing to me. It changed her. An enormous amount of time, years, were wasted before Papa believed her but in the end he did."

"People can learn from mistakes." His longing, clearly written on his face held a poignant sadness.

Lia remained silent.

"Some find it harder than others. But I believe we can learn from our mistakes. Your mother learned, and your father forgave her. I want the same thing. Convincing Gina and Domenico..." He shook his head despondently.

"You read the letters before they were sent back, didn't you," Lia whispered. A statement, not a question.

Lucio blinked, taken aback by her perception and the shift in conversation. "Yes, I did," he said after a long pause. "The pain, the honesty...the determination to change things, broke my heart and woke my heart."

"I..." Lia floundered, swallowed. "You resealed and sent them back."

"As Gina ordered. She doesn't know I read them."

"Why?"

"Because I wanted our family back, and reading the letters did that. He sent photos of you. I watched you grow up."

"Oh, Uncle Lucio. You did change."

"I think so."

"No more of the women Domenico accuses you of?" Lia had to ask but tossed it out with a tinge of humour to soften the effect. Gina put one hand to her mouth, the other to her heart.

Lucio laughed softly, not at all offended by her words. "Not for a long, long time, despite not sharing a room with my wife except for the odd times she will allow it. I think I grew up. I play bocce, work or share a drink with my friends."

"Why did you stay?" The question had to be asked as much for herself as the woman wiping tears from her face. He hesitated long enough to give Lia the time to put the pieces together. She asked again. "Why did you stay, why are you still here?" For a moment she thought he might not answer. She waited. Both women waited.

"At first because I had no place to go but then...." The silence was deafening.

"You love her!"

"Yes. She takes excellent care of me. I am what you English call *high maintenance,* like your mother. It takes a special person to understand this. Forgive though, I can only hope. And Lia, despite what my son thinks I would give my life for him." He shrugged, looking older and lost as he picked up his keys. Lia watched him leave and her aunt slink away.

I need to get my head in order. Ashlee and Greg would help. Meeting Greg on the flight to Italy had been a small miracle. Things had been set in motion and Lia wanted to see them through. Her hand caressed the smoothness of the table, while she considered the repercussions of remaining longer. Laura would not be happy, but their friendship would survive. Domenico would be a problem. Lia flinched, picturing the hard lines of his face. Like one of the military heroes on a romance book cover, the severe face defied logic, looking unearthly beautiful despite the weapons strapped to his body. *What would his reaction be?*

Chapter 4

"Greg called. He's organised the job interview at the base for this morning."

Lia could not believe her luck. An administrative job at the American Naval Base, Sigonella, had presented itself at the right time. The art classes she taught left her with time on her hands.

"So, is this babbling you're doing supposed to interest me in any way?" Nico asked from the recliner on the balcony.

"I need to be there sooner than anticipated. Greg wants to talk to me before the interview. I thought you might drive me. Please."

She had no illusions about him, but she could hope her excitement might be contagious. After all, he did act civilly these days in front of his parents. She sighed when he gave her the *look*. The one that said he barely tolerated her presence.

"Please," she asked again.

"I'm busy. You get the bus from here on the days you go stay with your friends or take a taxi."

"Not many taxis at this time of day and the bus takes too long. It'll be so much easier if you drive me, please. This one time."

"I'm busy."

Lia bit her lip at the blatant lie. He looked up from the newspaper, and as always, she had to fight to not react under his piercing scrutiny. Something in his directness, the way he blatantly inspected her body, what she wore and how she moved, rattled her peace of mind. At some level she accepted their bickering kept them both in some sort of check. Right now, all it did was increase her anxiety levels. She blew out a breath. He'd been more difficult of late, sensing the change in the atmosphere at home between his parents.

To him, she knew, it made no sense. His father had done the unforgivable; he didn't deserve any mercy. Lia also knew he blamed her for the changes. So many times, she wished she didn't have to power to get inside his head and feel sympathy for him. It messed up her own thinking. Asking him to help her had been foolish, additional ammunition to use against her. Yet last night he had brought home some of the sweets his mother loved and had included some for Lia. This morning, the jerk re-surfaced. Lia huffed. He smirked. Lia knew as she always did with him, that backing off achieved more, until the next round.

"Fine! I'll get the bus." Five minutes later she shut the door to the apartment aware if she missed this bus, she'd have an hour's wait for the next one and no guarantee of a taxi. Nico's laughter dogged her footsteps.

"Bus is close," she heard him say, in his perfect English, and fought to bite back a retort.

His position gave him an excellent view of the main street and giving him the finger from downstairs would be childish. Lia tugged at her hair, thinking her campaign to win back her childhood hero might have to be put to rest. Buried at least six feet under. Perversely, she noted the reluctance to let the idea go completely. Given his current obnoxious behaviour, Lia wondered at her own thinking, wondered why she bothered to analyse anything. *Fuck him*, she thought, as the lift reached the ground floor.

Upstairs Nico rose to his feet to watch her. Part of him felt bad at having refused to help her. Thirty seconds worth of bad. All that sweetness and light sickened him. He didn't believe the act for a second. *Look where believing Marissa had led.* Lia had his father wrapped around her little finger, and by the way his friends ogled her, it wasn't just Lucio who had fallen prey. *Brainless idiots, swayed by a body...* He stopped himself at that point, annoyed, because thinking about her body, or the way the bathroom smelled after she'd used it, a scent so essentially Lia lingering in his memory hours afterwards, disturbed him immensely.

Unclenching his fists, he reminded himself her cleverness wouldn't last. She'd make a mistake. To his mind, everything she did had to be premeditated, calculated, including the way she ensured she left everything in place in the bathroom. W*hy didn't she take the opportunity to annoy him further?*

Lia confused him with her fucking perfect behaviour and her perfect mouth, the same mouth capable of making him consider blushing, if he forced the issue. Not that his mother ever saw that side, no matter how hard he pushed for it to happen. *Had his mother seriously forgotten this irritating little brat had forced her way into their lives? And what the fuck was happening with Mamma and the old man now?*

Domenico felt it the moment Lia looked up, the four floors of distance unable to prevent their eyes meeting, his entertained, hers furious. He laughed when that finger went up. She chose not to react, her attention caught by the bus gliding closer. Seeing the opportunity, she darted across the road. *Stupid girl!* He knew straight away she'd forgotten they drove on the opposite side of the road. He grinned, enjoying her desperation. The humour quickly disappeared when Nico realised she hadn't seen the yellow Vespa.

"Fuck," he mouthed in English, then added a few words in Italian as the Vespa hit her. "God damn you, Lia!"

Still cursing, he raced downstairs, not waiting for the lift. A throng surrounded her, strangers, and an upset, apologetic rider. Like some waif Lia sat on the ground, re-assuring the old gentleman that it hadn't been his fault. Her legs were grazed, her stockings torn, and the long flowing head of hair failed to hide the nasty graze on her forehead. He pushed past the people standing around her and bent down in front of her, not sure of his reception, but unable to stop himself. The blame was his; he had steered her into carelessness.

"Oh Nico, I missed the bus," she wailed, and then did the unexpected: held up her arms towards him.

When had she started calling him Nico? Nico meant intimacy, a bond of sorts. He disliked the feeling his name on her lips created and he definitely disliked the way she fit in his arms. Carrying her back inside the building, he concentrated on trying to ignore how much he loathed the smell and look of blood. A weakness, one he couldn't control so close to her. *So typical of Lia*, he thought, taking refuge in irritation, and gritting his teeth. He couldn't enjoy a day away from work. Frowning heavily at the faintness of a memory triggered by the body in his arms, he retreated into ire. *Jesus! Trust her to rearrange his peaceful life into a fucking soap opera.* Opening the door, he quickly eased his way to the middle of the room and dumped her on the couch. The soft whimper of pain made him scowl as he walked to the linen closet.

Grabbing the first aid kit and some towels Nico donned gloves before touching her again. Most of the injuries were superficial. He grimaced anyway; the sight of blood had always made him queasy. *No tears, thank God.* For some reason, the tears had made him uncomfortable but thankfully after the initial wail, the tears had petered out. He tallied her injuries: grazes on both legs, a deep cut of some kind on the inside of her wrist and a scratch across the side of her face above her eye. Worried about the dirt she had picked up off the road, he patched her up as best he could, then washed her face and wiped her legs, pulling down the ruined stockings to facilitate the process. She wore stay ups. Transfixed, he slid the cloth up the tanned leg.

"It's okay," she said, flushing a bright pink, her stare fixated on the fingers spread across her thigh. "I can finish this. It's fine, but could you bring me the phone? I need to ring Greg. Please?"

Nico ignored her, continued wiping, pushed aside the flowing fabric of her skirt, and glowered at the glimpse of pink lace. As if sensing what he could see, Lia fiddled with her skirt, re-covering the soft smooth skin. He continued cleaning. *Pale pink high cut lace, probably with the matching bra*, he thought and barely held back another scowl. Sharing space in his home meant little escaped his notice. The washing drying on the balcony told its own tale. She had good pieces: lacy, more sensual than sexy, tasteful yet comfortable. No thongs, which he found fascinating for some perverse reason. Fuck, he couldn't believe his errant thoughts. She distracted him. His reaction, an abrupt, angry movement, caused her to recoil.

"I'll ring Marco." It came out sharp and she flinched. "The cut on your wrist looks nasty."

She worked her top teeth over her bottom lip. "No! It's not necessary. I'm fine, and in any case, Greg will know what do. He's a doctor. I don't want to ruin the chance for this...job." His fierce gaze intimidated. "Please, can I have the phone?"

Nico reached over, grabbed the handset, and dropped it on the sofa beside her. She smiled her thanks and dialled. He hated her quiet dignity. It made him the villain. At a profound level he knew she was genuine. *Why couldn't he accept that and her?* He sat down beside her.

"Thank you," she said, after a brief conversation, putting her hand on his arm and handing him back the phone with the other. "Greg is going to pick me up and take me back to the base for a few days." He stared at the spot where her hand and his arm met. She quickly removed her hand.

He let go a small sigh. *Why does this woman put me on edge?* "Good, in fact why don't you consider making that your home instead, or better still going home to Australia? My mother's read the damned letters. You've achieved your purpose so why are you trying to get a job?"

His abruptness hurt her. She withdrew into herself. He didn't care. The tic at the side of his mouth began a quiet beat as she held his gaze. Caught in the spell of those brown velvet eyes, his temper spiked. "For fuck's sake, go home."

"And the arsehole is back," she murmured, standing up shakily. She ignored the hand he offered and limped towards her room. "Fuck you! I'll go when I'm ready."

He grinned at the language, at her tone of voice. This Lia, he could handle. He refrained from answering, enjoying the return of a status quo he fathomed. She amused him especially the moments he managed to pierce her calm. Thus, he didn't resist the lure of another jibe. "Did you forget you told your friend Laura that the arsehole looks like a Greek God just yesterday?"

"I followed up with the manners of a baboon, or did you forget that part because you were too busy swaggering out in only a towel? A pathetic performance."

"It didn't stop you taking it all in, did it? Did you hope the towel wouldn't hold?"

Trembling with rage, she snapped back at him. "Please, of course I did. With the things I have told Laura, your arrogance being top of the list, we were hoping to see how small a dick you had. You must be compensating for something, to be so full of yourself."

"You'd know, you had the chance to feel it. I think you know you're lying but I can organise a tape measure if you need a reminder. You do understand it's a little disturbing to know you have a need to discuss my anatomy."

"Do you hear yourself? Do you know how childish your behaviour is? Why would you go out of your way to walk past me in a towel while I'm on the phone?"

"Why? Why not? This is my home, mine not yours. If you weren't here what I wore wouldn't matter, would it? Maybe you should take the hint? Neither I, nor my anatomy want you here."

She held her tongue, slamming the door on his laughter. Sometimes she hated him so much she feared for her sanity. Taking up the offer to move into the empty apartment might be a discussion when Greg arrived to pick her up.

Chapter 5

Gina insisted Nico and Marco take her with them. Having moved into Greg and Ashlee's spare apartment Lia looked forward to the weekends she came home. The tension living in the same home as Nico had wrought had been relegated in Lia's mind, to a nice, neat box. Until this particular weekend when Lia found herself coerced into a situation Lia wanted no part of.

"I haven't anything suitable to wear."

"We'll find something of mine to adjust."

"Aunt Gina. I don't have shoes, and it would take so much work to alter something of yours. I come here to see you and Uncle Lucio."

"Nonsense. You need to have some fun."

Seven months down the track, Lia was loath to upset Gina. An evening out clubbing with Nico, even with Marco there, pushed the boundaries, no matter how much Lia wanted the relationship with her aunt. *Would you be so keen to push me if I told you the real story behind my injuries that day I went for my interview, would you, Aunt Gina? Or the real reason I live on the base. Damn.*

"I don't have shoes." Lia said, instead.

"We take the same size in shoes," Gina said, "and I wasn't always an old woman. We'll find something."

Lia tried not to take notice of the look on Nico's face when Gina went to her bedroom and came back with a concoction of black lace. Upsetting his Saturday ritual hadn't impressed him at all. Normally, Marco came for brunch after a session at the gym or a game of squash. Then both men would go out somewhere for the afternoon, visit Marco's parents before planning an evening activity.

Not hiding his resentment at having her come to stay caused her plenty of consternation. Having her tag along could really break his balls. *Mamma, non mi rompere le palle, per favore* had been Domenico's exact words when Gina had insisted they take Lia out. Ball-breaking, a common expression, usually amused Lia, but not today. *If I had balls, today would definitely break mine.*

Marco, unsuccessfully masking his amusement, didn't help the situation. Wisely, she kept her eyes downcast, until the urge to see Nico's expression became impossible to resist, and she had to sneak a glance at the tight jaw and pursed lips. Caught by Marco, who proceeded to wink, had her smothering a giggle. The dark blond hair hung long enough to reach his collar, giving him an off-hand careless elegance to go with hazel eyes that never stopped smiling.

Scrutinising him against the other, harsher man Lia asked herself how someone so much fun, so charming, and down to earth could be Nico's best friend. Marco had been, if memory served her right, back then as teenage boys. She winked back and watched him try to smother a laugh in return. Nico's intimidating frown could not prevent their mirth. The frown became a scowl.

Nico, she suddenly realised, Nico. She had slipped from Domenico into Nico. She wanted to believe it simply a natural progression. Gina and Marco, depending on the conversation, constantly shortened his name. Gina distracted Lia from her musings and Nico's glare, with a pair of thin medium-heeled black suede shoes. The shoes would do. They did wear the same size. The dress, fully lined with three quarter length sleeves and much too large, would need work. Work Lia could handle, the enforced socialising was another matter.

"Fine, you win." Gina smiled smugly causing Lia to eye her suspiciously.

Lia held up the dress and studied it. Sleeves off, a few snips to expose the shoulders, some darts, slits at the side for easier movement and it might work. The beautiful fabric gave Lia inspiration for the shoes. Gina's excitement was contagious. Lia found herself smiling back at the excited older woman, not missing the look of affection Lucio sent his wife before turning it towards Lia.

She startled, an icy tingle causing a tremble along her spine. Without bothering to look, she knew exactly what caused the warm sunshine to pale. Nico staring, the sneer ever-present. The hairs on her arms helplessly responded, standing on end. The cold feeling didn't disperse until Nico and Marco had gone, and even then, a small portion of that icy tingle remained.

~

Marco couldn't dial down the intensity of his thoughts. He waited for Nico to retrieve the small black ball.

"What, Marco?"

"Do you have to treat her so badly?"

"I didn't say anything to her."

"Jesus Nico, you don't have to. The looks are enough on their own. Give her a break. She's lovely."

"Don't go there!"

"I'm not saying I want to fuck her!"

"Shut up Marco."

"What's your problem? So, she forced her way into your lives? Nico. Look at your mother. The change is incredible. Lia is not Marissa."

Nico closed his eyes, thinking about the way the shower had smelt after Lia had used the bathroom the Friday morning she had arrived. The products she used struck with visceral force. The fragrance got into his pores, followed him to work and overrode the cloying but expensive perfume Francesca used. The one he had purchased for her. He had almost forgotten the onslaught on his senses with Lia living at the base. *Liar*, he told himself. Even now, sweaty from the game and a day later, the clean fresh edible wisps of coconut and cinnamon were so attached to his skin, he could barely think of anything else.

"Shut the fuck up Marco!"

"Nico, is there more to this? She doesn't live at the apartment, hasn't for weeks. You're not sharing any space. She's not at the dinner table and she's polite when she's visiting, unless you rile her. What's the deal here?"

Marco, Nico thought, had a point. Marco however didn't understand the space Lia commandeered whether there or not. "I don't like her. She annoys me. Everything about her gets under my skin. I feel displaced in my own home. Why is she still in Italy?"

"That's a mouthful and hardly fair, Nico. She wanted a family. She makes your mother happy. You are not being logical. It's unlike you. Don't you remember when she was a small girl? She followed you around like you were God...doting on every little thing you did. She's the reason we stated calling you Nico. She claimed Domenico was hard to say. Not that she remembers."

"What's your fucking point?"

"No point except that after a while none of us minded when she tagged along. Such a funny, sweet thing."

"Determined, you forgot determined. And she's not a child now!"

"No, she's not but she's still that same sweet person, and after what she's been through, I understand why she came. Give her a chance."

"Can we play ball?"

Marco nodded, letting the subject drop. With Nico you had to back off or you would lose any chance to get through. Something felt off though. Marco had his suspicions. Playing ball was easier.

~

"Close your mouth, Old Man." Gina snapped, and then spoiled the effect when she grinned as he walked further into the room. "Doesn't look like the same dress, does it? She is a clever one, yes?" she asked her husband.

"Lia, you look so beautiful." He paused, looking doubtful, a frown appearing. "Maybe too good, Old Woman. There are some bad elements at the nightclub."

"What of it, Old Man? She has the boys to look after her."

Lia doubted the truth of that statement but kept quiet, preferring not to interrupt the flow of conversation. Affection oozed in the use of *old* and in their general tone with each other. A few times she'd caught the puzzled look on Nico's, Domenico's face she corrected.

"Uncle Lucio, can you make two holes through the top of these shoes?"

His eyes on Gina, heading for the kitchen, Lucio nodded absently at Lia's request. "I'm not sure what she'll do when you leave. I'm surprised you haven't gone home already."

"I know. I'm not ready to go and I love being here with the two of you. I love my job at the navy base and working online with Laura is going well."

She shrugged her slim shoulders and he nodded again. Lia and Lucio were in perfect accord.

Chapter 6

Lia shivered in the mild May night, feeling exposed and vulnerable, and wishing she had denied her aunt. A quick breath in and out turned into three or four before she stepped into the lounge room where the two men waited.

Marco had a demonic mouth, dedicated to making the situation between her and Nico worse. She suspected it gave him some kind of weird thrill to get a reaction from his friend. For once though, he seemed to be at a loss for words and opted for a loud whistle. Lia thought that alternative a bad one. Nico's face hardened. The tension palpable in his rigid stance worried her. In comparison, Marco looked thoughtful, if amused, judging by the gleam in his eyes. *What an odd friendship,* Lia reflected. Marco, she decided, would look after her. She could trust him in this.

They picked up Silvia, Marco's receptionist on the way. From what she knew, Marco often included her in social events. Tonight, Lia welcomed this whim because with Silvia's addition the atmosphere improved a few degrees. The atmosphere relaxed further when they met up at the club with the rest of the group, who were inclined to friendliness. Francesca gave her usual dismissive smile. Lia ignored Francesca until she gave Silvia a look of disdain too obvious to miss. Lia wanted to smack her perfect face. Silvia did look out of place with her wild hair caught at the nape of her neck, minimal makeup, and a grey tunic-shaped sleeveless dress. Most Italians, Lia had quickly discovered, were all about looking good. Silvia differed. Straight forward and shy, she had heart and did not deserve Francesca's bitchiness. Lia smiled, hoping to reassure Silvia and received a small smile back, and then a soft giggle when Lia poked her tongue at Francesca's receding back.

Francesca glowed. Lia thought she managed the right shade of tanned skin. Her dark, wavy hair and eyes looked stunning against the pink and black dress she wore. *Pity her personality didn't match her looks*, Lia thought, schooling her features, only to find herself the subject of Marco's knowing smirk. Francesca, Domenico's amica, was more than the girlfriend tag. A four-year relationship should have catapulted her to fidanzata, a fiancée. Yet the relationship remained on the edge of formality. Socially well-placed, Francesca had the manners of royalty unless the situation didn't suit her. Lia didn't suit her and neither apparently, did Silvia.

Lia wondered if Domenico hesitated to make the relationship permanent because of Francesca's attitude, the 'full of herself and her opinions' attitude. After all, if you suffered from the same complaint, the competition would be stiff. Chiding herself silently for the nasty thoughts, she couldn't stop herself from wondering why Domenico would be involved with someone so arrogant? *Did like really attract like?* Lia didn't think enough glue in the world existed to bind the relationship between two such hard surfaces. Then again Marco had shared some fascinating sexual innuendos about them as a couple. Perhaps they did belong together. The thought left a sour taste in her mouth.

Despite his caustic tongue Domenico's friends idolised him, accepting his stiff mannerisms, his haughty demeanour, and his dominant personality with affection. Marco's influence possibly to a certain degree, and Domenico's professional standing, Lia wondered? Allowing him to rule the roost testified to his position in life, something Italians seemed more comfortable with than perhaps her own Aussie upbringing embraced. Domenico fit the bill as a leader. Lia wouldn't, couldn't give him that type of reverence. She didn't care about his position; she cared about how he behaved.

Lia forced herself to relax, looking around, liking the open-air structure, the soft lighting, and the sizeable dance floor. A tall man dancing in the distance snagged her attention. His movements were precise, fluid. Lia harboured a guess he might be a professional.

He had the slick good looks and sex appeal male ballroom dancers appropriated when they were as good as this man. Marco, noticing her interest, leaned closer to speak to her.

"That's Lorenzo Rega. He was world champion a few years ago. Owns the dance studio where Nico and Francesca have lessons."

Lia looked up, shocked. "Nico dances?"

"And he's good," Marco leaned in closer, "Watch. Nico does this the same way he does everything else. He can't help himself. He's a perfectionist."

"Don't forget smug, irritating bastard."

Marco laughed. "You already know that part," he said and winked. "Unfortunately," Marco continued, "as good as he gets, something is missing. Lorenzo thinks he overthinks the movements, concentrates on technique and not heart. I can't tell the difference. Lorenzo, however, never lets him forget it."

Imagining Nico's frustration made her sad.

"Nico's determined and when he's determined he's dangerous." Marco punctuated the last bit by pulling faces.

Lia giggled, unable to resist him in this mood. Checking to see if Silvia agreed, she caught an odd look, one bringing the smattering of freckles on Silvia's face into prominence. *Interesting*. Lia made a note to investigate at a later date and returned her attention to the dance floor.

"That was wonderful." Lia clapped her hands as Nico and Francesca sat down. "Domenico, do you think I could have a dance later on?" When he narrowed his eyes, Lia's heart skipped a beat then stilled at the cold, hard stare. *A mistake, a stupid mistake. I'm an idiot.*

"I don't enjoy lowering my standards, so I don't think so," Nico meant his voice to carry. Silvia gasped. Marco blinked in surprise at both the abrupt and nasty retort and Nico's lack of manners.

"Okay." Lia fought to maintain her dignity but struggled to find a place to look.

Everyone at the table rushed into conversation, earning her gratitude as she focused on her drink. The hurt rubbed raw, opened wounds further. Midnight had come early for Cinderella, leaving Lia in her soiled gown for everyone to pity. *How could he be so harsh?* Marco leaned forward and put a hand on her arm, earning a glare from Nico as he shepherded Francesca towards the bar.

"He hates me, really hates me."

"No Lia, he doesn't." At her look, he shrugged a shoulder, knowing denial was pointless. "Correction, he only thinks he does. Or maybe he wants to think he does."

"Well, which is it, Marco? It doesn't matter, I shouldn't have come. Why, Marco, what have I done to him that he should be so awful?"

"Lia, he doesn't know what to do with you. You forced your way into his family's life, dredged up memories, caused a world war and yet somehow managed to bring his mother out of her self-imposed prison. He resents you."

"God forbid someone upsets his perfectly controlled life, even if the people in it were miserable. You do know he's not normal. You may be an obstetrician, but you're not obtuse, not where he's concerned."

"Lia, now you're the nasty one. It doesn't become you."

"You know what I mean. He's somewhere on the spectrum and I understand control of his environment is a big part. He is also a high functioning individual, so he knows better. His attitude makes no sense. He's holding onto...I don't know. I hate his mind is so closed when it doesn't have to be."

"That's just it, Lia. He has a set way of looking at things. You upset that. What's worse, you make him see things, especially where Gina is concerned. Somehow you make him question what seemed so simple to him. I think he really believed he was helping her by letting her make him her whole world. He takes some things at face value like a child."

"Bull shit! He likes having a willing slave, who wouldn't? He's a selfish pig. An arse. At his level he should comprehend the difference."

"That isn't fair Lia. One minute you blame it on the spectrum then you say he's an arse. He would die for his mother. You know that. And yes, he does like her attention. She doesn't question him the way you do."

"I know! Do you know how often he rearranges the pantry? He likes it to be in size and shape order which is fine except he will switch shelves as well. It makes me crazy. And the fuss he made when I mixed his white boxers with the black ones, instead of the separate piles he demands. Didn't matter I was helping Gina. I thought I would never hear the end of it. What?"

Silvia's struggle not to laugh failed as Marco's grin egged her on. Giving in, Silvia chuckled and Marco joined her.

Lia gave a careless shrug. "Okay. I admit it, I mixed them deliberately. But come on. People are starving, and he wants colour co-ordinated underpants?" Lia smiled when Silvia gave another quiet giggle. "It's not fair, Marco."

"I know, Lia."

"I really don't mind his ways. It's who he is but I do mind he won't try to get along."

"It's hard to shift his perspective once Nico decides. This with you though, I don't know. It is excessive. I have tried to talk to him. He won't listen. Anyway, why do you care so much?"

"What do you mean? He's family."

"Lia, are you sure that's all there is to this?"

Silvia glanced at Marco and frowned. The look they exchanged gave Lia an odd feeling.

"Yes, why are you asking?" Lia replied, her tone defensive.

"I mean that maybe it's become a competition as to who can do the most damage, and you want to win. You can't with him. Try being the sweet little pest of years ago instead. If you'd both kept to that, then all this wouldn't be happening."

"What do you mean?"

Marco didn't answer, choosing to worry his bottom lip, a gesture so alien to the clown. He looked at Silvia. She frowned again and shook her head. Instinct told Lia not to pursue the conversation. Instead, she considered the two people in front of her. Marco had a roving eye and yet a decent amount of trust bound the couple, more than an employer and employee relationship warranted.

"Let's not talk about it anymore." Lia leaned her head on Marco's shoulder as she spoke, testing her theory.

Taking note in the sudden tension of Silvia's body, Lia promised herself she would investigate but right now, moving away from Marco would be kind. Silvia relaxed but Lia couldn't. Thinking about this strange pair in front of her had provided a momentary distraction, but she needed more. She sat back, thinking, wanting, needing action. Marco had a point, but she couldn't help thinking she did need to win this. Domenico had to be taught a lesson. She quaked, remembering the last time she did that, it hadn't ended well. This time she would be the one to come out on top.

"Marco," she whispered, "can you do something for me?" She looked towards the bar, and satisfied Nico and Francesca were headed back, continued, "I want you to make sure Domenico stays at the table, makes sure everyone does, for the next...." she paused, again biting her lip, not sure how long it would take. "Mmm....maybe for at least ten minutes, or so?"

"Why? What are you going to do?"

Silence greeted him; Lia, weaving gracefully and purposefully had reached the other side of the dance floor.

~

"Excuse me? Lorenzo?"

The dark-haired man turned around, an eyebrow moving up arrogantly. *What was it with Italian men and that air of superiority?*

"I'm Angelia Lombardi."

"The Australian, the one making Nico crazy."

She nodded, uncomfortable and suddenly unsure of herself.

"From Francesca," he added, a sly tinge in his tone. "Nico doesn't exchange confidences about family matters. His arrogance forbids it."

She looked at him in surprise, and confusion. *Nico could have fooled her a short while ago.* Not knowing what to say, she remained silent.

"He is tight-lipped with his personal life. I think it comes with the profession he is in, and the fact he doesn't like me much."

The sudden grin held charm. She smiled back, relieved, knowing Lorenzo wouldn't be surprised at the reason for her request. She licked her lips and tilted her head towards him, not above using her looks. "It's the arrogance that concerns me and I am hoping you can help me."

"I am most happy to hear what you have in mind." When she hesitated at his obvious eagerness, he softened his stance. "Tell me, do not be afraid."

She faltered feeling a momentary conflict. Family loyalty and revenge didn't sit well together.

"Relax, little one. I know what he can be like. I imagine you have a good reason for coming to me, so please, tell me."

~

"Will you?" Her question hovered unanswered, his long silence unnerving. She shifted her weight from foot to foot, staring down at the lace bows adorning her aunt's shoes, and waited.

"I think the brilliant solicitor has made a tactical error, no? He didn't collect the evidence before he passed the judgement."

Lorenzo's words when he finally spoke had the quaintness often common when Italians spoke in English. Lia wondered if he had chosen English to be discreet, and it pleased her to think he might have had consideration for her feelings. She waited, concentrating on keeping her face impassive. His perusal of the room had an evil glint. A hand covering her mouth allowed her to set a small smile free. Lorenzo had no aversion to taking her cousin down a peg or two.

"How good are you, little one?"

She let out a relieved breath. "Good enough to make you look better than you already do."

"I see arrogance runs in the family."

"For some, for others, it's more problems with anger management."

He laughed heartily but his eyes were predatory. "Alright then, let's do this."

"What dance? Rumba?" Lia bit her bottom lip, feeling vulnerable and determined at the same time.

"I'm impressed, a difficult choice." He pursed his lips. "But if we want to make an impression, and with that outfit, an Argentinian Tango is better. The sharp movements will suit the splits either side of your dress and give you room for some sexy moves."

He leaned across, pulled out the hair tie, giving a pleased look as the heavy head of hair spilled to her waist.

"Okay, thank you. I think. You will be careful with those movements." She smoothed her hands down her dress, unable to hide the rise of colour as she met his eyes. The side splits would allow some leeway, but the short skirt worried Lia. She got the raised eyebrows as a reply. *Of course, she'd forgotten the man's profession, his peeved expression attested to the fact.* She offered him a blinding smile.

"You are stunning! When the dance floor clears go to the centre. When I come up behind you, lift your hands up through your hair. Let it fall around your shoulders slowly as you bring your hands back down. Let them skim your body. I will do the rest. You understand?"

Lia nodded slowly, intimidated by his take charge attitude.

"Are you sure you can do this?"

A hint of sympathy showed in his handsome face. He swivelled at her second nod and disappeared. She swallowed. A loud voice asking for the dance floor to be cleared for the Master made her laugh. *The Master indeed. Arrogance seemed to be in abundance.*

The sound of a sultry beat silenced the room. A shiny veil of dark hair slid slowly down the shoulders of the elegant creature on the dance floor, the one no longer Lia but instead, a siren. The tall impeccably dressed man pulled her close, holding her still. He released her slowly, only to engage in smooth, sensual and at times blatantly sexual displays of movement, echoing the words of the song. The black lace dress, sleeveless to expose her long slender arms, caressed each line of her body with clinging abandonment. It had joined the conspiracy to highlight the passion of both the dance and the music, ending only when Lorenzo pushed her slowly to her knees in front of him. The place erupted in a standing ovation.

"You are very, very good. You have competed?"

She blushed at the respect in his voice. "Not much, some medals. I did do a few competitions. I didn't enjoy the experience. I...I like to dance."

"Stunning, an exquisite dancer and a sensitive soul...the perfect combination."

The return of the sly tone she had detected previously, perturbed her. He had his own agenda. *Who am I to talk?*

"Come along, little one, and let's go play the game," he said.

The sudden sympathy in his face could not be mistaken for anything other than genuine. She allowed him to tug her firmly behind him, graciously accepting accolades as he wove his way through the crowds.

"You were amazing." Marco enveloped her in his arms and lifted her off the ground. Silvia laughed with admiration, the others surrounding her, smiling their appreciation. Lia blushed but couldn't stop her mouth turning up in delight.

"You did not tell me your little cousin was so talented." Lorenzo directed the remark straight to Domenico. "She has the instinct, the passion and talent. I can't remember when I have enjoyed a dance so much. Oh, of course I can. The last time I won a world championship. I had a brilliant partner then as I did now. She could teach you a few things."

He pivoted with a dancer's grace to wink at Lia. She rolled her eyes at the extravagance of his words, pleased and shy, horrified, and smug especially when Francesca's lips thinned until they became a red gash. Domenico, when she dared to regard him, remained impassive.

Giving a regal nod, Lorenzo slowly backed away, drawing Lia with him, his fingers tightening on her wrist until he felt the distance enough. He stopped, his face serious, bent to whispered. "Be careful, little one. Not everything is as it seems."

Lia stared at him, perplexed at his earnestness. "I don't..."

"No, you don't, do you? I didn't realise...You both haven't worked it out yet. One of you is close though."

With a kiss to her knuckles, Lorenzo gave an ambiguous smile to match his ambiguous words and disappeared, leaving only tantalising traces of expensive cologne behind. She wished she could follow him and ask what he meant. Instead, she sighed before crossing the distance back to the group.

"Quite the little exhibitionist, aren't you?" The sarcasm in the cold precise tone could not be ignored.

Tired of his behaviour, Lia forced her eyes to his, meeting his chilly expression with confidence. "Thank you for not dancing with me. You were right! One shouldn't lower their standards."

A collective inhalation was the only thing Lia registered, before Marco grabbed her and tossed her onto the dance floor.

Domenico did not dance for the rest of the night. He did disappear with Francesca for a while, only to return and sit grim-faced, mouth tight. Francesca, uncertain in a way she herself did not recognise, reflected her feelings by maintaining a permanent pout, until she left without him. Lia found herself grateful Marco had left his car back at her aunt and uncle's apartment.

Chapter 7

They dropped Silvia off. Marco had lost his exuberance, his smile half-hearted as he bid Silvia goodnight. Domenico barely acknowledged her. If the hold Domenico appeared to have over his friends had amused Lia, his current behaviour did not. The conspiracy to excuse what seemed ill-mannered and rude perplexed her. They eased the difficulties Domenico suffered when things took unexpected turns. He had their respect, earned through his position and because he had that kind of pull. *Hell, it explains why I keep trying to find that boy but this, this behaviour...I don't know. Marco's agitation is making me nervous.*

"I'm on call tonight," Marco put a hand on Lia's shoulder, letting her know he recognised her fears.

"How about making me some of your famous Australian cup of tea with milk? And maybe some toast, the one with fruit."

"You mean *raisin toast*?"

Lia made a loaf every week in the bread maker she had purchased. It reminded her of home, of Australia. Somehow it had become a thing between them. Marco would screw up his nose and sneak pieces from her plate. He'd laugh at her tea with milk, a *disgusting habit* he would tease, yet dunk the bread. She patted his hand where it rested, smiling in relief.

The quiet apartment and late hour meant Gina and Lucio were in bed. Lia prayed Marco's presence might delay the inevitable battle, at least for tonight. Tempted to disappear to her room, she knew she couldn't afford to give Domenico ammunition. Sighing with resignation, Lia switched on the range hood light and reached for some cups.

"A very entertaining night thanks to you, young lady." Marco hovered close by.

"Yes, but then you are easily amused." Lia pulled out the toaster from the side cupboard and shook her head when he winked. "Thank you. It was a lovely evening." She wanted to say more, wanted to tell him how much she appreciated his proximity, especially if it warded off an attack.

"Well, aren't the two of you cosy!" A caustic tone interrupted the small talk. Lia and Marco turned simultaneously to Nico. Steely glance fixated on Lia, he continued. "Of course, you enjoyed your evening. I'm sure your slutty display for attention had rewards."

"I beg your pardon."

She forced an even tone, fought the urge to smack that superior supercilious mouth with one of the cups. She put them down and clenched her fists at her hips. *What a fool to hope he would leave things alone.*

"Nico. That's not fair," Marco interjected, genuinely distressed at Nico's words and tone. He detested taking sides. Nico made it impossible not to in this case.

"It's okay, Marco. Let him have his say. He's waited this long. I don't know how he managed to contain himself." Lia moved towards the stove. She ducked, avoiding the range hood to switch off the gas. Facing Domenico again, she managed not to shake at the aggression evident in his face and body. "You're a total prick, you know that? You can't cope with the fact I can do something much better than you, even if it's only dancing."

"Oh, I would call the performance with Lorenzo more than dancing. I mean could he have gotten any closer? Could you have displayed yourself any better?"

Lia blanched. dismayed he made no effort to hide his contempt, however unfair. Carefully controlling the trembling in her hands, she poured hot water into two cups.

"I don't know why I am so surprised."

His annoyance at her refusal to take the bait had him pause in what Lia considered a dramatic courtroom ploy. Lia waited, her back to him.

"After all," he hissed, venom spraying into the night air, "Marissa was the mother of all sluts, fucking my father in the home he shared with my mother."

"Still, after all this time you can't let it go."

"Did you really think forcing yourself on us would change the truth? The *like mother like daughter* performance tonight proved my point."

"It was dancing, good dancing."

"It was a slut show, exactly what Marissa's daughter would do."

"Nico! Calm down. Both of you!"

Calm be damned. "Stay out of it, Marco. I can deal with this ego maniac."

Lia had barely spoken the words before her hand followed suit and made hard contact with Domenico's face. Using her body's momentum, she didn't hold back, and vivid red streaks met and held her eyes hostage. Marco's soft gasp, and her own action made her stumble back in horror. Seeing a raised hand and unsure of what Domenico might do, she angled away, smacking into the sharp corner of the range hood. The soft skin above her right eye tore on contact, eliciting a scream Lia could not hold back.

"Shit! God damn! Get me a clean cloth, Nico! Now!" Marco yelled.

"For God's sake! What's all this swearing? What is happening here? Oh my God, what did you do to her?"

Gina's voice targeted her son. Having thrown on the main light switch, she found herself confronted with a bloody Lia and a frantic Marco, and somehow decided the blame lay with Nico. He growled in response to the accusation.

Lia had never heard Gina speak to Nico in that way. Pain or not, Lia knew the last thing needed, was dissent between mother and son. She pushed the pain away. "No, Aunt Gina. I wasn't watching what I was doing."

Gina moved to Lia, her hands sliding gently over the dark hair, helping Marco hold the cloth in place. She made a sound that indicated she had a problem with the story Lia had fed her but said nothing.

"We have to get her to hospital. Nico! Now! She'll need stitches. We'll take my car. Lia, keep the cloth firm against the cut." He finished speaking as his phone rang. Marco answered with an impatient movement, then barked into the phone that he was on his way. "My patient," he explained. "Sorry to sound abrupt. Her baby is refusing to wait. Lia come with me. Nico, you follow us. Gina, please don't worry! Come on Lia." His professional manner dispensed with the clown.

"I'll come," Gina protested.

"No, Stay here. I'll be fine," Lia whispered to her aunt, kissing the soft cheek, and softening the impact.

"Go to bed. My things are here. Domenico will bring me back as soon as they sort this out."

Chapter 8

Nico ran his fingers through his hair, pulling at the strands as he followed the white Mercedes Marco drove. *I wouldn't have, it was a reflex action. I wouldn't have hit her.* He bit his lip in exasperation. Lia had been quick to soothe his mother. She had done the same thing when his mother had questioned the incident with the Vespa. *Fuck, the girl isn't normal.* He didn't know whether to be angry with her or himself. She turned him upside down and inside out and he hated her for it. She didn't have the decency to be malicious, and yet this was the second time she'd been physically hurt because of him.

Marco made sure they were seen to immediately. The doctor who met them at the ER seemed far too young for Nico's liking. Marco reassured Nico before racing off to his patient.

"Don't go, please."

Unable to pretend he didn't hear her, Nico faced Lia and shuddered as the full consequences of the evening hit him. The ugliness of the wound and the terrified look on her face, unglued him. He didn't know what he should do, how he should respond.

"You'll be fine, young lady."

The doctor's gentle tone held a soothing note. It didn't calm her at all. Nico thought her agitation out of proportion to the incident. She looked terrified, her eyes darting around the room. She blushed when she realised, he was staring.

"It's okay," she said, quietly. "Go."

The lack of emotion on her face and in her voice drew his feet towards her. Nico grabbed a chair and sat down, trying hard to hide his distaste for the blood, and the blend of hospital disinfectants surrounding them. She appeared to have shrunk, her face bleached of colour now that the flush had receded. Listening to the doctor explain about the local anaesthetic, Lia smiled shyly; a gesture clearly meant to appease the man. To

Nico watching her closely, the rigidity of her body and the trembling lips spoke their own tale. The barest touch would snap her in two.

"Goodness, it looks like you ran into Zorro, and I don't mean Antonio Banderas," the doctor spoke with humour, making an obvious effort to calm Lia. "Don't worry, I'm good. In any case nothing could spoil your looks." Lia gave another shy smile, smaller and sweeter in response.

It vexed Nico, the doctor's words, Lia smiling at the doctor. His mouth tightened. He felt her eyes on him; stared back at her until she quailed, shrank further into her skin. Ashamed of his behaviour, he reached over to her hand with his. She blinked with shock and then relief. He tightened his fingers, conscious of the way her eyes continued flickering all over the room. When he frowned, she lowered her eyes but the hand he held shook.

"Breathe, Lia," he told her, realising at last her reaction had to do with the hospital. Lacing his fingers with hers, his thumb moving of its own resolve over her wrist until the tension in her body slowly uncoiled. With his other hand he unobtrusively pushed at his chest, trying to ignore the niggle. *So much safer to argue with her than give her comfort.* It allowed him to ignore her skin, the shape of the long, delicate body, and the warmth that flowed from every pore.

Slowly she had edged her way into a heart that had long been dead, except for the portion Gina had given him. Until Angelia, nothing had been able to overcome his mother's bitterness with life. The fallacy he fed himself had no substance. In no way did Lia replicate Marissa. The looks may have been inherited but none of the vanity or superficiality. Lia's sweetness and determination, a strange mix, were real.

He felt the tug of each stitch, followed the silent tears on their path down her pale face. Using the thumb of his free hand he wiped them while the other stayed linked to hers long after the doctor had finished, and Marco had checked on them.

~

The attending physician had suggested leaving it a while before taking her home. Nico found himself alone, uncomfortable, and unable to ward off unwelcome thoughts. Compassion for the woman whose hand he currently held and a jumbled collection of other feelings and emotions. He and Lia were...what was the English expression? *An... accident waiting to happen?* His mind drifted back to earlier in the day.

"She comes here and spends time with two old people. She needs to have fun. Take Lia with you tonight," his mother had demanded.

Since when, he wondered, did his mother think in terms of fun? Whilst amusing at first, when the tone in her voice reached a certain level of determination, Nico had no option but to give in. Brusquely he'd told Lia to be ready by nine o'clock. His mother had then held up the monstrosity of black lace. Nico unable to resist, had glared at Lia, satisfied at her air of despondency, and had pushed away the tinge of guilt trying to surface despite his irritation with the entire situation.

~

"So, is she ready?"

"A few more minutes," his mother had replied, ignoring his black mood. *"Marco, come give me a kiss and promise me Lia enjoys herself." Gina had pinched Marco's cheek as if he was still a small boy.*

About to comment, Nico found himself silenced. It couldn't be the same dress, Nico thought, taking in the short, sleeveless black lace moulding itself sinfully to her body. The lace could have looked cheap, yet with the minimum of makeup, her hair tied up in a high ponytail, and her bare tanned legs in black heels, it looked expensive, and sexy. Marco, standing beside him whistled.

With downcast eyes, shyness turning her cheeks a soft pink, Nico found himself forced to concede Lia genuinely did not know the effect she had, or if the awareness did exist, it did not sit well with her. The insight angered him.

"Let's go. Let's get this damned night over with."

Lia paled. Marco grimaced. Gina sent her son a sharp look before proceeding to wave them on their way. The unhappiness etched on her Lia's face pleased him enormously.

Chapter 9

He slipped back to the present. Lia slept on. Nico wanted a coffee, but he didn't like the idea of one from a hospital. He adjusted his position in the chair and went back to thinking about the previous night.

The women in his group had been entranced with her sweetness, the sweetness he refused to see, and the men with her striking looks, the ones she never flaunted. Francesca who hated competition of any kind held her tongue. Unfortunately, her possessiveness had made itself felt in place of any comments she might have made. Nico counted on a foray onto the dance floor to distract her. He and Francesca partook of lessons and partnered well. Dancing had become a respite from the demands of his profession, a challenge of a different kind. He fought to master the steps, well aware that an aspect eluded him. With Francesca as a partner, it didn't matter. She excelled; it reflected on his lead. It satisfied him.

Lia moaned in her sleep, the sound an unwanted intimacy. *The look on her face when he refused to dance with her confirmed his cruelty.* Now instead of satisfaction he felt ashamed to have embarrassed her in front of other people. Nico had crossed a line. Hurt by his words she had remained dignified. Nico hadn't known how to repair the damage, hadn't wanted to. Her pull on his being addled him; he wanted her gone. A respite at the bar had been pleasant. Casting an eye briefly back to the table, he'd wondered idly about her disappearance.

An insistent Marco wearing a worried expression had tugged the group back to the table in time to the DJ announcing a *Lorenzo Special.* Lorenzo did the special only if he had a superb partner. Other than Francesca who was right beside him, Nico had not noticed anyone good enough for the spotlight. With Lorenzo's arrogance, nothing less than perfection, on and off the dance floor, would do.

The lights had dimmed; the floor cleared to reveal a figure bathed in a soft, pink light. Hands wound their way sensuously up her hips, skimmed past her breasts and into her hair, lifting it and letting it fall. A curtain of soft, shiny, black satin had caressed the length of her body. The light then shifted focus to the man sliding up behind her. Bodies had swayed, closing the distance between them. Lorenzo's hand had moved to her waist, had bent her into his space – two disappeared and became one.

Nico had ignored the murmuring at the table, his eyes glued to a glide of slick and sensual limbs. Lorenzo wrapped a long, slim leg around his hip, the movement mesmerising. Nico's groin had tightened in response. He remembered he'd been grateful to be seated. Caught up in his recollections, Nico forgot the uncomfortable hospital chair, reliving the moment.

A sensuality of skin on skin, muscles contracting as she lifted, sharply slid, and shaped herself around Lorenzo. Nico steeled his face to hide the turmoil in his head as he watched the duo undermine his normal control. Agitated, his dick battling with the zipper holding it down, and the paralysing desire for the woman on the dance floor, destroyed detachment. He slid his hand under the table, rubbed harshly against the fabric with the heel of his palm seeking to regain some semblance of relief. Rock hard, oozing and aching, he wondered if a penis could snap in two.

"Nico. Nico?"

Marco's voice intruded, bringing his thoughts back to the table. Nico focused on maintaining a bland expression.

"Did you know she could do that?" Marco asked, his voice annoying, caught up in the show like everyone else at the table.

Nico shook his head, words impossible because the ache in his body overrode everything, and then Lorenzo had pushed Lia to the floor in front of him, putting her eye level with his crotch. Nico's cock went crazy, pulsing and throbbing against his pants until he was literally forced into grinding his teeth together to not cry out.

In his imagination he saw himself spilling into a mouth glued to his length, a mouth prepared to swallow every drop he had. The visual nearly had him surrender to the moment. With controlled precision he swivelled his head to watch Lia walking back to the table, and let his rage take over. In that blinding moment she became Marissa, bare-arsed and locked in his father's embrace. The memory of that day deflated him, despite the fact Lia's skin glowed, misted and caressed by the moonlight in the outdoor venue.

He ignored her, ignored Marco, and ignored Francesca being snide in his ear, and he ignored the arrogant and satisfied look from Lorenzo. He also ignored Lia's little jibe. He deserved it. What he couldn't ignore was how much he wanted her. He needed to calm down. Francesca smirked as he dragged her beside him. She'd reminded him of a cat anticipating cream. Well, he'd give her that. They went to the usual place. Her mouth only improved when he thought about another face, another mouth. She squeezed him hard the way he liked it. He pulled her hair and pushed further down her throat giving himself over to the ruthless battering his cock demanded, uncaring of the person in front of him. His release came jetting out in furious spurts. It didn't change things. Francesca was not the name he'd wanted to yell.

Helping her up, he pushed her against the wall thrusting his hand up her dress to shove aside the string *she wore as an undergarment. She moaned, loving the feeling of being dominated by the slim digits, not concerned by his rough manner. Francesca wanted his tongue. Nico could hear it in the pathetic, desperate panting but she wouldn't ask. Half her fun arose from never knowing the outcomes; his fun arose from being in charge. With Francesca he could take things as far as he wanted whenever he wanted. She moaned again, and he was grateful she wouldn't ask. The thought of going down on her revolted him and he wouldn't be able to hide that fact.*

He liked control. It didn't mean he wanted to hurt her. He knew it seemed a contradiction, but he wanted the players in his games to be aware of the rules and want them willingly. Nico thrust his fingers faster, taking pleasure in her surrender to his whims. She wouldn't come until he allowed it. The more the restrictions, the more she loved it.

"I hope this is a sample of what to expect later," Francesca panted, begged, desperate to pin him down.

"Not tonight," he leaned in and whispered in a voice that would not tolerate argument, "but tomorrow night might be a different story if you're a good girl." With that

he tugged the ring on her nipple once, with enough force to hurt. He thrust faster, using his thumb in the way she loved. "Now, behave like a good girl and come."

He left her to find her way to the ladies' toilet and tidy up. In the men's toilet he scrubbed hard, needing to remove the smell from his fingers. Absently he accepted the fact that washing so ruthlessly had become something he did all the time these days. Somehow in the last few months he had begun questioning many things including the relationship. It disturbed him. The fact his body had enjoyed itself while his errant mind had not, disturbed him more.

Nearing home had served to darken, to intensify and twist his mood. Marco had sensed it, inviting himself in, afraid to leave Lia alone with him.

Lia waking brought him back to the present. He squeezed her hand and she sighed, happy to see him and not afraid to let him know. While it unnerved him at some profound level, it also gave him a sense of rightness.

Nico helped her to the car. She voiced her thanks, a soft whisper in the still night air, before leaning back into the black leather. He started the engine, and she closed her eyes. He lifted her out when they got home and carried her upstairs. Asleep, she fit like she belonged in his arms, a welcome and comfortable weight reminding him of years ago when he had carried the sleeping child. He needed to remember she was family, and nurture that relationship; the alternative a place he couldn't go. Something inside him disagreed. Nico ignored it like he ignored most things he didn't like.

Chapter 10

Nico strode into Lia's room. Surprised at his intrusion and at the purposeful footsteps, placing him directly in front of her, she stared, mouth agape.

"Tomorrow, swimsuit, towel and whatever else you need! We need to be out of here about nine," he said without preamble.

Lia still in stunned mode, closed her mouth positive the goldfish look didn't flatter. Nico's face reflected her thoughts before he shuttered his face into the familiar bland zone. Any hope of reading him vanished. This room, her sanctuary, now acquired an uneasy atmosphere. His foot tapped an impatient tune. She dug deep for something to say

"I don't have my swimsuit with me. Why do I need it and why do I have to go anywhere with you?"

"Time for a truce, and I thought the beach would be a pleasant location to talk. I have a house I own with friends. It's peaceful, private. We can have lunch, enjoy the sunshine."

"I see!" Her hand moved automatically to the small scar. "If it's about this, forget it. No offence but I'm fine and not keen on getting to know you better."

"We need to talk." He frowned at the scar. "You're coming."

Lia had once sneaked in, on Marco's advice, to watch Nico in action. She recognised the courtroom voice, the closing argument. Though specialising in corporate law, he also accepted pro bono criminal cases. Lia had catered to Marco's whim, curious, knowing Marco wanted to shed insight into Nico's better qualities. The irony had not escaped her. Contrary to Marco's beliefs Lia didn't doubt Nico had good qualities; unfortunately, they didn't apply to her.

"Fine!"

Gritting her teeth at his satisfied expression, Lia wished she had stayed away longer, but after two weeks Gina had been difficult to refuse. Lia loved living close to Greg and Ashlee in the apartment above their garage and loved her new administrative position. Combined with teaching arts and crafts to the wives and children from the base both jobs allowed her time for Laura's projects back home. Lia found it disconcerting, this lack of desire to return to Sydney. She bit her lip, in a constant little motion until she caught herself. *No point doing damage.* Aware her motives about staying went deeper than the obvious, and unwilling to dwell on it, she shrugged slim shoulders and focused on the man now apparently focused on her mouth.

"Is there something else?" Uncomfortable, Lia laid the book down on the bed beside her, hoping he would take the hint when the book remained open. Those few moments she had given in to her thoughts had left her feeling exposed. The glint of amusement in those dark eyes worried her, clouded her thinking. "I was trying to catch up on some reading."

"I like what you have done here." He ignored her dismissive tone and let his gaze rove around the room. When they returned to her, they were hooded. "He was right, the doctor, that night. On you the scar doesn't make a difference." With that he abruptly left the room.

She picked up her book, folded the page, a habit Laura detested, and closed it. She thought about his words. Nico liked simplicity both in his surroundings and on his person. He wore beautifully cut black suits with crisp, white linen shirts demanding forever to be ironed, or black jeans with pristine white T-shirts. The only relief were the bold, block coloured ties he had for work, usually a variant shade of red.

Lia acknowledged his choice of strong colours. Patterns were too busy for someone like him, and heaven forbid a mark or stain. Those items were instantly tossed. Annoyed with him or not, she found herself pleased he'd liked the way she had made this room her own. His actual spoken approval mystified her. Then again, he always noticed the things his mother did. *What an irritating puzzle of a man!*

Though she also loved simplicity she allowed flexibility. Persuading Nico to make changes – impossible like pulling teeth. Though common for adult children in Italian households to live at home, Nico's reasons were complex and based around the need to have things a certain way. His mother had no problem indulging this. Fiddling with her forehead, she sighed. The doctor had indicated the scar wouldn't affect her looks. *Did this mean Nico thought her nice looking? Wow, an unnerving thought!* Lia found herself torn. She didn't want to go but she hated the way things were.

"Why do you care so much?" Marco had asked her. She'd answered Nico was family and of course she wanted his acceptance. Had she given an honest answer though? The look on Marco's face as he had glanced at Silvia, suggested he didn't think so.

~

Nico had organised Gina to pack lunch, an appetising array of coffee, fruit, and fresh salami-filled rolls. If Gina had been surprised by Nico's request, she hadn't said a word. Gina wanted them to get along, wanted Lia to have less reason to leave Sicily. *Truce it is then*.

The house proved a pleasant surprise. Small, well-landscaped, a perfect holiday home, sleeping six people and boasting both an outdoor shower and a decent sized bathroom indoors - a prime piece of real-estate. Nico, Marco, and another friend had purchased it a few years earlier, and modernised without going to extremes. Sturdy, timber furniture, soft, black leather couches, a desk, and scattered bookcases reflected good taste and comfort. Lia helped Nico put the food away in the fridge before he grabbed a blanket, some towels and handed her two bottles of water. Concentrating on the path, she followed him quietly as they made their way to the sun-kissed stretch of sand and sea.

"Did you find a swimsuit?" Nico asked as they neared a spot near a tree.

"No, but I'm not going in the water, so it doesn't matter.

"Lose the dress then and get some sun. You need a bit of colour, and your underwear doesn't look that different to a bikini."

She pulled at the T-shirt style dress, wondering if he could see through it, glaring at him at the same time for his take-charge attitude.

"I can't see it through what you are wearing, Lia." He sounded exasperated.

"Domenico, I'm sorry..."

"Nico, I like Nico better," he said interrupting her, and stopping near one of the few trees.

The thought she referred to him already as Nico in her mind made her uneasy. *What would addressing him as Nico do to her frazzled nerves?* Hoping her face wouldn't betray her thoughts, she watched him spread the blanket in his swift, precise manner before she chose the corner in the shade as suitably distant from him and sat down and reached for her bag.

"What's this?" Moving closer, as she delved inside the oversized raffia holdall, he followed the abrupt question by grabbing her notebook. "I see you writing intensely or sketching all the time." He flicked through the pages before she could prevent him.

"They're notes, nothing important."

"You still draw butterflies I see, and doors. What a strange creature you were with those rainbow doors on every page. These are dignified, not a unicorn in sight."

"You remember that?"

"There were some good things to remember though..."

"Exactly. Some things are best forgotten." For a brief heartbeat she thought he would labour the point. *Let it go. Please let it go.*

"Mamma said you were writing a book."

"No," she replied. *Take a deep breath.* She softened her tone. "I'm writing another book."

"That would imply you have had one published, at some stage?"

"Yes, exactly!" She wanted to tear the notebook from his hands. He'd never made the slightest effort to get to know her before this, why now? She exhaled sharply, thought about her aunt and uncle and making peace, and added calmly, "I've actually been commissioned to write a series of children's books. This will be my third."

Nico handed back the notebook without asking further questions. His narrowed, piercing stare spoke for him. *The doors had done their job activating memories, remembering that day, the little girl begging to use the keys.* Pushing away the tremor the memory evoked, she turned to stare at the pale green sea water contrasting against the haphazard placing of pebbles and small stones.

No abundance of golden sand here, not like beaches back home, but it had a beauty all its own. The only blight, the man staring at her, waiting for a reaction. *What did he want?* Lia found it unsettling to go from a tumultuous relationship without real conversation to a semblance of cosy normality.

She trembled despite the heat, remembering his comments about her father's funeral, damning her without knowing the details. Her mind switched to Nico changing the television channel for her when her favourite game show came on. Granted he would also leave the room, giving her the evil eye. Lia uttered a small sound of frustration. *I don't know what to think.*

Bending her head to write in her notebook seemed wise. Beside her Nico stripped off his jeans and shirt and walked down to the water. *Black swimmers* she thought, *of course.* Ignoring him also seemed wise, but a losing battle. She touched her scar, prodding at it as if it could divert her attention from the beauty of the male in front of her. She knew he and Marco hit the gym often between their schedules.

How did he manage to look so sexual, and sophisticated at the same time? Until Domenico, she had thought the mix of bad boy vibes and facial regrowth sexy, whilst the clean cut 'pretty boy' look lacked sensual substance. It didn't, she realised, when combined with that slightly sullen mouth and powerful brown gaze, a gaze capable of setting fire to anything in its path.

Did looking sexy automatically make you good at sex? Lia pouted at her wayward thoughts, continuing her appraisal but consciously stepping back a little. She needed to be objective, not personal. *At just over six foot, unusual for an Italian or at least the ones that she knew, and that golden skin...*

She halted, conceding she needed coffee badly, and reached for the thermos and cups he had thoughtfully provided. With conscious effort she settled her attention on her notes and not the man determined to do her head in.

~

"So, tell me about this writing. I thought you and your friend did something with home decorating?"

She hadn't heard him come back and started as he bent to grab his towel, droplets of water demanding her attention as they made their way down his body.

This Nico made her nervous. "Yes, that's all true but writing is my preference these days. Laura is more the business. She's got the talent and passion for designing but performs better with someone to bounce her ideas off. I like doing that for her. My consulting for her satisfies us both, and I can do that anywhere." Lia wished he would sit down. All that golden skin and muscle on display seemed irritatingly indecent.

"Isn't it a partnership though?"

He sensed her discomfort, found amusement in the fact, the evidence in his voice, in the lines of his face.

"Yes!" she snapped. "Why all this sudden interest when you seem to know so much already?"

"My mother. She thought telling me things about you might help us get along. Hasn't she been telling you things about me?"

"No, I try to discuss you as little as possible." *That was nasty, damn it.* "Sorry, I didn't mean that the way it sounded."

Nico stepped closer, seriously entertained by her mistrust and discomfort at his proximity, and her inability to be mean. She looked cute, scrunching her mouth into a contrite smile when she wanted to scowl. "I think you did, but I forgive you."

"True, and thanks, I think." Lia accepted the olive branch he offered, smiling genuinely at him for the first time that day.

Nico draped the towel around his waist and sat down beside her.

"The writing is something I kind of fell into. I wrote a few magazine articles that tied in with the business and it became a regular feature which grew into a monthly question and answer segment. And then one day a reader asked about involving kids in projects around the house, and somehow it became a book. Things grew from there. Suddenly my time narrowed, and we hired some extra staff and I moved into a consultancy role. The arrangement works for both of us."

"Clever little thing, aren't you?"

"Yes, I am. Why is that such a surprise to you?" His attitude bewildered her. *How could it be anything other than an attack with the obvious smirk in his voice?* "I admit my arrival may have been traumatic, but it's taken a stint at the Emergency room for you to decide

I'm worthy of being a family member, and even then, you can't resist the smart comments?" She shook her head. "Look this isn't going to work. I don't think we have anything to say to each other."

"You're wrong. We do. I think we both know that."

She squirmed under his penetrating gaze. "I don't know what you mean."

"Yes, you do. Don't pretend you don't feel this tension between us."

He watched as she swallowed uneasily, the colour rising in her cheeks, her eyelids fluttering. *Would she deny it?* Idly he noted her breasts, a perfect size, made for firm hands to fondle. He wondered if her nipples would be a pale, delicate pink like her full lips. Her hair, in one of those side plaits today, defined the oval shape of her face, leaving her features on show. Nico's interest drifted down. He reined it in before salvaging a relationship became impossible.

"Give me a chance," he said quietly, "give us a chance to be friends."

Moments like this with his eyes roaming, the heat radiating, made it difficult to deny the tension. *Talking to him might help*. Allowing herself the luxury of calming breaths, she began a discussion of her life in Australia. The antipathy marking their relationship absent, Lia discovered Nico could be stimulating company. She teetered on regretful when he got up to go to the house to complete some work on his computer. Caught up in her thoughts, she looked up to find he hadn't moved far.

"I wasn't going to hit you that night."

"I know. I overreacted. Can we forget it?"

"No, I shouldn't have said those things. I'm sorry. To see you physically hurt has never been my intention even when you try my patience, and you do."

Warily, she eyed him. Cracks in the stone face reflected sincerity. "Thank you."

Nico hesitated. He didn't want to leave her; he resented the feeling. A flash of anger, a now ingrained if undeserved reaction to her, escaped him. Her expression altered. The fleeting sadness shamed him. He reached out, pulled back quickly, smiled briefly instead. "Will you be alright here on your own?"

Lia nodded, and hesitantly returned his smile.

"I'll be about an hour. Stay in the shade."

Shaking with relief at his retreating back, she watched him disappear towards the house. With deliberation she tugged her dress over her head. The warm sun on her skin appealed. She laughed. He'd mentioned staying in the shade; it made her want to do the opposite. Spreading sunscreen on her face and arms didn't hide the fact that getting on with Nico enveloped her with a sense of foreboding, and a perverse desire to see where it would lead. She hovered, uncertain - the adaptation from enemy to friend a strain.

Chapter 11

"Feel like something to eat?"

"Finished your work?" She hadn't heard him come back. Reaching casually for her dress, she slipped it back on. He grinned at what she presumed he thought shyness. Now if only she could avoid more heart to heart, she might survive the day. Sociable could be bearable, a serious discussion another matter and not one she wanted. If, however, it broke the hold of the past, it would be worth it. Her stomach churned, not with hunger.

"Most of it thanks to the phone and the computer. I'll still need to go in this afternoon though." He put the basket down on the blanket.

"Why don't we call it a day and go home then? We can take lunch back with us."

"You truly struggle with my company, don't you? I won't bite, I promise."

"Yeah, well, we'll see." Lia's face creased in doubt. She raised her eyebrows at his laugh, pursing her lips. Her stomach growled. Nico laughed again. Begrudgingly, she reached over, helping him unpack the basket. Her stomach growled again. This time she laughed with him, using the lightened mood to start the conversation. "What else do we need to talk about? We seem to have done a bit already."

"Okay. So, let's not beat around your shrub, then."

"Bush!" she corrected, rolling her eyes, "beat around the bush."

"Isn't *bush* an American expression for..."

"Shut up, Domenico."

"I'll not say another word."

She made a rude gesture.

"Look," he said, amusement in his voice, "I thought if we knew more about each other we could get on better."

"We don't need to, we know enough."

"Are you backtracking, Lia? You're the one wanting happy families."

"We're here, aren't we? We're both still alive. Does anything else matter?"

"Yes, it does matter. I think we've gone off track." She coloured under his gaze, remaining silent. "I have questions, more a question, to help me understand you better. Is that so bad?"

"No."

"Then tell me Lia, why all the drama with the letters? It's been twenty years and your father...your father isn't here to know."

Lia stared at his face, watched him reach for one of the fresh rolls. She knew he didn't mean to sound callous. He had loved her Papa, but Domenico was a practical person. "Straight into that shrub?" She sighed, considering how best to answer. "I know he isn't here, but he wanted this. And twenty years? Exactly the point! Hasn't it been long enough? Two of the main players are dead. Your mother has led a half-life and your father..."

"Deserves everything he gets for what he did."

"You asked me a question so let me answer it. I want a family, my family."

"You have all those friends in Australia and now your American friends. In fact, you seem to have a talent for collecting champions, including my parents."

"Yes, I do. Is it wrong though to want something more closely connected to my Papa? How long do we let the past impact on the present? How long does the punishment go on for? And it is punishment." She held her hand up as he went to speak. "Look, Mama told me what happened all those years ago."

He flinched, his face reforming into a piece of ice. She handed him the container holding the salami and sliced cheese, keeping him on track with food so she could continue talking. She had learned many things living in the same house with him.

"I didn't remember much about the day for a long time. I just knew everything had changed. We weren't the same family and I thought it my fault. Mama sensed it. I had turned eleven when she told me enough to help me understand why Papa treated her the way he did. She trusted in my maturity, I guess. Do you know she described herself as emotional, impulsive? Grown up words. I loved her, and I know how much she loved me. But it didn't stop me knowing what she meant. Despite that Domenico, she was a good person. Don't give me that face. To be honest with her young daughter required courage."

"Nico, not Domenico. And do you honestly believe what you're saying?"

"Yes. Yes, I do. She wanted me to know what she did cost her dearly; she lost the right to a family, a husband, a happy life." Lia paused to look at him. "She accepted her punishment, living in the same house, doing the necessary household tasks, looking after a child, used to satisfy a sexual urge whenever her husband felt like it."

Nico snorted. She ignored him.

"No, she didn't tell me that part. She didn't need to be explicit. I figured it out myself. Papa was a good man who could be uncompromising. Mama trusted in him enough to hope for the good again, and it came. For him she fought hard against the cancer, and for me." Lia paused, her throat tight, her head aching, her eyes stinging from the battle not to cry. "Friends are wonderful, but Papa and I would've given anything to have family. He wanted more for me, wanted this trip." She gulped, slowed to allow herself to settle. "All those letters he wrote, he kept hoping Gina would understand and want him back in her life. I couldn't let all that hope go to waste. I couldn't."

"Sentiment isn't enough to erase the sins of the past."

"So moral, so inflexible, so high and mighty. Does it make you feel superior? Fixating makes you forget to be human. You miss the essential. Instead of the whole picture, you get your portion. I'm not defending anyone here. I'm answering your question. My way. Marissa and Lucio were young. What they had, fragile. Gina wanted Lucio. The pregnancy got her what she wanted. Don't growl at me! Your father had no choice. My Papa manipulated the situation to his advantage. He wanted Marissa. Is it so strange then that when Lucio and Marissa met again, things happened? They paid for it, twenty years of payment. Time to move on, push it all into the past. Let it go."

"You make it sound easy. Let it go? No. People do, people pay."

"Black is black. White is white. No. Grey exists whether you like it or not and sometimes grey allows a little peace in our lives, allows forgiveness. My father taught me that. If you can't let it go, why are we here? We didn't need this private tete-a-tete."

"You know why we're here, Lia. For now, let's stick to the present conversation."

"This conversation is the only agenda I'm interested in. So, alright then. Let's finish it. How much is this about pride, your pride? How much is ego?"

"Little girl, you have no idea what you are talking about."

"Don't patronise me. Don't treat me like I'm stupid. And keep your temper under control. You think...you think I don't know you were in love with my mother, or thought you were? A teenage boy's idea of love, pure and from afar. It made betrayal worse, didn't it? That pedestal, the goddess fell off. Your father, well, he was never on one. I get it. I get what it did to your ideas of how things should be. You were wrong and you can't stand a flaw in the pattern you created in your head. Like I said, you fixate. You were fixated on her and then you fixated on what she did. Your mother paid the real price, her health, and her baby. Your pride seems a poor second to those things."

He moved so quickly she gasped after the fact, his tight grip pulling her body into his. The connection, intense, more than skin on skin, his head to the side of hers, his breath, warm against her cheek. If he turned a small fraction, their lips would touch, and his arousal would be impossible to ignore. The fact he smelled of the ocean bothered her. Underneath the salty flavour Lia could detect his aftershave, the same fragrance he had worn since his early twenties according to his mother. The irony of their similarities did not escape Lia. Her lotions and perfume, both a concoction she had dreamed up with Laura, were the only products she ever used.

He let her go abruptly, picked up the roll he'd dropped and threw it into a container in the basket. His face smoothed. Lia wasn't fooled. The anger, both at her words and the betrayal of his body, simmered, not masked by his stillness. His agitation, whilst it made her nervous, wouldn't let her put the conversation to bed. She shivered again at the thought of a bed, a disturbing connotation. Shrugging the errant images away, she concentrated on choosing her next words with care.

"She didn't mean to hurt you. She was...Marissa."

Nico stretched his legs out in front of him, a semblance of relaxation she didn't believe.

"She told you a lot, didn't she?"

The coolness in his voice had the hairs on her arms stand to attention. Much of what he did had that effect. She wanted to smooth them down but then he would see how much he unnerved her. The urgent, sick-to-the-stomach feeling held a warning. He resented how she made him feel, didn't understand it. Neither did she. This was a conversation they needed to have before the day's end.

"Yes. Yes, she did," Lia said, answering his question with calm.

"Nothing justifies what they did."

His voice and clenched jaw signalled the resurgence of anger on the topic of Marissa. It had no place in the present. Lia's perspective differed to his. She had witnessed the changes forgiveness wrought. Needing him to understand, she reached over unthinkingly, and put her hand on his thigh. He recoiled; she drew back.

"Nico..."

"Let's finish our lunch."

"I'm not justifying. I'm trying to explain how things can get out of control." Lia had to make him see the truth of it, for his sake as much as her own. "I thought you would understand that. Isn't it the other reason we are here?"

She picked up her roll and chewed quietly. It had no taste, but she needed something to do. The slight flush in his cheeks told her she had made her point.

"Why do you pronounce mamma the way you do?"

The random question threw her off balance. Realising he'd offered an olive branch, she thought about her answer, not wanting to upset the moment.

"I don't know. I couldn't say it properly when I was little, couldn't manage the double letter and it stuck.

"I remember we teased you about it."

"You said I sounded like a lamb."

"You remember that?"

"I remember everything," she told him quietly.

Nico didn't reply, choosing to finish his roll and pour a coffee. A short time later he began asking questions about the business she and Laura ran. They were complex questions and didn't allow for one-word answers. Lia followed his lead until his mobile rang.

The call stole his attention, taking him up to the house and giving Lia time to gather her thoughts. *Has today made things better? Papa, I don't know. I really don't.* She removed her dress and lay down to doze under the lulling warmth of the sun.

Chapter 12

Lia, he could see as he neared the blanket had decided to take advantage of his absence and relax. Not wanting to startle her with his approach, he kicked at the sand and small pebble mixture with his bare feet to give her warning. She didn't stir. Nico sent more pebbles flying. No movement but he could hear murmurs, small, pained groans, garbled words.

"Lia, wake up," he said, bending carefully so as not to frighten her with his sudden presence. "It's only a dream." Nico gentled his hands on her shoulders, perturbed by the depth of sleep, her inability to waken.

A familiar voice teased the edge of her subconscious. She fought it, afraid to leave despite the pain of the dreamscape. "Papa! Papa!" She fought harder to stay, "Papa, please. Don't make me leave you."

The dry sobbing had an obscene quality. Not knowing what would be appropriate, he sat beside her until her anguish put an end to his patience. Not able to withstand the level of her suffering, he pulled her into his arms, rocking her gently until the harsh sounds eased into whimpering. Preoccupied with her distress blinded him to her semi-naked body. Now conscious of warm skin he wondered at the reason why this beautiful woman could be modest to the point of paranoia where he was concerned. Or perhaps he shouldn't wonder, he thought. Instead, he focused on a quiet litany of comforting words.

Cocooned in his arms, her brain enticed her with visions of safety. Drowsy eyes lifted tired lids. Nico's face loomed close. Embarrassed she immediately pushed away, scrubbing her face with trembling hands. Looking down she spied the dress she had tossed aside. Panic overwhelmed her, her hands searching blindly.

Nico thought Lia's furtive effort to find her dress, ridiculous. *Her underwear covered more than most swimsuits.* And then Nico saw it. "What the hell is this?"

he asked, his hand gliding the length of a jagged dark pink line reaching from the front of her hip to the small of her back. "Lia? Is this from the accident? Fuck! Is this what the nightmares are about?"

Mortified and still in the trembling throes of the aftermath the nightmares caused, she couldn't answer. Hanging her head, she clutched her dress like a shield.

With one hand Nico lifted her chin. The other tugged the dress away from her body.

"Don't. Don't hide. I want to understand. I wondered at the panic you displayed at the hospital. I assumed an association with the accident. Not that you had been a part of what happened." Long, gentle fingers traced the line of the scar again.

Her body tightened, clenched with emotion, pushed against him, desperately trying to break free of his arms. "How would you know? You've been busy trying to keep some stupid vendetta alive because your ego hurt."

He let go of her. "That isn't fair, Lia. We've come a long way today."

"Have we? To your way of thinking perhaps but not mine. One normal conversation in all the time I have been here. How nice! Can we go home now?" Lia went to rise; her legs buckled. Nico's arms snaked their way around her body and dragged her back into a sitting position beside him.

"Lia. The dream, tell me about the dream." Instinct told him not to say the accident.

"No. Domenico. I'm sorry to spoil the day and the fun we're having. I want to go home."

"Nico, I like Nico. I want to understand. I honestly do. I did love your father. I'm sorry I haven't made that clear. I don't like reminders of the past, but it doesn't mean I don't care."

Lia stared at him, eyes swimming in unshed tears. "Really, forgive me for not having noticed."

He reached for her then and enfolded her in strong arms, ignoring her truculent tone. "I'm the one who should be asking for forgiveness. I'm sorry, sorry about everything including that night. I should have danced with you."

Lia tucked her head down, her thoughts jumbled, her body raw. Finally, the childhood hero surfaced, and she didn't know what to do with him.

"Nico, it doesn't matter."

"It does. I haven't made it easy for you. I do struggle to let go of things. I do find it hard to forgive and forget."

Lia's thoughts flashed back to the courtroom and the Nico she had witnessed. He had controlled the room, working it for his client. Marco had told her Nico did this frequently without compensation. Lia always came back to one word – enigma. A contradiction, Nico was a contradiction. It must be so hard to be him, she thought. The intensity that drove him, the need for order and control over his world. Whilst keeping him strong it also kept him away from the real world. Nico believed emotion undermined his abilities and thus needed to be rationed. Yet that same man had offered to listen to her. *Should she trust him?*

Lia trembled; she always did when she had these insights into his head. Stranger still, he had the same ability to get inside hers. She laughed. Rather than take offence, he tightened his hold. Her lashes fluttered. She allowed their gazes to meet. So good-looking, so approachable: another courtroom ploy, or real interest in her? Liking him presented a danger she could do without. Right now, she liked him a damned lot.

"We were on our way home from dinner." She gulped, shocked at herself for speaking. Papa driving, Laura in the backseat. The light had just turned green. We kept going. Papa and the car beside us. A truck turned in front of us both, the driver thinking he had time I guess." Lia stopped for a second, as though seeing it.

"Go on."

"The truck hit hard, spinning our car around and against the other one. The truck's load, mostly timber, crashed through our windscreen. I felt its weight, but it didn't hurt. So strange. Shock, I guess. Papa's voice was frantic. I kept repeating I was fine. The timber blocked his view and mine."

Lia laughed, a chilling, bitter sound.

"Laura answered slowly. She sounded strained. I was scared she might be hurt more than she wanted us to know. As it turned out...that wasn't it at all. From the back seat, she saw what I couldn't. Sirens, people, shouting, and Papa talking on the inside, telling me how much the trip to Italy mattered all blended. I remember being sick but from then it became a jigsaw, where pieces didn't make sense. The smell in the car, Laura crying, more voices, loud banging, tearing sounds, all of it so confusing."

Nico reached up and stroked her hair. Her body softened, then immediately tensed. Frustrated, he drew his hand back.

"Three people in the other car died including the driver."

The coldness of her tone shook him. Taking a risk, he tugged her fully into his body. Icy skin met his fingers. Instinctively Nico skimmed over the parts he could touch to share a modicum of heat.

"The truck driver walked away without a scratch. I know he didn't mean to cause...still, it's hard to forgive. Anyway, they got Laura's door open. She argued, screamed her protest, wanted me out first. The rescue team seemed to take forever moving the timber off me, something about reducing pressure too quickly. I didn't understand, kept dozing off and calling for Papa."

"Then what?"

The richness of his voice, smooth like the slide of wine comforted and enticed her to nestle closer. He tightened his hold. The feeling of safety strengthened.

"All this time I couldn't see him, couldn't turn my head until hands were reaching for me and then I saw him. He was pushed up against the steering wheel. A piece of timber had somehow pierced his chest and the blood, so much blood. I screamed, clawed, begged not to be taken away. Nico?"

"Yes. I'm here."

"I want my Papa. Nico. Tell him to let me stay with him. Tell him."

"Lia. Hush. You're safe." Oblivious to his voice, she kept calling for her father. Nico thought she might have forgotten his presence completely but then she quietened, melted against him, and gave one last shudder. He sighed in relief.

"They gave me something. I woke up in hospital," she whispered, wanting to get all of it out now she had begun. "First, I would feel disorientated, so confused about the events and then I would remember, and I would scream until something jabbed me. Then, oblivion until I woke up again. I don't know how many times. Lexi and Laura sitting there, Connie, Lexi's mother, with her endless knitting, they were my reality. Papa's death I couldn't accept. And then..."

Nico caressed her arm lightly. "What Lia, what happened?"

The pleasant voice, a cool breath against her ear, soothed. "Mama was there. She said Papa had to follow the butterflies. Mama had this thing about butterflies. The night she died she told me the butterflies had come. I swear I heard rustling. I heard them again or thought I did that night. I stopped screaming when I woke up and began to heal, my body anyway. The nightmares started once I got home and haven't stopped." Lia lifted her head, afraid and yet needing to see his reaction to her words.

"That's why you missed the funeral, isn't it?"

Surprised he didn't take the opportunity to belittle the butterflies, she relaxed, accepting his sincerity. A part of her stirred, still angry as she recalled the dreadful things Nico had said to her about missing the funeral. Then again, she hadn't refuted his words.

"I wasn't in any condition to go anywhere for a long time."

Her reply, calm and straight-forward, made no reference to waking up with a thousand tubes connected to her body, or the fact she only had one kidney now or the long convalescence period. She only knew missing the funeral had left a brand, a bigger scar than the one he'd seen.

"A video does exist. I've never watched it."

"Your Papa would understand, and you will eventually, or you won't. Either way he'd understand."

Sincerity and sympathy? From him? Lia's fragile hold on sanity broke; she fractured.

Chapter 13

The heaving of the slender body reverberated in his chest. The sound messed with his mind, demanding a response. The only person he might have allowed this kind of intimacy would be his mother, yet memories were awakening. He'd done this before with her, held her, comforted her. When Lia moved away, wrapping her arms around her body, looking fragile, small, and broken the dots began to connect. Small snippets of the past, relegated to dark recesses of his mind surfaced, reminding him of the child she'd been, and the tears shed that terrible day.

Nico tugged Lia fiercely back into his embrace. Her cold trembling body felt brittle. All the sassiness, her determination and strength washed away in sad memories. If she shattered, he wasn't sure the pieces could be put back together. Guilt gnawed at his insides. He hadn't helped at all with his attitude. His lips moved to her hair. Inhaling the fresh fragrance, he gave his hands freedom to roam and warm her shaking limbs.

Lia's frantic effort to breathe vibrated into something primal inside his head. *Mine.* He alternated between rubbing along her arms, with gentle fingertips and open palms, and giving freedom to his mouth and lips to explore the velvet feel of her hair. He hovered, like her precious butterflies, then moved to the base of her neck, keeping kisses soft. His mouth wanted to touch her soft cheek, clamp down on her beckoning jaw line. She turned a fraction towards him, enough to allow a melding with the luscious mouth. The desire to taste had haunted his dreams long enough. Hunger demanded attention, his because he had denied it, hers because she wanted to flee from the haunting memories, and then theirs, bending to inevitability.

From comforting caresses, wandering hands greedily latched onto the softness of skin. Her taste, her essence on the tongue duelling with his, bewitched him. Swallowing her whole would not sate his desire.

Her lack of resistance, a lure beyond his imagination. When her hands clawed ownership of his body, his desire escalated. He ignored the final threat to sanity and let mouths cleave. Nothing mattered more than fused mouths.

Clothes disappeared. With great care Nico pulled the long braid apart, threading his fingers through its silky softness. He let it spread between them and breathed in the aroma of chocolate and coconut and something he couldn't identify. Hands glided in search of promises. The laboured breathing, an erotic film soundtrack. Nico refused to relinquish the thrill of her fingers digging into his skin as a way to deal with grief. This was about her wanting him, a perverse satisfaction he intended to enjoy. Passion pumped the flow of blood in two separate people, blending, morphing them into one being.

Nico's length nestled against her belly, a hard, hot determined part of the man holding Lia possessively. Finesse faded and gave way to a selfish driving need. Nico had to be inside of her soon. Using his knee, he spread her legs apart. One hand drifted down to touch her where she glistened with invitation. She arched, and Nico wished he had time to investigate further but he was ruled by insanity to thrust so far inside her that she would be ruined for anyone else. Lia's clinging hands and sharp fingernails taunted Nico to make it happen.

Nico ignored the ache demanding he enjoy the glide of his fingers inside her, to keep feeling how wet she was for him and brought his hand back to her body. Not holding her was unthinkable. He would let his cock fend for itself. Nico thrust into the beckoning warmth. Her moan of pain shocked him, putting him in limbo. Nico's attention shifted to the unexpected. He grimaced. Half-way home, pulsing with painful need he realised what he should have known.

She whispered his name, a plea, a guttural yearning. Then, understanding his predicament, she rose, impaling herself the rest of the way.

The ever-alert voyeur in his head screamed perfection in her tightness, in the clenching of her muscles and the wicked, wet made-to-order slide housing his length. His release thundered at him, wanting the warm flood unleashed. He wanted to mark her forever his. The thought, emotionally irrational, angered him. He cast it aside, concentrating on making the experience right for her. His ego demanded it.

Lia, lost in a daze of blissful agony thought herself in heaven and hell. The more it moved inside her the more the hell receded, like Nico's shock. She opened her eyes to find harsh planes in the passionate face as he fought to slow down. His lashes fluttered, rose. Caught up as she was in this blazing moment, the thought he worried for her managed to thrill. She didn't care if the thought shared the limelight with a now fragile and determined male ego. Spirals of pleasure would replace the pain. He would not have it any other way. She smiled at him, closed her eyes, and tightened her hold.

Slowly and steadily the sweep of intimate parts picked up the universal rhythm. The need to be deeper, go harder, impossible to resist. Nico groaned, and she instinctively recognised the effort to hold himself back for her. She pulled her mouth from his and opened her eyes again to discover a vortex of need matching her own. She held his gaze, wanting her own eyes to say the words she couldn't say and licked her lips. Satisfied, he pounced on her, making it clear there would be no stopping now. Lia opened for him, allowing his tongue to mimic the furious pace of his body.

Nico pushed her legs wider apart. The savagery of his grip served to ignite her further. A heat flared, burned. Sparks of pleasure became flames spiralling her further into the unknown. Nico roared her name. Lia splintered, burying herself in his body. He held her tightly and she gripped back, pleased at the way she felt treasured in his arms. When he finally moved, Lia panicked, dug fingernails into his skin. He sighed and moved onto his back, taking her with him so she could lay her head on his chest. Nico's hands trailed soothingly down her back. Safe, she closed her eyes.

"Lia." A hand traced along her cheek and stirred her awake. "We have to go."

She opened her eyes, met melted chocolate, and smiled, at ease with the unexpected person who had managed to chase off her nightmares and bury them for good. The universe had dictated a strange way for Lia to find peace. She and Nico definitely needed to talk.

Chapter 14

"I guess this is the discussion we needed to have." Lia, a shy confidence adding a pale pink glow to her cheeks, put a hand on his chest and used it as leverage to face him.

"I'd hoped to talk before this."

"Well, tact isn't your strong point when dealing with me, is it?"

"Lia." Watching the colour drain from her face, Nico brushed the back of his hand across the smoothness of her cheek. "That came out wrong. I wanted you and I'm not regretting a moment but..."

"It shouldn't have happened."

"Exactly. I take full responsibility. I fought you being here. If I had accepted you, at the beginning..."

"I think it would've happened anyway."

"No."

"Yes."

"No. Maybe. No."

"Nico?"

He sighed. "From the first day I felt this pull towards you. You represented problems on so many levels and I'm not sure I comprehended any of them. I still don't."

Lia felt a pang of sympathy. A bewildered Nico drew on her emotions. Nico had principles, a strong sense of right and wrong. The current situation didn't fit his vision, his parameters. She rubbed her head against his chest before laying it down. His heartbeat, a slow, determined sound, echoed his resolve. Nico didn't want to believe in the power of the chemistry between them. Correction, she thought, he didn't want to believe in a situation he had no power to control.

"I wanted you to be my boy wonder again, my superhero, my family. Yet, I didn't make it easy for us. Maybe if I had behaved differently? Truthfully, I think we both fucked up."

He laughed, and she gave him a small, shy grin before falling into a companionable silence. Lia palmed his chest, lifting so their heads were once again level. In his arms she'd found a haven, and whilst she felt the turmoil, a tangible satisfaction she hadn't expected tempered it. Nico, on the other hand, had a jaw about to snap if he didn't relax. His eyes were hooded. Lia wondered what they hid, glanced away to ease his tension but couldn't resist looking back. When their gazes locked, her insides went up in flames.

"What?" Not bothering to disguise annoyance, he grunted the question.

"You know what."

"Lia." Her name, a soft but this time, angry sigh.

"I should feel...I don't know," Lia ran her fingers through her tangled hair, let the dark mass veil her expression.

"Lia, I don't know either. My common sense has disappeared, leaving my libido in charge. It's pretty impressed it got to do what it did. And, to make things worse, it would like to do it again." He pushed her hair back off her face.

Lia blushed. "Nico."

Her use of his name said more than she realised. "Did you think I would be smug, or that I'd hold you accountable?"

"I thought you might like me even less." Her voice held a slight quiver.

He laughed, reaching up and using his hand in her hair to bring her closer. His lips grazed across hers. She lowered her head to his chest.

"Lia. Don't hide from me."

She let her chin caress his collarbone. "You're not angry then?"

"We had sex, great sex. I'm definitely not angry, but the fact logic no longer resides in my brain where you're concerned doesn't thrill me." She laughed. He tugged on her hair. "I'm glad it makes you happy because it annoys the shit out of me." He used his grip on the long, dark strands to manoeuvre her, stare into her eyes.

"What?" she asked at the small frown creasing his forehead.

"Nothing."

"You want to know why, don't you?"

Her small exhalation ruffled the sparse amount of hair on his chest as she lowered her head. She found the nearness distracting. Warm and smelling of the sea he tantalised her senses. She wanted to inhale and lick her way from one nipple across the expanse to the other. Instead, she settled for using his chest as a pillow.

"Lia. You're a beautiful woman. So, yes it does seem strange to find you've never... that you were still a...?"

"Stop! Don't say it." She blushed, burying her face further into his chest.

He tugged on her hair, bringing them both back to eye level.

"Sorry," she whispered, "hearing that word from you is going to make me crazy. I'm already feeling foolish."

"No! Never foolish, but I would like to understand."

Nico moved his hand to her cheek, his smile widening when she leaned in to rest on his palm. He missed her touch when she sat up to answer him.

"I never wanted to go that far. I can't tell you why. Family history? Something in me? I don't know. I mean

I liked the idea of sex, but the final act always put me off."

"But not today?"

"Apparently not."

Lia reached for the nearby towel to cover herself. The turn in conversation while naked, hiked up her vulnerability. Nico on the other hand sat comfortably, and if anything, seemed amused by her modesty.

"Interesting. I'm honoured."

"Now you're being your usual obnoxious self. Nico, it wasn't your charm. I was upset."

"Liar. That wasn't the only reason."

"Shut up Nico." His answer, a snigger and a rise in those eyebrows, a typical Nico action, made her laugh. "You're such an arse. Alright. It may not have been the only reason."

"You're admitting it."

"Nico, all that tension? I did recognise what it meant. I was a virgin, not dead. Acknowledging it meant trouble, ignoring it seemed the best solution consciously or unconsciously."

"Let's not make too much of this, Lia. I haven't made it easy for you. Today maybe, I've made it up to you. Why don't we leave it at that?"

"I like the idea, but can we?"

"We have to, Lia. Whatever drives...fuels this...?"

"Attraction?"

"That's as good a word as any but it doesn't excuse it. We're not just two people. Damn it. If my mother...it's...this is so fucked."

"I know. Thank you though, for today..." Lia put her hands to her cheeks. "I mean..." She rolled off his body and onto her knees.

"I know what you mean. But now you need to stop looking at my dick."

"Fuck off, Nico. I'm not interested in your stupid cock."

"Language please."

"I'm not afraid of the word and here's another one. Arsehole!"

He laughed.

"Nico," she said hesitantly, "do you think maybe now things can be different? I don't want to fight anymore."

"I can't change how I feel so easily, especially about my father. Can you accept that?"

"Please, ease up a bit on him. Something is happening at home. And it's a good thing. I don't want you to interfere...and when we fight...the tension it causes..."

"I know what it does. And I'm not blind to the development with my parents," he interrupted, placing warm fingers over her lush mouth. "I don't want to be angry. Something about you makes me want to keep you at arm's length. Maybe if we act like normal people, my penis will stay where it belongs." He sighed and got to his feet. "I'm far from happy about my parents but I won't interfere."

Lia also rose but unlike him, she wrapped the towel tightly around her. She reached down to help him pick up their belongings. Nico grabbed the towel from her with a malicious grin. She rolled her eyes, he widened the grin, a comfortable companionship between them. They made their way back towards the house, neither one speaking.

"For now," Nico broke the silence, "let's concentrate on today as progress in getting along."

Lia couldn't hide her pleasure at his words.

Amused, he couldn't resist the opportunity to continue teasing. "You're still staring." Her outrage was worth it.

"Shut up about your dick. It's not that impressive."

"Yes, it is."

"Hey, I read, I look at pictures, I don't think so at all."

"You know, you shouldn't have said that."

He dropped the things he carried, advancing on her. She dropped her things and ran. He caught her, threw her over his shoulder, then tossed her under the outdoor shower, turning on the cold water before she could protest. Ready to berate him, she lost her train of thought in view of the enormous arousal pointing directly at her.

"You do know what happened today can't happen again."

She wasn't sure whether he was speaking to himself or to her. Enthralled by his hand working its way casually up and down the impressive erection, she didn't much care. The way it came alive, the head wet with fluid captured all her attention.

"I know it can't."

All the same her eyes followed every movement. On show, recognising appreciation, his erection became even more impressive. Her mouth opened, a shocked half-moan escaping. The sound drew his eyes to her mouth, to the pink tip of her tongue. She reached out from under the cascade of water, sliding her thumb over the moisture seeping from the engorged head. Captivated, she moved her thumb to her mouth. He drew in a ragged breath. She smiled.

"Fuck, Lia. You definitely should not have done that."

Lia smiled again. "We have a saying in English. It's an old one but appropriate for this moment. In for a penny, in for a pound. It means, Nico..."

"I know what it means Lia."

"Today then Nico, for today let's pretend nothing else exists. I haven't felt so alive for such a long time. I want this, want you and warmer water, and not in that order." She grinned.

His brown eyes flashed danger. He prowled forward, adjusted the water temperature, halted to regard her, watched her faltering under his intensity.

"What, what is it?"

"I'm not sure I can be gentle this time. I don't think I want to be."

"Nico. I'm a big girl. I know what I want and for today, it's you. I want you."

He growled, barely letting her finish before swooping on her mouth. His fingers roamed through the strands of her hair, enjoying the slick wet feel of it. Something about her called to the primitive male inside of him. Her unexpected bravery, the manner she'd faced him head on without losing her sweetness. A virginal air in a body made for fucking had the whole of his body responding.

Her mouth opened to him, to his desire. Dislodging their mouths, he turned her to face the wall, imprisoning her hands, nailing them high above her head. "Keep your hands right here, on this wall," he whispered harshly in her ear, biting it, not stopping short of causing pain. She yelped and immediately brought her hands down. "Put your hands on the wall and keep them there!"

His sharp and succinct tone commanded instant obedience. The hardness at her back signalled its approval by jerking. Nico moved his hands to her hips and then moved them closer together. His thumbs met, and he slid them down, brushing the small opening they found on their wandering path. *God, the things he wanted to do to her.* Hands gripping her hip bones, he entered her with one hard slide. The small sound she made, vibrated throughout his body. He froze, waiting. She exhaled, a satisfied sound. Permission, he thought, and began a pounding rhythm, his body revelling in the way she met him thrust for thrust, celebrating the fierce savagery as much as he did. Nico wanted her mouth, needed to watch every reaction on that beautiful face.

Lia gasped when he pulled out. Nico turned her to him and plastered his mouth over hers, simultaneously lifting her. She knew instinctively what to do, what he wanted, no, needed from her. She tightened her hold on him sliding down over him and taking him back into her body. She wrapped her legs around his waist and let her tongue delve into his mouth with the same furious intensity his cock delved into her.

Lia's hunger for him matched his. Wet where she encased him, and wet where the water poured over them, a mindless intoxication of sensations spiralling him out of control. He wanted to slide down and put his tongue on her, in her. His legs weakened at the thought. Lia, a danger to his orderly life; one taste and he'd be ruined. His thoughts increased the perfect rhythm of their bodies, put him over, spilling liquid fire. Paradise, Lia transported him to paradise he thought as she quivered around him. He tightened his hold, her hands coming to rest in his hair, her voice a melody of pleasure in his ear.

"Right or wrong, I can't regret today, Nico. I can't."

He acknowledged her with a slight movement of his chin as he allowed her to slide down his body. Turning off the tap, he reached for and handed her a towel. His phone rang. His eyes continued to watch, absorbed by her actions even as he spoke to the person on the other end. Graceful, he thought, from wrapping the towel around her body, to bending and picking up their things, she was fucking perfect.

Chapter 15

"I need to sort something out." He drove the black Citroen the way he did everything, methodically.

"This has to do with the phone call?"

"Do you mind coming with me? It's on our way home." Nico nodded absently in her direction.

Lia wondered if he realised, he hadn't given her a choice. *Why argue?* Lia watched the road until they reached their destination, a building close to the city centre. Two boutiques, one each side of the mosaic tiled entrance spoke volumes about position and prestige. Inside, he put a hand to the small of her back and directed her towards the lift.

"What do you think?" Nico asked her sometime later, having been greeted by a man in a tailored

Armani suit, led inside, and given a tour of an extremely spacious apartment.

Lia brought her perplexed gaze back to him, considering his question. He waited, expectant somehow.

"This is yours, isn't it?" He didn't answer. "It is, isn't it?" Lia asked again but before he could answer, she cut in. "I can't believe you don't live here."

"Yes, well, it brings in a nice return and I'm too much of a mamma's boy, or is that mama's boy to leave home, according to some people."

"Very funny. You can't deny the grain of truth though, can you?" She smiled when he grinned, delighted to see the sixteen-year-old boy alive in his eyes. "Ah, I get it."

"What?" His stance now had a hint of curiosity along with the humour and she detected a touch of defensiveness.

"Home is comfortable, deflects ideas Francesca might get." She felt a distinct sense of satisfaction at his expression. She loved surprising him.

"That's perceptive of you. Do you know how annoying that is? And do I detect hesitancy about the place in your voice?"

"Now who's perceptive? But yes, you have a point. As a rental it's fine. As a home the floor tiles are dated. A timber floor would give it a more modern look. An off-white or cream on the walls and ceiling to contrast would lighten the atmosphere and make the apartment look bigger. The bathroom tiles need something. Perhaps a coloured border, edging of some kind, new taps and accessories, and extra storage wouldn't go astray. The bedroom shutters could be re-stained to match the floor..."

"Christ, Lia. You worked all that out in five minutes?"

"Sorry. Laura and I have done this for a while now. It's second nature." Lia smirked, satisfaction rising at his reaction. "You are good at underestimating me, aren't you?"

"What else?" he asked, his tone serious, his hand on her shoulder, moving her forward.

She rattled off some other suggestions and tried not to notice that her skin burned at his touch. Lia wondered how she could move out of range without making it obvious. "You're not making the situation easy, you know?"

"Sorry, I keep getting these flashbacks of you up against that wall, naked, me inside you."

"Nico!"

"What?"

"You like to push my buttons. You..." Lia halted, moved to the side as the real estate agent stepped back into the room minus his clients, demanding Nico's time.

Minutes later an unhappy Giovanni, Nico's real estate agent, left. An intrigued Lia swivelled to face Nico. "You do want to live here," she said, watching his eyes rove around the apartment. He continued pacing, restless or agitated, or both.

"Maybe," he said after a long pause.

"Have my *mamma's boy* comments got to you?"

"Lia, we seem to have reached a reasonable stage in our relationship, don't spoil it now by being childish."

"What, you don't think a thirty-six-year-old man living at home isn't a bit much?" Verbal sparring provided welcome relief from the sexual tension not lessening with the day's advancement.

"You know damn well it's not uncommon here in Italy, so stop trying to get a reaction and let me think."

"Sorry, I guess some habits are hard to break. I mean I can understand how having someone cook, wash your clothes and generally be your slave would be hard to leave behind."

"Bitch!"

She wrinkled her nose, shrugged a shoulder, not at all put out.

"It gave my mother purpose."

"It kept her from living her life."

"You don't know everything."

"Nico, I'm sorry. I won't tease anymore."

"I never meant to do anything to hurt her."

"I know Nico. So, living here...?"

"Francesca. I don't know if I'd be comfortable with her knowing I lived here."

"You're afraid she will take it as a sign of the next step in your relationship? And you don't want to hurt her." She put a hand over her mouth, stifling the horror as the events of the day hit her. "Oh God, I didn't consider her once today."

"Neither did I and I should have. She and I, it's a big step Lia, and today...today proved I've been right to hesitate." He shuddered. "Four years together...I wondered so often whether it was right for me."

"Four years is a long time in a relationship going nowhere. It seems unfair to Francesca. How could you not realise?"

"Funny, I don't remember you being so concerned about Francesca earlier."

"That's not fair. How...why do you have to turn everything on me the way you do? I don't want to fight. I didn't stop to think about Francesca today. I've already admitted to the fact. Today was pretty emotional for me in many ways." Her bottom lip trembled. "But your attitude doesn't show you in a good light. So blasé! I asked a simple question, perhaps because I'm feeling guilty. Maybe I'm not the only one feeling guilty."

"Meaning?"

"You turned it on me. Maybe you're feeling guilty. Maybe it's not the first time you've cheated on her?

Stupid me, thinking you had integrity. Should I be worried now about catching something?"

"So snide. Should I be worried about pregnancy?"

"Why are we fighting?"

"Answer the damned question."

"No, I don't think so. I haven't had a period since the accident. Anyway, it's too late now. You should have thought about that earlier."

"No, I haven't cheated on her, or she on me. No matter what you may think of me I assure you in this, I would never.... Today was, fuck, I don't know what today was. I do know I forgot to be careful. In four years, I've never had unprotected sex with Francesca, or anybody else for that matter, ever. Today with you I didn't even think, not the first time and not the second time."

Lia paled as images flashed into her mind. "Today is over. We agreed it won't happen again. I didn't question you to be nosy. I want to understand you better. I want us to be friends."

"Friends? You want to be friends. In that case there's no reason not to tell you. Sex, Lia, pure and simple, hardcore, and the kind in which Francesca excels. The kind of sex, Lia, where she does what she's told to do, the kind of sex that satisfies my need to be in charge and satisfies her need to obey, to be my virtual slave."

"Sex?"

"Yes, sex. Are you surprised, shocked?"

Lia remained calm; he needed a reaction. She would not provide it, as difficult as that might be.

"Francesca has specific desires. She likes to be dominated. You do know the kind of things I mean, don't you, Lia? Or...," he said moving closer to her, invading her space, his breath hot against her skin, "or maybe you don't. After all there aren't many twenty-eight-year-old virgins around." He slid behind her, close enough that she could feel him hardening against her, his hands locking her in place.

"Stop it, stop trying to intimidate me." She fought back tears. "Why are you so angry?"

"Poor baby. Francesca now, she would be revelling in the onslaught, waiting for my next move."

"Okay. I'll bite." Unwilling on one level, Lia found herself fascinated and aroused on a baser level, by a body tense and so close she felt the vibrations. "What happens next, I mean what would happen next?"

"You play a dangerous game, little girl. Let's see. I'd force her to her knees and make her suck my cock, taking it as far down her throat as I could get it while I pulled on her hair roughly, so roughly that she'd have tears in her eyes, not that I'd care. She likes it that way and she likes sucking my cock, more than I can say. I make sure she never knows when she may get the opportunity. Of course, this is tempered a bit for your innocent little ears."

He slid his hand down her hip. "If I slid my fingers inside you Lia, what would I find? Would you like to do what she does? Would you like to suck...?"

She cut off his words by reaching behind her, grabbing hold of him, and twisted firmly. Caught by surprise, he let her go.

"That's twice you've done that. You won't get a third chance."

"Actually," she told him, spinning around to meet his eyes, "that was the third time. Stop being an arsehole and you'll avoid a fourth."

"That's the other thing she likes."

"Enough. You're too twisted for me."

"I don't know about that. You have hidden depths no matter how you pretend otherwise." He sighed and let her go. "I like order, Lia. I like dictating the when, and I fucking love dictating the where."

"I get it. But this conversation is out of control. Please stop."

"I hope it's that easy."

His cryptic tone teased her mind all the way home.

~

Nico dropped her home. True to his word, he maintained a cordial note with his father when he got home that night. Lia watched, secretly amused but trusting him, as he narrowed his eyes every time Lucio spoke to Gina. Less amusing were the eyes turned on her, following her every move.

The next morning when they met in the kitchen, she knew they had a problem. Gina's presence did little to dispel the tension between them. When Nico placed his cup in the sink, standing behind her, she couldn't look at him. When she finally found the courage, she wished she hadn't. The look on his face, a copy of hers in the bathroom mirror, strained and pale, failed to hide a burning need for things best forgotten.

From enemies to friends, friends to lovers, and lovers to confidants all in one day had taken a toll. The pull to each other tugged hard, merciless. As soon as he left, she would pack her bag and head back to the base, even if she had to lie to her aunt about the reason. She needed the comfort, the sanctuary the navy base provided.

Chapter 16

"What's wrong with you?" Ivana, his administrative assistant, hovered over Nico.

"What do you mean?" Nico didn't bother to mask his irritation at the ambush. He recognised her *dog-with-a-bone* look.

"You know."

"I'm busy. This contract is a big one."

Ivana remained resolute. He hadn't been himself for weeks, even here at his office, where things ran like clockwork. She ensured they did. His office ran with military discipline, and because of this it provided him a soothing environment in which to thrive professionally. With her magical organisational skills, she had created the perfect working environment. It kept him on an even emotional plane no matter how demanding the work but not over the last few weeks, and he'd made the mistake of letting it show.

"Listen. In ten years, I've never seen you this distracted."

Nico's temper escalated a notch. "What are you talking about?"

"Don't worry, your work is fine. I don't know how. You can talk to me. You do know this?"

"I do know. Get me the file I asked for."

He regretted the brusqueness immediately. The pinched look, the lowering of her lashes to hide her reaction spoke for itself. He'd helped her out of a nasty marriage, and possibly something more sinister. Choosing not to ask questions, he employed her instead for her uncanny ability with languages and clients, and for her ability to remain calm under incredible emotional duress. She did struggle with Francesca, a mutual antipathy between the two women which amused him when it didn't grate on his nerves. These days Ivana tolerated Francesca because Francesca's father encouraged new clients and therefore more business. Francesca tolerated Ivana because she had to.

"Nico."

Ivana and his mother were close. Somehow Ivana believed this meant she had the right to comment on his personal life. Normally also amusing, in his current mood it fuelled his irritability, making curbing his temper difficult. "Please, just get me the file."

"Your moods are bad enough at the best of times, but lately? Is Miss High and Mighty withholding sex, you know, trying to bring you to heel, holding out for marriage?"

"Holy Mother of..."

"Don't be sacrilegious. You know how much I hate it!"

Bosoms heaved theatrically from her position at his shoulder.

"Can you take you and your breasts out of my face and get me the file. Now! Don't make me ask again."

"Have it your way."

He wondered what Ivana would think if she knew the truth. *Would she drop the bone to yap at him?* He almost chuckled aloud at the thought of her as an...English bulldog? It suited her tenacity. He supposed he could lighten up and give her something else to think about.

"I'm not seeing Francesca. We're having a break while we decide where things are going."

"Ha!" Ivana snorted. "Like I believe that! You mean while you decide. Maybe you should spell it out clearer because she hasn't gotten the hint."

"Let's say she's having a struggle with the concept." His continued hard stare prevented a reply.

She left his office huffing and muttering under her breath. Francesca had inundated him with phone calls or casually dropped in on her father's behalf every day since he had spoken to her a week ago. She thought it part of a game, although uncertainty had clouded her eyes the last time she'd turned up. Marriage had been discussed. The familiar and irksome tic near his jaw signified his distaste for the whole situation.

Francesca would make the perfect partner. Beautiful and an excellent hostess, she came from an influential family and as a bonus she obeyed his directives. He needed the controlled sexual play to keep him grounded. A marriage between them had possibilities. So why did his mind keep wandering to soft, silky skin and an explosion of pleasure so unexpected that no matter what he did, he couldn't shake it from his mind? Apparently not from his body either because he had woken up every morning with a raging hard-on that nothing could satisfy, most especially not Francesca's very skilled hot little mouth.

~

"Well, your temperament hasn't improved so I might have to call Francesca myself." Ivana sniped again two weeks later.

"What the fuck are you going on about?"

"Exactly the bad attitude and bad language you're currently displaying! Just because you use English doesn't make it any politer. You should have more respect for my age." She put the contracts he had asked for down on his desk with a thud. "You're impossible to be around. This break and your sexual frustration is playing havoc with my work environment. How long is it going to last?"

"I could fire you and solve your problem, you know, or you could act like an employee and do your job and mind your own fucking business!"

She laughed. Ivana knew he'd never let her go. All these years together also told him she wouldn't be put off much longer. Maybe he could throw her a bone. Again, the image of her as the bulldog came to mind and he sniggered.

"Francesca and I, well the truth is...we're no longer an item in a more permanent sense."

Her shock warred with a satisfied gleam before Ivana switched to a neutral expression. She knew he wouldn't react well to emotional displays, especially smug ones. *Cunning bitch.*

"Does Gina know?"

"I'm telling you first, so you can prepare yourself to comfort my mother. She will be heartbroken."

Picking up his black leather brief case and giving her a stern look that boded badly for her if she questioned him further, he left. He could hear her frustrated grunts all the way to the lift, the click of her fingers as she dialled and then the Gina word. He couldn't resist it. He turned around and strolled back.

"That's what he said!"

Nico grinned; schooled his face back to bland and cleared his throat. "A reminder to...oh sorry I didn't realise you were busy."

Ivana gasped.

"I can wait." Nico could barely keep a straight face.

"Can you hold the line a moment, please?" Ivana looked up at Nico, her colour high as one hand covered the mouthpiece. She swallowed nervously.

"Did you need something?"

"Ring Gabriella. The bathroom needs doing again, and the carpet. Some dusting won't go astray."

The briskly spoken commands reassured her until an eyebrow casually swept upwards.

"So which client are you talking to?"

She eyed him suspiciously. "Mrs. Danoni. You know how she is, always a million questions. I'll get right on to Gabriella. Is there anything else?"

He shook his head, amused at her efforts to conceal her relief. "Tell the Signora I'm having dinner with Marco tonight, so I won't be home till late."

Ivana choked before smoothly turning it to a cough. Nico gave her a wicked grin and she had the grace to blush. He strolled back to the lift pleased with himself. Discussing Francesca would keep Ivana and Gina occupied for some time, days perhaps. It might give him the time to pull himself together.

Chapter 17

"You have a visitor."

Ivana's tone had him glance up. She, and his mother, had been snarly since he had refused to discuss his former relationship in any shape or form. Ivana, upset with him made sense; Ivana agitated, did not.

"Well?"

"It's your cousin."

"Lia?" Sweeping his eyes down to the papers in front of him, he hoped he had conveyed minimal interest.

"Yes."

"Well, what does she want? You know we have this client coming in. Can't you handle it?" Nico asked, drumming his fingers on the desk, in time to his accelerated heartbeat.

"She didn't say, but maybe you should see her, or at least, I don't know, do something."

Nico couldn't prevent his eyes turning momentarily towards the small waiting area. His attention shifted smoothly back to his normally unflappable personal assistant. Knowing the importance of this contract Ivana should have handled the situation. *Where was her normal curiosity?* Ivana's lack of calm efficiency fuelled the churning in his gut.

"Domenico, I know you don't like her, but you should see her. She doesn't look well."

The churning became a burn. Lia's last visit to see his parents had been a month ago and it had been two weeks since they had visited the base. By his calculations it had been five and a half weeks since that day at the beach. The silent conspiracy to avoid each other could not have worked better if he and Lia had co-ordinated down to the last detail.

"Bring her in but let me know as soon as Claudio arrives." Waiting till Ivana left he methodically thumped at his shaking thigh until it stopped. Flustered was not something he did and certainly not something he could allow anyone else to see.

~

The apparition in front of him had translucent lilac shadows under her eyes. Not even make-up could disguise the pallid skin of her face. Ivana's concern made sense. The long hair tied back severely at the nape of her neck only increased how unwell she appeared. She flushed under his perusal of the clothes, thrown together, different to the poised self he was accustomed to seeing. Her style whilst on the trendy side nevertheless held a certain charm. The blue singlet, short white skirt with flat sandals made her appear like a waif, a colourless waif, the brown belt weighing the skirt down; a testimony to at least a good four kilos missing from her frame.

Lia's trademark butterfly scarf attached to the brown leather satchel looked in severe danger of disintegrating under the fingers of her right-hand. A terrified Lia angered Nico. Pointing to the nearest seat, he shut the door and turned.

"What the fuck, Lia, have you done to yourself?"

He'd forced himself to accept the impossibility of their relationship. He couldn't accept her looking like some phantom in a ghost story.

"Lia?" She wouldn't look at him, choosing to increase the manic motions of her hand. "Lia, look at me." His insistence had her obey.

"I'm sorry. I know I should've called. I know how busy you are. I had to come, to do it now...I knew it had to be now or I wouldn't do it."

He focused on her hand and the scarf. The intricate silver butterflies seem to take flight under the restless tugging. He leaned over, took her handbag away from her and put it on the floor.

"I knew if I didn't tell you, you'd figure it out, if you hadn't already." She stopped talking, nervous at finding him so close and biting down on her lip the way she did when upset. When he stood and moved away, she breathed a sigh of relief and continued. "I thought I had a virus," she whispered, "but it didn't go away. I couldn't eat. I couldn't drink. Finally, Greg did some blood tests. Everything's been so crazy since the accident, I didn't know. I assumed..."

"Lia?"

"I'm pregnant," Lia blurted, wrapping her arms around herself, bending her head, and giving way to tears.

"Fuck! Such a fucking idiot." Nico's body spasmed, tightened again to a stillness before he began pacing.

"Nico," she began. He wasn't listening.

"Unprotected sex? I made light of it. Jesus, what the hell was I thinking? Fuck! I can't believe this!"

He stopped directly in front of her. She hadn't looked so lost even when talking about her father. He didn't recognise her and then he inhaled, and the familiar scent of coconut mixed with cinnamon and chocolate disarmed him, silenced his thinking. Not so for his demon. *She's here,* it reminded the pathetic human. Nico's brain snapped to attention. His demon had a point. In perfect accord his cock, controlled by his demon, jerked against his zipper. Both of them agreed they liked her fragrance, and the battle to stay away was no longer an issue.

"Lia," he said, needing to reassure her. He lifted her face with his hand. Instinctively she leaned into the movement and his cock quivered. The luscious mouth, soft and swollen owned him. *How did he not realise?* She swallowed. He inhaled.

"Two people were there that day." Nico gently punctuated the words by letting his thumb roam her lips. "Two of us, and one of us should have known better." The thumb swept across her cheek, wiping the tears. "Let's try to discuss this calmly."

"I had to come. I didn't know what else to do."

"I know, Lia. I know. You did the right thing. Fuck!"

"I think that's what caused this in the first place, so maybe you could find another word or at least use the Italian equivalent. It sounds better," she retorted, sniffling.

For the first time that day, she sounded like the Lia he knew, and he laughed, his relief immense. "I can't seem to use Italian around you. I don't know why."

"Liar!" she replied, feeling more like herself, something she hadn't felt like in weeks. She could trust in him. The intercom buzzed interrupting the moment.

"Damn! Lia, I have to answer this as much as I'd like to continue this discussion. I have a meeting scheduled. It's important. I need to speak to this client."

"Sorry, sorry," she whispered, suddenly crestfallen, gathering her bag from the floor in a panic.

"Lia, listen to me." He reached for the intercom. "Please, listen to me and this once do what I ask. We can work this out but right now I have this appointment." He pointed to the door near the bookcase. "I have a bed in there. You look exhausted...I want you to go lie down."

Ivana buzzed again. He pressed down on the button, "*Un attimo*, Ivana."

"I can come back later." On her feet and ready to run, she hesitated under his fierce gaze.

Her fragility had no right to affect him the way it did. He stared, his jaw rigid, angry but not at her. She blushed and looked down.

"You aren't going anywhere till we sort this out." Rising, he strode over to the door of the small room he often used when working late. "Get some rest, I'll do what I have to do and then we can talk and have some lunch. God knows you look like you need it."

She paled, flashing her eyes like a cornered animal.

"Please, Lia. Please," he added gently. "This appointment can't wait. Promise me not to come out until I tell you. I'll be about an hour or so. Okay?" She seized the hand he held out. His demon backed off, agreed not to squeeze the slim fingers in his possession. She was skittish enough. His head reeled from the lure of the fragrance she wore. Needing his head in the game for his meeting, he pushed thoughts of her desirability away. Even now, pale and wan like some tragic Gothic heroine her appeal shattered him.

Returning to his desk once she was inside, he found it impossible to stop staring at the door. He had an insane urge to mark it somehow, pee on it so that everyone would see it as his territory. Irrationality around Lia came naturally. *Unprotected sex?* The idea - abhorrent. *That's not how it felt.* Even after four years with Francesca, he'd never risked it. He needed to think, no he needed to do. He leaned across the desk to the intercom.

"Ivana?"

"*Signor Donelli è qui.*"

"*Va bene,*" Nico switched to English. "Can you apologise for me and ask him to wait for a few minutes, and then can you come in here? I have matters that need urgent attention."

Motioning her to take a seat on her entry into his office, Nico didn't miss the covert glance she gave the closed door. Ignoring it, he continued writing, numbering, checking and double checking he hadn't missed anything on his notepad.

Ivana waited, used to the way he did things, getting them straight in his head by making a list. Something had him rattled. Ivana quickly scanned the notes he handed her. Engrossed, she failed to register Nico still standing beside her. Perturbed, Ivana looked up sharply, watching the intense gaze as it moved to the closed door of the room. "Do you know what you are doing?"

"No! I just know it has to be done, and straight away."

"I know you have good reason for this..."

"Don't!"

Her eyes roamed over him, searching for answers. Ivana had no doubt he trusted her, knew he hated having to explain himself, yet she sensed more to this. Meeting his eyes, she glimpsed confusion,

confusion battling...elation? *What's going on?* Her heart skipped a beat, panicked because she loved this man like a son. To be holding all this tension in his body, and Lia looking so frail, suddenly made sense.

"Ivana..."

Sensing his difficulty with the situation, she weighed her words. Nico agitated was never a good thing. Firstly, she had to reassure him of her dedication to him. Secondly, her analytical brain insisted, she had to point out pitfalls without revealing what she now suspected.

"This won't be easy for some to understand. Domenico, the suddenness of the situation...it's all so unexpected...it might be confronting, even misleading."

"Believe me, I know, but I'm hoping that the *unexpected factor* is what will pull us through. Help me weather this, especially with my mother." At Ivana's quick nod the furrows in his brow lessened. "Thank you. Do as much as you can. Can you send downstairs for coffee and biscuits for Claudio? It will soften the delay and give me time to get myself into deal mode. I don't want to risk this contract."

Her head snapped up. Nico met her stare, his discomfort evident in the rapid blinking. He never admitted uncertainty. Though compassion engulfed her, Domenico needed her strong. Ivana scanned the list again. "Consider it done."

"It's an impossible feat no one else but you can accomplish. Please. And Ivana," he stressed, using a tone he knew she would interpret correctly, "today, her appearance here didn't happen. This is not open for discussion with anyone, not now or possibly ever, even between us."

She frowned but bowed her agreement. He could trust in her.

Chapter 18

Lia removed her skirt and top. *Lunch!* She hadn't dressed to go anywhere. Creased clothing would not improve things. Walking to the chest of drawers, she rummaged inside and discovered a T-shirt, and smiled wryly. *White. Of course, it's white. It's Domenico. It couldn't be anything else, could it?* Out of curiosity she slid the wardrobe door open. Inside, four pristine white shirts hung next to suits, both black and expensive. *Not surprising and so predictable.* Strangely that predictability reassured her. A yawn overtook her. She stripped her clothing and donned the T-shirt. Pulling the soft quilt over herself, comforted that it smelled like Nico and far too exhausted to question the thought, she closed her eyes.

The swish of the door moving over the thick pile of cream carpet filtered through her brain. Opening her eyes, her breath hitched. His skin, a shimmering gold against the white of his collar, came courtesy of the sun's rays drifting through the small window. She sat up. His eyes moved, drifting to her breasts in his T-shirt, and back to her mouth. Her heart hammered, became frenzied, waking parts of her body in the same way a plant might react to water. *Is it my imagination his eyes are glazed, his jaw about to snap?*

"I've booked a table for lunch."

He looked vulnerable. To Lia, witnessing the way he watched her, it seemed as if he didn't know what expression to assume. The lines and planes of his face finally re-arranged into a puzzled frown. She swallowed, nervous at his penetrating stare, wanting to break it but afraid to move out of the bed. His presence loomed, his eyes following the outline of her body under the quilt. Silent and wary Lia chose to stay motionless.

"You look better. You have colour." He shook his head, re-settling his features into neutrality.

Lia in turn, let out a relieved breath and waited.

"Why don't you have a shower while I finalise some work? The restaurant is about fifteen minutes away and we have time." He turned, shutting the door behind him as he exited. She sighed, not sure what she had expected. Taking his advice, she headed for the shower. Knowing him, it would be well stocked.

~

Lia paused, unbuckled her belt, opened the wardrobe door, and reached in for one of his linen shirts. She put it on, buttoning only from the waist down, allowing the singlet top to show. Carefully, she folded the cuffs back to her elbows, then buckled her belt over the shirt. Knotting the ends of her scarf she let it hang around her neck loosely before pulling her hair into a high ponytail. Rummaging in her small makeup bag she found her blusher, a lipstick and a black eye pencil, and earrings. She treasured her earrings and always kept a spare pair of plain silver hoops. The knock at the door startled her. Inhaling, she breathed his name. He entered. His eyebrows immediately lifted at the sight of his shirt.

She had lost count of the times he had given her the same look. She disregarded her angst when the eyebrows levelled and his eyes gleamed approval. She saw him glance around and into the bathroom. Nico didn't bother to hide his further approval at what he found. He tempered it with amusement when she raised her own brows, prepared for this habit to check, for his obsessive fetish with tidiness.

She grabbed her bag and, putting on her sunglasses, gained the courage to walk past Ivana. *What was she thinking, sitting behind her desk with that intent gaze in that well-schooled face of hers? Schooled to not show emotion, and yet I feel she's trying to reassure me. Is paradox the right word?* She offered a tentative smile and received a surprisingly supportive one back.

The feeling warmed her, and it stayed with her as Nico led her to his car, to the restaurant and to the table. Lia knew his confidence to handle the situation had foundation. Knew he thought she should have faith in him. Lia wanted to believe. This once she decided, she would forgo annoyance at the way he moved his hands and shrugged his shoulders at her when he sat down. *Such flourish, such an arrogant declaration of his superiority.* She bent her head and fiddled with the napkin, allowing herself a small smile.

~

"Domenico?"

"Later, and I prefer Nico, you know that." He rasped in a voice that prevented further discussion. "Let's eat first, you need it."

He signalled the hovering waiter to fill their glasses with sparkling mineral water and proceeded to order without consulting Lia.

The typical arrogance made her feel better. Familiar ground, she thought, unlike the hypnotic gaze making her heart flutter. He smiled smugly. Something else familiar, she realised and hid her smile. She'd had plenty of practice navigating her way around him and his ways. Secretly, the constant challenge he presented amused her as much as it did Nico although two months ago, she would have denied the idea with vigour.

A plate of linguini topped with thin slices of tomatoes and parmesan, a local speciality, done with fried breadcrumbs, chilli, basil, and plenty of olive oil teased her nostrils with the combination of flavours. *Impressive and I bet Ivana's doing.* Smaller plates containing meatballs, zucchini, and eggplant, along with slices of fresh bread gave the scene a touch of the surreal. Lovers dining out, came to Lia's mind.

"Nico?" she began. He put his finger to his lips. Lia stopped, intimidated by his ability to distance himself from an issue until he chose otherwise. Compartmentalising, a skill he had in abundance.

"Later, I told you we eat first!"

She lifted the fork to her mouth, hungry for the first time in days, and allowed the first mouthful to go down. The second proved harder. He frowned. To appease him she chewed, she swallowed, and she stayed silent. A tear slid down her cheek. Fear, confusion, frissons of excitement, and uncertainty at the repercussions of the situation, overwhelmed her. She couldn't shove her feelings aside like he did.

"Lia," he sighed in exasperation. "Can you at least keep eating while we have this discussion?"

She forked another mouthful and waited for him to say more.

"Why did you wait so long to come to me?"

"Why do you think, Nico?"

"Take the food to your mouth Lia," he insisted. "And I'm asking the questions."

"Why did I wait?" She didn't bother to disguise her annoyance, rebelliously putting down her fork. "I waited because I didn't know who I'd find if I came to you. Perverse Domenico who thinks I'm to blame for bringing the past back to upset his life? Obsessive Domenico who likes everything in its place, whether it's the way a towel sits in the bathroom or where the knife is placed at the table? Imagine how little a baby would suit this person, or perhaps suit Brooding Nico who watches every move I make, as if I contaminate the air around him."

She frowned. "Then there is Sexy Hot Nico who looks at me as if he could swallow me whole and make me enjoy it. Wait a minute, he did. He put me into a crazed state of arousal and the result is why we're here. Common sense, mine, dictates it's not right. The chemistry shouldn't be this strong, but it is, was, even before the beach."

Taking another breath, she narrowed her eyes to signal her growing frustration. "Stop with the eyebrow lift thing! I swear to God, it makes me crazy. It's the most irritating thing ever."

He let his eyebrows sit where they were. She raised her brows back.

"Well, aren't we the clever one?" Clipped words, cold and precise.

"Goodness, how could I forget Supercilious Nico, or should that be Domenico?"

"Can we get rid of Domenico and keep the Nico?" He laughed, unable to keep his exasperation hidden and unable to keep the coolness in his manner. She entertained him so beautifully.

This was Charming Nico, and despite herself, his charm worked its magic and she laughed with him. "Then," she continued, confidence building, "there's Sweet and Gentle Nico who can hold you and make you feel nothing bad can touch you, a Nico who is loyal and adores his mother. Sweet and gentle Nico is the one I had sex with..."

"Only the first time. The second time I was..."

Lia rolled her eyes and finished her sentence: "...and the cause of this situation."

"I had no idea I occupied so much of your thoughts."

"Well, to give you credit, you have managed to make my pity party disappear."

"*Pity party*, I like that. So, which of us has created this miracle?"

"Sexy Hot Nico of course, who is liable to turn into Perverse Domenico, sorry I mean Nico, who will blame me at any moment now for getting pregnant and creating this problem. Wait a minute, it might be Brooding Nico, considering you're watching every move I make."

"I don't know what to say. It appears you have appointed yourself judge and jury."

"You sound hurt. At least your words do. That smirk and the raised eyebrows suggest you're not taking anything I say seriously. And, as for your judge and jury comment, isn't that what you've been with me since the day I arrived? Do you honestly not see how I might have dreaded coming to you?"

"Can you loosen the death grip on your knife?"

"Now you're pissing me off."

"Lia, I'd hoped we'd moved past all this."

"Stop saying 'Lia' in that superior tone. It's aggravating. Look, I appreciate the lunch, but we have a problem we need to solve. I came to you, didn't I? Now what?"

"Have some more pasta, Lia. We have plenty of time to assassinate my character after we eat. We might even assassinate yours a trifle. I don't know which Lia I may find either. The Lia crying in my office who knew I would help her, the sharp-tongued cat here with me now, or the virginal Lia who didn't hesitate to impale herself on my cock?"

Lia gasped at his crudeness then sighed. "I suppose I deserved that. Less explicit would be nice."

"Well, that's surprising coming from you. I've never been able to work out how someone that lives up to her name in looking like an angel, can use the language she does."

"Funny, I can't figure out how someone so clean cut, with such an obsessive, compulsive personality can have such a kinky bent on sex. I would've thought you'd be more particular."

"Now I know why I wasn't inclined to be nice to you. Nasty girl! Marco might talk too much but you do too much listening. I wonder why." His shrewd eyes didn't miss her guilty flush. "Keep eating. We're at an impasse, and you look like, what is the English expression, like a wind can push you over? You're so thin!"

At her scowl, he shrugged, so she forked some more pasta to give herself something to do other than hitting him.

"While you were sleeping, I did some organising."

She chewed slower, aware of the sudden chill along her spine, a warning. Lia knew she wouldn't like what came next. His ability to decide and do without discussion was ingrained.

"Today is Wednesday. We have until next Friday to clear up some minor details that may arise. Otherwise, we're getting married at 11am Saturday week. At the church near my parent's home."

She forgot she had a mouthful of pasta, shock causing her mouth to open wider. Strands of linguini fell back into the plate.

Disapproval on his face softened as he perused the room, reassured her culinary performance had gone unnoticed.

"Are you insane?" she yelled, uncaring of her surroundings. His displeasure returned, became comical. He had picked a public place to avoid this kind of drama. *He'd got it wrong.* "Holy fucking shit!" she whispered, putting down her fork.

"That mouth again, in more ways than I want to witness. Please swallow what's left and don't say anything else!"

She stared, stunned, and did as he asked, wondering at the same time why she was obeying him. The rustle of movement had him in the chair beside her. Having him suddenly so close further silenced her powers of speech.

"Thank you," he said more gently. "Lia, listen to me carefully. Please allow me to finish and then you can speak."

She nodded, not knowing what else to do.

"I know that these days, people are more accepting and open-minded. However, we're not two ordinary people, are we? We have a family history of drama. We're cousins, Lia, if reasonably diluted. Many will still consider our relationship inappropriate including myself. Put it down to Conservative Nico. I suspect at heart so are you, and we won't even think about my parents at this stage. A pregnancy? Even if you went home to Australia, we wouldn't be able to hide it, especially from my mother. Someone would be sure to work it out."

He held up his hand to stop her from speaking, and though his high-handed manner vexed her further, she stilled, choosing to mutter words that sounded like 'Controlling Nico'. He rolled his eyes this time and she did the smirking. Their joint humour settled them both.

"Seriously, Lia. With the amount of people to fuck around with, we choose each other and do it carelessly. I'm sorry, I can't have it. My mother would never understand."

"And she'd blame you."

"Shut up, Lia."

"Sorry, old habits die hard. Marriage, though?"

"If it was someone other than you, maybe not. But it is you and I won't hurt my mother. Let's get in first and make it seem it's what we want. If, after the baby, it happens that we don't get along then she won't be happy, but she will accept it."

"That's a long time to be in a relationship we don't want. And where will we live...do we share a room, live as a couple? Nico, it means putting our lives on hold, and what exactly are you planning on doing with Francesca? Damn it! I shouldn't have come."

"Lia. *Basta*. Stop panicking. And Francesca is not an issue. This is my child. You did right to come to me. If you had kept this from me..."

"I wouldn't have done that. It wouldn't have been right. Marriage though? It's not like anyone is going to believe it. Let's face it, most of our time is spent arguing, and people know that. How are we going to explain this sudden shift in our relationship? And what do you mean, Francesca isn't an issue? Shit. Shit."

"Calm down! One thing at a time and we can start with Francesca. I ended it a month ago, to be exact. Don't even think about it, Lia. It had nothing to do with what happened between us. The relationship wasn't going anywhere. It wasn't fair to her." *That wasn't the only reason.* "Look, we don't have to explain anything to anyone. But if it makes you feel better, we can say we kept it quiet because it felt awkward, considering our connection and so soon after Francesca. To be frank it amazes me this dubious tension between us has gone unnoticed."

"With your rigid self-control?"

"Then how did you know?"

"Because I felt it as well, you idiot." She sighed. "I'm sorry. I'm acting like a child. Nico, your parents, Marco, they won't accept anything less than love. How can we possibly make this work? You can't decide and arrange something like this without talking to me."

"Lia, I have it under control. You're right. They won't understand anything less than love. We give them that. The chemistry between us has been veiled in aggression and arguments but it existed. Now we turn it around. We can make this work. I know we can."

"Why, Nico?"

"Why? Because I can't get that day out of my head, and I doubt you can either."

"No. That's not true."

"Liar. You know for a beginner, you...never mind. Don't tell me you haven't thought about it. I won't believe you. I can feel, smell, taste how much you want me, and it's not half as much as I want you."

Hunger echoed in his voice along with fury. The chemistry had been so unexpectedly profound that day, blurring common sense, and he spoke the truth now even if she was loath to admit it. His words seducing every nerve in her body proved it. She had to be insane, surely; they both were, weren't they? "No. It's not true," she repeated needing to put up an argument. They both heard the lie in her voice.

"If I touched you now, would I find you wet and willing?"

The desire etched in his face overwhelmed her. Lia gasped, grabbed her throat unsure if the shock was for his words, or the warm hand moving up under her skirt.

"Stop, please. Please, Nico."

She put her other hand over his to prevent him wandering any further. Reining in his actions, she felt the hand leave her, watched in awe as his face re-arranged itself into the familiar hard planes. Grateful, she entwined their fingers, demonstrating she wasn't immune to the attraction, and sighing, laid her head on his shoulder

When he moved his hand back onto the table, taking hers with him, she allowed it. Tightening her fingers around his, she accepted she owed him the truth. "It's not...I mean...I can't deny...it's true, all of it. I haven't had a day where I didn't think about you or what we did. Nico, that's not the point. Marriage? That's crazy."

"Marriage is the only way out of this with dignity."

"And if I wasn't pregnant?"

"I don't know, Lia. I'm not sure I would've kept away. I hate not being able to control how I feel around you, but as much as I hate it, I want it. Right now, my dick is yelling to be let out, to be inside you. If this gives me an excuse, I'll take it."

"For how long? What if this attraction burns itself out before the baby even comes? There has to be another way."

"What, Lia, an abortion?

"God no, I never even considered that."

"Thank you for that much. Look, I can't answer how long this attraction will last. I don't care. I only know a week, a month or even a year won't be long enough to do the things I want to do to you."

"How did we get here?"

"Does it matter?"

"Yes. No! I don't know." She stopped talking, looking around the restaurant blindly. She blinked, bringing her gaze back to his face. "I give up," she said, feeling exhausted and unable to fight how he made her feel. "You're right about everything: how your parents would feel, especially your mother, how much I want you, want you to want me...everything."

"I'm sorry, Lia. I'm overwhelming you."

"A church wedding?"

"It has to be formalised Lia. It's the only way to avoid questions. Have you forgotten my mother had to marry Lucio? Do you want the same situation in front of her? A church wedding makes it real. The church kept her going all these years, the one constant in her life. I won't have her hurt or suspicious."

"Domenico..." she began.

"Nico," he interjected, "I like it better when you call me Nico."

"I don't think I can keep up with these changes."

"It's easy, Lia. Vary the pace; it makes it so much more interesting." With that he moved her hand underneath the table and over the bulge in his pants.

"You're enjoying this, aren't you?

"Fuck, yes, and I'd enjoy it better if I could feel your hand on my skin, on my...."

"You truly are an arsehole! You're trying to shock me with Perverse Nico." She squeezed him hard and twisted, enjoying a moment of satisfaction at his in-drawn gasp and the way his eyes glazed with pain.

"You need training. If you are going to persist in grabbing me then you need to learn how not to traumatise my bits and pieces. I may have to teach you some manners."

"Oh really? What did you have in mind? Putting me over your knees and spanking me?"

"Yes, and then I would find the nearest four-poster bed and tie you up, open to anything I want."

"Okay. You win. You've got an answer for everything. I haven't the energy to fight, not when I know you're right. Now let go of my hand or I swear to God you won't have a dick left. Nico, the waiter is coming back! Let go of my hand!"

Nico huffed and released his hold. "Fine. I'll let you off without getting me off. We do have things to before the day is over. In any case this is a family restaurant and even Perverse Nico has standards. Clever, right? The way I can manipulate your language?"

"Are you asking a question? It sounds to me more like you're giving an answer. I don't know about Perverse Nico, but Childish Nico is certainly present. It's a male thing, right?"

"Eat up!"

Chapter 19

"**Angelia,** what are you doing here? What a surprise!" Gina enfolded Lia with warmth and enthusiasm, and only then turned to kiss Nico's cheek. "And you are here too, Nico?"

He did his best to suppress the twinge of jealousy at his mother's greeting order. The woman had come a full one hundred and eighty degrees with Lia.

"How did you two meet up? Are you staying, Lia? Your bed is made up if you are. Dinner is simple but we have plenty. Lucio, Angelia is here, and she looks so skinny. We need some meat. Can you go buy some cooked chickens? Lia, have you been sick? What have you been doing, what...?"

"Stop! Mamma! One question, at a time, please. It's not like she left the country. You saw her two weeks ago." Exasperation in his voice had Gina pouting.

"But she looks thinner."

Lia smiled and hugged Gina tighter. Nico watched his mother quieten, melt into the embrace. Love and honest affection banished his last wisp of fear. Lia would not risk hurting his mother. Nico saw the agreement when their gazes met and held. His lids lowered, he broke into speech, not wanting her to see his relief. Lia saw a great deal, too often for his liking.

"I asked Lia's advice about my apartment. I think it's time I live in it."

"You're moving out? When? When did you decide all this? Lucio, did you hear him? Did you know?" In response Lucio shrugged. Lucio, Nico noted, knew he'd be the last person to know his son's plans. The thought simultaneously gladdened him and made him sad.

"Mamma, it's been a long time since lunch. I'm starving. How about we eat and talk all you want later?" He laid a hand on her shoulder. "Mamma, you said it yourself, the girl needs feeding."

Gina complied readily, speeding towards the kitchen, followed by Lucio. Nico shook his head. If it concerned Lia, his mother had no argument. Peering closely at Lia, he heard the tiny gulp, and noted the way her hands trembled. She'd crumble if he didn't step in. He pulled the cornered kitten Lia resembled, into his arms. It worried him to read her so well. It worried him more that she could do the same with him. These were considerations for a later date. Whilst he appreciated her determination to do her part, Lia's pale and flustered face made her an easy target for his determined mother. Gina's perceptive nature, and if he had it correct, Lucio's penetrating look, had to be deflected. *Or perhaps the opposite needed to happen?*

Sitting down at the dining table Nico tugged Lia onto his lap. The shocked expression and the squeal had him laughing, his amusement furthered when she hung her head in embarrassment.

"Relax Lia, we can do this. Try to act like you like me," he baited, unable to help himself. She sucked in a desperate breath. "Lia, a picture is worth a thousand words, remember." She wiggled as she nodded, the movement unfortunate. It woke the part of his anatomy he'd had to battle all day, a very long day, he thought, reflecting back to the afternoon.

~

"This is a jeweller!" She'd been complacent on arrival, having recognised the store as the one on the ground level of his apartment building, but once she ascertained they were going inside she'd been horrified.

"Yes, I know!"

"Oh no, Domenico, no."

"Nico." He had whispered against her ear, taking hold of her hand leading her inside.

"Lia? May I call you that?" Seppo had asked in a beautifully cultured voice Nico knew had women weak at the knees. "Domenico tells me you normally wear white gold or silver, but he would prefer yellow. I have taken the liberty to gather together some pieces that may suit both of you. I am hoping by his description I have your measurements correct as well." With that, he lifted the glass lid. "Please look and feel free to touch and try. If there is nothing here you like, I have some other ideas that might suit."

"No," she whispered, bending closer. "These are superb."

Nico wondered which one she would choose. He'd already decided the moment Seppo had opened the case. Exactly as Seppo had described by phone, the square cut ruby with the two smaller matching square diamonds, sitting either side, were perfect. Entwining both the platinum and golden hues, it had elegance and simplicity. He curbed his instinct to decide for her. Sitting close beside her he felt the tremble vibrating through her body. Nico put his hand on her thigh. She tensed then settled.

As if reading his thoughts through their physical connection, she reached over and picked it up. He prised it from her, sliding it onto her finger. She looked at him, piqued, as if she knew she had pleased him but wasn't sure if it had made him happy. How he knew he couldn't say. He wondered whether being inside her body had let him inside her head. The ring fit perfectly. Nico felt torn; happy they were on the same page yet uneasy. She blushed under his scrutiny.

Nico followed the path of pink moving across the smooth cheeks. He motioned Seppo to bring the wedding bands. She selected a double set, yellow gold etched with white, and then lifted her head with a question she didn't voice. He shrugged, an elegant movement of one shoulder, and reached for a matching larger single band. She frowned, surprised, and ducked her head but not before he'd seen the elation, caught her desire to brand him. His beast rose, anxious for her touch. Taking her hand, he placed it under the table to the place desperate for her. She reddened further, embarrassed, and aroused, her eyes glowing. As Seppo led them back to the front of the store, she slipped the hand wearing the ruby into his, and made sure she stayed in front of him, giving him a welcome privacy.

As if aware his thoughts had drifted, Lia rubbed her head in the curve of his neck, waiting patiently till he was back in the present. She didn't question his thoughts. Instead, she quietly accepted the way he tightened his hold, the way he hardened further and the thoughtful way he adjusted her clothing to cover as much as was decent.

"Why does this feel so natural despite what's happening under my dress?" she asked, puzzled, and satisfied at the same time.

He shook his head and laughed again. She always did the unexpected. Like now, acknowledging his dick, enjoying his obvious difficulty in dealing with her effect on him. Her humour, her insight made his heart stutter. He concentrated on her question, one not easily answered, considering the complexity of their situation and the day they had spent together. From Seppo's small but distinct establishment they had gone up to his apartment.

"You didn't rent it. You did decide to live here."

"Ironic isn't it, given our current predicament."

"Ironic? Yes, I guess. I do like the changes I suggested."

"Shut up. I improved on them."

"True. I can admit it." She said but added a smirk.

"You think you're so clever, don't you? And...?"

"It's beautiful, perfect in fact. I've had a thought. In all your machinations today, have you stopped to consider we have no furniture?"

"Fuck. No! I actually haven't given it a thought."

"I'm disappointed. I expected more from you!"

"That mouth of yours..."

She smiled. "Let me take care of this."

"I'm not sure I can do that."

"Trust me. I know exactly where to go. I promise to keep your tastes in mind. Please, so I can feel we're in this together. Please, Nico. Trust me to look after this."

And, now here they were in his parent's apartment with her on his lap, a most unusual deviation from normal behaviour for him. He hated public displays of affection unless orchestrated.

"Isn't it enough that it does feel that way?" He spoke into the top of her head. "Do we need to question it?"

Lia's body gave a tiny quiver at his reply. "I bow to your wisdom."

His answering smile, small and unobtrusive said he had assimilated the fact he made her feel safe.

Her words had lacked her usual fire. He found he liked that fact enormously. Uneasiness forgotten, at least momentarily on her part, he pushed aside his own questions to deal with later. Instead, he allowed himself pleasure when she leaned further into his body.

Chapter 20

"**It's** unnerving how well your parents reacted, isn't it?" Lia's soft words drifted across the silent companionship of the night.

"Except for the screech when she found you sitting on my lap."

"Yes, that picture painted more words than I could come up with." She rolled her eyes at his smug satisfaction, her eyes cat-like with an almond bright glow in the car's dark interior. "Seriously, though...it was strange, or is that only my impression?"

"No, I agree. She loves you. I think she'd be happy with anything you did, as long as it meant you stayed. As for my father, he's been your slave from the first day." Nico paused, reluctant to say more but he owed it to her. "She cornered me while you were talking to Lucio."

"What did she say, Nico?"

"That she didn't care about how and why, but if I hurt you, she would hurt me."

His annoyed growl had made Lia laugh. "Don't sook. I can't help it if she likes me better than you."

"Don't be ridiculous. Sook? What kind of a word is that?"

"It means cry like a baby!"

"Don't push it Lia, or I will give you something to sook about. A spanking would sort you out."

"I'm so scared," she said, laughing wholeheartedly at his grumpiness until he narrowed his gaze to her breasts, and back to her mouth. She swallowed; he grinned. She narrowed her own eyes, daring him to comment further, determined not to be intimidated. He turned away with a snort. She huffed. He ignored her, concentrating on parking the car, and staring at the path leading to the apartment above the garage. She sighed. "Do you want to come in? I can tell you're curious."

"I am. I'm not keen on meeting your American friends at this moment though."

"You don't have to, Nico. It's a totally separate living area."

He followed her up the external stairs into the space Lia called home, noting how nervous she'd become. It amused him, tantalised him, this constant change from spitting skittish cat to soft unsure kitten. She had strength; she had timid, shy moments. She oozed a lazy sexiness; she possessed an air of innocence. The contradictions, once so irritating, now held appeal. With her, things were *unexpectedly more,* never simple but always intriguing.

"It's lovely, Lia. I can see your touches. The bedspread is your work, a larger and more complex version of the one at home. I think my mother would be devastated if you tried to take that one away." He paused and cocked his head.

"So would Ashlee."

"You are a clever girl, aren't you?"

"You've said that before."

"I mean it, Lia. Why would you doubt it?"

Lia stilled. His gaze roved over her in much the same way it had perused the room, listing items in that notebook brain of his. Her body reacted by trembling. She sought strength from the wall, leaning on it for support.

"I haven't been nice to you at all, have I?"

"Nico, that's a leading question."

He laughed. "You're distinctive and it has enormous appeal."

She swallowed, nerves surfacing, and waited for him to continue.

"And it would appear we're not so different, as our little shopping spree today demonstrated."

Glad her steely determination to pay her way with the furniture had impressed him, she found herself not so glad at the amusement it had provided him at her expense.

A large comfortable three-piece black leather lounge, a black timber table that would sit eight with comfort, and a matching black buffet with glass doors had been easy. Two black stools for the breakfast area, a queen size bed for one of the spare rooms, and various bits and pieces had also been easy. But the choice for the master bedroom proved to be the most interesting purchase, with emotional repercussions.

The black four-poster he'd discovered in a large alcove of the store had him giving her intense, sidelong glances. His imagination had her sprawled across the bed and he didn't bother to hide it. She'd scowled but couldn't prevent the slow burn, the liquid pooling between her legs. Fear and desire made her clumsy. The laughter gleaming in his eloquent eyes had made it difficult not to squirm and show her trepidation. Nico hadn't asked if she liked the bed or not. He had simply told the salesman they were buying the bed. Lia had not argued, happy to have this one thing entirely his way.

Back in the present and in her apartment, Lia let her eyes drift over him now, in his black suit and an emerald-coloured tie. Normally he favoured red, a rich ruby red. His ties were the only colour concession he made in his formal business attire. They were always bold, no pattern but of the finest silk, statements contrasting against the purity of the white shirts he wore. She wondered if his ties would hurt her wrists. Raising spiky lashes, she peeked at him, and blushed, thinking mind-reading might be another of his skills.

She fought not to worry her lip with her teeth as he drew closer, holding up her hand, warding him off with her palm.

"If you keep looking at me like that I won't be going home soon, if at all. I'll have to reassure you, and that could take all night."

Fear and desire had plagued her at the furniture store; they plagued her now. Her insides quivered in response to the silky, sensual voice. Nico had a beautiful voice: the tone rich, his diction clear.

"Don't play games with me. I need to understand more, know the boundaries, and know what I can and can't do to suit both me, and you."

He prowled closer, a frown puckering his brow. She lifted both hands this time and moved back. He shook his beautiful head as if she were a naughty child and reached for her. She sighed and let him pull her into his arms.

"I need order Lia, you know that. But I am prepared to be more...accommodating. I can try not to be so pedantic. I don't know how successful I will be, but I will try."

"Does that mean you might introduce colours to your underwear choice? I mean black and white is good but...what...?" She raised her brows at his look. "I helped your mother with the laundry, and the cooking and the cleaning. I lived with all of you long enough to notice lots of things," she said, daring to tease and hoping it would offset the sexual atmosphere. *On reflection, underwear is a poor choice of topic, Lia.*

"No! But, speaking of underwear," he told her with a grin, "I like comfort, style and simplicity and can live with the virginal air. Some variation in your lingerie would be appreciated and I would be happy to organise it." At her small gasp, he smiled. "What, you can discuss underwear, but I can't?"

"Funny Nico has surfaced. What did you have in mind, a black lace thong?"

"Wouldn't go astray," he replied with a wicked look.

"Like I want to waste my time, picking things out of my arse."

"Aha! My potty mouthed girl has surfaced. Language, Lia. And, I don't know," he said, moving his hand down slowly and firmly to her well-shaped behind. "You might enjoy certain aspects where that arse is concerned, that might surprise you."

"Stop trying to scare me with sexual innuendos! It won't work. I would have to be stupid not to suspect you might be slightly more demanding than the average male."

"Is that what I was doing? Trying to frighten you? Maybe. Lia, maybe. I like a controlled environment, strict guidelines. It keeps my world, my personal and business world ordered and private. I limit my choices but not the quality, but yes, I limit them. With sex...with sex my limits are not so limited, but I promise you I won't do anything you won't like."

"I know. I also know you don't like explaining yourself. I'm...I'm not worried about the sex. I trust you. It's the rest...living on our own."

Both his hands cupped her backside now, sliding her closer into the lower half of his body. The hard length pressing against her felt right. She made a noise, a pathetic mouse-like squeak. A hand lifted her chin, brown stared at brown, one searching for reassurance, the other, perplexed and irritated.

"Stop worrying so much. I don't want you to be different. I've noticed the changes in my mother since you arrived." He stepped away, fingers and hands running through his hair.

She missed the fiery heat of his body. Her heart hurt, beating in distress to see the dark strands ruffled, disordered, and to notice the frown lines returning to furrow his brow. She did that to him and did it often. His determined search to find the words gave him a child-like quality.

"I didn't realise how rigid I was, how inflexible. I don't, didn't see it that way and she never said, still hasn't. That's why you bring out the worst in me, you make me see it. Lia, I can't change the way I am. I don't want to. Can you understand? But I can try to be more tolerant, less demanding, well at least in some things. I can't promise though, when it comes to your delicious, enticing body."

Conceding this much demonstrated a huge shift in their relationship. She had to acknowledge it. Her hands slid around his neck and into his dishevelled hair, hesitantly reaching for his mouth with hers, wanting to show him her willingness to bend to his wishes. She moved slowly, wanting him to understand he would win only if he gave her the opportunity to decide for herself. Nico had to understand the difference, she thought, breathing in his cologne, or it wouldn't work.

Nico moved back before their lips met. She stilled. He pulled the tie from her hair. Tangling his hands in the length, he used it as leverage to tug her roughly away from him. Nico wanted to read her like a book. Knowledge would make keeping a distance possible. *What was it about her? Not tall but certainly above average height, full breasted yet slender. Hands long and elegant. Just as well considering the amount of talking she did with them, and her nose, small, contrasting with her full, pink lips. She reminded him of a young Monica Bellucci, only better. He was obsessed. He had to be.*

Nico pulled himself from his thoughts to the woman in front of him. Her skin, sporting a light golden tan, still managed a porcelain delicacy with its tiny dusting of freckles across her nose and cheekbones. It added sweetness to her expression. She watched, waiting quietly, mouth slightly parted. Nico suspected she recognised his need to analyse her. He drew in a breath. Exquisite. Everything about her, he thought, came together to form this little bit of perfection he had hungered for all his life, without ever knowing he lacked such sustenance.

His kiss, all-consuming when it came, sent Lia's emotions whirling. A gentle stroke to her cheek with his thumb, and he left the room. She remained in the same spot for a long time, her mind a comfortable blank. Thinking might provide answers, but did she want to ask the questions? Did she even know what they were?

~

He let himself into the apartment quietly, hoping, but it proved useless. Awake and waiting, the shadows failed to shield her as he opened his door.

"Ma, please, it's late and you should be in bed. I don't want to..."

"Don't panic," Gina cut across him, "I'm not going to ask awkward questions. Well, maybe one."

He sighed in frustration and fear. He didn't want to explain but mostly he didn't want to lie. "Do it then!" Resignation tinged his tone.

"Do you know what you're doing?"

The one question he feared most. He looked at her, meeting her eyes, without wincing, without blinking. Here, another woman waited but unlike Lia, his mother's face and eyes held little expression, at least on the surface. "No, I don't," he said, not prevaricating. "Mamma, I don't know how to not do it. I have to keep her."

"I see."

"Are you upset?"

"No, I want to keep her too. Goodnight, Son."

He wanted to let it go at that. "Mamma?"

She stopped at the doorway, turned a shoulder towards him. Her face he noted, she kept carefully in the darkness of the hallway.

"Ma, why? She represents everything I shouldn't want."

Gina's chest moved up and down in time to her heartbeat. Her breathing held a strand of agitation. "I don't know. It's the same for me. But around her something happens and all of it good. Don't let her go."

He waited for the sound of the door to her room shutting before he left the kitchen. Nico put his keys on the chest of drawers, right next to his wallet, a nightly ritual. Reaching across he pulled the fresh pair of pyjama pants out from under the pillow. He found a fresh pair every day. For him, logic dictated that if he showered every night why would he put on something he had worn the night before? It occurred to him since he also showered in the morning, he may be giving his mother extra work. Would she tell him? Damn Lia, what had been normal now had become questionable.

Looking around the room, he scrutinised everything carefully. The relief in finding all his things in their rightful place overwhelmed him, forcing him to give in to the need to sit down. Perched on the bed he finally, painfully allowed himself to let go of the tension haunting his mind and body. Lia would understand. She'd seen his need for order firsthand, and if she didn't, it wouldn't matter. He wanted her. He would make it work.

Chapter 21

"Do you know what you're doing?" Ashlee asked, watching Lia pin the hem.

Lia wished she could ignore the question. Ashlee did not mean the dress. "Yes. Not really!"

"Have you spoken to Laura about this yet?"

"No!"

"Y'all are certainly a library of information, this morning,"

Ashlee, the picture of the traditional belle of the south with her gold-spun hair and sky-blue eyes, eyes both her children had inherited, drifted into a southern accent when things became serious. Lia knew Ashlee had trepidations about the wedding.

"It's hard, Ashlee." Lia thought carefully about how to phrase her answer. "I could say I can't do anything else given the situation, but it wouldn't be true. It's like my body is determined to melt in his direction. He's more in control of course, but even Nico doesn't understand what's going on. It's not the pregnancy directing this. The pregnancy is incidental to the drama. Does that make sense?"

"Yes. But is it enough for a step like marriage?"

Lia blew out a frustrated stream of air. "I can't talk to Laura. She would jump on the first plane and drag me home. I can't let her do that. I want this. Wrong or right, long term, short term, I want this, and I can't hurt my family. Gina and Lucio are so happy. If we do this right, then the baby will be all of Gina's Christmases at once. I hope Laura will forgive me. I've never kept anything from her, ever."

"I love my dress." Ashlee glanced down, skimmed her hand down her body, drawing attention to the fabric. The sensual stroke of her fingers showed both appreciation for the creation, and the way she looked in the simple pale pink crepe V-neck sheath. She smiled at Lia, and turned her gaze towards Lia's dressmaker dummy, scrutinising the wedding dress from top to bottom in the same way she'd been doing all morning. Underneath the lace, the soft white lawn underskirt gave the dress a solid base to shine. The lace neckline was high but the lining neckline low. The illusion of flesh added allure to an otherwise pristine purity. Sleeveless, the delicacy of the lace followed a smooth path down the body. At the hips two chiffon panels inserted in the front and back gave the skirt a beautiful shape as it fluttered down to calf-length.

Ashlee's silent contemplation set Lia's heart beating. *Had she missed her own brief?*

"It's truly beautiful. The mantilla in matching lace instead of a conventional veil is a brilliant touch," Ashlee said finally, bringing her eyes back to Lia, smiling. "I love the miniature of yours for Melissa; love the pink ribbon along the waistline, matching me. I can't believe how you've managed everything including sorting out a church wedding."

"I simply had to make it work. As for the church bit, my aunt would've gone ballistic at a civil ceremony. Red flags all over the place. You know, she's into religion."

"Ballistic? Interesting word, is this an Aussie thing?"

Lia lifted her brows at the jibe.

Ashlee winked, then turned serious. "Honey, are you sure you can handle living with him?"

Lia lowered her eyes to the hem, aware her friend would continue the conversation no matter what she said.

"Hey, I've met the man twice and I freely confess to lustful thoughts. It didn't stop me noticing how tightly reined he is. He will control you if you're not strong enough to hold out against him."

"Ash. Don't underestimate me. Don't think because I can't stop this, I'm weak. I'm on a surfboard the size of my thumbnail riding a wave so high it has its own flight path. I can't afford to fall off. Look, it's a done thing. It's happening even if Nico and I aren't happy about certain aspects, like the church." She paused aware she hadn't answered the real question. "I know what Nico is like. I have to show him what I'm like. I will."

"Nico, not Domenico, hmm...why does that sound so...affectionate and totally sexy?"

Ashlee drawled the words, simultaneously scrunching her nose so much that she reminded Lia of a rabbit. Lia didn't know whether to be exasperated or amused by the American.

"Ash, cut it out."

"You want him, don't you? And you truly want this."

"Something in him calls to me. Always has, I think. Even as a child I felt drawn to him. Laura was the same with Robert. Sometimes, sometimes I think we make a connection with people and over time it becomes so much more. I can't say I understand it but Nico, strange as it may seem, makes me feel safe. So yes, I do want this."

"Y'all will talk to Laura soon though?"

"What's with the southern accent?" Lia countered, hoping to distract.

"Soon?"

"Yes, I will, and soon. Now shut up or I will stab you with these pins."

"Yeah, yeah. You love me. You won't hurt me."

"Don't bet your cotton fields."

"You know," Ashlee said with both humour and warmth, "my husband sure has good taste when it comes to picking up strange women and…"

"I know," Lia interjected, "and bringing them home." They both laughed.

~

Lia met Greg on the Sydney to Tokyo flight. Needing the time to herself, she hadn't been overly impressed with his friendliness. He had been impossible to resist, with his American accent and affable charm. She had let him ramble on, mostly about his wife Ashlee, their seven-year-old daughter Melissa, and six-month-old Jacob, and slowly her tension melted. Coincidentally, it turned out he was headed home to Sicily where he had been stationed for the last three years.

Naval Air Station Sigonella or NAS Sigonella located west of Catania had been maintained as a permanent presence there since 1959. Sicily, as a strategic centre of the Mediterranean Sea made sense to Lia. Most of her information about the island had come from Papa and he had concentrated on the local area he grew up in, and on Mount Etna, the volcano.

Papa claimed it puffed and groaned with the temperament of a true Italian.

Shortly into the flight, Lia had found herself confiding in Greg, unsure if the reason occurred because he happened to be a doctor, or purely because of his warm personality. A long stopover in Tokyo cemented the bonding. He had rung Ashlee to ask permission to take a new friend to dinner. Lia had been captivated by the sleepy voice on the phone. Landing at Catania, Greg had waited till she had her bags before dragging her to meet his family. Lia had fallen in-love at first hug.

Laura of course, had thought she had lost her mind, threatening to come get her. Moving in with an American family she'd only just met, did sound strange, Lia supposed. The confidence boost had made it worthwhile. That last email she had sent to Laura before facing her aunt and uncle for the first time had highlighted the confidence Lia had gained.

Dear Laura,

Using email so I can add the notes in the attachment. Hope you're both doing well and not working hard (HA HA).

I'm heading in tomorrow. Can't believe I've been here almost six weeks. These people are amazing. I'll miss Ashlee and her mother-hen tendencies and my hip little set-up.

Stop worrying, please. I'm fine. This may change tomorrow. I accept that. At least I have some place I can come back to.

The fabrics are perfect, better than I envisaged for the new project, and I agree completely about the small bedroom. It's all in my notes. I like the sound of these new clients.

Miss you both, will Skype soon to give you an update.

Lia (AKA Angie)

PS. Get a dog to mother or better still, have a baby. I'm a big girl now.

Coming out of her reverie, Lia smiled at the thought of Laura, her safe place from the first time they'd met. Laura, now a source of regret because she wouldn't be present at the wedding. Shaking off the feeling of loss, Lia asked Ashlee to find Melissa, so she could complete the finishing touches to the very excited little girl's dress. Nico was coming to dinner tonight with his parents, and Lia had promised to help with the cooking. Laura would understand.

Chapter 22

The wedding ceremony went to plan, a simple service in beautifully presented surroundings, Gina and Ashlee's work. Pink and white ribbons on the ends of the pews closest to the aisle matched the stunning mixture of pale pink and white roses sitting at the altar.

As Lia walked the centre aisle of the church on Greg's arm, and Nico turned his intense eyes on her, she could believe in the fairy-tale atmosphere. She smiled, enjoying the warm affection radiating from the people attending. Gina and Lucio had been taken with Lia's American friends, especially the children. Melissa, spreading rose petals and charged with ring-bearing, had stolen the limelight. Jacob had smiled contentedly from Gina's arms whilst Ashlee had led the way towards the waiting audience. Seeing the look on Gina's and Uncle Lucio's faces, Lia wished the reality had more substance.

Marco, his parents, Silvia and her mother Cinzia who sat proudly in her wheelchair, had all chosen to sit alongside others from Gina's church group, one of the few things Gina had maintained over the years. Having these people and Ivana attend had given Gina a special glow, a queen holding a well-photographed court. Ivana had been free with winks directed with great affection at Lia. Also invited were an interesting couple, Gianni, and Annalisa Meoli, who had come down from Padua. Nico and Annalisa were old friends. Gianni intrigued Lia. He watched Nico like a hawk when Nico moved in close vicinity to Annalisa. Though Lia couldn't detect anything to warrant this, she did have certain suspicions. Lia hoped she'd have answers once the small reception got under way at the restaurant.

She and Nico had barely spoken all morning, but at the ceremony he had linked her hand to his, and the look of possession and desire had been unmistakable. Marco, she knew, had found this painfully perplexing. His demeanour at the church, the looks she caught directed at both her and Nico, reflected his battered emotions. She hated the air of hurt he wore, knowing full well Laura would wear the same. *Marco's right to feel left out and God knows what Laura will say.*

Despite her best efforts, Lia found herself colouring every time she caught Marco's eyes. The same blush had Annalisa narrowing her remarkable grey eyes, constantly swinging from Nico to herself. Lia's nerves began a slow fray, growing stronger in the confines of the black sedan.

"Tell me again about your friend?" Lia asked Nico, eager to be distracted.

He reached over to grip the slender hand playing restlessly with the fabric of her dress and squeezed it. "You look like an angel, an incredibly beautiful one. Did I tell you that?" He hadn't been able to take his eyes off her. Nico envied the soft material hugging every line of her beautiful body. Soon, he reminded himself, he would follow suit and more. His hunger gnawed at him. He pulled her hand onto his thigh and dragged it upwards, close enough for her to feel the tightness in his black suit pants.

"Not in words," Lia replied shyly, unable to control the blush or the trembling caused by the slight vibrations under her fingertips, grateful his eyes were on the road.

"Words are overrated. I think there may be better ways to demonstrate the fact."

A small turn of his head gave him visual access to the pulse beating furiously in the slender throat. He knew she would find his intensely masculine look of satisfaction overwhelming. The small trembling grew. Taking pity on her, he moved her hand away from his growing erection.

"Annalisa and I were at University together. She struggled to settle into Law. She wanted to please her parents, but preferred history and architecture. Anna finished the degree but became obsessed by travel. Australia was the last country she visited before coming back and looking into tourism. She found a job at a travel agency for a while, did some courses in business. She has a photographic memory which makes whatever she does, easier."

"You obviously kept in touch?"

"She was and is my closest friend, after Marco." Nico looked over at Lia and smiled. "Surprised?" He gave a short laugh when she ignored the sly taunt.

"Anyway, she completed her courses and disappeared on her travels again, emailing every so often. Then she decided to live in London for a while. I had the opportunity for some postgraduate at the University and decided it would do wonders for my English."

Lia felt his eyes on her, watching, waiting for a reaction. *London, living together, even for a short while?* Lia decided on not commenting as prudent. Keeping her sudden insight into Gianni's demeanour around Nico private also seemed a wise decision. "And...?"

"Two years ago, she came to me with an idea and a need for some money. The rest is Paradiso Tours. History, travel, and all the architecture she could find, combined in perfect harmony."

"Gianni is wealthy, isn't he?"

Nico grunted in agreement.

"So, why do you still have money invested in her? You do, don't you?"

He glanced at her, the look a penetrating one. She kept her composure. Lia must have satisfied him because he continued.

"She wants to maintain her independence, and I like the diversity of the investment. I do all her legal work free and get ten percent of the profits. It's a nice return. She could pay me back. If things continue this well though, she will be expanding early next year and running two coaches. Anna will need the cash, and I am more than happy to keep my small share in the business."

"You care about her, don't you?"

His head revolved. He gave Lia a searching glance. Satisfied again at what he saw, he nodded before returning his focus to the road ahead. "I'm not like you. You draw people in because you're so easy to be around. It's harder for me."

Lia's raised eyebrows gave him pause. "I have a following but they follow my power, my position. They are good people, but my real friends are few. Not many people are comfortable with my...moods." He shrugged at her look. "Fine, I'm difficult."

"Well, you don't always make it easy." Lia hesitated.

"And?"

"Sometimes it's not so hard either."

"I wouldn't agree," he quipped, then laughed at the return of her blush, pleased that she recognised his innuendo.

"You make me crazy. You are so determined to make this sexual every chance you get."

"It is."

"Yes, it is. It's also more than that."

"I know. I don't have to like that part; the sex part I can indulge in happily. And I intend to." He laughed again when she gave in to another scowl.

Lia sat quietly wondering, not for the first time, if she hadn't taken on more than she could handle. Her path though had been set the moment her body had accommodated his. In him she had found shelter. Why it had to be him had been decided a long time ago when he'd found her under those stairs.

Despite her willingness to face situations head on, the truth remained. The world made her feel too much, perhaps because of what she had been through or perhaps because it was in her. Regardless of the whys, it took a toll. Nico's single-mindedness, his disciplined approach to life reassured her, had done so all along despite their verbal skirmishes.

~

"You're not at all what I thought you would be," Annalisa said not unpleasantly, considering her sharp, shrewd perusal. The main courses had been served and cleared, and the atmosphere more conducive now to moving from their allocated seats. Lia could see Annalisa had been waiting for an opportunity. She smiled at the diminutive woman and indicated the chair Nico had vacated.

"You are." Lia said firmly and clearly, refusing to be intimidated by short blonde hair gracing a face designed for magazine covers. Flawless tanned skin, dark lashes surrounding deep grey eyes glinting silver specks of light, perfect teeth in a perfect mouth presented Annalisa as an extraordinarily beautiful woman. Her dress, navy in colour, looked sexy and tasteful on her curvy, full-breasted body. Navy was a strong colour, one that provided a dynamic and powerful statement. You didn't trifle with Annalisa.

Oh yes, Lia thought to herself, *there was reason to be intimidated*. Along with her looks Annalisa exuded the same feeling of power Lia felt in Nico. Both had supreme confidence in their abilities to feed and maintain that power. Nico must have slept with her, Lia thought suddenly, making more sense now of the way Gianni's body seem to ooze possession every time his wife made a move. Annalisa narrowed her eyes at Lia's appraisal, as if reading Lia's mind. Lia added perceptive to a growing list of qualities.

"You're a far cry from Francesca," Annalisa said cryptically, sitting back, her manner pensive and penetrating. "Why does it feel as if more is going on here?"

"Does it? I'm not sure I understand what you mean."

"I think you do. It's your business, yours and his. I've watched both of you all afternoon and I see his fascination with you." She paused, deliberating. "And, what about you? Nico is a most difficult man."

"I thought you were his friend." Lia challenged, not intimidated by Annalisa.

"I am. That's why I'm asking the question. I love him. I want the best for him. Give me a reason to think you are."

"By asking what I see in him?"

"Yes!" Annalisa's abrupt answer spoke volumes. Genuine concern existed without a trace of malice in the melodic voice. Lia decided on honesty.

"On the surface, he and I are different. Underneath, not so much. We fit. We ground each other, but I will admit Nico still has a way to go with this. Beyond that I won't comment."

"I think I like you." Annalisa smiled, and any fears and reservations Lia had, fell away. "Did you truly make your dress, and that gorgeous creation your American friend is wearing?"

Lia laughed, enjoying the honest appraisal and the quick shift to the more casual. She had an inkling of why Nico thought highly of this woman. Her novel business concept and its implementation reminded her of Laura. The two women would like each other. The thought saddened Lia, reminding her of the reality of her situation. She shook it off before the clever Annalisa drew conclusions, choosing to reflect on the information she had received from Nico earlier. Annalisa's company visited places both famous and off the beaten track. The sleeping arrangements varied from home stays to beautiful and exclusive hotels, giving their clients a real feel for the countries they toured.

Annalisa insisted Lia and Nico join them for a couple of days on the next tour as Gianni would be joining her and Lia would be able to see how the tours functioned. "I promise you will love it."

"Is this because you think I can convince Gianni that Nico has no desire to sleep with you again?" Lia asked slyly, unable to let this perfect opportunity to show her mettle pass her by.

Annalisa pulled a face. A host of expressions flitted across the perfect oval shape. Without warning Annalisa released a raucous laugh, surprising in one so small in stature. She continued to laugh until Lia had no choice but to join in.

"I think Nico may have won the lottery with you."

"I'm glad you think so. It's important to him that we get along. But also, he's interested in what you do, and I think that's good for him. He lives for his job, and with someone like him...it's important to broaden his..."

"Horizons?" Annalisa looked searchingly at Lia. "You do understand him. It makes me happy. He's single minded sometimes. Well, all the time and it can make relationships for him..."

"Difficult?"

"I think the four of us will have an amazing time together. But for the record, and I told Gianni the same thing: it was once, a long time ago, and both Nico and I decided our friendship meant more. I don't make friends any easier than he does." She grinned and continued, "I share many of Nico's characteristics but I'm probably not as anal, at least on first meeting. Anyway, Nico and I work better as friends." She winked at Lia. "Unfortunately, Gianni cannot believe anyone who had known me in this fashion would ever let me go, so he always has one eye on Nico. But not anymore, I think?"

"I don't know about that. I am inclined to feel the same way about my new husband."

Annalisa laughed again, drawing attention from the two men gliding towards them. When she stopped laughing, the gaze she directed at Lia held affection.

"I see how he looks at you. I see the difference in him, subtle but to a good friend who wishes him well, noticeable. And the chemistry," she paused, and as the colour rose in Lia, winked again. "Like a bomb. Like what I have with my Gianni. I'm so glad we came. It's been a wonderful day, a beautiful wedding, small and intimate, perfect for Nico. You make him...happy."

Lia looked up. Dark eyes were focused on her. Annalisa's words held a truth to them. She did make him happy. Nico's intensity, an intensity ingrained in his pores, tonight had absented itself from that overworking brain. He had wrapped their relationship up into a neat bundle marked *sexual attraction,* and now thanks to the *pregnancy* he could have what he wanted, legitimately ignoring societal taboos. These days, taboos were not set in blood. People were more accepting, but not someone as rigid as Nico, at least under normal circumstances. If it suited him, bending the rules wasn't a problem. She wondered if the time would come when he realised his beautiful logic contained flaws.

For now, it didn't matter. The situation held more difficulties for her. She could see underneath the surface of the neat package. If it had been simply chemistry, then the kinship taboos, distanced by generations, would have held. Living with her truth wasn't going to be as easy as living with his. Nico craved her. She craved reality. Nevertheless, Lia took his hand when Nico extended it and wove her fingers through his.

Chapter 23

Later that evening, a nervous Lia inhaled, peering intently into the mirror. *What would get him off balance? Breathe, Lia. He's deliberately making you nervous. You know he likes the upper hand. Damn it, I made this nightgown for this reason, didn't I? It's supposed to give me an edge. I can do this.*

Smoke drifted like a halo above his head. She knew about the cigarettes, an idiosyncrasy he nurtured. Not the smoking itself but the idea of controlling a habit. One packet lasted him a good two to three months, if not longer. In fact, she didn't know why he wasted the time. Aunt Gina had once told her he had been doing this since he was about seventeen years old. He enjoyed the challenge against the addiction and winning; he enjoyed all challenges. Lia knew he considered her one.

On the balcony, he looked sinister, a pirate in his white shirt. Her jaw dropped. The unbuttoned linen shirt, his belt buckle and the top button of his pants also undone, allowed the showcasing of the fine dark hairs on their downward path. His tanned skin contrasted sharply with the purity of white, both at the forearms where he had cuffed and rolled up the sleeves, and at his abdomen where the muscles gleamed sleek and firm. Nico, a fantasy come to life, a stereotype of smouldering looks designed solely to reduce Lia to a teenager. Her courage verged on disappearing until his in-drawn breath revealed his own fascination. His eyes darkened in appreciation, a balm to her frazzled emotions.

"You leave me without words," he whispered, failing to disguise the tremor in the quaintly spoken English.

His desire drifted in scorching waves to prickle her already sensitive skin and undermine her determination not to quiver and shake. Behaving like cornered quarry to his hunter on the prowl persona did not bode well for the evening. Acting swiftly become imperative.

"I've been thinking," she began.

"How interesting! A touch only of wine, in this," he said in an amused tone, referring to the mixture of sparkling mineral water and white wine in the crystal goblet he held towards her.

Once again, the quaint use of English words did something to her insides, side-tracking her determination to stay in control. "Thank you." She stepped closer to take the drink and to show she wasn't afraid.

"I confess I was somewhat worried that the bathroom would have the honeymoon I'd envisaged. Now I see it was a place to think. Should I be insulted that you prefer thinking?" His eyes roamed over her, the piercing stare highlighting the sardonic gleam.

"I don't want to disappoint you..."

"Are you hungry?"

She shook her head, blushing at the intensity of his gaze and his control of the situation. "I've been thinking..."

"You said that already," he interrupted, not bothering to hide the entertainment derived from her obvious nerves.

He had morphed into the Nico she knew, a Nico she'd sparred with. She could handle this.

"As I said, I've been thinking about how much my inexperience puts me at a disadvantage. Nico! Don't look at me like that. Being pregnant doesn't mean experience. It means we did the deed."

"True..." At her annoyed click of tongue and teeth, he wiped the grin away before it began. "My attention is yours."

"You obviously wear the mantle of the expert." She concentrated on her words, refusing to be flustered by his teasing, and the appealing way he phrased things. The little something off kilter in his pronunciation heightened his sex appeal.

"How do you know I am expert?"

"Please. I lived in the same house with you for months, so give me some credit. You're an expert in everything you do, Nico. You know you can't stand it any other way."

"Perceptive and clever, a combination I like. This is a new you."

"A new me...?"

"Yes, a change from the annoying, irritating, pain in the..."

"I get the picture, except you're talking about yourself, aren't you?" She couldn't help a snigger at his mock hurt expression. "So," she continued more firmly, "I thought we could play schools."

He gave her a sharp look, followed by a frank sexual appraisal. Heart-stopping. Sexy Nico, a danger to her peace of mind had come to visit.

"Are you trying for kinky? Is this some intellectual form of seduction?"

Husky throaty tones taunted her.

"Will it be legal? I do have a reputation to maintain."

"Yes, it's legal." She shook her head at him, biting the inside of her cheek and hardening her voice. "I thought we could play student, in my case mature-aged student, and teacher. A small roleplay to ease me into things. I figure I'm out of kindergarten or I wouldn't be here, but if all you can do is make fun of me..."

Nico moved a step closer, allowing him to reach out and gently touch her chin with his long lean fingers. "Mmm...it sounds kinky! Do we get to dress up as well?"

Lia sighed, feeling clumsy and awkward. He could be so damned annoying, and hurtful. She hid her hands behind her back, so he wouldn't see the way they trembled. "Can you please stop this, whatever you're doing?"

"Lia?" His voice enthralled her with its soft silkiness. "Trust me and relax. We will make this work." He paused. "Our history perhaps makes it hard to accept but I promise, you can trust me in this, in tonight." She released the air in her lungs as his thumb moved over her bottom lip. "However, since your suggestion does sound interesting and has merit, I'm willing to...explore."

Somehow that last word sounded exciting and menacing at the same time. Butterflies assumed permanent residence in her tummy.

"Nico, don't tease."

"Trust me. I'm not teasing. If our first session was also the first lesson, I think you may be a star pupil." Nico bent closer, letting the heat of his breath ghost across her throat, and whispered. "Where do we start with this role play of yours?"

"Well," she began, only to pause and re-consider. An understanding Nico didn't mean he wouldn't control this and every facet of their lives. "I think it's important to understand I'm not Francesca."

"I know very well you're not her." He stepped away, unable to prevent the tinge of anger at her words.

Lia held up a hand. "Hear me out. I'm not a prude...I..." To her horror she found herself unable to continue. Lia felt the heat in her cheeks at the same time her eyes welled. She moved away, covering her face with her hands, embarrassed and furious to display weakness.

"Lia."

"Blushing, tears...I'm so stupid. I don't know how to do this."

"You are such an intriguing mixture of innocence and strength. Annalisa commented on it. I think she's become your number one fan."

"And you are the master of mockery."

"Lia, I'm not mocking you."

"Maybe mockery is too harsh. Stop making fun of me, then!"

"Lia." He gave her a smile, small, without any agenda other than to reassure.

She returned his gesture with a small sigh.

"I like the way you are. You're thoughtful and you're passionate. I won't ask anything of you that you won't be willing to give. Trust me, Lia."

"I do." She felt her body sag in relief; she did trust him. He wiped a tear with his thumb and moved the thumb to his mouth. The butterflies fluttered, prickling her internally.

"That's not to say I won't demand things of you. But you'll enjoy every minute. I promise you. It will be about pleasure, yours as much as mine. Now tell me about this idea of yours." Noting her rise in colour and the quivering chin, he couldn't resist a sly smile. "I won't bite, not the first time, anyway."

"You're making fun of me. Again."

Stepping away from him, letting her eyes roam over the golden skin, she slowly lowered her gaze to the rising tension in the softness of the fabric below his waist. Heat hit, and she licked dry lips. *Perhaps he didn't have the upper hand.*

"Definitely intriguing."

A cryptic comment and tilt of the head indicated his suspicion. He didn't know what she was thinking and didn't like it. His lashes lowered. Nervously she licked her lips again and in accord his lashes rose. His irises now black with emotion, shifted to her mouth. Round one to her. His expression turned suddenly smug. Her breath hitched.

"You're thinking how to change things to your advantage, how to get on top, aren't you? I do like the idea, of you on top," he told her making no effort to hide his returning amusement on knowing he was right.

"I'm so happy to be providing entertainment."

The touch of malevolence in his answering grin reminded her how much he liked winning. Right now, he felt like a winner. She could accept the situation, or she could make a surprise move of her own on the chessboard. The face in the mirror had drawn little confidence in her own beauty and capabilities. *Maybe I'm only in kindergarten but I'm a bloody good student.* Lia stepped back, reached for the bow on her shoulder, and tugged. The white one-shoulder gown had been designed and made by her with him in mind. Between making the wedding gown and this little number, she had barely slept in the last ten days.

She felt like a pagan goddess as the soft sleek fabric slithered down her body and pooled at her feet. She stepped over the fabric and moved purposefully into his arms. Encircling his neck with her hands and digging her fingers into his dark hair, she embraced her fears. The tightening of hands on her body made her smile. She wouldn't be catching up on sleep any time soon.

"Lia."

The husky whisper could not disguise his hunger. He bit down gently on the lobe of her ear, and at her answering quiver, moved down to the juncture between her neck and shoulder, sucking and licking at her skin. He seized her right hand and placed it on his heart. "Feel it," he said. "It's going crazy being near you." Nico moved her left hand to the hard bulge straining for freedom. "Feel it," he repeated, the rasping quality of his tone melting her insides as much as the feel of him. "It's going crazy from wanting inside of you."

Surrendering to his demanding mouth, she pushed the shirt from his shoulders, exposing the glistening body and flex of muscle. In retaliation, he nipped her bottom lip. She opened to the sweep of his tongue. Nico picked her up and carried her to the bed, eased her down, eyes holding hers, daring her to make a move. Satisfied his prey recognised the predator, he reached down and let his hands take hold of her feet.

His teeth grazed one foot and then the other. Nipping at her calves, he smoothed over the delicate skin with his lips. The onslaught increased, his dark eyes hypnotising her. She relaxed, allowed him the invasion of her body's privacy, delighting in his fierce possession until his intention sent her heartbeat spiralling out of control.

The carnal mouth both frightened and entranced. Lia couldn't breathe. The pull of pleasure radiated through her skin, beading it with a fine misting of perspiration. Her heartbeat continued to accelerate; her pulse became a living thing. Nothing mattered more than to know the glide of his tongue. She had no recollection of him moving her legs over his shoulders, knew only the moment he flattened his tongue against her, because it was then she died.

Hands locked onto her hips keeping her prisoner. She screamed, shattering into tiny, fragmented pieces. When she finally opened her eyes, she found herself faced with the reality of his arousal, long, thick, and as arrogant in its stance as its owner. Nico's mouth climbed its way to hers. His hard length found her entrance and then she discovered those little pieces were capable of disintegrating further.

When his fingers dug sharply into her hip as he released his essence into her body, she smiled, knowing he felt the connection as strongly as she did. In one smooth, silent movement, he reversed their position, so she lay with her head on his chest. If this is higher education, then let the lessons never end, she thought as she inhaled the delicious fragrance of his skin.

~

Lia opened her eyes slowly, stretching carefully, conscious of his male body lying beside her, one arm possessively draped over her. The filtering light spoke of the coming dawn giving her a clear view of the long lashes shadowing his cheek, the fall of the dark hair across his forehead, and the long body carelessly naked and so desirable. She thought back to the moment she had stepped into his arms: his breath, hitching at her sudden boldness, his face losing some of the smugness to a feral desire and recalled the feeling of power at knowing she could please him.

Lia thought it exhilarating being this free to look at him now, to gaze at the width of his chest, the fine hairs snaking down the taut stomach, past his belly button, winding a path to the thicker curls nestling the part of him he had used so well inside her body. Fascinated by the contrast in size from the night's activities, she slid down the bed and ran shaky hands lightly down the insides of his thighs, skimming skin slowly, coming to rest against his balls. She lifted, testing texture and weight gently with her palms. She ran a finger up the length of his penis and watched it give a slight jerk, smiling at the result, and pleased sleep still owned him. Lia wanted time to gain confidence, to navigate her way slowly into his pleasure. Last night he'd made it about her. This morning she wanted it to be about him, wanted to keep things on an equal plane.

Her mouth breathed him in. The slow tensing turned to lengthening, to hardness, to an increase in his breathing, to a timid excitement Lia embraced. Focusing on the fit, the salty flavour as he continued to extend in her mouth, dazzled her senses. A small amount of leaking liquid forced her to swallow. The pulsing length pushed eagerly, intent on the back of her throat, demanding her gagging reflex be set aside. Fingers wove into her hair and tugged.

Gliding her tongue around the thickness of him, she raised lashes to find glazed eyes. Smug satisfaction enveloped her, giving her the courage to vary the pace. Hands in her hair tightened, loosened, tightened again as they followed the rhythm she set. She knew the minute he relaxed, accepting that her schooling though still new, would be enough. Lia had seen the willingness to give her leeway this first time, but she wanted to finish it this way, wanted to reciprocate the amazing sensations of the night.

She felt the growl begin in his belly, grow until her name left his lips as she swallowed everything he had to give. Peaceful, drowsy, and proud of herself, she barely noticed when he shifted her, enfolding her in his arms. Almost asleep, she felt his warm breath as he bent to whisper, his nose tickling her and his mouth moist against her skin.

"Hmmm! Imagination and flair! How could I have underestimated you so badly? I think you jumped straight to high school."

She laughed softly, amused as he meant her to be, and drifted off to sleep only to lunge out of bed, and barely make it to the toilet bowl. Buckling under the crippling spasms, she nevertheless managed enough strength to keep her long hair out of the way and to wave Nico back with the other. He went green at the sight of blood; vomit wouldn't thrill him either.

"It's okay. Go back to bed," she said sharply and promptly vomited again. "Please. Go away."

She sagged against the wall waiting for the nausea to subside, naked and humiliated. Nico continued to stand beside her, the struggle on his face to not show his distaste admirable but not helping Lia's abject misery.

"It must have been something I ate," she said, hoping to lighten the mood.

He paled, then flushed a crimson shade of red under the golden tan. Lia sighed, the acid taste in her mouth burning her throat, his expression hurting her eyes.

"Nico, come on, I'm joking. I'm sorry, that was a stupid attempt at humour." She leaned back against the bathroom wall, exhausted. "I think it's over."

His tight demeanour relaxed a fraction and then with surprisingly thoughtfulness, he grabbed her toothbrush, added toothpaste, and handed it to her along with a glass of water. Helping her to her feet, he guided her to the basin then flushed the toilet. She rinsed her mouth and brushed her teeth, glad to rid herself of the sour taste, wishing it as easy to get rid of the smell permeating the room.

"Does this mean you're putting me back down to middle school?"

"No. I think it means I may need to watch my diet in case you need a snack again."

"Now that would be considerate." She blushed before grinning weakly. "Nice to know you have a sense of humour."

"You don't know when to keep your mouth shut, do you?"

"You didn't seem to mind my mouth earlier this morning."

She looked up, crinkling her nose at him. He laughed. The sound filled her with relief. With a nice little ironic twist, her tummy chose that moment to growl its need to be replenished. He laughed again.

"School is out for the moment while we get you fed, with real food this time. Also, you stink!"

He held out a hand as he stepped into the shower. What followed was neither romantic nor sexual. The idea of pampering appealed to Lia, and she relinquished herself into his hands, revelling in his gentle ministrations. He sighed when she returned the favour. The comfortable atmosphere continued as they dressed for breakfast.

~

The word picturesque suited the town of Taormina. Lively bars, fine restaurants, antique shops, and beautiful clothing stores with their exquisitely presented windows lined the streets. Lia kept thinking how much Laura would love the old-world feel. Italian towns were such a wonderful blend of historic periods. She tore herself away from thoughts of Laura for the moment, knowing she would have to say something soon. Instead, she gave herself over to Nico when he stopped and pulled her close. The instantaneous physical connection vanquished the little remnants of the awkwardness of the morning.

Chapter 24

The passing days fed the rapport between them, the ease strange when bickering had been a large portion of their lives. Moments of doubt about real life in a real home arose to be rapidly quashed. There would be time enough to give them consideration. *Like the current example.* Lia sighed, giving her attention to Informative Nico, well acquainted with history and architecture and in perfect English. Why he continued to speak to her in English she preferred not to question, hoping fervently it had become a habit and nothing more. On a positive note, it provided privacy from his family though not from Marco.

"Bored?"

"No. Absolutely not. I was thinking how nice it was..."

"Not to indulge in our habitual fighting?"

"Yes, exactly. Now drop the eyebrows down a notch and tell me more." She slid her hand in his, smiling when he entwined their fingers.

The present town of Taormina overlooked two bays. These formed part of the Ionian Sea and provided a breathtaking panorama. The town itself provided Lia with constant delight, offering a host of fascinating architecture. Each new piece bore witness to the numerous invasions over the centuries. History revealed itself in the Greek Amphitheatre, the Renaissance doorways disguising dark Gothic interiors framed by rose-coloured windows, and piazzas honouring medieval times. Sicily had been invaded so often that the symbol of its capital, Catania, was an elephant.

Like Nico, Lia loved the intricacy of history particularly having grown up in Australia to less dramatic changes. Not that one place was better than the other, just different, Lia thought as she listened to Nico. Sharing similarities though could be a double-edged sword. Lia found discomfiture in the fact they had so much in common, their blood tie niggling despite how well her new mother-in-law accepted things.

"I thought you might be upset with us."

"I see the difference in my son. Francesca filled his time. I would have accepted her for that alone. But she wasn't enough to stop his restlessness, the one in his mind. This last month he's been different, expectant but not restless. Now I know why." She laughed softly. "He was such a strange child. Handsome, intelligent, and inflexible. His intellect accepts people see things differently. His logical side does not quite follow through with understanding. Marco balances Nico to a degree, takes the time to pull him up. Yesterday when you came here with him...I don't know. You calm him; make life better for him. You did it before as well.

"What do you mean?"

"As a child. Once you got his attention, he melted at your every word, would have done anything for you. You accepted him so readily. It made him...feel...less out of place."

"I had no idea."

"Lia, you were a child, a sweet one. Not that you didn't argue with him, but he listened to you, didn't want to hurt your feelings."

"I must have missed that part, this time round."

"Now, now, don't be mean."

Rather than reply, Lia just stared at Gina who stared straight back before her mouth twitched and she smiled.

"Not unless he needs it," she said, "and he will."

"You're truly not worried about the kinship?"

"Lia, it's generations ago. If it had been closer, I don't know. Enough serious talk, show me that ring again."

Back in the present, Lia sipped at her orange juice, enjoying the sun on her skin as she watched Nico swimming in the pool, his body glistening, the muscles flexing, reminding her of the previous night. The memories stirred her in places that ached from use, Nico's use. She wriggled, closed her eyes, and tried to ignore the heat in the lower part of her body.

Lifting her lashes, she found the man responsible for her pleasurable discomfort staring at her from the pool. She bent her head, letting the fall of her hair hide her face, but still she felt him smile. He knew exactly where her thoughts had been.

~

For their last night in Taormina, Nico had suggested a nightclub. Excitement had her buzzing. Tonight felt like a date, and she found herself tossing outfits in a flutter of nerves. Deciding on a white sleeveless vest over a red three-quarter-length skirt she added a string of beads, and her silver hoop earrings. With a touch of mascara, her hair loose, she thought the outfit sophisticated enough to please Nico's more conservative tastes, and colourful enough to suit her own bohemian bent. Confident, she turned to Nico for confirmation, and received the raw, brooding look that usually led to undressing. Lia ducked to the side, evading his arms. His eyes glinted. There would be punishment. She grinned. The idea had merit.

~

Thankfully, Lia thought as they looked for seating, she seemed to be turning a few heads herself because her husband certainly made an impression on entry. Sexy and debonair with the black jacket over a plain white linen shirt and black jeans, he looked right at home in the dark edgy venue.

"The free-spirit, hippy look you've adopted tonight seems to have a certain charm," he rasped in her ear, letting her know he had seen the looks she garnered.

Happy at his words, she relaxed into the warmth of his body, shivering at the soft nip of her ear lobe. The desire to dance teased her mind. Lia knew she had little hope despite sensing her husband's curiosity. *Would they be good together and of course the real question - would she compare him to Lorenzo, and find him lacking?* She suspected the latter plagued him the most.

Pulling her back further into his arms Nico adjusted his position on the stool so she half sat on his lap. She rubbed his arms, absent-mindedly moving to the rhythm. A rumba began its slow siren song: the purer beat, rich in melody, a welcome change to the previous song. Lia knew this one, an old song given a modern sensual twist. Each note of music demanded she move in time to the rhythm, and against the hard body behind her. His breathing picked up speed and volume, fluttering against the back of her neck.

He wanted her. Lia could feel his body hardening in response to her nearness and the music, and she could hear his displeasure in the little hiss he gave. During the last few days, she'd come to terms with the fact Nico disliked the strong physical effect she elicited as much as he enjoyed it. He didn't stop to think how difficult it made things for her, how confusing. Nico loosened his hold, leaned further back, drawing away from her. Lia's desire to override his control spiralled, fuelled by hurt. The hands resting on his thighs clung tighter, her body heated, little beads of sweat forming along her forehead.

His mouth nuzzled at her ear and without warning, bit down hard. She barely had time to wince when with an angry inhalation and a smooth rising movement, he dragged her onto the dance floor. The flawless perfection of dancing with Lorenzo disappeared in Nico's arms, replaced by highly charged sensuality. Their bodies complemented each other, meshed, slid into a perfect unity of limbs and mind. Every time he spun her out, she regained herself only to dissolve against the possessive hard, hot pulsing length.

The mixture of rage and potent desire on his face intoxicated and dominated every ounce of will and suddenly afraid, she missed a step. He caught her, placing her in front of him, needing protection from prying eyes, as much as the need to hold her up and stop her falling. The music ceased; the applause started. Lia blinked, caught in the sexual thrall. She trembled. His urgency to avoid the crowds bruised the wrists he tugged.

The air heated, scalding Lia with rage, a rage blaming her for his lack of control. His selfish anger left no room to acknowledge her feelings. She didn't question how attuned she had become to his thoughts. The fear ate all her energy. Astonished, she realised they had left the club a long way behind and had reached the quieter section of the town. The residential section. Villas and their high stone fences shut off the busy world of tourists and locals roaming the piazza. She turned to Nico to comment, uncertain but wanting to break the stony silence.

"Not a word, Lia. I don't want to hear a word."

He pulled her hard against him, moving them further into an alcove. Nudging her forward, her bottom flush against the hard heat of his erection, he bit her neck, his teeth sharp, painful, a vampire seeking gratification in her every flinch.

"We're going to fuck, right here, right now and I want you quiet, not a murmur. No moans, no groans, nothing. Keep your hands on the stone."

A swift movement lifted her skirt, shoved her underwear aside, the only sound, the zipper sliding down and then him, inside her, hard, unrelenting. He bit her again on the same tender spot, determined to mark her. Lia shuddered; the wall cold against her palms. She shuddered again at the sting of pain. A fierce, guttural moan filled the air at their fit, replaced by a heavy pant in her ear. Nico pulled out, plunged half-way, poised, teasing, a taunt to ensure she recognised this moment as a punishment. Of course, she thought, she deserved punishment for making him feel good.

His ragged breath testified to his lack of control. This would be quick, and all about him. *So why can't I fight or deny the rising thrill?* The fear and arousal confused Lia until she realised this was the Nico Francesca had known, and one she'd secretly hoped to meet. Marco's whispers and insinuations, meant to scandalise, had burrowed into her mind, giving life to subconscious desires.

Lia tried to reach back, to touch him. He wouldn't have it, shrugging her touch away as if venomous. She clung to the wall in front, hoping her thighs would hold up. In all this time he hadn't uttered a word, hell-bent on delivering the message that Lia had no substance except for the wet warmth she provided. Pumping one last time, his release sent a burning trail into her body and brain. Disorientated, a shocked moan escaped her when sleek fingers reached inside, and pleasure exploded. Sagging against him like a rag doll, grateful he hadn't excluded her, she held herself still, puzzling over the fact. Nico made no sense.

They remained like that for a long time. He sighed deeply, painfully. From a pocket he pragmatically pulled out one of the many crisp white linen handkerchiefs he owned. Nico had a collection, all of them the same. The pure, white, softness of the fabric, only ever used once for any purpose, and then tossed because no amount of washing could get them clean enough in his mind. With surprising gentleness, he wiped the mess sliding down her legs. Lia interpreted the nature of the act as an apology. Standing perfectly still she waited as he proceeded to do the same for himself before stuffing the piece of fabric into the jacket pocket once again. *Would he toss away the jacket for housing the offending handkerchief? Probably.*

Like a child, she allowed him to adjust her clothing and pull her along. Turning to look at her from time to time, his face reflected a battle between irritation and bewilderment at her silence. Nico's mouth set in a hard line and the perplexity in his eyes demanded something be said. *But what? I don't know what to say.* Following him quietly, she smiled when he next looked at her. Her reward: quickly veiled relief. He had control issues he needed to re-think, at least when it came to her. For now, she would hold her tongue. She needed time to think how best to handle the situation.

Chapter 25

Time with Lia ran to a calendar Nico didn't understand. Married for a month, the living together arrangements reflected comfort and normalcy. The smooth transition made him uncomfortable, and it made him anxious. When anxious his concentration suffered, his disposition more so. Logic dictated living together should've been harder. He liked the way she cooked, looked after things, how she knew when he needed quiet, and their sex life would have overruled anything in any case.

That last night of their honeymoon, his libido had exploded, created a life of its own, a world where control failed. The battle to regain it had not yet been won or he would not be this creature obsessed,

obsessed with her. It went against everything he had carefully constructed in his life. With Francesca, everything had run like clockwork. He had decided the time, the place, and more importantly, how often. Sex mattered but it didn't rule him. He ruled it. *Until the day at the beach, and the night in Taormina!*

The first he could live with, the second made him afraid. He'd wanted to hurt Lia, use her as nothing more than a means to gratify his desires and yet at the last minute, he hadn't been able to lose himself in her without giving back. Fury raced through him. He couldn't leave her wanting, not then and not now. He couldn't wait to have his day end and be in her vicinity, a sexual addiction and to his consternation something emotional. With Lia, the after-sex intimacy, the closeness, the sweaty mess didn't bother him, a universe away from the meticulously planned sessions with Francesca.

He stared at Lia sprawled naked in his bed, their bed. Her hair, in the loose plait she favoured, her extraordinary body lax and well sated, stirred his beast again. Angry, he narrowed his eyes, not making any pretence to disguise his distaste.

"Okay, Domenico, enough. I've had a gut full." Lia sat up, not caring about covering herself as she leaned back against the headboard.

"What are you talking about? *Gut full*? Is this one of your little *Australianisms*?" He shrugged his shirt on and began the buttoning process, not oblivious to the use of his full name, and the sudden sharpness in her voice. He didn't know why but somehow this conversation needed deflecting.

"You know exactly what I'm talking about. That look you give me. The one blaming me for your lack of control, for not being able to keep your hands to yourself. How considerate of you to save the disdain for after the fucking."

"You have such a way with words. I would remind you that you weren't exactly complaining."

"Neither were you during the process. This isn't about the sex. It's about the look you give me after sex, like I'm nothing or worse still, contagious."

"What the hell are you talking about?"

"When sex isn't involved, we're best friends. Mostly when sex is involved, we're... you know what we are, and you've managed the right balance...almost.

You're clever. And I am so tempted to leave it alone, but I can't."

She paused, watching him methodically tuck his shirt into his pants, his attention a token, nothing more.

"You finished?" She had shadows under her eyes, he noticed idly.

"You know, I'm used to your looks. I had enough of them when I first got here to last a lifetime. I thought we had moved past it. And instead, we've gone backwards. I'm pregnant. I'm in a position I wasn't expecting, and you're acting like an arsehole. I comprehended you saw Marissa in me, comprehended you hated the way I reminded you of the past. I even comprehended you hated feeling an attraction for me, but things are different now. So, here's another expression for you – cut the crap. Stop blaming me because you can't keep your dick in your pants. Tough titties if you can't control and relegate fucking to the weekends, like you did with Francesca. Don't look at me like that! Don't treat me like I'm stupid. I know where your head is."

"You think you know."

The cold, methodical voice stirred a sense of violence so strong, it frightened her. "If you keep this up..."

"What? What will you do, Lia?"

Reaching for his tie he turned his back only to feel the jolt of an unexpected physical attack when she leapt off the bed and pushed him. He ignored the immediate response to grab her, afraid he might hurt her.

"That's very mature," he said coldly.

She glared at him, a naked goddess, a naked angry goddess.

"Are you done?"

She continued glaring but her body softened. He wanted her to be the 'bad guy' and she would not allow it.

"This is a strange situation for both of us. It's more complex than either of us expected." She battled to stay and sound calm. "You're doing my head in with your behaviour. I have a baby to think about. You dictated the terms of this relationship. I agreed because I believed it was the right thing to do, and because we do have...chemistry. You're angry because what we have is good. Seriously? Where the fuck is your logic, Nico?

Grow up. I'm confused too. Sex between us is, I...I don't know...it's like making love has become as necessary as breathing, necessary to survival."

"So is taking a shit."

"Fuck you." She stalked into the living area and pulled out a suitcase from the cupboard. "You're a spoilt brat. I nearly lost my best friend, to make this work. So did you. Marco still doesn't understand about us. You married me as much for the right to fuck me as you did for the pregnancy and now it doesn't...suit you?"

He picked up her robe from the foot of the bed and handed it to her. Seeing her naked, emotionally, her face wet with tears, flushed with anger, and then also physically exposed, made it hard for him to breathe. Like a robotic doll, Lia accepted the robe, slipped it on and turned back to the suitcase. Even now, distraught, she deciphered his emotions, put him first. His elated ego did nothing to help the man. Lia drew out emotions he didn't have the equipment to examine. She had no idea what it did to him knowing he couldn't leave her alone no matter how hard he tried.

"You're overreacting!" he said at last.

"For fuck's sake! Don't bloody patronise me. I don't deserve your black moods. Have you any idea of how cruel you can be with that look, how it makes me feel? I won't tolerate it, Nico."

Her tears didn't sit well with him. He didn't want to hurt her, but he struggled with how he felt around her.

"Lia..."

"No, let me finish. That first time...and you know what I'm talking about, that night you dragged me through Taormina, I comprehended you needed to punish me. I didn't like it, but I comprehended. Naively, I thought, hoped, we could get past it. I thought you would see you don't need to hold how you feel, against me. Do you really want less than what we have?"

"No! Yes! No, I don't know. I hate not having control."

"I don't have any either."

Lia sighed. He looked like a little boy, a sulky confused one, and it made her chest ache.

"Someone is going to notice this tension. My guess. Your mother."

Her level voice at odds with the heaving chest, the sag of her shoulders, and the tears destabilised him. *See, this is the problem.* Her effect on him mystified him completely. *Why the fuck did she appear so fragile instead of angry which made more sense?* He closed his eyes, awareness dawning. Lia's concern revolved around him, on the toll his behaviour and emotions took on him.

"Lia."

"I understand. Our blood tie bothers you. Lying to Gina, the pregnancy, and on top of everything...there's this insane attraction. These things are hard for you to digest. Well, your behaviour is difficult for me to digest."

She gripped the suitcase handle tightly, desperate to feel something solid.

"Nico, you're hurting me without reason. It's the way to failure. I'm on your side, our side."

Without conscious thought his hand moved to cover hers.

"Everything with you is so untidy," he muttered, struggling to explain himself. "I like boxes with clear definitions. What I know is disappearing under a mountain of wanting you. I can't cope, it's overwhelming. Sometimes it feels I can only breathe properly when I'm inside you. Nothing prepared me for this. I don't understand it."

"Neither do I."

"Lia."

"I remember asking you how we'd gotten to this point...at the restaurant the day I came to your office. You said it didn't matter. You were right. We're here. Let's deal with it."

He remained quiet, his breathing highlighting his obvious exasperation.

"This can only work if we go with it, Nico, not against it. Resenting me won't make it go away any faster, and you don't want it to go away. That's the real reason you're angry."

He shook his head in agreement. The opposing actions only emphasised his little boy sulk. She stilled, waiting patiently for the outcome.

He breathed her in. Coconut, chocolate, and cinnamon, and even though he wasn't someone who loved sweet things, he wanted to eat her, absorb her, and if he were honest, control her.

"You're impossible to dislike, you know that?"

Lia sighed. "But it doesn't make you happy?"

"I don't like surprises. I get the irony of the situation. This is good; I want to punish you for it. Right now, I really want to punish you by pushing you down to your knees and filling that overactive mouth with my cock, so you can't talk and justify everything in that annoyingly reasonable way you have."

"That was a long sentence!"

"Did I mention overactive smart mouth?"

He growled as she unzipped his pants and unleashed him. She stared into his eyes, her wicked smile mocking his unreasonable behaviour, her appeal even more unreasonable.

"I guess I'll be late for work again?"

"You poor thing having to suffer." She had the audacity to wink before she continued. "If you keep this look and not the other, you're going to be very late," she replied and squeezed him hard before sliding down his body.

He sighed and let his mind go blank to everything but her. *Fuck, she felt so good.*

Lia opened the shutters and stepped onto the balcony. From this vantage point she could see the shiny black vehicle heading down the road. Leaning against the wall she watched until it became a black speck. Slowly and deliberately, she rocked her head against the concrete, not enough to hurt but enough to feel it. She kept it going, reminding herself to breathe. *That's what you do at the gym, breathe through the pain and then the repetitions don't seem so hard.*

Lia inhaled then exhaled slowly. "It's not and never has been about fucking, no matter how good it is," she whispered to the air around her. "He can't see it, won't let himself see it. I wish I smoked."

She smiled wryly. It would feel so good, she imagined, to viciously stub that cancer stick out. A stupid idea, she admitted fiercely, to even joke about smoking but she craved an action. Nico was such hard work. Lia's fingers glided over the back of her head, rubbed the tender spot. *How ironic to feel so well used, sated by the very thing that makes life seem as if I am on a permanent precipice waiting to fall.*

Chapter 26

"**So?** Two months as a married man?"

"And your point is, Marco?"

Little had been said about Lia and the wedding despite meeting every Wednesday morning for their squash game. Nico knew Marco had been biding his time. He took their friendship seriously. Sensing Nico's reluctance to discuss the matter, resentment oozed from his pores.

"So, how is it?"

"Fine, how should it be? You ask the same question every time."

"Do you think that's because I get short, clipped answers telling me nothing?"

"Marco, there's nothing to tell. Lia and I are doing fine but that's not what you're asking, is it? You won't be happy until you know every little detail of the before, of the how it all happened. I told you. Between the family connection and Francesca, it seemed wiser to keep it quiet. Enough. It's that simple."

"I'm guessing she fucks the way she dances. It started that night, didn't it?"

"Shut up, you idiot, and hit the ball before I'm tempted to use one of your balls in the game instead."

Nico slammed the racquet with more force than usual, irritated by the crude, childish behaviour.

"How good is she at giving head? I know how much like you like it. I've seen it firsthand."

"What? Shut the fuck up!" Nico couldn't control the angry response.

"You never minded sharing information before."

"What's got into you? I let you watch, you let me watch, we shared, and it was also a long time ago. Talk about my wife like that again and I will make sure you can't walk out of this court on your own."

"Oh yes, the good old days. How long have we been friends, shared things? Maybe that's the problem;

she sucks at sucking, and you didn't want to share that? Is that it?" Marco smirked.

Before Nico knew it, he had dropped his racquet and slammed Marco into the wall, hands around his throat.

"Dom, you're hurting me. Let me go." Marco gasped, struggling to pry himself loose from Nico's hold.

Nico raked his eyes over Marco, breathing hard. His knuckles bone-white under the stretched skin of his clenched fists, Nico let go and walked to the other side of the court.

"You need to grow up." Nico rasped, struggling to control his breathing.

"I'm sorry," Marco rasped, holding his hands to his throat. "That was going too far, even for me. I didn't mean it. You know how I feel about her."

"You're such an idiot, Marco, a danger to yourself. Look I'm sorry you feel hurt. This is private though, between Lia and me."

"No. I'm sorry." Marco risked a hand on Nico's shoulder. "I guess I'm pissed at how quickly it all happened and without a word. You didn't even tell me you had dumped Francesca, never mind that you and Lia were a thing, and every time I try to talk about it, you shut me down."

"Marco please. Don't push this." Nico found himself oddly protective of his relationship.

"Alright. Will you at least answer one thing?"

"I don't know." The defeated look on Marco's face did not sit well with Nico. "Fine."

"Why do you look so torn, so uneasy?" Marco's puzzled tone held a genuine note of concern. "You hide it well. Gina is overjoyed with the situation and doesn't see it, but I do."

"It's complicated." Nico said, hoping Marco would let the subject drop.

"That's the most honest you've been around me. Thank you." He paused, an awkward silence. "Is it the sex games you miss? I can't imagine Lia playing those games."

Nico couldn't forestall the small, annoyed grimace. "Marco, you don't learn, do you? If you want to live, don't mention your imagination and Lia in the same breath. Understand?"

"Can I say anything?"

"Probably not!" Nico huffed out a breath, concentrating on the concern behind Marco's flippant tone. "Look, with Lia, it was difficult, awkward. It happened quickly and we weren't sure how my parents would react."

"Because you're related or because of Francesca?"

"A little of both." Nico felt pressured to answer, uncomfortable at bending the truth.

"Nico. The family ties are diluted but I do understand about Francesca. And for what it's worth as far as Lia goes, I think I got it before you did, or at least I had suspicions."

"I don't think so!"

"Don't go getting all hot and sweaty. I know you. I have eyes."

"Why didn't you say something then?"

"This is you we're talking about. I know when to keep my mouth shut, believe it or not." Marco gave a rueful bark. "I wasn't sure. And I didn't think it would go anywhere. Nico, you have rules and fucking in your own backyard isn't a rule I thought you would break. Francesca's father wouldn't have been happy."

"Actually, he wasn't surprised, but he was disappointed."

Marco snorted. "You did keep her in line. So...tell me. You don't miss any of the...party tricks? There's little Francesca wouldn't do. Don't get angry, I'm just saying."

"You're worse than a woman! You want to know everything." Nico sighed in exasperation, slamming the ball at the wall.

"That's a sexist remark! You're better than that. Nico, come on, we've always discussed things, so now what...I'm not allowed to ask questions?"

"No, I mean yes. No!"

"Which is it?"

"It doesn't feel right to talk about Lia."

"I'm not being an arse. I want to know things are good with you. This whole thing has been a big change in your life. You don't like change."

"No, but I like her." Nico allowed himself a wry grin at Marco's expression. "I'm as surprised as you. And it is good between us, incredibly good. I'm fucking addicted! Around her, my dick has its own agenda."

"And that's bad because...? Nico, I've watched her watching you. It's subtle but she knows when you need easing. She knows to put a hand on your shoulder or move closer, and she does it without making a production of it."

He laughed as Nico raised his eyebrows.

"No, I'm not a stalker, I notice things. You need me to do that because you can't or refuse to." Marco paused, thinking it through. "You know what I like most about her?"

"What?"

"Lia's not competitive. She defers to your mother, allows Gina her place, and does the same with me. That ability to allow others their space...it demonstrates strength, a sense of security in herself and you. She's genuine. I'm jealous. I want the same from someone. Don't look so shocked."

"It's not that." Nico shook his head, his face a network of tension.

"What then? What is it, Nico?"

"You don't get it Marco! She's beyond anything I've ever experienced. With her I don't need the thrills, the build-up, or fucking fantasies. She derails me. I am so fucking caught up in her and her vagina, nothing else matters. She's buried her way so deep...it's like she's soul deep."

"Soul kissed."

Marco's voice, a barely-there whisper confused Nico. "What? What did you say?"

"Nothing. An old story about the sea. A mermaid and a sailor kissed, a kiss so true, it bound their souls together. There's also a poem of some sort."

"Really? You want to talk about stories? Poems?" Nico gave an annoyed huff. "Let's just play." With that Nico positioned his racquet, ready to resume the game. The bewildered look on his face remained.

Marco, uneasy, had to say something. "She's not a threat. Lia's a dimension to your life I think you needed."

Nico served again with more precision, less heat, relieved the conversation with Marco had come to an end. The game soothed him like Marco's words. Lia did add a dimension. *I don't know why I'm threatened by something so good*. Nico wished he could explain more to Marco. *But then how do I explain something I don't understand myself?* He confined his thoughts to the ball, putting his energy into keeping Marco occupied and avoiding the way the words *soul kissed* floated to the surface of his mind and niggled.

Chapter 27

Lia sat brushing her hair. She had said little since they had left the home of her American friends. Methodically, she began the intricate plait she preferred when sleeping. Such a waste, as he had every intention of pulling it all apart.

"Lia? What are you thinking?"

Lia fiddled with the long dark strands, weighing her words. "Greg is overcautious... I feel fine...I don't think..."

"I detect uncertainty. I don't like that from you."

"Liar. You hate it when I know things."

"True. But I like to be the one to make you quiet."

"Quiet. You know how to make me quiet?"

"Well, I know how to occupy that beautiful mouth. It's the same thing."

She rolled her eyes at him, daring him to continue. He grinned as she made her way over to the bed, stopping in front of him. She bent down and bit his chin. He scowled.

"Serves you right." She kissed the spot and sat down on the bed beside him. "You make everything about sex. And you take a perverse delight in shocking me with visuals."

"You love my dirty talk and," Nico said slyly as he slid his hands up her thighs, "you love my visuals."

"Surely someone else will do?" Lia replied, slapping at his hands.

"Not for this, they won't."

"A comedian, you think you're a comedian." She crinkled her nose at him finding Nico in playful mode irresistible.

"Are you saying someone else because you're worried about my reaction, or because you might find it embarrassing?"

He spoke calmly in opposition to the furrowed lines on his brow. Knowing him as she did, it oozed possessive male on the prowl. She leaned into his body, answering with quiet deliberation. "Both reasons apply. I know you won't like it. And, as for having Marco manhandling," she cupped his cheek, "my vagina, well, it doesn't fill me with joy. He's also the best so I can deal with the idea. Does that upset you?"

"Yes. It feels wrong on so many levels. And yes, I know it screams possessive and yes I know you're not my personal toy."

"Do you? I wonder sometimes." She rolled her eyes at him again.

He laughed despite his tightly wound body, welcoming the intimacy of talking freely. She made it easy with her humour and acceptance.

"This pregnancy is suddenly like an octopus with tentacles spreading to places we hadn't imagined. It's a strange coincidence that Marco is conveniently a renowned obstetrician." The tightness in his jaw increased with his words.

"Greg is my friend and my doctor. He knows my history and he knows Marco's reputation."

With Nico you had to be careful how you presented things; short and sweet worked best. *Time to stop speaking.*

"Can we sleep on it?" His thumb strummed a pink peak as he spoke.

She nodded, her insides tightening in response to his touch, bent her head to meet his mouth knowing full well sleep would be a while. His tongue sneaked in to play with hers, his hands climbing to cup her face. One hand threaded itself in her hair, using the braid as leverage to look directly into her eyes. While lust might rule his body, his mind was another matter.

"Why don't we ask Marco to recommend someone instead? He could oversee, and everyone would be happy." Before he could answer she swooped down and elegantly enveloped him with her mouth.

~

Nico turned off the lamp. The minute he settled, Lia snuggled closer, drawing his arms into a cocooning position. Never one for wanting emotional closeness, his body disagreed time and time again. Lia thrived on space invasion, walked in on private moments, would watch him shave or search for him at odd moments and then sit in his lap. He favoured the latter and relished the closeness when her head lay on his shoulder. With Lia, Nico found himself aboard a fast train to intimacy; you either got on or it rolled over you. Climbing on board had infinite rewards.

Greg's words, medically precise, drummed inside Nico's head. Lia's body had suffered trauma. A baby this soon after the accident could take a toll. Marco's reputation had long outgrown Sicily and now included a major part of Europe. Yet, the thought of Marco having access to Lia's body stirred dark things in him.

He nodded off to the soothing sounds of Lia's quiet breathing, only to stir a short time later rock hard and with a disturbing need to brand her. Disturbing her seemed selfish. He settled for proximity, his fingers on her hip, and closed his eyes.

"Nico," Lia whispered, her voice a siren's huskiness, woke him close to dawn. She positioned long slender limbs to accommodate his aroused body. Sometime later, sated and still inside her body, he fell asleep again.

~

"Why am I all sticky and glued together?" She raised her dark, delicate brows, blinking sleepily against the morning light. "You're one sick man, Domenico Morrelli."

He strolled into the bathroom, returning to the bed with a warm cloth to clean her up, amused and aroused by the way she lay, every inch a contented feline. Christ, he thought, catching himself before falling prey to never ending urges. He frowned. She laughed. He rolled her over and smacked her bottom hard, grinning as she turned her head to look at him and pouted, a token gesture, knowing well she responded nicely to a little paddling.

"I need breakfast, I used up a lot of energy last night. *Harder...Nico, harder...oh...*" He grinned again as she stuck her tongue out, rising from the bed. She sniffed disdainfully, heading for the bathroom. He slapped her bottom again.

"Can you leave my behind alone?"

"No. It's mine," he answered arrogantly. She tossed her hair. He tugged her so her back lay flush against his front, her heat potent through the fabric of his suit. "It's mine and sometime soon I am going to have it. I don't know why we haven't already. We've done everything else." He moved his finger down her spine, gently outlining that part of her until her breath quickened.

She turned her head to look at him over her shoulder. "I don't think so, Mister. What on earth makes you think you can decide what we can and can't do?"

"Because I can."

"I repeat. I don't think so."

"Wrong! I know so. Don't think that tone is fooling anyone. I can hear the acceleration of your heart. Consider the experience as working towards a Masters."

"Not interested." She made a disparaging sound and tried to pull herself out of reach. He hung on tightly.

"Little liar," he said, unable to resist one last slap on that already rosy behind, before he turned her and kissed her.

"Can I please pee now?"

He let her go, thinking he seriously might not survive if they added more to the mix. His cock stirred again with ideas of its own, completely ignoring its master's complaints about stamina. Nico frowned. He needed clarification. Could indulging in so much sex be harmful in her condition? Lines deepened at the thought of asking Marco.

The coffeemaker warming greeted her entrance into the kitchen. Lia smiled in anticipation. Her watered-down version of coffee because of the pregnancy had him cringing. The pink silk robe he'd bought her hugged every curve and gave a subtle shine to her skin. He might buy her a robe to match each tie in his wardrobe. *So many possibilities.*

"What are you thinking so hard about? Don't tell me! I know that look." With fluid efficiency, Lia popped the bread into the toaster, ignoring his laughter. "You have a one-track mind. How many pieces?" She shook her head, laughing at the four fingers he held up. "I've turned you into a raisin toast aficionado. It's so un-Italian."

Lia made a fresh batch once a week. She had turned out to be an extremely good cook who, much to his surprise, broadened his palette, commencing with raisin toast, Lia's religion. She found the sweet pastries that were the custom for breakfast in Italy unappealing at the early hour, and now, so did he.

"So, what else are you thinking so hard about, and not that," she asked, directing her gaze down and back up to his now serious face, enjoying the play of emotions as his thoughts tumbled in his overactive brain.

"Can you do something for me today?"

She grinned in answer, rolled her eyes, and looked down at his groin again. His lips twisted in the effort not to look annoyed. She knew he hated the eye-rolling.

"You're so amusing. Don't do that with your eyes, and no, not that, at least not again this morning."

"Just as well, I may not be able to walk. What did you have in mind?"

"Can you ring Silvia and cancel Marco's game with me tomorrow? Tell her he's got a new patient, a difficult, smart-mouthed patient."

"Nico. Are you sure?"

He liked the fact she didn't pretend to misunderstand, didn't hide her relief. "I'm sure."

"I thought we were going to ask him to recommend someone?"

"He's the best, Lia. And I don't think he would be happy delegating."

After he had gone Lia sat with her weak, non-coffee coffee, staring into space. It had cost her every bit of self-control she possessed not react, to keep her face impassive. She had what she wanted. Marco was the best, and she wanted the best. With Nico you had to tread carefully and wait, trusting in his sense of fair play. *Why is it then, he still surprises me?*

Chapter 28

"**Any** more secrets?" Marco asked.

"Marco, please. We're sorry…we…" Nico shook his head at Lia. Understanding Marco's negativity and anger had nothing to do with her, she deferred to Nico and stopped trying to apologise. They sat opposite Marco in silence.

Marco stared hard at them both and looked back to the referral letter from Greg. He continued reading. Once he finished, he returned to staring at them both.

Lia, uncomfortable with the heavy atmosphere, shifted in her seat. Nico reached across and covered her hand with his. She calmed; they waited. Minutes later Marco switched into what Lia assumed to be his 'professional mode' and began asking for medical information. Lia relaxed further until Nico asked for the birth timeline to be kept vague. The professional faded as a disgruntled Marco re-surfaced. Nico, Lia thought to herself, would have to talk to Marco soon.

~

Nico's parents had been ecstatic, Gina beside herself with joy. Nico and Lucio were still on rocky territory, but the changes Lucio had made to the apartment on Lia's request had impressed Nico and mellowed him a little. Lia hoped time would do the rest. Lucio had done a brilliant job converting their dining room into an office for both Lia and Nico to share. Lia had her own sewing and computer area with hinged doors to keep her section tidy. The other half of the room held a desk for Nico, and a tall bookcase, a floor-to-ceiling masterpiece to house his legal texts. The smooth, black surface, the final touch.

She found herself thinking about her sometimes-difficult husband as she brushed her hand along the same wood and smiled. *Did Nico suspect Lucio had progressed to once again sharing a permanent bedroom with Gina?* He hadn't said a word to her. Today Nico would be bringing a client, Andrea Chiari, home for an informal business meeting. Andrea apparently, believed in a more personal acquaintance with the people he engaged. Nico, at first uncomfortable with the idea, had conceded. The amount of business Andrea offered, enough for Nico to take on a junior partner, had figured greatly in his acceptance.

Aside from business, Lia had the distinct impression Nico liked the older man. He'd fussed about the menu, the apartment and even about her. *Then again, once Nico decided, he went all out.* Placing a small tray with a bottle of Chianti and some glasses in the office area, she gave it a last look before returning to the nursery.

~

A small commotion drew Lia's attention away from the scene in front of her.

"Oops," she whispered checking her watch.

"Lia? Lia?"

Wiping her hands as best she could, she headed towards her husband's voice. "I'm here." She lifted her face to meet his kiss. Nico's eyes slid to the paint on her oversized t-shirt and frowned. Lia kept her smile in place, turning to their visitor. "Signor Chiari, it's a pleasure to meet you. I've heard so much about you. Please forgive my appearance but I have been working on a small project in the nursery."

"The pleasure is mine. And you, I must say are even lovelier than your husband has led me to believe. May I call you Lia?" At the small inclination of her head, he smiled. "And you must call me Andrea. My dear, is this a bad time? Domenico and I can make other arrangements..."

"No. Not at all! I have everything ready; well, everything but myself."

She indicated the way to the small office as she spoke. Stopping at the fridge she took out the oval dish with the appetisers and continued to the study, opening the sliding doors. "Please help yourself while I go change. I'm afraid I lost track of time."

The gleam in Andrea's gaze might be reassuring, but her husband's mood was harder to gauge.

"Andrea, may I offer you a drink?" Nico asked, picking up the crystal decanter, his tone neutral, his eyes directed at Lia, displeased.

"Thank you, I would love an aperitif."

The voice, fastidiously polite, belied by the twinkle in Andrea's eyes had Lia wanting to laugh. *It seems you have my husband all worked out.* He cemented that impression by slyly winking at her. Lia smothered the laugh once more. Nico didn't react well to subtle jokes. Lia on the other hand found the snow-white hair and matching well-trimmed beard charming and his humour appealing. Salvaging the situation would not be difficult.

"I have been working on something special. In fact, so special even Nico has been banned from a viewing until completion. The paint hasn't dried but I think the full effect is possible. Would you like to have a look?" Andrea took the hint, winking his understanding.

"Do you mind, Domenico? I confess to being intrigued." He bent closer to Lia and whispered, "This might be a wise move before settling down to business with your husband, in his current mood." This time Lia did the winking.

"Of course," Nico replied, leading the way, his tension barely in check.

Lia felt sorry for him. In his office environment he might have coped. At home, his vulnerability surfaced. Andrea's joviality perplexed him. She bit her lip anxiously, and hoped she'd been correct in thinking the room would soften his mood, convince him things could still run smoothly if not rigidly to plan.

"Would you mind," Lia asked Andrea as they reached the nursery, "if Nico goes in first?"

"This becomes more and more fascinating, my dear. Domenico, please don't keep us in suspense."

Nico face tight, his body tense, opened the door, and found himself unable to utter the smallest sound.

"Dio! Che meraviglia!" Andrea, following close behind, managed to speak Nico's thoughts for him.

Blushing, she whispered back in Italian. "Grazie."

"Of course, you had to finish it." He turned to Nico. "Your wife is a very talented woman."

The top half of the facing wall, painted a soft pale blue held white fluffy clouds, dotting the sky, staring down on a soft, grassy scene filled with baby animals. A small koala sat on an alligator wearing a tiara. Two small kookaburras rode on the tail. Mother kangaroo held her baby safe and warm inside her pouch while friendly wombats crouched beside two echidnas wearing nappies. The stunning creatures were focused on a gum tree full of brightly coloured lorikeets. Building blocks, a bucket and spade, a goal post and a big beach ball completed the panorama.

"To ensure this baby will be able to look at his or her heritage every day?" Andrea reached for her hand and brought it to his lips and turned to Nico. "Complimenti, Avvocàto. If she cooks half as well as she paints, I am a fortunate man."

Lia blushed again, pleased with his comments and the fleeting look of pride that crossed Nico's face.

Lunch proved an enjoyable event, if later than had been organised. Lia had returned free of paint smudges, wearing some light make-up and a flowing pink dress instead of her painting attire. Whatever Andrea had been searching for in Nico's personal life had obviously been satisfied. Lia had been sorry to see him go when his driver had come to collect him.

Smiling, she turned to find Nico leaning on the breakfast bar, watching her place the last of the things into the dishwasher. The narrowed focused look, one she recognised, liquefied her legs and sped up her heartbeat.

"It's not unreasonable to expect your cooperation, is it?"

"Of course, not."

"So, your inability to adhere to my wishes shouldn't go unnoticed? Unpunished?"

"Nico, I've apologised. It went well."

"Still, you might do it again if I let it go and next time...who knows?"

"No! It won't happen again."

"I can't trust you. I think unless you are chastised, you will transgress again."

~

"From now on, what will Lia do with my requests?"

Nico returned to his previous stern stance. The timber shutter filtered the last of the day's light, enhancing the beauty of the woman in front of him. He untied her hands, removed the blindfold before stretching out beside her, his pose deliberately intimidating.

The effect he'd hoped for, in Lia's opinion, was spoiled by the delicious nudity at her fingertips, making it hard to keep a straight face. "Ignore them so I have to be punished?"

He rolled her to her side so that he could give her bottom a hard slap, not once but twice, before he spoke again. "You do understand that this isn't the way this is supposed to end, that it's not the way the game is played?"

"What should I have said then?" Lia replied, not the least bit daunted by his words, rubbing a soothing hand over her now pink bottom.

He shook his head, thinking briefly of Francesca. He would have dressed in brooding silence, leaving without a word or a sign to signify a next time. All of it orchestrated carefully to tease and taunt in a highly disciplined game. The rules kept her under his control, wanting more, a power game he'd fucking loved. Nico looked down at the woman in his bed, at the long limbs, at the swollen belly that only highlighted her beauty, at the sleek sheen of sweat covering her well satisfied body, and lastly the part of her, soft and wet, evidencing his thorough possession and grinned.

"You gave me the right answer."

"Then why this?" She grumbled, rubbing her behind again.

"When I ask for something, I expect it to be done."

"Yes, Master. Three bags full, Master!"

"Mouthy, aren't you?" He gave her bottom another smack.

Laughing, she got up and headed for the shower. He followed, reaching out to put a hand on her shoulder and swivelling her around to him. "That room is incredible."

Not answering him vocally, overcome with emotion at the awe in his voice, she tugged his hand with hers and pulled him into the bathroom.

Chapter 29

"Where are you going?"

"Bathroom," she replied. Nico closed his eyes knowing he wouldn't succumb to sleep until she had returned to bed. Now in her last few weeks of pregnancy, the nightly restlessness had become routine. A sudden frantic cry had him leap out of bed.

"Lia?"

"Call Marco," she croaked.

The small whimpers from Lia and the pervading dank, dark coppery smell of blood registered trouble. He scrambled for the mobile, dialling for an ambulance first and then Marco. Covering Lia with a small blanket, he held her hand and with the other rang his mother. The ambulance and his parents arrived simultaneously. Sitting in the ambulance he heard garbled medical jargon about placentas and blood pressure. All Nico comprehended was no-one could look so pale, be so cold and live.

The baby, male and tiny didn't interest Nico. Lia had broken her word to Marissa and gone chasing butterflies. Over and over, she had whispered about the tiny creatures, about the way they were urging her to follow them. He'd wanted to shake her, yell at her to shut up, to concentrate on him. Watching the warmth seep out of her swollen body Nico thought he could hate her easily. Perhaps he did. At the hospital he even ignored Gina but perversely he noted Lucio did not leave Gina's side. He continued making lists in his head, the same way he always did when he needed to regain control of his thoughts.

Later, someone led him to a room where Marco had arranged a portable cot. He preferred the armchair beside the bed holding Lia and the wires and tubes swamping her fragile body. He sat in the same spot for three days. Lucio made it easy for him by bringing a change of clothes and Nico's computer.

"Thank you." Nico whispered, grateful for the first time in a long time, for the presence of his father.

Nico appreciated the silence. His father he realised had never been one for unnecessary words. After a small pat on the shoulder Lucio left him to the distraction of work. Relieved Nico stroked the equipment now on his lap. The computer and work meant he could stop listing periods of history and it kept him from thinking about the body in the bed, the body needing to disappear, so Lia could come back.

~

"Nico?"

Shocked, fingers reached for the small hand. His chest ached when she squeezed.

"How long?"

"Three days." He cleared his throat.

"I'm sorry. I wanted this different for you. The baby?"

"Our son is beautiful, I've been told."

"Does he look like you, then?" Despite the mask muffling her voice, her humour rang through.

"Of course."

She gave a small smile. Something flickered in her eyes when she searched his. Did she guess he hadn't bothered with their child? He would bet his life on her insight. He swallowed, waiting. She looked around instead, taking in her surroundings and inhaled sharply.

"They're tubes and wires, Lia, don't panic. They'll take them away as soon as they can. Breathe." His voice, strong and reassuring, calmed her. "It's fine, you're fine, I promise."

"I'm alright. Too many memories."

"I know. I've buzzed for the nurse."

"You look terrible. Have you been here all this time?" She frowned. "Of course, you have."

The arrival of a nurse, followed by the Registrar took precedence. Having established all was well for the moment and freeing Lia of the oxygen mask, the room returned to silence as the occupants stared at one another.

"You need to go home."

"It's four in the morning; I'll stay a while longer and then go straight to the office and organise things so I can come back."

"I knew our baby would be a boy."

"Antonio, for your father."

Her smile lit up the room. "Thank you."

"It's a good name."

"Nico?"

"Yes?"

"I heard you," she whispered, "I heard you tell me not to chase the butterflies."

"Go back to sleep. I'll be right here."

Nico, tempted to lie on the cot, walked over to the window instead. The relentless pain in his head yelling migraine, refused to be silenced. To distract himself he thought back to the last migraine he'd had.

"You look shocking," Lia winced at the sight of him. "Ivana rang, told me you were on the way with a migraine. I don't know how you managed."

"Practice."

Soft hands helped him remove his clothes. He barely registered the closing of the shutters and Lia quietly leaving the room. She had seen him like this a few times when living with his parents yet this time, he felt diminished, less of a man especially with her advanced pregnancy.

"It's no better, is it?"

He hadn't heard her come back. Wincing with the effort to lift himself, he managed a mouthful of water and to swallow the tablet she handed him. He would give anything for the oblivion of sleep instead of the small drifts of piecemeal naps and rude awakenings. Small hands intruded on his thoughts, roamed his body while a sweet tone told him to keep his eyes closed. He dreamed of a warm, wet mouth enfolding him. Wanting to protest, he lifted his hand and found soft, silky hair instead. He liked this dream. Later Lia would tell him about studies concerned with constricted blood vessels and he would see a certain logic.

In his dream though all he knew centred on a delicious sensation pushing the pain into the background. He slid his hands to her scalp, not thinking but feeling and she felt so good, so fucking good. He could die happily encased in the velvet moisture of that mouth. Sleep pulled at him, the pain slowly diminishing but not before an orgasm rocked him, stole his breath.

"Stay with me," he whispered, "stay until I fall asleep."

The beeping of the machines, softer now, less intimidating, brought him back to reality. He couldn't live this life, could not be with this woman. She made it impossible to shut himself off. Lia had dug her way so deep into his life, too deep and it could not continue. Infiltrating every corner of his existence was not acceptable. Sitting there, instead of lists, he pictured scenarios. If a way to stop this thing he couldn't name existed, he would find it.

~

His normal taciturn behaviour paid off, both pleasing and infuriating him. The people around him were accustomed to his moodiness and attributed most of it to his caseloads and of course, the new baby. Both those things made sense, but he would have expected more from Lia. His anger and confusion increased his moodiness and took on a self-righteous edge directed to a large degree at Lia for allowing the baby to matter more than he did. He recognised the unfairness of his thinking, that it was irrational, and he knew he should discuss things with Lia; he chose not to. *Lia should have noticed* became his mantra. Francesca noticed, made it a point to be around his office under the proviso of filling in for her father. An idea formed, one that offered an interesting challenge and Nico liked a challenge.

"Nico, what's wrong?"

Lia had been home two weeks and though he touched her often, those same touches felt off in some way. An air of premeditation, of purpose tinged his caresses. Lia couldn't make sense of the situation and it bewildered her immensely. The birth had taken a toll physically not mentally.

"Work is busy, demanding but these are clients from Andrea."

She cupped his cheeks with delicate hands. Her thumb stroked his bottom lip and in reply his body quickened. The cinnamon in her lotion tickled his nose and he drew in a breath, inhaling slowly and closing his eyes to absorb it better.

"Nico...?" Fingers traced from his heart down to the bulge he couldn't prevent.

"Don't. Please." He moved her hand away gently. "Not until Marco gives the go ahead. I want it to be about both of us."

"You know I get as much pleasure out of pleasing you."

"I know. But for now, this is more than enough."
As if it was that simple.

"You don't seem yourself. The situation has been a lot to take in." She searched his eyes, learning further into his embrace.

To distract her he kissed her – a mistake. One taste and he wanted it all. He would always want it all. He pulled away slowly. Their gazes held, hers warm, her lips plump, entrancing. *What*, he wondered, *did she see*? He waited, hoping his half-lowered lids hid the heat, and the effort to deny her. When she chose to rest her head on his chest, he smiled. *Perfect. She knew something was wrong. She should have followed through. It was on her shoulders now.*

Lia would have called him Perverse Nico. Under normal circumstances, subterfuge held little appeal. He didn't know why he didn't take the opportunity to tell her things had changed. What could he say? *It's your fault, all of it. You make me feel too much. It's not acceptable. You had no right to nearly die.* The intellectual knew the dialogue in his head made no sense; the man didn't care.

Two weeks later, after her final check up with Marco, Lia did exactly what Nico knew she would do by heading straight for Nico at his office. Detailed planning included giving Ivana the day off and checking with Marco's office for the time Lia left. Watching for her car, organising to be found in the small room on the bed in the kind of compromising situation that could not, would not be misread, had been easy. Meticulous timing was his specialty. Fixated on the reel, the one where he thrust into Francesca, he ignored the thoughts in his head telling him his machinations were sadistic and sordid. Lia didn't say a word. She'd spun on her heel and walked out. He stood, ignoring Francesca, still hard, unsatisfied not about his dick, but about what he had done, and yet perversely pleased.

Lia couldn't wait for the lift. She raced towards the door to the right and sped down the stairs. Reaching the bottom, she leaned against the wall, breathing hard.

"I have to calm down," she panted to the empty staircase. *God damn him*! She had miscalculated, been fooled by her baby brain. She'd felt his fears, been aware of his panic but she had needed more time. He'd been smarter, quicker, and more devious than she'd expected. He'd ensured her hand was forced. "I can't back down."

An hour later Lia called Nico's mobile. Her voice cool, her tone calm, she asked him to not come home, to give her a space. He owed her that much. He said nothing.

"Please don't say anything to anyone, especially your mother. I'll tell her we can use some privacy. I need a couple of days to myself."

Frozen limbs and fractured brain hung up the phone. He had agreed, exactly as she knew he would. Now she could do exactly what he thought she would do, and all of the action read like a bad scene in a bad film.

Chapter 30

Nico went home three days later. The beguiling scent hovered, the combination of scents from the body lotions and creams she favoured, and he inhaled all of it with greed. The apartment felt cold, colourless. Retaining its elegance and comfort didn't make it a home; her warmth, her personality did. Nico chewed the inside of his cheek thoughtfully. Having promised Lia a trip home after the baby's birth, passport adjustments would have been easy.

Nico sat on the bed, stroking the clean white spread. Lia had made the quilt herself, cleverly edging it in black satin. The pillowcases matched, their austerity softened by small sprays of cherry blossoms, painstakingly hand embroidered by Lia. The Japanese simplicity of style soothed him, symbolising the combination of both their tastes. He clutched the quilt, let it go again and went back to stroking the smooth fabric, his other hand tapping with a rhythmic fury on his thigh. Easing his head onto Lia's pillow, he inhaled again with the same greed he had displayed on entering the room. The mobile beeped, a message from his mother, reminding him about dinner. She knew Lia had gone but what else she knew, he had yet to find out. *Had Lia told them what happened that day? No! Not Lia, the perfect woman, incapable of a malicious act even when deserved.*

~

"What did you do?" Gina screeched at him as soon as he arrived.

"How do you know it has anything to do with me?" Nico's brusque reply shocked him, but he wouldn't accept histrionics, not even from her.

"She asked me to look after Antonio, said she had things to do. I had never seen her look the way she did."

"Gina, don't." Lucio put his arms around her. She leaned in and sobbed. "Sit down, Domenico," his father asked but his voice held a stern note. "Please."

"What did she tell you?" Nico asked them both, not hiding he annoyance at their unity.

"Nothing, nothing that makes sense." His father's devastated voice echoed the look on his mother's face. "Gina, get some plates. You need to eat. We can talk with Nico at the table."

"Nothing! Did you hear that? She told us nothing. She rang us from Japan, said she was on her way home and gave us some rubbish about it being for the best, said she would be in contact. She didn't give me a chance to ask anything."

"Then there's nothing to talk about. She's gone. That's it."

His mother narrowed her eyes. "You think I can't imagine what might have happened? That I'm too stupid, too old, too much your mother not to have realised you had done something disgraceful and been caught. I rang Ivana. Francesca's perfume was all over that room." She pulled a face, a twisted ugly scowl.

"So why ask?" He should fire Ivana.

"I wanted to be wrong." Anguished, she looked away. Her head snapped back instantly. "With trash? I don't care who her father is. Trash is trash. Why?"

"Whoring around seems to run in the family." Nico answered, looking pointedly at Lucio. The force of the slap Gina delivered shocked him into silence. His mother had never hit him.

"You are nothing like him," Gina spat out through her tears. "There were reasons for what happened. What your father did, as much my fault as his. And my business, not yours. What you did...what reason could be good enough to destroy the best part of your life, and ours? A comparison does not exist. Now unless you're prepared to show the respect your father deserves, I suggest you get out of my home."

"Gina." Lucio faced his son, reaching out to his arm. "Nico. She doesn't mean it. She's upset. She loved Lia like a daughter and the baby..."

"Stay out of it, old man, I don't need your help." Nico stepped away, ensuring the hand didn't touch him. "What happened is between Lia and me. You can forget any cosy little discussions. If you and my mother can't accept that, I'll go, and I won't be back. Now, what's it going to be?"

He stayed that night and slowly their lives developed a routine of sorts. Dinner became a ritual where his mother spoke only when necessary. Nico found himself accepting of Lucio efforts, to maintain the peace, grateful in the face of the devastation he saw in his mother. She looked older, sadder, relying on Lucio a great deal. Every discussion highlighted the absence of his wife and child, and the need for two old people to know the reason they had been denied the joy in their lives. Tempted to say something, hating the weight of silence, Nico failed every single time to think of a plausible explanation.

~

"You bought a computer?" Nico moved closer for a better look at the equipment. Gina had found him a housekeeper but dinner with his parents one night of the week had become a ritual.

"Why not? It's time we were more modern." Nico ignored the prickly tone, choosing to whistle in appreciation at the top of the range equipment gathered in front of him. Gina eyed Lucio. He in turn shook his head. Gina frowned. Both of them defensive in their stance.

"I'll help you set it up, if you like." Nico said, doing his best to ignore the chill in the air.

"No, that's not necessary. Thank you, anyway." Lucio stepped between him and the computer. "We have someone coming to help us tomorrow."

"This is impressive." Nico ran his hand over the smooth black keyboard. "I'm here now. Why pay someone, or is it part of the deal?" Another look passed between his parents.

"It's a gift, delivered this morning..." His father began.

Gina interrupted him. Her voice cool; her words final. "Lia organised it. Ashlee and the children will be here tomorrow to help us put it together. We don't need your help but thank you for offering. Now do you want another meatball?"

Nico stared at his mother.

"Nico..." Lucio stopped speaking, unsure of what to say.

Nico continued staring at his mother. *Who was she?* She wasn't the woman who had made Nico her sole reason for living. Thousands of miles away, Lia somehow managed to push him out of his own life. *Not that I don't deserve it.* The introspection unwelcome, he steered the discussion to general things surprising both his parents, had dinner with them but cut his visit short.

~

The first time he saw the pictures on the desktop he ignored the pain. The next time it hurt more. Nevertheless, his eyes rarely strayed from the woman and baby flashing across the screen. He thought about all the people close to him: his parents, Ivana, Marco and Silvia now officially a couple. and Annalisa, kilometres away, and how they had become a unit privileged to intimate details, he could only obtain second hand. Always an outsider with his exacting nature, his path had been smoothed by his mother and then Marco. Nico had, with their support, prided himself on his self-sufficiency, grown to appreciate his differences and made use of them. Why, he wondered, did being an outsider hurt so much less than being someone alone?

Chapter 31

The months drifted into a year and then a year became two. Life settled into a less uncomfortable pattern. Nico accepted that Lia, whether in Australia or Italy, would be a permanent fixture. What he hadn't expected were the memories and the merciless pull on his emotions. Reminding himself, his handling of the situation had resulted in the desired outcome, didn't, couldn't erase the look on her face that day. It haunted him, and the effort to deny his feelings and hide them exhausted him. *Did his confusion show?* People around him appeared kinder these days.

"You're more creative than usual." Lia's tone held a *question. "Not that I'm complaining."*

"Marco said it might be...better to vary things so that you are more comfortable considering..."

"Considering?"

"Considering how often we do this."

"The 'this' being...having sex? You discuss how often we have sex, with Marco?"

"Yes, the same Marco who, in case you've forgotten, is your obstetrician."

"I see." She ignored the mocking tone, thinking how to get more information from her husband and deciding teasing might work. "Do you want me to take over because you seem to enjoy this too much?"

"Meaning?" His hand slid along his length, increasing in speed despite her success in distracting him. She rarely said things without a reason.

"Coming all over me...it's like branding me, marking your territory, isn't it? I'm surprised you don't pee all over me too."

"Don't need to. You already know you belong to me. Coming all over you is a different story. I like it. It's that simple."

~

The mornings never varied. He would wake hard, finding release only when he called her name. Short, hollow satisfaction no longer enough, had him admitting he needed her, craved her essence; the way she fit against him, the way she laughed and the way she accepted everything he did to her with abandon and voracious appetite.

"I like these cushions. I'm leaving them here. Suck it up! You have to give a little."

"If I don't?"

"Please," she said, *drawing the word out and pulling a face at him before going down on her knees in a begging position.*

"You're a comedian now? Get up."

Her answer had been to unzip his pants.

"That's not going to work."

She had rolled her eyes at him and laughed, knowing he found it hard to refuse her regardless of what she chose to do or not do next.

"For fuck's sake," he whispered to himself. "It's been nearly two years. When does it stop?" Everything in the room reminded him of her. The unyielding pressure in his head told him he could not survive like this. The crashing and splintering of the items from the dresser didn't assuage his anger. The cloying sweetness of the shattered perfume bottle permeated every corner of the bedroom, making his head spin. *The only thing she left behind. Had it been deliberate?* Frustrated, hurting, he didn't blink at the hole or at the blood smeared across his knuckles and the pristine white of the bedroom wall.

~

"Ivana," Nico said into the intercom. "Drop everything and get in here now. Bring your notebook."

The door flew open to a smile so wide, he had to take a step back. He kept his face impassive, ignoring the knowing, gloating gleam in her eyes.

"Can I sit?"

He didn't know why she asked him; she'd already sat down.

"Coffee is on the way, and I can clear about five weeks for you over Christmas. You will need to take your computer."

"Jesus," he said in English, forgetting she spoke it better than he did, "one day I'm going to fucking fire you."

She stared at him with a smug look on her face. "English, Italian, it's all the same. Don't use the Lord's name in vain, and don't swear at me because I'm a good assistant and can anticipate needs. It's what you pay me for."

"Smart arse. How the fuck did you know what I wanted? I didn't know."

Ivana gave him the look, the superior, obnoxious look of someone who knew her worth.

"It's about time you came to your fucking senses. Let's not waste any more time talking about things that don't matter and get you on a plane. All this fucking talk is holding up progress."

Chapter 32

The Sydney summer heat had less bite this weekend, and in response Centennial Park offered a world alive with hibiscus flowers at the Oxford Street entrance. Butterflies and bees danced above a panorama of golds and reds, soft pinks leaking to a pale white, and the burning orange found only in a sunset. Anyone with eyes and a sense of smell could easily become inebriated on the proffered gardens and their lushness.

Marissa's superstitious nature had obsessed over butterflies. She believed them to be omens of happiness and love, but only if you left them alone. Antonio, Lia's father, and Lia had never ascertained where Mama's ideas came from, especially the idea of chasing them as being dangerous. Papa believed Mama to be a smidgen psychic, and a great deal crazy. Marissa hadn't wanted to go to Italy all those years ago. Papa and Lia had laughed when they had found her in tears over the kitchen sink. A butterfly had landed briefly on the passport sitting on the kitchen table before flying, straight into a sink full of water, and drowning. Butterflies never came into the house. Mama cried and cried. *We can't go to Italy. Bad things will happen.* Papa listened, then explained the butterfly had most *likely* come in with the flowers Marissa had picked, become disorientated, and flown to an early demise. Mama did not stop crying for a long time.

Lia's memory faltered when it concerned events before the age of seven. Brief flashes of laughter, hugs and kisses, hands pinching her cheeks and the boy who scowled at her but later become her best friend. Her reality began with their return to Australia with Papa and Mama in separate rooms. Sometimes though Papa would sleep in Mama's room. Things were confusing. She had nightmares about a dark staircase and a door. The butterflies had been right, and a bad thing had happened. But what? *I wish I could ask Mama,* fluttered around inside her head. *Maybe,* she thought, *the butterflies are inside my head.*

Lia bristled. *Such misery for a small child.* Easing her death grip on the handle of the pram, grateful Antonio remained oblivious to her moods, she caught a whiff of lavender and other enticing scents. Another tug from the past - the herb garden, the day before her eleventh birthday.

"What are you doing, Mama?"

"Wait and see," Marissa had replied in English, with that wonderful lilt in her voice. They always spoke in English during the day and Italian at night. Papa said they had chosen this country and they needed to accept everything about it, especially the language.

"But your herbs, Mama. You pulled them all out. Why?"

"I want to make a different garden, add new herbs so I can try some Asian cooking."

"Mama look." Lia, distracted by a pretty pink and smatterings of blue butterfly, rose from her kneeling position. Ready to chase the pretty creature, Mama grabbed hold of her hand.

"No, my angel, don't frighten it away. Butterflies are fragile; you can kill them with even the softest touch. They need to be free to go on their way to wonderful places, their places not ours until we are ready. Promise you will never chase them."

"You're so silly, Mama." Lia replied, snuggling closer to the perfume of her mother's body. Biscuits, dirt, and perfume. The best combination, unlike Mama's strange words.

"Promise me."

Frightened by the intensity radiating from Marissa, Lia would have promised her anything.

As a child Lia hated the fragmented recollections. The Butterfly Garden - a sliver of a memory where colour and laughter ran riot. Aunt Gina and Mama, one either side of little Lia, all of them happy until the black shadows dispersed it all. *Something had happened the next day, or had it? The door, why the glimpse of a door?* The truth if painful, brought relief and cemented Lia's own obsession with butterflies. The one tattooed on her shoulder, she found to her amusement, annoyed Nico. For him, it marred her perfect skin, yet he hadn't been fazed by the scar from the accident. *Why then had both places drawn his equal sensual attention? Nico, always the enigma!*

Laura, comprehending Lia's fixation, willingly agreed to naming their boutique, *The Butterfly Bazaar*. Leaning forward, Lia grinned at the little boy engrossed in his surroundings before allowing her mind to drift, this time to the herb garden, now Laura's pride and joy.

The centre of fragrances housed lavender, a variety of basil with dark purple leaves, oregano, marjoram, rosemary, mint, and many other herbs. The feel of Marissa as close by, never disappeared. Lia loved how the white, wrought-iron park bench beckoned to those in need of sanctuary. Long ago the magic had whispered, enticing two people to seat themselves for a while. And it was there, protected by the garden's air of tranquillity, that the young girl and the sad, beautiful woman who was her mother invited Truth to pay a visit.

Chapter 33

"Faffaaaalaa" said Antonio, drawing Lia back to the present.

"Farfálla" Lia corrected his pronunciation, glad to let go of the past for a little while. He laughed and refused to say it again. That a two-year-old could tease and out-smart his mother floored her. She leaned closer, kissing the top of his head, enjoying the way Antonio had come to love the atmosphere by osmosis. Through her, this place had become his. These days he began clapping his hands and chuckling the word *park* over and over the minute she angled the pram into Oxford Street. He knew the way; they did it every weekend.

"Ducks. Mummy, ducks." He squealed, knowing they had finally arrived at his favourite spot overlooking a lake.

Antonio's excitement had him climbing out of his stroller. Lia sighed. He had learnt how to undo the restraints. She shook her head at him. He pouted, and she giggled. He flung himself into her arms laughing. "Naughty boy. Next time wait for Mama, okay?" She had to be content with his nod.

Despite the throng of noisy people, the lake worked its magic. An hour later, Lia wiped Antonio's face and chin free of the remains of strawberries and coaxed him back into his stroller. Badly in need of a distraction, she decided to amble her way the length of Oxford Street. Saturday meant markets, with music and street entertainers and more than a fair share of second-hand clothing stores. Today a vintage creation of red roses on a white background, feminine and fresh, but in need of tender loving care, provided the right kind of dressmaking challenge to distract her.

Coffee at Ecco's would give her time to consider how best to reconstruct the garment and indulge in the best coffee in Sydney. The Greek owners were renowned for their sweets, a culinary mix of Greek and Italian. Across the road, the bustle of people wandering the markets blurred Lia's eyes. A wave of longing overwhelmed her for the Italian marketplaces, the loud voices selling wares and for her life in Italy.

"Aren't you perturbed at all?"

"No, Marco. He's just dancing."

"He is," Marco answered drily and narrowed his eyes, *"but Francesca has wandering hands. She needs to be put in her place."*

"He's old enough to handle this by himself." Lia winked at Silvia.

"Tell her to do something, Silvia!"

The redhead rolled her eyes at Marco. *"What do you want me to tell her to do?"*

"Put Francesca in her place." Marco growled, annoyed the women weren't taking him seriously.

"Marco, you're such a 'stirrer'!"

"Silvia! What did you call me? A what? What's got into you?"

"Stirrer," she repeated rolling her 'r' in a way Lia found an absolute joy. *"Lia taught me the word. It's very Australian, no?"*

"Bah! I know what it means. Lia, you need to stop corrupting my assistant," he pouted. "This is different. Francesca is showing disrespect."

"Marco, relax." Lia patted his arm.

"I'm going to the bar," he announced with a huff, and shook off her hand. "Too bad you can't drink; it might help you come to your senses. I know I need one, with that show going on in front of us."

"Stirrer!" Lia winked at Silvia again.

"I'll have hers and yours. You're on call tonight," volunteered Sylvia. Pulling a face, he walked away.

Lia turned to find herself scrutinised by Silvia's warm dark eyes. "You think I should be chagrined as well, don't you?

"What do I know, Lia? I don't have a husband! Hell, I don't even have a boyfriend, and look at me. I'm not exactly competition the way you are. I would be daunted by someone like Francesca."

Lia sighed. She needed to weigh her words. Marco had told her that Silvia's father had been a hard man, a strict man who had fostered a lack of confidence in his daughter. Lia also knew Silvia's widowed mother had numerous health problem; confinement to a wheelchair *being only one of them. It fell heavily on Silvia to be the caregiver. Lia doubted Silvia had much time to herself. Marco's popularity with the opposite sex contributed to keeping Silvia in her shell. Lia hadn't missed the longing looks cast his way when Silvia thought no-one watched.*

"Silvia, my looks aren't a magic potion. Nico will do what he will do. I can't stop him. I have to be more than my looks to ensure he doesn't want something else."

"I don't...understand."

Silvia looked solemn. Lia's instinct told her the other woman would sense if Lia embellished. "Someone secure in what they have to offer."

"Exactly. Nico chose you, someone who looks like you."

"Is that all you think I am?"

"No! I know you are more than that, but it's what he saw first, isn't it?"

"It was a trifle different with us but yes, he saw the surface, but he found someone who wouldn't take any shit either. Nico, like most people, wants to know he is wanted and appreciated. Men like him, and men like Marco, want and need someone who is confident but not necessarily someone who bends over backwards to

please, despite merit in that idea at other times." Lia smiled as the other woman blushed. *"Sorry, I couldn't resist that. Silvia, beauty isn't enough on its own."*

"I'm still not sure I understand."

"I think you do. You're afraid. Silvia, you know who he is. Show Marco who you are. You make his professional and sometimes even his social life easier...but you still hide from him." She held Silvia's gaze. *"Marco wants more than looks. That's why he is so annoyed with Francesca. He hates her type. What she sees as confidence is ego. To trade on your looks, is ego."*

"But they still want the whole package, don't they?"

"Do you think yourself less than the package?" Lia countered, watching the colour in Silvia's face now match the shade of her hair. Hazel eyes glittered.

"I'm not like that," she whispered. *"I mean, like what you said...I'm not confident that way."*

"You need to be if you want Marco."

Silvia flinched, her skin paling, throwing the freckles into prominence.

"He doesn't know. Let's not worry about him for the moment. You can't expect to mean something to someone if you don't mean something to yourself."

"I know, but I have horrible hair. I'm short so clothes are difficult, and I have a red-head's skin..."

"And you're smart, articulate, funny and fantastic at your job."

"But I have to change to be noticed? Why do I have to change?"

"You don't. You need to be true to you, maybe. You hide behind your clothes and lack of make-up, and that crazy beautiful head of red curls. You need to own who you are. Silvia, you're already halfway with him. He genuinely likes you and your mother, and she adores him."

"Cappuccino?" Julieann roused Lia from her thoughts.

"Yes, please."

Chapter 34

Julie delivered an impressive cappuccino before darting away with a promise to come back for a chat as soon as she could. Lia sipped, sighing with pleasure. In Italy, the cappuccinos were served lukewarm; Lia preferred hers hot.

"I can help you change your look, Silvia. But the rest is still up to you."

"I know." Silvia hesitated. *"I don't know if I can."*

"You don't have to do anything other than own who you are by looking how you want and wearing what you like. Stop hiding."

"Louie," Silvia quoted, *"this could be the start of a beautiful friendship."*

"Casablanca. One of my favourite films." Lia grinned in response then grimaced. She swivelled Silvia's chair around, so Silvia could see what was happening.

"Now that is annoying! Lia, you need to do something."

Lia nodded. Both girls watched as Marco caught up to Francesca and Nico, only to step between them. He mouthed 'I told you so' at both women. He then slipped his arm through Nico's, and not so subtly shoved Francesca further away. Lia and Silvia swivelled towards each other and gave way to giggling. Nico merely looked bored.

"Marco loathes her."

Lia thought Silvia commented on the obvious. Marco didn't hide his feelings at all well. It hadn't been easy to appease him about the baby. He'd hated being left out, hadn't hesitated to vocalise the fact over and over. "Hmm, maybe I should make him happy then."

"Who?" Silvia asked. "Make who happy?"

"Marco!"

"Marco?"

"Lia. Wait! Where are you going? What are you going to do?"

"Remind Francesca about my place in Nico's life, like Marco wanted me to do." Lia patted her small lump, grabbed her bag, and winked once again. *"Watch and learn. The secret is doing it nicely. I'll ring you about a time to get together."*

A sip of her coffee in the present, a quick glance to ensure Antonio slept and then she was back there again, back to that night.

"Were you worried?" Nico arched his perfect brow, steering his wife towards the dance floor.

"About her?" Lia rolled her eyes. *"Should I be?"*

"I don't know. Should you be?"

"You want me to be jealous, don't you?" She laughed and rolled her eyes again.

"I wish you wouldn't do that thing with your eyes. How many times have I told you, it's incredibly unattractive?" His arms drew her closer. *"You and Silvia. Some intense moments. Anything you want to share?"*

"Making a time to assassinate her hair and wardrobe and enjoy some girl time. Nothing for you to worry about."

"Ahh!"

"Ahh? What does that mean?"

"Poor Marco! He doesn't stand a chance, does he?"

An irritatingly typical Nico statement proving he noticed everything.

"Sometimes you're too clever."

"Nice work, by the way."

"Meaning?"

"Darling Francesca, would you mind if I danced with my husband."

"You obviously don't want sex tonight or you would know better than to mock me."

His answer had been to tighten his arms around her.

Damn, Lia thought, how did things go so wrong? She knew the answer. The birth had spooked him; she should have realised he would panic.

"Lia. Are you alright? You're muttering to yourself."

"I'm fine, Jules. It's one of those days," she said, wiping her teary face. "A catch up would be a lovely distraction. Sit down! What's been happening?"

Chapter 35

"I can't believe this child is still asleep."

"He loves the park. He'll sleep for hours afterwards. How's Lexi?"

"Nice one, Angelia. Deflecting from the tears."

"Julieann," Lia pouted at her friend's sarcastic use of her full name and replied in kind.

"With Lexi these days, who knows?" Julieann sighed. "My Aunt, your godmother hasn't been well for a long time now but since Yiayia's death…what can I say."

"She's gone into a shell."

"Yes. It's scary. Lexi's vibrancy, that big personality has been missing for a long while. Mum and I are trying to get her to take a trip, something catered for. One of those tours, maybe, so she's not alone. We hope being around strangers might pull her back into a politer frame of mind. She's so testy these days."

"I love your family, but they left too much to her. It wasn't fair."

"I know. There's resentment, anger, and a wee bit of bitter in amongst the grieving. My Dad and my aunt took advantage because she didn't have a family of her own."

"She needs a change and I think I know the tour and the person to get her out of this black mood. No-one can resist Annalisa."

"Great. Oops, sorry, gotta go, customers. I'll come back as soon as I can."

Annalisa would be perfect for Lexi. Lia pulled out her diary and searched for the details to give to Julieann. Her fingers caressed Antonio's soft cheek. Wistfully she wished... *What do you wish? Sydney's home, isn't it, Laura, and Sydney?* Time to go home to Laura, because when the loneliness crowded her mind, Laura and only Laura gave her stability. Lia stacked her cup neatly to one side from habit. Both she and Laura had waitressed here, many years ago. She pushed the stroller towards the counter to pay.

"On the house," Julie said with affection. "You're our favourite customer, especially since the new cushions and wall hangings. Mum loves the updated look."

"It's pretty good, if I say so myself." Lia answered, as she looked at the rich burgundy and golds, carefully chosen to give a Renaissance charm to Ecco's.

"About before. Are you sure you're okay?

"A momentary weakness, Jules. I don't know why, but today he's in my head."

"You should have stuck it out with James. He was good for you."

"No, Missy. His heart is set on you. Always has been, since grade two, if I remember correctly. You guys got out of sync somehow. Why don't you give the man a break? He and I marked time. Jules, don't you think it's time to put the Chris thing in the past?"

"I'm trying. It's difficult; he was everything I thought I wanted for four years."

"The same years James was unavailable."

"Don't. Don't go there. Anyway, the arsehole marries an eighteen-year-old Greek virgin his parents picked out and still comes sniffing around. I'm so over relationships."

"He's a manipulator and you let him manipulate. And you knew his mother was a devil woman from the start."

"She was, wasn't she?"

"Go out with James."

"He and I are the best friends. I can't take the risk."

"Take the risk."

"What and give him an opportunity to compare our vaginas?"

"Julieann Marie Georgiou, you did not say that! I'm out of here." With that, Lia poked out her tongue at her friend and started pushing the stroller. Julieann's laughter followed her home.

Chapter 36

Lia's Papa had split the house into two sections thinking to have a tenant bring in extra money. It had. The double garage had become a self-contained two-bedroom unit with a beautifully hand-carved timber gated separate entrance. The loneliness of the big house after Papa's death had been unbearable. Thankfully, Robert and Laura, who at the time had been renting the unit, jumped at the opportunity to swap. Though some thought it odd, it worked for them and that was all that mattered.

Laura, currently poolside with her sketchbook, resembled a fairy-tale tsarina. Pregnancy had added to her Nordic heritage, enhancing the perfect cheekbones, and giving a particular glint to her sky-blue eyes.

"How are you?"

Laura shrugged. "Tired of wearing this huge balloon. I still have a month to go." Putting her sketchbook down she reached eagerly for Lia's carry bag. "Give me. What did you find, and can I have it when I lose my baby-fat?"

Laura smiled slyly at Lia.

"No. I might let you borrow it though," Lia gave Laura's big belly a rub before adding, "if and only if you make me a beautiful goddaughter."

"I have. I need to wait for the oven to ding though, according to my husband. Let's get Antonio out of this hot sun. Cup of tea? I baked a pineapple ginger cake," Laura called over her shoulder as Lia followed with the pram.

"You want me to get to your oversized state. Just a tea and only because watching you use Lucinda's tea set, and brew the tea the old-fashioned way, is so soothing. Seriously, your Mum should have been English."

"I know."

They sat in the breakfast nook catching up on boutique business and Robert. A first-time dad and a medical degree didn't mix. He fussed like an old woman around his wife. Jokes made at his expense were a regular occurrence. Today comments were few by a subdued Laura.

Had Laura and Robert argued? Laura and subdued didn't mix any better than new dad and a medical degree. Glancing over her friend's furrowed brow, Lia saw the subtle look Laura directed towards Lia's abode and the nervous way she bit down on her bottom lip. Noticing Lia watching her, Laura attempted a small smile and Lia's heart sank.

"He's here, isn't he?" The cup in her hand fell, smashing into tiny slivers on the tiled floor. "I'm not ready." *But then, would she ever be ready?*

"He's something." Laura's words were accompanied by a guilty blush.

A smitten Laura didn't surprise Lia. Photos were one thing. Nico in the flesh, something else again.

"So dark and broody," Laura continued her ramble, "and all that gorgeous golden skin combined with sexual intensity, stole my breath away."

"I'm glad he made an impact."

"I don't think anything prepares you for the kind of impact he makes." Laura ignored the sarcasm.

"No, nothing can." Lia replied with an irony Laura couldn't fail to miss. "You liked him, didn't you, or at least you let your hormones dictate for you?"

"I didn't want to because I know how much he hurt you, but he is..."

"What...what is he, Laura?"

"He's spectacular," Laura answered wryly. "Those eyes and the way they penetrate, the easy elegance, the total control over his body, the economy of movement...I get it now. I get what draws you together. You're so alike. And it's not the diluted kinship. It's the people you are."

"Sometimes I've wondered if the tie of blood no matter how long ago, did lead us astray."

"Bull shit, Angelia. Like attracts like, we both know that. Or maybe I should call you Lia now? He did." Laura reached across to take Lia's hand. She squeezed gently. "Angie, relax. You've been waiting for this. Keep your head."

"You know me so well."

"Blood sisters, remember."

"I remember. Mama said she understood we wanted to be family. But she and Lucy weren't impressed with the blood part." She lifted her arm. Laura did the same. They touched scars. "I have to go. It's a wonder he hasn't come out."

"Gorgeous he may be, but the man looked drained. Dark circles under those smouldering eyes."

"Oh please, you sound like a groupie. What did you talk about with him that has your knickers knotted?"

"Very funny! Nothing, everything! He was interested in me, Robert, the baby. He loved the house."

"I can't believe you let him into my home."

"I know, but I liked him, he has so much ..."

"Sex appeal!"

"Charm, but yes, that too. Angie, tread carefully. He's a man on a mission and you are the prize. I know what he did. But I feel sorry for him. He won't react well."

"That's the whole point."

"You have frightening ideas about fair play. Goose and gander, and all it entails, is great in theory. In real life, I'm not so sure and I should know."

"Leave it. Laura. His way would be to gloss over everything. He'll say he's sorry, and according to his logic, we move on. No. There are consequences. He needs to learn my logic."

"Angie...okay...I'll shut up."

"Good. I obviously tell you more than I should. Stop pouting. It won't work." She moved to the pram and undid the restraints that held her son. She needed the solid warmth of her baby close to her, to selfishly draw strength.

"Angie?"

"I'm sorry about the cup." Lia didn't bother to answer the unspoken question. She couldn't be certain of outcomes.

Chapter 37

Nico stood by the bay window looking out to the garden. She opened the door; he reversed his stance to face her. A flashback to the first night of their honeymoon. He wore the same look, the hunter not afraid to put his sensual hunger on display. Then the look disappeared into an implacable mask, or perhaps not, if that tiny tic near his mouth meant anything. Stoney-faced, he monitored her every move, the way she strode in, shut the door, then continued to Antonio's small bedroom. Lia felt him behind her. When she wheeled her body around, her heart stuttered at the way the stony face shattered.

"He's grown so much." A whisper.

"Yes, he has." Ice in every syllable.

"Does he talk much?" He followed Lia as she left the room.

"Yes."

He sighed, looking a combination of edgy, nervous, and a tad angry in his black suit and white linen shirt. He resumed his previous position near the window. The fine, delicate tug of a spider's silky web floated towards her, insidious and dangerous. Lia knew how the story ended. The spider always ate the fly. This fly ignored the trembling snaking its way across her traitorous body.

"So, Nico...what brings you to Australia?" Pleased at her tone, one suggesting he was no more than a passing acquaintance, tested his self-control. Not a muscle moved but she knew him, knew the tightening of the jaw, what the secret clench of teeth meant.

"Obviously, I'm here to take you and my son home. How long will it take you to pack?"

"Nice," her eyebrows lifted, harmonising with the vocal disdain. "Straight to the point. I see you still haven't learnt the difference between demanding and asking. Forgive me if I am not thrilled."

"No games, Lia. You come home; my son comes home."

So many emotions raged inside her head at the sound of his voice. Satisfaction at the further clenching of jaw, anger at the way her name sounded so intimate rolling off his tongue. Hatred, for his looks, for his arrogance, and for the amount of hurt he had inflicted with his dramatic parting scene.

"Lia. I'm sorry."

Gentle persuasion oozed from every pore, a hand raised to appear contrite, a plea. Tactics. She'd watched him use them in the courtroom. If the hand shook, she didn't care.

"Of course, you're sorry. You behaved like an arsehole."

"I want you home where you belong."

"That's right, Nico. Ignore what I'm saying."

"My mother and father are devastated at losing you and Antonio. They need their grandchild, they need you. Don't punish them for my mistake."

"Don't you dare use your parents against me, not when it's taken you two years to decide they're hurting. I talk to them every day. You think all it takes is to say you're sorry. You snap your fingers, I obey. I'm not a pet. You were the one, that day at lunch, the one who made it sound so easy, made it sound as if we could handle anything, and you fucking lied. You made a fool of me with Francesca, in the most humiliating way possible. Saying sorry will never be enough!"

Somehow, she had moved closer. A mistake. His proximity allowed a weak version of Lia to rise despite her anger. Weak Lia, the one who cried herself to sleep, missing this impossible, overbearing man. Strong Lia fought back wanting desperately to keep the upper hand.

"Lia, everything got messy. I wasn't prepared for what happened with you. I wanted it ended, finished. Too many emotions, too much drama. I did what I thought would work best. You would have tried to convince me otherwise. You would have been right, but it's taken me a long time to work that out. I never meant to hurt you."

"What the fuck? You never meant to hurt me! What did you think would happen?"

"I'm sorry. I wasn't thinking."

She knew his little scenario had been about forcing her to make the decision. Now, like then, he had no intention of explaining why she'd needed to go. *Did he even know?* Her heart ached with disappointment. He would win, she would concede defeat and go back with him. First though, he would pay. Choosing Francesca as an *out* couldn't be forgiven, and the way he did it, the precise planning, deserved punishment. His penance - to feel what she had felt, and then they would see.

His impenetrable façade showed signs of weakness, small frown lines he tried to hide. Her silence unnerved him.

"Lia."

"What exactly have you in mind. Start again, same bargain and pretend nothing happened in between?"

She felt his gaze on her lips, hungry, urgent, wanting, and fought the flashes of memory. They undermined her determination. *Nico: that first day at the beach, their wedding night; Nico lifting her onto the dining table, Nico holding her every night.*

"You want to come home. Don't pretend otherwise. I see it in your face, in your eyes." He inhaled a tense breath and released it. "I'm not suggesting we forget anything." He spoke firmly, slowly. "I want us to begin knowing our mistakes so..."

"Our mistakes?" Lia laughed at his words. "You are an arrogant prick."

"You could have tried harder. You knew something wasn't right."

"Fuck you! I did try. I tried as soon as I had some strength back. I nearly died, Nico."

"Exactly. You should have known how confronting that would be for someone like me. All those emotions...it doesn't matter. I want us to begin again. We had something; we can have it again."

"All those emotions? You poor little thing! I deserved everything I got, didn't I?"

Pull back, she told herself. *So hard to breathe with this much anger. Breathe in. Breathe out. Fuck it.*

"You bastard! You orchestrated the whole thing, that disgusting tawdry scene. I was the string section, so innocent, so predictable to arrive punctually for the 'heartbreaking' finale to the concerto you controlled. And it was heartbreaking. How the fuck did I deserve that?"

The look on his face was worth every bit of energy her rage demanded. He flinched unable to hide the hurt caused by her disdain. His piercing regard roamed her body, hot and fierce. The bastard was also aroused by her performance and struggling to keep it from showing.

"Do you know what it felt like, watching you? No, you don't. You, Lia, were somewhere chasing butterflies for two days. You didn't hear the fucking machines fighting to keep you alive. I'm sorry I am not wired for sensitivity. I thought it best we went separate ways. My methods were…questionable. It's in the past. We start again."

More tactics – a sidestep into emotional blackmail. Her turn to sidestep. "Do you want some lunch?"

He stared. Shock or surprise, Lia didn't much care. For a moment, Lia found the temptation to grin irresistible. Her abrupt change of topic caught him off guard. Nico at this moment appeared more like a child than a grown man. Confused, annoyed, his wishes thwarted, he didn't know how to react. She took perverse pity on his perplexed half-nod. "I'll take that as a yes."

"Antonio's a little boy, not a baby," Nico said quietly.

"Yes."

"You cut your hair."

"Yes."

"You don't like me very much."

"Yes."

"Do you know any other words, other than yes?"

"No."

He laughed. "Alright Lia, let's have some lunch then." He removed his jacket and threw it on the couch carelessly, without taking his eyes off her. "Your hair suits you. I loved it long." He stopped speaking. She would deliberately misconstrue anything he said in this mood. Instead, he followed her movements as she methodically cut salami into thin slices before adding tomato and lettuce.

Yes, Lia thought to herself thinking about the comment on her hair. *I cut it for that reason*. Pouring them both a glass of sparkling mineral water, she sat down on the stool, glad of the bench between them. She picked up the bread roll and nibbled. The repetitive actions of chewing, swallowing, and taking another bite soothed. He did the same, taking his own small bite, perching on the edge of the stool, wary eyes reflecting his discomfort.

"I do get the emotional upheaval." She began with a casual shrug of her shoulder. "I know you struggle. How though, did sex with Francesca put things into perspective? Because that's also why you did what you did, right? You wanted to prove that what we had was just sex. The fact your little performance would drive me away without fuss, a stroke of genius."

Nico stopped chewing, lowered his lashes, but his skin lost colour, the tiny tic working overtime.

Lia's eyes narrowed. *Was he remembering that day? Frozen, an iceberg in the ocean of her body, her head controlled by her masochistic mind, she had witnessed a smug Francesca partake in his sexual performance. How had Nico dared to look her in the face? Even now, two years later Lia couldn't fathom how he had kept his eyes, cold, stagnant pools of nothing, level with hers. Had a small part of him died that day too?*

Francesca's lipstick had been intact, either a good lipstick, or he hadn't kissed her.

The urge to throw up what she had already swallowed rose in her throat. She forced it down.

"Lia, it was...Lia. It's in the past."

Nico's distress at the direction of her thoughts fuelled her anger. She knew it had to do with his reluctance to discuss the issue.

"And I'm supposed to accept it?" She asked, her voice deceptively calm.

"We need to move on. I don't see we have a choice."

She almost felt sorry for him, almost. His refusal to embrace exactly how much damage he'd done overriding any pity.

"And does the same thing apply if our positions were reversed? Would you want to move forward?"

"It's a moot point."

"I tried it. It did nothing for me."

"Tried what?"

Frown lines creased his forehead. Lia had once again changed the direction of their conversation. He struggled to keep up with her, hurt at her offhand attitude, and her ice queen persona. Acknowledging he deserved her taunts, to his way of thinking, would serve no purpose. He had admitted his regret. Further discussion would complicate rather than resolve.

"Perspective, of course."

"Fuck, Lia. Enough of this useless rambling and let's get to the point. You knew I would come for you. Admit it, you were expecting me."

"Okay I was. But can I get to *my* point?"

"Lia." He rose, came round to her side of the bench, angling over her and curled his hand around her neck. She pulled away, rose, and strode across to the lounge room. He followed.

"I met someone three months after I got home. It wasn't that hard. I had a life here, remember."

Her back to him annoyed him. A hand on her shoulder spun her around. He couldn't hide his irritation at another change of conversation.

"I knew people, had friends and I caught up with them. One friend." His cologne drifted across. She stepped away. He dropped his hand. "Don't look so surprised. What did you expect me to do? Sit in a corner, pull my hair out and cry?"

He wanted to close his eyes; he couldn't. His head shifted to the side, listening intently.

Nico, child-like once again and for a split second, she felt bad. "James, well he was going through some things. We'd been friends for years so gravitating to one another was easy. Perhaps not the best idea but sex is sex."

"What are you doing? What are you trying to prove with this rubbish?" He crossed the room to the bay window.

His couldn't help himself, not even now. *You arrogant prick!* "I needed to know what someone else might make me feel. I needed to understand why you would imagine sex with someone else could put things into perspective. I do seem to be using that word a lot, don't I? Perspective! I like it, it fits."

She paused dramatically, her eyes blazing and obliterating the ice queen.

He swallowed. Waited. The tic prominent.

"You spoiled me, unfortunately. His creativity although impressive, didn't quite match yours. Well, actually that's not true. I think with the right person, his right person, it might. All the same, I did gain some perspective. His appreciation showed me I had what it takes to satisfy someone." Nico hissed. Tempted to laugh, she lifted one shoulder and both hands to signify confusion. "What? Obviously, I had doubts about myself. I believed the chemistry between us was special. I found out, not special enough to counteract day-to-day reality, like babies or wives dying. Oh, wait a minute, I didn't die."

"What in fuck's name are you playing at?"

Nico pinched the area between his brows, his forehead creasing in response to her words. The thought of someone else touching her - abhorrent, unthinkable. Lia would not do something so demeaning. He laughed, shook his head at her.

"You wouldn't. Games like this? Making up stories is beneath you."

He paced the room, his actual movements uncoordinated, unlike the cat-like fluidity his body normally displayed. Annoyed, frustrated and Lia realised, afraid.

"Hmm.... beneath and games...that does conjure up images. James liked me beneath him the most, so he could watch my face as I came. That was sweet of him, don't you think? Did I mention we used condoms? I'd hate for you to think I was reckless."

Nico, a silent figure near the bay window, bothered her for some odd reason. With clenched fists, tense body, and ragged breathing, he looked capable of smashing the window. She should've been frightened instead of perversely excited.

"Liar, you would never, never betray what we had, that way."

"What did we have? Seriously, what...did...we...have? You never gave it a name. Worse, you were afraid, afraid enough to force the decision to go on me. I knew you'd be sorry. And I, I'm not above revenge. A levelled playing field in my opinion gives us better odds to succeed the second time round."

Déjà vu. Lia found herself back in front of the range hood at his parents' home. He wouldn't hit her. She knew it then; she knew it now. He half-turned and swung his arm away from his body - a purely reflexive move, not aiming to hit anything, a way to purge his anger. The proximity to the window and the force of his arm making contact sent glass flying. Shattered bits landed at his feet, distracting her at first from the blood pouring down his arm.

Nico blanched at the crimson flow, anger dissipating, replaced with a recoil of distaste at the seeping liquid. Allowing Lia to minister to him, he began making lists in his head – the number of scattered bits of glass, a good place to start.

Wasn't it winter in Europe? Why did he have a tan? The random thought made her sad for some reason. *Damn it.* The intention had been to hurt him, to show him she was capable of repercussions, of action but not this. He'd stolen her moment of glory, sitting there, bleeding, arranging and re-arranging things, in his head. She supposed she deserved to feel bad. Laura had tried to tell her. She walked over to the phone and dialled Laura's number. Robert would know what to do, at least about Nico's arm.

Chapter 38

"**Nico's** at the surgery. Robbie says they'll be a while. I rang the glass people and organised it for the morning, like you wanted."

"Thank you." Lia refrained from raising her head, obsessed with scrubbing at the spots of blood on the wall.

"You had the conversation, didn't you?" Laura impatient for an answer, moved to crowd her into replying. "Look at me."

"Yes. I did. He had a choice. Me or the window. The window won. It was closer."

Laura ignored the attitude. "He wouldn't have hit you."

Lia's tongue poked at the insides of her cheeks, not wanting to give in to her irritation. "A few telephone hook-ups a couple of years ago, and one brief meeting this morning, and you're suddenly an expert on my husband?"

"Oooh. I'm scared of the big bad girl on her knees. I may not be an expert on your husband, but I am an expert on you. It tasted bitter, didn't it? You two are quite the pair. You know where to stick the knife and dig it deep and then neither of you can live with it. You know, I'm pretty positive this behaviour is deep, dark, and obscenely erotic in some bizarre way."

"Pregnancy has definitely warped that brain of yours." Resignation in her scowl, Lia glanced up. "You're not going to leave me alone, are you?"

Laura took the cleaning cloth away from her and helped Lia to her feet before enfolding her in her arms.

Lia leaned her forehead against her friend and let the tears fall.

"If you two communicated, no one would get hurt."

"There is no communicating with him."

"You chose a difficult man."

"I didn't choose anything."

"Please. Neither one of you had a choice if it comes to that, which is why you need to communicate with each other."

"Laura, do you know what you're talking about? God knows, I don't."

"Yes, you do. If you two are competing, concentrating on tactics, you don't have to talk, really talk. If you're having sex, everything is tangible. There's no need for words. Lia, I get that you get him, but you both need to talk to each other. And sooner is better than later."

"Bloody smartarse! I don't even want to try and work out what you mean."

"He's lucky he didn't cut a tendon." Laura thought it wise to change the subject. "You did what you had to do. You wanted equality. You got it, so now what?"

"I go home with him!"

"Are you sure it's what you want, really sure? You sound pretty shaky."

"I've no choice. There has never been a choice. Like you said, deep, dark, and obscenely erotic. How can anyone resist that combination?"

"You need to talk."

"It's not that easy with him. You have to bring him to that point where he can see the bigger picture, Laura. Don't be fooled because you can have what appears a normal conversation with him. He's high-functioning but he has boxes and getting inside takes patience and time."

"He's high-functioning. Find a way. I'm going to make us some tea while you have a shower. You've got blood all over your clothes and your son will be awake soon. I might take him with me. It's good practice."

When she didn't move, Laura began unbuttoning Lia's shirt. Lia smoothed her hands over the rounded belly in front of her.

"Take your shorts off as well. I'll soak them while you take that shower. I don't know who has more blood on them, you or your clothes."

Lia unzipped them, dropping them to the floor. Bending to pick them up she felt Laura's hand trace the long line of the fading, pink scar, a feather-light touch. Stepping away, Laura's fingertips pushed her blonde hair aside and automatically roamed to the small scar at her temple.

"Mine is tiny. It's unfair. I'm so sorry." Laura's blue eyes dulled.

"Don't say that. We didn't get to decide. The other driver did that."

Lia bent to kiss the small reminder that Laura had been in the car. "It makes me happy you walked away with so little, Laura. I couldn't have borne it if something had happened to you as well, couldn't have survived these last two years." Lia's chest rose and fell with her emotions. She gave a small, sad huff. "I'm so sorry about your cup and saucer though. I know how much the set means to you."

Laura kissed Lia's cheek. "It's crockery," she whispered. "Mum would understand." She gave Lia a gentle nudge. "Come on, both your boys will need you soon."

The water felt wonderfully soothing as it flowed down her back, warming her body. She'd been waiting for him for so long. Her life for the last two years had been an arctic hibernation. Bears protect themselves from the cold by sleeping through it. A baby had made that impossible so instead Lia had allowed herself to become a consummate sleepwalker. With eyes open she had created a home, warm and inviting but a hollow icy den all the same.

The flowing water coursed down in a torrent of hot, wet, slicing pain. The heat mirroring her thoughts: Nico's face as the blood poured down his arm, and Marissa, her mother, her incredibly beautiful and sad mother. Loving them had been and was painful. They demanded enormous emotional patience but the rewards...the rewards were endless.

"Mama, was it my fault?" They were outside working on the new herb garden, a huge mess like always, when Mama started a new project.

Lia wondered if her conventional Papa had ever understood his wife. Marissa's creativity when the mood for new struck, became obsessive. Not able to keep still at the best of times, a new project unleashed turmoil for everyone until completed. Mama and Nico. Different yet the same. No wonder Nico had become fascinated.

Mama had turned to Lia at the question and put down the plants in her hand. "Oh, piccola! Farfálla mia, is that what you have been thinking all this time?" Lia loved her mother's eyes, loved how clear and green they were. Lia's eyes were the same shape with the same long lashes but a deep brown like her Papa. Secretly, not to hurt Mama's feelings, Lia loved she had Papa's eyes.

Piccola in Italian meant 'little one', and farfálla meant butterfly. The fact that Mama had mixed her languages and had gone so still made Lia's heartbeat jump around inside her body. Stillness, a rare thing in Marissa, meant she had decided something important. Mama in this position reminded her of a butterfly landing on a petal or leaf, but the similarity lasted only for the landing. The small motionless creature enchanted her like a fairy princess might. Not so Mama. She was a buzzing bee. Marissa captured her small hand and led her to the white park bench.

"My mother," she began, "left me with my grandparents when I was five. She never came back. Nonno and Nonna did their best with me, but I was wild."

"I have a grandmother!"

"She's dead now, not that it matters, but I will tell you another time. Lucio, your uncle, lived next door. He was five years older than me, handsome, wild, but being a boy, it didn't matter. I loved him," she said. "He used to

laugh at me, call me a child, a vain child. It made me determined to change his mind."

Mama's hair spun from side to side as she spoke. She had become the bee. The hair contrasted sharply with the alabaster skin. Papa had taught her that word and had said she, Lia, had the same skin. Mama was beautiful but Lia felt a sort of sick feeling in her tummy, and it had to do with looking like Mama. She didn't like it at all.

"Piccola," Mama said softly, "where have you gone?" Sighing, she stroked Lia's cheek. "This conversation is for grownups, but I want, no I need you to understand. Your Aunt Gina, Papa's sister liked him the same way I did. He preferred me. I knew it even if he called me a child. I tried to make him jealous, flirting with his friends. It made him angry, made him treat me more like his sister. Then I would get angry, so angry with him."

Mama paused and stroked Lia's hair. "When I turned sixteen, my Nonno needed a part for his car. It meant going into Catania. He asked Lucio if he could go for him. I begged to go along and look at the shops. Nonno gave me some money and told me to buy *something nice. I made sure Lucio noticed me that day, but Gina was already pregnant. Lucio married her. I went crazy when I found out. My grandparents sent me north to stay with my Aunt Maria. When Nonna died I went back to look after Nonno, and met your father, Gina's brother."* Mama had shaken her head, upset with herself. *"It became complicated, everyone knowing each other; but your Papa was a handsome man and he wanted to live in Australia. A big adventure with a handsome man. I married him. We came here, bought this house, had you. The trip home scared me. The butterfly tried to warn me, but your Papa wouldn't listen."* She stopped, making the sign of the cross.

"What are you doing in there?" Laura's voice shook Lia back to the present. "Lia? Are you alright?

"Thinking of butterflies. I'm nearly finished. I'll tell you about it when I'm dressed."

After Laura had left with Antonio, Lia sat down on the lounge to wait. Restless fingers reached for the spot where the small scar sat. Such a small incident to trigger such a complicated situation and with such a complicated man. Domenico Morrelli, as difficult to read as a summer storm, would be back here soon. Lia might not know how she had lasted without him, might long to be back in the heaven his arms created, but they had a child and people who loved them. Making mistakes was not an option.

Chapter 39

"**You** don't say much, do you?" Robert commented quietly in Italian. Nico gritted his teeth. Robert efficiently removed slivers of glass, making Nico feel ungracious but not less resentful. From the moment Robert had stepped inside Lia's cosy abode, his first objective had been to ascertain Lia's welfare, the blood pouring from Nico's arm, a secondary consideration.

His smile grim, Nico admitted to himself, Lia's words had cut deep. Unlike the pieces currently housed in his skin. His movements, if aggressive in appearance, were about what he felt. Not about what he might do. Robert had eyed him with suspicion. If positions had been reversed, Nico admitted he might have felt the same.

"You came pretty close to the tendon with this piece." Robert's words were more a grunt.

Nico looked at him dispassionately, upset at having left his jacket, holding his wallet and the keys to the hire car at Lia's home. Having to go back there looking dishevelled suited him even less than sitting in front of this man did.

"So, you're the strong silent type?"

Nico ignored the jibe. The arm, a throbbing mess, stole all his energy. His jaw ached from the effort to remain stoic, to concentrate on clock hands, on counting the seconds, instead of his naivety in not expecting the unexpected from Lia. *Why am I surprised?* Her tenacity in remaining in his parent's home affirmed her resilience, making her a hell of an opponent. It hurt though, more than he thought possible. She belonged to him.

He had fucked up. What was the English expression? Royally. Nico had fucked up royally. Perversely he couldn't dismiss his perfect execution of his perfect plan. Perfect until he discovered life without Lia to be intolerable. *Fuck, his arm hurt, hurt* as *much as his pride had when he discovered two years down the track, he had outsmarted himself.* He winced.

"Sorry, not much longer,"

Nico's gaze returned to the man in front of him. When he let his eyes drift down, he winced again at the sight.

"You don't like blood much, do you?"

Nico huffed, not bothering to answer. These people had no respect, no comprehension of the word privacy. *Did the man know everything, and if he did then why the fuck couldn't he keep the fact to himself?* Keeping still made Nico claustrophobic despite the pristine surgery. No environment could have been better designed for Nico.

"How much longer? Or rather how long is your, *not much longer*?"

Nico huffed again when Robert laughed in reply and chanced another look at the arm. His linen shirt had stains, ugly red stains. Robert tugged another stitch into place. Nico continued to stare at the shirt sleeve. *What a pity! The shirt would have to go. Now he would need a new one. Where would he get a replica?* The thought unnerved him, made him feel vulnerable. *How much longer?*

Robert grumbled to himself about how much damage a supposedly grown man could do. Nico smiled then, grateful for the diversion. Robert must have forgotten how well Nico spoke English. His current aloofness seemed childish. This man who had grown up with Lia was not the enemy. *What if Lia preferred this life, to life with him? Having Robert offside would end up strategic suicide.*

"Tell me about the girls, how they got together," Nico asked, choosing English for the interaction.

"I would have thought you knew most of it."

Robert answered with surprising speed leading Nico to suspect Robert liked to talk.

"I do. I want to understand things better."

"It bothers you, doesn't it, this bond we all have with your wife?" Robert didn't wait for an answer. "Angie...Lia. Sorry, I've always called her Angie. Anyway, Lia said you were possessive."

Nico's defences kicked in, too swiftly for him to hide his sullen reaction.

"It's hard for you to accept how much we know about each other, isn't it? It shouldn't be." Robert paused, deliberating. "Let me finish this. I have coffee making facilities in my office."

Nico sat back, grimacing occasionally, silent until Robert declared himself finished.

"Done! Time for that coffee. Come on through. The armchair is comfortable. I can testify to that."

"Thank you!"

"Prego."

Nico winced on standing.

"Easy, you did some damage." Robert winked as he led the way through the waiting area. "How much do you know about this tight little group that has you so worried?"

"I didn't say I was worried about any group."

"You didn't have to. It's normal. This is her territory."

Nico's edginess, never far, surfaced again. This person knew too much. The familiarity, the ease with which this man spoke of personal things had him in retreat.

"Nico, relax. We're her family; we want the best for her. Trust us. Now give me a few minutes to get the coffee going and we can talk." Robert grabbed two blue ceramic mugs from an overhead cupboard. "Let me fill these."

Two minutes later he handed Nico one of the mugs.

Nico tried a sip and half spat it out. "Milk and sugar." Nico said, cringing in horror.

Robert chuckled, the chuckle becoming full-blown laughter when Nico took another sip and shuddered further. "Sorry I should have asked. You're a 'strong black' aren't you?"

"Instead of amusing yourself at my expense, you could start talking."

"Yes sir. Growing up," Robert began, "we all lived close to one another. My parents were friends with Laura's, meeting not long after they all arrived in Australia. After Laura's father was killed in a work accident, we kept an eye on Lucy, Lucinda, Laura's mother. Sorry but we do have a habit of shortening everyone's name."

"I've noticed."

Robert laughed again at Nico's tone. "Lucy," Robert continued, "didn't speak much English but you couldn't fault her for industry. She started off cleaning homes, and then got a job cleaning at the local primary school. Her husband had left her a small life insurance policy, but Lucy wanted that for Laura's education."

"How did Marissa and Antonio fit in with this?"

"Marissa and Lucinda had chemotherapy at the same hospital. Pure coincidence but my Mum knew them both and sat with Lucinda when she could. Marissa and Mum lived around the corner from one another. Things took off from there. Poor Laura, a gangly teenager with braces, and all her mother could talk about was this incredibly beautiful girl, the daughter of her new friend. Laura may have been intimidated at first. A mutual passion for hot chocolate and marshmallows and the girls became inseparable. I should have known something was up when they asked about sterilising a knife."

"The blood sisters?"

"You know about that. Crazy girls! Lia sterilised the knife. Laura did the cutting. We are talking about two intelligent girls and an extraordinarily stupid stunt. They were obsessed with being family. Anyway, both women went into remission and stayed friends. Like most people from Slavic countries Lucinda spoke other languages fluently, including Italian. My Mum had the same ability, so between them, they were their own United Nations. Then of course, they were joined by Lexi, and Fran and Mona. We had Croatian, Greek, Italian and Samoan, and Japanese. Lexi's brother met his wife in Japan. These women all had children who attended the same school. Friendships grew. By then Tonio had become a different man. I think the way Marissa handled herself before cancer, and certainly afterwards, cemented something. They were happy. A year later the cancer came back."

"So many people involved in everyone's business."

Robert flicked a sharp glance Nico's way. Whatever he found in Nico's face satisfied him. He shrugged. "It doesn't suit everyone, but in this case, it made the end easier."

"Yes, I see that." Nico, not wanting to offend, exhaled slowly before speaking. "I'm not comfortable with so many people knowing things."

Robert reached out and gave Nico a reassuring pat on his good arm before taking up the tale. "Lucinda helped care for Marissa. Having her close worked miracles. Antonio asked her to move into the apartment at the back of the house. Having Laura close was good for Angie...Lia. Marissa lasted longer, almost eighteen months longer than her doctors thought possible. I think Marissa fought because of Tonio. They were very happy; she glowed with his forgiveness. And of course, she fought for Lia."

Robert paused, eyes glazed, voice unsteady.

Nico waited, reflecting on his own perspective on Marissa. *A world apart.*

"We worried for Lia. Imagine growing up as a little girl in that household. She navigated some big emotions to survive, only to have it taken away just when it changed. We had to get her back a teaspoon at a time. Do you understand?"

"I think so, or at least I am beginning to better understand." His arm throbbed. His heart did the same picturing Lia, so young and so hurt by losing her mother.

"She missed six months of school. Lexi and Laura caught her up, arguing, pleading but persistent. You've met Lexi on..."

"Skype, briefly. She's an interesting woman."

"She's one of a kind. These days...that's another story. Anyway, everyone helped where they could."

"Of course, they did."

"You sound dubious, or is it uncomfortable? These people, including my parents, were and are a big part of Lia's life."

"A small community, all of you connected in some way or another?"

"Lia barely ate, barely spoke. They pulled her through." Robert said quietly, but nevertheless shooting Nico a warning with his eyes.

"I'm trying to understand."

"Then, you also need to accept you can't take Lia away from here if you're not intending to look after her. She's not a toy. You're not her owner. You're her husband."

"I know," Nico snarled. "This isn't any of your business for that reason alone."

"Wrong. That's how it works with us. Scale back on that temperament, with me and with her. She accepts your beast. That's what she calls it. She won't bow to bullying. You want to possess her? Let her decide you can."

Nico looked away, unable to prevent the colour flashing a furious path across his cheekbones. *How had a simple discussion become a reason to attack?*

Ascertaining exactly where Nico's head had gone, Robert reached across and patted the good arm again. "I'm on your side. Believe it or not. She's been lost without you. But you need to change your approach."

"I'm not sure I can."

"We're not so different. I understand possessive. I also know it's much sweeter when they let you possess."

"I won't hurt her again, not intentionally. You have my word on that."

"When Lucy died three years later, Laura had her turn." Robert picked up his narration. "Drugs, alcohol. Her behaviour - hard to watch. I think she needed to feel connected to something, and Lia and Antonio without Marissa weren't enough. Lia thinks with her head, Laura reacts. She wanted things from me that were difficult to give. Don't think I didn't want to. I've always seen Laura as mine. She was still so young, and she saw it as rejection and turned elsewhere, often."

Nico looked up, surprised.

"People do strange things when they're hurting." Robert glanced across pointedly at Nico. "Lia hadn't heard from her all week. She rang me, and we went over to the University dormitories. Laura had moved out of Antonio's home by then. We found a bedraggled, hung-over mess. Lia lost it, threw her into the shower to sober her up. *Robert, I refuse to let you marry this junkie-slash-slut my former best-friend has become.*

"Harsh," Nico interjected. "I can't imagine Lia saying something like that."

"Somebody had to. It worked. A mortified Laura listened. I moved Lia out of the way, told her to mind her own business because I was willing to take my chances."

"So then, a happy ending?"

"No. Six months, six months of persuasion to get Laura to even look at me. She hated the way she'd behaved, and she was behind in all her studies. She wanted to work things out for herself. Once she did, she went home. I decided then and there I didn't care about the whole letting her have a life first and staked my claim."

"Did you mind about the things she did?"

"That's a fair question. Yes. No. I had to accept some of the responsibility. My decision impacted on her badly. I'd decided for her. I had no right." Robert glanced sharply at Nico, gauging how much Nico had comprehended.

"And their business kept running?"

"I think Ang... Lia took on the bulk of it and it was still small at that stage. Laura did do her part, if erratically at times. I think in the end, it was the business that saved her."

"A clever idea, this business of theirs."

"They helped an elderly friend of my mother's get her home ready for sale and impressed the real estate agent. He recommended them to another client. They were in high school when they started. My wife's creativity never ceases to astound me, in all areas."

This time Nico did the laughing. "Two extraordinary women."

"Yes, they are," Robert replied. "Look, I won't interfere with things that are not my business but...."

"But" Nico interjected, "you're going to?"

"No, I only want to say we, us, the people who love Lia, we're not the bad guys here. All we want is her happiness."

"I know. What if I'm not enough?"

"You were before. Don't fuck it up again."

"And, what she did?"

"You deserved it." Robert frowned, gave Nico a hard, penetrating glance tinged with surprise. "You must know that, surely? I'm not saying it was right. We worried, even though we knew James. They were both hurting for their own reasons and were adults. Laura and I had to stand back and just be there. You hurt her. The only reason I haven't punched you in that arrogant face, is because you hurt yourself more."

Nico admired Robert's efficiency. Caught up in the narrative, he hadn't noticed the coffee mugs had been washed and put away and everything wiped clean. Wanting to say something, he found himself at a loss.

Robert risked a hand on Nico's shoulder. "She has us whether she lives here or in Italy. You can too."

Nico allowed the hand sit on his shoulder.

Robert delivered Nico back to Lia shortly afterwards, leaving something to dull the pain and help with sleep. Nico had intended going back to the hotel. Exhaustion ruled. He didn't resist when Lia helped him undress and put him in her bed. He could smell the lotion on the sheets, that coconut and chocolate fragrance mixed with whatever was essentially her. He liked the fact she hadn't changed her fragrance, found it reassuring.

Chapter 40

She left Nico sleeping and strolled over to the main house for dinner. Laura had made Antonio's favourite, a vegetable lasagne. He wore it with style on his face and clothes, giggling at his mother's mock scowl.

"So, do you think Lexi will go on the trip?'

"I hope so, Laura. Julieann will certainly keep pushing the idea. I suggested the August-September tour in the new year. Lexi put up a list of negatives. We can work on her. That's all I managed to get out of Julie. James had thrown her into a panic by calling and asking her out to dinner."

"Is she going?" Robert asked.

"No. It's too much like a date. She has friend-zoned him, and I don't think that will change any time soon." Lia played with her bottom lip, teeth lightly scraping back and forwards. "Everything has its time. I don't think the right time has happened for them, not yet anyway."

"He's a good guy. They'd be a good fit. Between her relationship with Chris the Dickhead, and his with Olivia, they got out of step. Dickhead's marriage is in trouble so he's sniffing around again confusing things further. Damn! Talking like this, I feel like one of the girls."

Lia gave him the evil eye. His wife slapped him in the chest.

"Ouch." The trio resumed eating until Robert cocked his head in Lia's direction, breaking the silence. "Was it worth it, Angie?"

She glowered at him, not prepared for the change in topic. "We tell him more than we should, especially you," Lia muttered to Laura.

"Of course. Laura's my friend and my wife, my best friend when you're not around." He gave Laura a lewd wink before giving Lia a superior look.

"Then I guess it shouldn't bother you that I can tell you the exact length of your penis in centimetres before and after. Wait a minute which is smaller, centimetres or millimetres?"

"That is so not true!" Laura shrieked indignantly, spoiling the effect when she dissolved into laughter.

"What, the measurements or that you told me?" Lia couldn't resist putting in with a smirk. The humour at Robert's expense gave her breathing space.

"It's alright darling; I know she's making that up. She's seen it in the before state when we skinny dip and…" he added slyly, "she's seen it in full throttle when she caught us…."

"Stop," Lia yelled, trying to keep a straight face. "I've worked pretty hard to forget that particular image."

Antonio picking up on the jovial mood began chortling and clapping, sending them into more fits of laughter until Laura's sudden sobs jarred the atmosphere. Robert grabbed a cloth, cleaned the little boy's face and hands, and removed him from the table. Not straying far but comprehending the girls, particularly the hormonal pregnant one, needed to sort this out, he waited and kept the baby amused.

"I won't go until after the baby is born, I promise." Lia had shifted seats to sit beside Laura. "I promise," she crooned again, pulling Laura into an embrace. "I'll answer your question now Robbie. A bittersweet victory, to be honest. He had to learn what I am capable of. Having him physically hurt, not what I intended. Nico doesn't mean to be high-handed or selfish. He see things a certain way, it's part of his make-up. I don't want him to change. He is who he is. However, he needs to think more laterally, consider the aftermath."

"Are you sure he's what you want?" Robert ambled back to the women.

"What is it with you two? Laura asked me the same thing."

"You know, Nico's going to want to pee on you pretty soon. He can't cope with what you did until he does."

"What? Do what?" Laura and Lia asked simultaneously.

"After your little revelation, he's going to want to mark his territory, and he'll want to do it as soon as possible. Are you ready?"

"I'm ready. But honestly Robbie, your choice of phrase lacks finesse and makes me want to seriously rethink all this sharing we do. The terrible thing is that it sounds like Nico."

Robert gave her a smile which reeked of smug because in one short morning he'd managed to acquire a handle on Nico. She shook her head at him and then glanced across at the lounge chair where Robert had placed her son. Antonio could barely keep his eyes open.

"I'd better go. Dinner was great. Thanks both of you."

Laura shuffled her way to Antonio and picked him up. Both friends followed her to the door.

"Lia," Robert stopped abruptly on reaching for the doorknob. Two heads, one with hair the colour of sunshine, and the other a midnight black, turned in unison. Their identical stares, disconcerting in their intensity had him hesitate. "In...in all this time you've never doubted he would come for you. I can't manage to assimilate how you were sure enough to plan and execute a revenge.

"Robbie!" Laura wrinkled her nose in semi-annoyance.

"I'm not having a go, I promise. I know why she did it." Robert looked at Laura, reassuring her before focusing back on Lia. Laura made an annoyed sound and tucked her head into the little boy in her arms, her protective streak humming.

"It's okay, Laura. I don't mind answering." Lia reached over, and smoothly slid the sleeping Antonio into her arms. "I just did. I knew. This was never a trope in a romance novel. We didn't look across a crowded room, we didn't date, we didn't get to stop and know one another and then decide. The attraction, chemistry simmered like a fuse waiting to be lit and when it happened, we just were, both of us drowning in something fierce. What's between Nico and I, has a life of its own, and is all consuming. I didn't know when he'd come. I knew he would, and I had to be ready because this time it would be forever. As for revenge? Is it revenge Robbie? He needed to know my measure, and I guess doing something kept me believing he'd come. Nico needed rattling."

"I love you. You know I do. But honestly, you scare me."

"I know, Robert, I know." Lia didn't miss the concerned look that passed between her two best friends. They would always worry about her, just as she would about them. Their relationship went beyond the friend tag; they were family. Nico had no idea what he would be getting into, she thought and allowed herself a touch of smugness as she headed back towards the small apartment.

~

"Don't take this the wrong way, darling, but I'm glad we're normal."

"I know exactly what you mean. Their individual intensity is bad enough. Together, I don't want to think about it." Laura paused. "Robert, what is it that makes them so...I don't even know how to express it...other-worldly..."

"What are you worried about, love? Them or the fact we're so different?"

"I know we love each other, Robbie. I know what we have but..."

"They appear on another level. Maybe. It's not better, I promise you. It's different. And I don't know why. It just is."

"She will be alright, won't she?"

"Yes, they belong together. He's afraid. She's not. Not now. They're opposites in so many ways, and so similar in others. Wrong or right, she showed him her mettle. She'll be his constant challenge. He'll never let go."

"I want to believe that." She worried her bottom lip.

"You'll feel better tomorrow, trust me."

"Why?"

"He'll pee on her at some stage tonight. Mark my words. *Mark*, get it?"

"For an intelligent man, your analogies suck but you're right. It's how they connect, communicate. I told Lia. They need to use words."

"Speaking of words?"

"Okay. I bow to the Master. Your play on words was clever."

"Thank you."

"You're so needy."

He came up behind, enfolding her with his arms and warm body. Laura leaned back, rotating her head to look at him as she spoke. "I like him. I trust him. He's arrogant, he's possessive and not as nice with it as you are but he's... straight? Like an arrow. Do you know what I mean?"

"Yep. Ironic considering how he handled things," Robert grunted, the edge of disapproval evident. Laura pouted at the reminder. "Stop worrying," he whispered at her ear. "They're well suited."

She hesitated, rubbing her head into the curve of his neck. "How can you be so sure?"

"They're a rare fit. She said it herself. Stop nibbling at my chin. You know it makes me horny."

"You're always horny. Let's get this washing up out of the way and go pretend I'm flexible despite this tummy."

"Hell yes," he replied, and began hurriedly stacking things into the dishwasher. Besotted, a mild word to describe the way he felt about his beautiful wife. He revelled in the feeling.

~

Antonio woke up as she let herself inside. She smiled at his tiny frown and made her way to the rocking chair beside her bed. She knew what he wanted. Her son latched on eagerly. Lia caressed the soft hair.

"Isn't he a little old for that?"

She didn't react to his voice. Her insides did, a slow-moving burn. She swallowed hard, focused on answering in a steady voice.

"Yes, but it doesn't happen often these days. He's close to being weaned." Proving his mother's words were right, Antonio's mouth dropped away to be replaced by tiny snores. She got up to put him to bed.

"He's a beautiful little boy, and it seems I've missed much," Nico said gingerly as she re-entered the room.

Lia chose to ignore the edge of regret. "How do you feel? Robert left some tablets."

"It hurts but I'm more...hungry, I think."

"Well, you didn't finish lunch. Maybe something light, some tea? Tea's good for shock, I hear."

"And is it good for other things?"

"I wouldn't know about that."

"Fine then, bring the tea." He tilted his head, eyeing her intently. "You're not going to make this easy, are you?" She didn't answer. "In that case I don't suppose you have some…"

"Raisin toast?" She finished the sentence for him.

Looking pale and drawn, he'd managed to pull himself into a sitting position by the time she got back. She placed his tea and the plate with toast on the bedside table. He attacked both items, sitting back in satisfaction when he finished. She removed the cup and plate and replaced them with a glass of water and the tablets Robert had left. As she went to leave, he grabbed her wrist.

"Lia. I wasn't going to hit you."

"I know. You lash out around you. Like with this," she said, running her free hand up to the scar on her forehead. "Your body tightens up and your arms go back automatically, a reflex."

"I'd appreciate it if you explained that to Robert."

"He doesn't know you like I do."

"Do you Lia, do you know me?"

"Well enough to know you would never hurt someone."

"Thank you I suppose. I'm not sure I know you." He put the glass down and shuffled further up the bed until he was eye level with her. "I wouldn't have expected such a callous act from you. And yet, it was the perfect comeback."

She looked down at her hands. Hers were wedding band free. Nico wore his, a flash of gold on the left hand. *How odd.*

"Perfect comeback should tell you everything."

"Look at me."

She obeyed immediately, a habit when he used that tone. *Look at me; don't take those beautiful eyes off me.* How often had he said those words to her?

"You knew I would come for you."

"You still don't get it. Because you like to control, to have things on your terms, and our relationship can't work that way. Things are going to be messy sometimes. We need ways to compromise if we value what we have. I can live with you not verbalising what this is between us. I can even live with you not wanting what is between us. I will never ask more than you can give, but I can't live with you dictating terms."

"That's not the real reason." His gaze, fierce and demanding, didn't waver.

She took her time answering. "I needed to prove you wrong, for my sake."

"Meaning?"

"Nico, I think you knew what we had was more than sex, but you clung desperately to that idea. What if you were right?"

"I wasn't."

"You know that because you've been with others. I hadn't." She saw his jaw clench. "I needed to see if better existed." She heard his painful intake of air. "You asked."

"You have a nasty streak. Why does it make me want you?"

Her body came alive at the depth of longing in his voice. Her arms were quick to cover the tightening of her nipples. He reached out and tugged a hand.

"Nico, don't. I don't want this." She didn't resist when he tugged harder to bring her closer.

"Take off your top. I want the same privileges you allowed my son."

The rise and fall of his chest fed the excitement already out of control. She allowed her shirt to drop to the ground.

"Take everything off. I want to see you, need to see you," he groaned, his voice hoarse with desire.

"I suppose you want me to take your clothes off as well?"

He let go of her and attacked his pristine white boxers. His frustration her undoing. His cock sprang free. She had forgotten how beautiful the long hard length could be, especially when blatantly aching to be inside her. She liked him impatient. Slowly she removed her white shorts and white lace panties. She stood naked, letting him look his fill.

"You are so beautiful." His hand reverently circled her breast. His breath hitched. "I don't think I can wait. I need you."

"Nico." His fingers had drifted down, following a path that would let him access what he needed. Her breathing accelerated as he neared his target.

"You're so wet, so ready for me."

He slid his hand upwards to her waist. Intent on drawing her closer, he jerked and then groaned as his arm protested. His pain vibrated through her, seared, branded her.

"We can't. You'll hurt yourself."

"Then make it easier for me. Help me Lia, please. I need this, need you so much."

Gently, she eased her way over him, straddling him, lowering herself, foreplay redundant. Nico hissed; she wondered how he could possibly fit inside her. He did, he always did. Her walls tightened around him. His answering pant of pleasure gave Lia pause to ask herself how she had survived so long without him.

"You feel so good."

His husky whisper echoed her own thoughts. He latched on hard to her breast, and she reared up in urgent response to the pleasure and pain of his mouth. Riding his sleek golden body, his good hand holding her captive, she leaned forward to whisper against his ear. "I'm sorry you got hurt."

"What, my body or my ego?" He bit down gently on her nipple, let it go as he met her eyes. "Liar, you're not sorry at all." Another powerful thrust, distracting her briefly but not long enough to miss the rest of his words. "You might be sorry about my arm. You're not sorry about anything else." Placing a soft swift kiss on her mouth, he retrieved the small eager peak.

"Is that so?" She breathed in his scent, the cologne faint, but pleasant. "Kiss me."

He didn't hesitate to trade her nipple for her mouth. The taste of him: how could she have forgotten? *Was he drowning in her nearness, in her smell, the way she was in his?* Trembling limbs spoke a depth of need. *Was it his body or hers that shook and burned?*

"*Dio,*" he moaned in Italian. "Lia, I'm so sorry. I can't hold back."

Nico didn't stir when she rose to search the jacket she had hung in her wardrobe. She found what she wanted, grabbed a robe, and quietly left the room, stopping momentarily to make herself a cup of tea. *Well*, she thought as she sat down in the small porch area outside the front door, *Robert had been right about marking me.* The wet streaks running down her legs proved it.

Lia pulled a cigarette from the packet she had confiscated. Three were missing but that meant nothing. He could have had the packet for a year or three months. Smoking was a challenge against addiction for him and not about the cigarettes themselves. *Such a puzzle. The man was a puzzle.* She lit one, took a drag and coughed. *It tastes so shitty. How did people do this long enough to get addicted?* The comfort of habit could become dangerous, she speculated. *No wonder Nico enjoyed the challenge. Nico. Nico who had surprised her.* The moment when he had let himself go, she'd known he hadn't been with anyone else since she'd left.

Her throat welcomed the sweet honey taste of her tea. Tonight, the facing garden had a moonlit glow that blended pleasantly with the aroma of mixed herbs in the air. Lia shook her head, desperate to clear her mind. Nico confounded her. He hadn't got rid of her because he didn't want her; he got rid of her precisely because he did want her. *What do you do with a man like that?* She took another drag, spluttered, and stubbed the offending object in the pot beside her. The small amount of smoke she retained, she let out slowly in time to the flow of her memories.

Chapter 41

The truth had always been there. Taking on the blame had shunted the memory into a padlocked box. Of course, Lia had not wanted to remember the events. She's been a child, a confused little child. The ingrained graphics needed only a brief nudge to unlock a rusty padlock. Mama may have sugar-coated some of the facts; Lia's eyes had borne witness that terrible day.

Mama had opted not to go and instead because she would be at home, would have dinner ready for them. With Uncle Lucio at work, the group narrowed down to Lia, Papa, Aunt Gina, and Domenico. She had been so excited, getting up early to help Aunt Gina make the sweet sugary biscuits that were Lia's favourite. The day out had been perfect until Lia fell over on some rocks, and they ended up at the nearest hospital for stitches, instead of harvesting grapes. Cutting the day short had been disappointing. Lia didn't mind too much because her big cousin Domenico carried her on his back. Papa had said she looked like a monkey.

Lia loved doors, had a strange fascination for them, sketching and drawing. The oddness of her passion, especially when it came to using keys, amused her parents. Lia's pregnant aunt didn't hesitate to hand over hers that day.

At first, Lia had thought Uncle Lucio was hurting Mama. He had her up against the wall, her legs wrapped around him as he pushed her. Mama had been making funny noises. Lia yelled for him to stop. Her aunt let out a shriek and run towards the door. Domenico yelled bad words and Papa froze, a funny look on his face. More loud voices, all of them hurting Lia's ears. Someone screamed. An awful sound with people running and more shouting. Lia crept outside. Her aunt had fallen down the first flight of steps. Blood, lots of it, lay on the ground. Aunt Gina clutched her tummy. Nobody noticed Lia.

"Call an ambulance," her Papa had yelled, as he hovered over Aunt Gina. Mama had gone over to him, but

Lia's Papa had slapped her across the face and Mama had run away, down the stairs. Uncle Lucio bent down to Aunt Gina. Lia thought she heard lots of bad words from her Papa. Lia gulped, scared. She didn't know what to do.

"Go after your wife," Lucio said to Papa. His voice different, hard, made Lia more afraid. Papa went, forgetting Lia. Domenico kept yelling at Uncle Lucio.

"Go wait for the ambulance downstairs," her uncle shouted at Domenico. Lia crept under the alcove of the stairs. She stuck her thumb in her mouth and lay down on the cold floor, crying quietly.

A long, long time later she heard footsteps. She opened her eyes to darkness. Someone leaned down. Scared, she started crying again.

"Hush," a familiar voice told her.

"Nico." Sobbing she held out her arms to him, "I wet myself." With that, she started crying in earnest. He picked her up and carried her inside. "I smell bad." He tried hard, but he pulled a face anyway. She sobbed harder. In the bathroom, he ran water in the bath, threw in a cloth and some soap.

"Can you manage by yourself with your clothes?" She nodded, removing them gingerly. Wet they clung and

she felt such a baby in front of him. He grimaced when she handed them over. "I have to go put these in the laundry and use the phone. Will you be alright?"

He sounded sad so she nodded and climbed into the bath. By the time he returned she had dried herself. She dressed quickly in a t-shirt he'd brought back, a soft one and long enough to be a dress. When he produced a comb and began untangling her hair, she sniffed hard and tried not to cry again.

"Did I do something wrong? Is Aunt Gina hurt? Where's Mama and my Papa? I don't understand." He shook his head, his face distorted, looking about to cry himself. He scrunched down to her level, but any reply went unsaid at the sound of the front door opening. Hearing her father's voice call for her, she went running to him.

"Thank you," Tonio said. Papa was crying as he spoke to Domenico. She hid her head in her Papa's shoulder and put her thumb in her mouth again. She lost track of things then. Vague memories of a plane, of Mama telling her Aunt Gina had lost her baby and hurt her leg and how once home, Papa stopped hugging and

kissing Mama. Lia remembered being afraid to ask question and she remembered being sad.

A breeze had come up, chilly enough to send her back inside. Her fingers reached out and briefly caressed the dark wood of the door. Butterflies and doors still held her captive, the doors for the diversity of materials and for the new worlds that offered on opening, and the butterflies for their wisps of fragility. The vulnerability on Nico's face before he fell asleep reminded her of the sixteen-year-old boy he'd been that day. Nico had been right behind her when Lia had opened the door. They had both been shaped by those events. They simply handled things differently.

Given the rigidness of his nature, he'd seen the events in black and white. Nico had judged the deeds committed: the protagonists deserved no mercy. He'd dismissed the agony of repercussions and regrets. She hadn't. How confusing and painful for him to discover that the straightforward wasn't straightforward at all. His own actions demonstrated the harshness of the lesson.

The urge to pee woke him. In the bathroom he swore softly, hating the handicap of his right arm in bandages. The awkwardness of having to do things left-handed, from finding light switches to lifting toilet seats, irritated him. Trust him to mutilate the wrong arm. That's what happened when you let emotion rule instead of common sense. He padded on bare feet to the open doorway. He laughed softly when she pulled a face at the taste. *Lia and a cigarette? She must have checked his pockets.* The intimate act pleased him.

Her unexpected actions never failed to surprise him. Nico wanted her warmth in his life, had missed it despite not understanding the logic of his need for it. Lia destroyed all his carefully constructed rules about relationships. From the beginning every touch maximised, brought a sense of completeness. No wonder he had fought so hard to deny her power. Fear and longing battled constantly. Silently he withdrew and hoped she wouldn't be long.

Lia had a quick shower, used the bathroom, checked on both her men, one sleeping, one pretending. Grabbing a pillow and a sheet, she lay down on the couch until need overrode common sense and she found herself slipping in behind him.

When her hand slid around his waist, he closed his eyes and settled.

Chapter 42

Nico and Robert were missing. Something about the expression on their faces, struck a suspicious note she couldn't seem to shake. Her instincts already on high alert, hit their peak when Nico walked in unable to hide a limp behind a sheepish Robert.

"Okay, what's going on?"

"Nothing rest, and an ice pack won't cure."

"What the hell does that mean?" Lia folded her arms across her body, not satisfied with Robert's blithe reply.

Both men declined to answer.

"Male bonding sucks. Robert? Why is my husband limping? Someone start talking."

"I had a vasectomy this morning."

"Well, that's my cue to leave. Don't say I didn't warn you." Robert directed his comment to Nico as he edged himself closer to the door.

"Robert? What the hell?"

The door slamming shut testified to a fast getaway. Lia, relieved Antonio napped, stomped behind Nico. Pivoting in front of him, she placed a hand on his chest. "Are you crazy? You make a decision like this without discussing it first?"

"What is it women say: it's my body, my choice?"

The haughtiness in his voice, his sheer arrogance made her want to smack him hard across that superior face. Instead, she mangled the cushion she hadn't been aware of picking up. She threw it at him, enjoying his groan at the effort to dodge it. She felt no sympathy.

"You're an arrogant shit! Don't worry, Robert will hear about it from Laura. Why, Nico, why would you do this?"

"I told you I wouldn't risk a pregnancy. Stupidity the first night, understandable but still stupidity. Abstaining is not up for debate, and I hate condoms. Breast feeding can only do so much and you're at the end of it. I asked Robert for the best option and fixed the problem."

"Without discussion?"

"I made a practical decision. You would have made it an emotional one. Don't blame Robert. He told me to talk to you. Now I'm going to lie down because this is incredibly uncomfortable."

Lia left the room, ending up on the porch where she sat, shaking her head, and clenching and unclenching her fists. The reasoning she comprehended. Marco had stressed the risks. Nico's high-handed attitude she could not and would not tolerate. His propensity to decide things, and not discuss them had the power to undermine their relationship. Lia had an urge to grab him, shake him, rattle the stones passing for brains in his head until they rearranged into something resembling good sense. *Talk. Laura said we needed to talk. Sure, if the arrogant shit would give me the opportunity. God, give me patience. I've waited this long.* She walked back inside, pulled the sweatpants away from his body, inspecting the results of the mornings sojourn. *Ouch, a swollen tragedy.*

"Are you alright?"

"I'm not up to doing what we did last night," he replied in a tired tone. "I did the right thing Lia. I don't want another child."

"That's not the point. It's the way you went about it. You should have discussed it first. What about what I want?"

"I didn't make a spur of the moment decision Lia. It's not a petulant rebellion against condoms.

"You stole my choice away."

"I don't want another child."

It didn't take a genius to work out his anger came as much from pain as having his decisions questioned. The defensive glint in his eyes, she more than suspected, meant he knew he had done the wrong thing in not speaking to her.

"Nico."

"I don't see the problem?"

"Don't you think Antonio was worth it?"

"For fuck's sake. Why would you ask that?" The depth of feeling in his answer left no room for doubt.

"I know it got complicated with us. I'm wondering if that contributed to this decision. Did you need to do it now, in view of the mess you made of your arm? I want to know."

"Lia, wanting you and our child has never been in question. I struggled with the responsibility, the emotional demands the situation called for but it was never about not wanting, at least not the way you mean it."

"Emotional demands are part of life, especially family life. If we go with you, it's important you accept that." She wanted to argue a different point. *Why, she wanted to ask, didn't you talk to me then and now?* She couldn't. It meant backing him into a corner, an emotional one he was nowhere near ready to face.

"No, there's no 'if', Lia. I know what you're saying and despite what you may think or how I act, I am prepared for that."

Then why did you do what you did? "Do you want something to eat?"

He shook his head but the crease in his forehead indicated he knew her thoughts. She eyed him, knuckles transparent with the effort to rein in his temper. Nico had beautiful hands, long and slender without losing masculinity. Hurting, and he was, judging from the taut jaw and the fine sweat along his brow, did not bode well for a serious conversation. Beating up a miserable, one-handed man with balls the size of oranges had little appeal.

"Tell me how it all works," Lia asked, sitting down next to him.

"We keep using condoms until we do the deed a reasonable amount and don't need them anymore." He raised his eyebrow at her. "Simple so it shouldn't be a problem, should it?"

"I don't think we need to worry about condoms or anything else for a while."

"Lose the attitude." Peeved at the lack of sympathy, he scowled.

She raised her brows. "It might help if you lost yours and explained instead of glossing over details." His arrogance niggled, cut inroads into her good intentions to be sympathetic.

"Fine. We need two sperm-free samples, and we throw the condoms away."

"Until then, knock off the grumbling every time the word condom comes up."

"You think you're so funny, don't you? What about some of that, what do you call it? TLC, is that right? Robert said I should ask you for some and an icepack."

Tender Loving Care? I don't think so. She laughed as she headed for Antonio's room. *An ice pack on the other hand, maybe.* She lifted Antonio out of his cot. Their son, who had been entranced with his father from the first meeting, immediately ran out to leap on Nico. Catching Antonio before any damage could be done, he patiently explained Papa wasn't well. On told to fetch some toys, Antonio raced to his room nearly bowling Lia over. She laughed, anger lessening with Nico, when his sorry attempt to ease himself against the bed head resulted in a grimace taking over his whole face.

"You play so well with him."

"Why not? You know how much I like to play."

The hot look he gave her disappeared rapidly when he moved the wrong way. She wrinkled her nose at him, and stayed silent, sure he could work out for himself that she thought it served him right. He did and he scowled to prove it. Antonio's explosion back into the room wiped the look from his face as he fought to both, control the little boy's eagerness, and not reveal his annoyance in case Antonio turned it on himself.

She laughed but then stopped sharply, replacing it with a quizzical stare. "Nico?" Lia hesitated to voice her question. He reacted by eying her warily in much the same manner Antonio did when he'd misbehaved. She stifled a giggle.

"What?"

"You had a tan when you arrived. It's winter in Italy."

"So?"

"So?"

"I had a week to myself before I came to see you." His wariness increased when he caught her narrowed stare.

"I see," she said gently, her tone belied by her belligerent stance.

He looked daggers at her over their son's head, before sighing in resignation. "You want blood?"

"Maybe."

"Alright you can have it. I wasn't sure how it, this, us would go."

"Nice. I can live with that."

"Shut up Lia. You've got your pound of flesh."

Not quite. "Not so tough, are you? You deserve to feel bad."

"I know, Lia."

She nodded, acknowledging both his words, and his need for her to leave it alone.

~

His arrogance in thinking he could decide for them both, still in contention, moved to the back burner. Lia made the decision to trust he would eventually accept that railroading her would only alienate. She belonged to him by choice, and by the way her soul thrived on his nearness. The time to go home drew nearer, dependant on Laura having her baby. She obliged by having a perfect little girl, a blonde, with huge blue eyes and her grandmother's dimple, earning the right to sharing her grandmother's name.

New Year celebrations, with Laura and Robert and other friends, brought sadness and excitement. Time had run out. Nico had extended their time once and Lia knew it couldn't happen again. Tomorrow, at Lucy's baptism, Lia would take on the role of a godparent alongside Nico and Robert's older brother.

Nico had been happy to be asked though he tried to shrug it off. Trips back home to see Robert and Laura would not be a problem.

"I can't believe we're leaving. I'll miss them...so much. I can't imagine their reaction to what I've done, can you?"

His answer, a slide behind her. She put down the tube of hand cream, tilting her head to meet his mouth, not noticing until too late the way his hands on her body had positioned them. The corner of her left eye could see the reflection of their bodies displayed in the wardrobe's mirror doors. Lia swallowed, kept her eyes lowered, her emotions hidden, and carefully began to distance herself. He tightened his hold. She swallowed again. In a typical Nico-smooth movement, he let her go, pushed both straps off her shoulders, forcing the nightgown to the floor, and quickly folded her back in strong arms. She tensed.

"Don't do that!" he whispered, nipping gently at her earlobe, moving down to kiss the favoured spot on her shoulder. The small butterfly tattoo now sported a smaller one beside it, to symbolise their son. His tongue circled the small design, slid up to the juncture of her neck and shoulder. She tensed further. He responded by moving closer, his body imprisoning hers, his presence inescapable.

"I don't like watching us," she said, maintaining an even tone despite the change in her breathing.

"It's not worried you before."

"That was *before*," she said, meeting his gaze in the dressing table mirror. "Now I don't want to see it. I don't want to watch a performance." He increased the pressure of his grip, holding her eyes prisoner when she tried to move away. She pulled harder. Nico loosened his hold enough to slide down her body with one hand and showed no mercy as he plunged two fingers swiftly inside of her. Evading him impossible, she still fought, trying hard to wriggle out of his grasp.

"*Dio, quando sei bella.*" Nico's appreciation of her, spoken in Italian, undid her more than his touch. Sensations poured into her body until she shook with need. No matter how hard she tried, resisting this impossible man - an impossible feat.

"The bed will be more comfortable."

"So considerate but I like it here," he mocked in his rich tenor voice. "These drawers are a perfect height."

"Please, Nico! Please! Not like this, I don't want it like this." Her head and heart were afraid, no matter her willing body.

"What don't you want Lia? Say it."

"Stop it. I don't want to see it."

"Why, Lia? Because you saw me with Francesca? Because you watched with morbid fascination, creating a film reel in that beautiful brain of yours. You think because I didn't physically witness your own little scenario that it's any easier for me, that I can't imagine it, see it?

He thrust in roughly, seating himself fully so his balls slapped her buttocks, the visual unnerving and hypnotic all at once.

"Is this punishment then? Please, let me go. I'm not saying no to the sex, just not here."

"No Lia, it's not punishment and no, I will not let you go, not now or ever. Do you remember our little game, the teacher and the student, your brave suggestion on our honeymoon? I thought our lessons were over. They weren't. They're not. This is one more. I'm in charge and I want you to watch. Look at us, at you and me. This is the way it will be from this moment on. I need you to see it, accept it, I need you to hear me while I can still talk. We're making new memories Lia, for both of us, before we get on that plane and go home."

Her insides tightened around him. His ragged breath spoke volumes, drawing her into a lust driven dimension, one so much more than either of them had bargained for. She couldn't not look at their reflection. She couldn't not watch him, watch him command her body, master it as only he could. Through deliberately narrowed eyelids to thwart his arrogance, Lia surrendered to their new history.

When she relented, smiling at him in the smaller mirror in front of them, the one allowing them to view their coupling, the answering blaze destroyed her ability to stand without help. Together they soared and alone she gloated. No-one else would ever do for him, no-one but her. His hold, firm enough to snap her in two, wouldn't hurt her; he would never hurt her again.

"I think they will be emotional but happy. You made the right decision." Nico said, finally answering her question about Laura and Robert.

Lia shook her head, irked beyond reason that he could regain his equilibrium so easily, until she realised that the closeness of their bodies couldn't hide his trembling limbs, couldn't hide the fact that without a death grip on the beautiful and solid pine chest, he wouldn't be able to stand.

"Fuck you!" she whispered on a sob, totally overcome, knowing he had made his point. They belonged together. Nothing else mattered. *Fuck you to hell* she repeated silently as a token protest. Even as she said the words, she welcomed the fact she would never be free of him again.

"You just did." Smug satisfaction oozed in the quietly spoken words.

"Why do you always have to win?"

"Because I do."

He said it with such firm logic that she gasped, a tiny sound, before sighing as his mouth swooped down to prove his point.

Lia allowed her misgivings to be absorbed in his kiss. For the moment he could have this victory. She had time, all the time in the world. Little wars were exhausting. Saving her energy for important battles might show prudence.

Chapter 43

The day of the Baptism, though tinged with sadness, brought everyone at the ceremony great joy. Smoothing down her white lace dress with the burgundy roses, the one she would leave behind for Laura's pleasure, Lia and Nico assumed their places at the altar.

The celebratory noise had disappeared with their family and guests. The four of them were sitting comfortably, waiting to share the champagne Nico had poured. Something about the demeanour of both Nico and Lia didn't sit well with Laura. Contemplating the minute portion of liquid in her glass, she swirled it around, monitoring the other couple before subtly motioning her head at Robert. He lifted his brows, signifying his own curiosity.

Taking a breath, Lia passed a large envelope each to Robert and Laura. Nico had helped her with the legal side. For Lia's purpose, the difference in the laws of the respective countries hadn't mattered. "Something extra for both of you to share with Lucy."

"But you gave her a present. The bracelet was a lovely gift." Laura's features creased, a sudden anxiety taking hold.

"Like I said, this is extra." Lia sat back down next to Nico on the sofa. He took her hand and squeezed gently.

"Are you fucking crazy?" Robert stared at the documents in his hands.

"What, what's going on?" Laura asked, her hands twisting and rubbing nervously. She hadn't attempted to open her envelope yet.

"She's basically selling us the house." Lia found Robert's stricken face ironic considering how much he and Laura loved the house. Sometimes he reminded her of Marco. She hoped the men would meet one day. No, they would meet.

"I don't understand." Laura's hands were now busy tearing the envelope open, but her eyes were on Lia. "We haven't anywhere near the money for a house, not with the business. We're happy renting here. I love this house."

"Exactly." Lia's interjection silenced Laura.

"Angie, I still don't understand." Laura's blue eyes glittered with unshed tears. She stared at the documents as if they were alive and ready to take a bite. She pulled at the *please sign here* tag. Whatever these papers represented, they were a finality that Laura didn't want.

"We can't let you do this, Lia."

"Do what?" Confused, Laura looked at her husband. "I still don't get it."

"She's sold us the house." Robert had moved from his previous position on the single armchair to sit next to his wife. "We continue paying into the same account. Only now it's a mortgage at a ridiculously small amount of interest. I don't know why...fucking hell Angie...what are you doing?"

"Well, pay me more. I don't care. I want my goddaughter to have a house of her own to enjoy. You both love this place. I'm going to be living thousands of kilometres away. You were planning on buying in the next couple of years anyway. And you were dreading leaving here. So, what are you whinging for?"

"Angie," wailed Laura before bursting into tears. Lia moved swiftly to sit beside her, opening her arms. They held each other for a long time, Lia finally being the one to break the embrace.

"I do expect the apartment to be kept ready for any visits we make. And there will be many." She looked at Nico for confirmation and he nodded.

"Promise you'll visit, promise. You not owning this house scares me. It's too much like an ending. You won't have a reason to visit."

"Don't be silly. Of course, we will, Laura. Nothing is changing. As long as you are here...I...we will always think of this as home."

"It's such a big step. Are you sure, Angie...Lia? We'd be happy to go on living here and paying rent forever if you wanted."

"I know that. I want this for you and Robert and Lucy. It feels right." She reached across, and Nico took her hand. "Believe me, I'm certain. Italy will be home from now on." Lia looked at Nico as she spoke. He squeezed her hand firmly, turned to both Laura and Robert and nodded. When his eyes returned to her, the reassurance she found in his glance said more than words could possibly say.

~

Lia checked on Antonio one more time and lay back in the seat. Travelling business class certainly made a difference. Her hurried, economy trip home two years ago with a newborn had been challenging. She grinned to herself, remembering the look on Laura and Robert's faces when they had finally accepted the house as theirs.

The man sitting the other side of Lia smiled. "Thinking of them, aren't you?"

"Yes."

"Pleased with yourself, aren't you?"

She shrugged trying to be casual. It didn't work. "It was the right thing to do," she replied, blinking away tears and grinning widely at the same time. Despite a smirk at her expression, tell-tale lines appeared on his forehead and his jaw tightened. Highly attuned to him, she reached out and stroked his arm.

Nico didn't like being confined. Even travelling as extensively for work as he did, he couldn't get used to it. Nico suffered the displacement only because he had to. Singapore had given them respite but the next leg of their journey would not be easy. The drifting aromas of airline food had no appeal for him. He'd refused the first meal with barely concealed distaste. The smells and limited space tested his good manners. She'd confidently bet he hadn't eaten anything at all on the flight coming over. She exhaled softly. *This isn't going to be easy, and it's not because we're travelling with a toddler.* She put her hand in his and squeezed, then leaned over and whispered in his ear.

"If I eat something next time they come around?"

"Yes, and only then." She winked, happy to see some of the tension leave him. Sex for him was the answer to everything.

"I guess I can suffer some food. Do you expect reciprocation?"

"Don't be ridiculous! You know I can't keep quiet."

"Fine, but don't say I didn't ask."

"I'm married to a comedian. Don't push your luck, smartarse, or you'll be crying out and it won't be because you're having fun." Nico gave her that look then, the one that melted her insides. She interlaced her fingers with his, laughing quietly when he moved their hands over the interesting thickening in his black jeans.

Chapter 44

"You don't know how happy we are to have you back."

"I've a fair idea," Lia replied, as she accepted the cup of coffee her mother-in-law handed her. Gina looked good. Her charcoal grey hair, longer, beautifully styled in a straight bob, her face fuller, she glowed. "You look wonderful."

Gina blushed. Lia put the delicate white cup down on the table. She ran her hand over the area in front of her, loving the familiar feel of the wood and the texture of the timber's rich brown colouring.

"The apartment looks good. Lucio did a wonderful job repainting. Lucio is doing a wonderful job all around, I would say."

"I never thought to be this happy. It was my fault, you know," Gina said, her voice a hush. "Our marriage happened because of circumstances I forced. I wanted him. There were women before Marissa, not many, I'll grant. I didn't care. I had him so I forgave. After Marissa, I couldn't forgive. When he struggled with Nico's personality, I did nothing to help him. I fed Nico's resentment. Punishment maybe? Still, he stayed."

"Aunt Gina..."

"Your arrival forced us to put the past in perspective. If I had to go through it again to be this happy, I would. But my Nico, he took a long time to accept and even now it's measured."

"He wants your happiness, that's all that counts. Aunt Gina...Gina..." Lia stumbled over what to call her aunt, a topic they hadn't got around to sorting out the first time. Mamma, a possibility but not yet. "Gina, thank you...thank you for not demanding answers. I hated leaving here without explanation when you and Lucio had been so good to me."

"You pushed your way into my heart. Such an endearing little bully, and I thank God for it. Those letters and your determination changed my life. Don't leave us again."

"I'm not going anywhere."

"Gina is good. You can call me Gina...for now." She eyed Lia carefully and continued. "You have other questions, don't you? You still wonder about how quickly I accepted everything with you and Nico?"

"Gina, even Nico and I had trouble accepting the situation. You made it so easy."

"Lia, my son is a difficult man. The Lord knows he was a difficult child. He makes up his mind about things and getting him to shift his ideas is impossible. In his career and studies, that single-mindedness is an asset. Living with him, another story. Angelia, I love my son but I'm not blind to his faults. I've always suspected there may be some underlying reason for his behaviour. It didn't matter to me. He functioned, most of the time on his terms, but he functioned." She gave a small laugh and then her smile lit up the room. "With you though, he 'lives'. When you were gone, he became a shadow. He didn't know where he belonged. He couldn't go back to how things were. He couldn't go forward without you. You centre him."

"Gina," Lia began. But Gina wouldn't be stopped. She took hold of Lia's hands and brought them to her cheeks.

"No, please let me finish. His abilities fool people into seeing confidence. He has it. It doesn't mean he doesn't see he is a puzzle piece, an awkward one. He doesn't fit, and he knows it. He's always known, and it has always made him restless. He learnt to cover it with arrogance, something I'm not sure he will ever lose." Gina gave a small chuckle. "I worried for him, especially with Francesca. I know she had her uses. What?" Gina asked at the face Lia pulled. "Did you think I was stupid? That restlessness had Nico chasing ... what do you call it in English, an edge? Is that right?"

Lia went to speak, but Gina held up a hand.

"Whatever he was looking for, he found some relief on those weekends or nights he spent with Francesca. And to be fair, I think she genuinely accepted him for more than sex. And then you came. Even in the beginning with all the disagreements, I saw it. You challenge him, stir his curiosity and senses. You bring out a more human side, make him feel comfortable with himself, despite or is it in spite of those marks along your neck."

"Gina!"

"What? Again, you think I'm stupid. Please, we're all grownups, or at least I finally am. My point is, Lia, around you Nico has a life, a real one. How could I not accept a relationship which gives him normality? What I do question is what do you get out of this? He's hard work. The sex must be good. He is his father's child."

"I'm going," Lia said, unable to look at her mother-in-law. "I'm not so sure Lucio has been a good influence, after all."

"He has, trust me."

"I'm happy for you and Lucio. As for your question, all I can say is that knowing I can do that for Nico, makes me happy. I've always felt...felt a piece of me had somehow been misplaced. I've never had trouble fitting in. I know that and yet in my own way, I've been restless, not knowing where I belonged. I think I was created for him. Even the times I stood up to him, fought with him, I was on the journey to him. He makes me mad, and he makes me laugh. He is impossible. Yet without him I can't breathe. I can't explain..."

"Then don't! Let's talk about my handsome grandson." Gina punctuated her comments with kisses as she bent down to the little boy whose cheeks were flushed from driving around in his miniature car. Gina pulled him out and into her arms. Antonio lay back against her warm body, content to be cuddled by his Nonna.

"I can leave him with you while I go to the market and to see Silvia?"

"Forever, if you want." Gina replied. "But only as long as you stay close."

"I never meant to hurt you."

"I know. I also know my son and he will never let you go even if he still has a lot to learn. Don't make it easy for him," she said with a wink.

"We call it a work in progress in English."

Gina narrowed her eyes. "You look wonderful today, even more so than usual. I was afraid the cold might make you regret coming back so quickly."

"I don't mind the cold. Everywhere we go is heated."

UNEXPECTED OBSESSION . 472

"No. There is something."

"I think you're biased."

"Maybe."

"Definitely."

"True. But today...you look particularly...I don't know. Glowing?" She went to say more, but Antonio tugged on her skirt. She bent and reached for his hand. "Come, my little darling. Nonna has a new toy for you." Nevertheless, Gina paused and gave her an odd parting look.

Lia bit her lip, puzzled and put out, but uncertain as to the reason. She eyed her coffee and discovered the appeal had vanished. Giving her cup a quick rinse, she picked up her handbag and let herself out of the apartment.

~

Silvia had blossomed under Marco's hands. Lia may have helped by improving her wardrobe and persuading her to cut the unmanageable mess of curls into a red halo, but the rest could be credited to Silvia, thriving under Marco's affection. Silvia's mother beamed at Lia. "My favourite young visitor has finally arrived and looking most beautiful today. Have you done something new?"

The long quizzical look disconcerted Lia. She shook her head, choosing to accept the words at face value. "Thank you. Where is our girl?"

"Come," Cinzia said, pushing on the fancy wheels of her new wheelchair. "My daughter is impatient to show you her new dress. She is excited about the party Andrea is throwing tonight."

"And your dress too, Mamma. She is coming with us," Silvia yelled from inside one of the bedrooms. "You have to help both of us with some make-up hints, please."

Lia laughed. She had created a makeover monster who had managed to snag her man. Two doting women, and Lia had to admit she doted as well, had placed Marco in his own female paradise.

Chapter 45

"I thought you'd decided on the red dress?" Nico perused his wife intently.

"Don't you like this?"

"Black velvet like your hair. I love it enough to want to take it off you, slowly. The red one on the other hand I'd have ripped off already, so perhaps a wise choice."

"You're sick, obsessed."

"And look here, an extra special treat; the stay up stockings with the lacy tops I bought you." Lia slapped away the hand he had insinuated up her leg. He laughed but let her be.

"I bought these."

"With me in mind."

"You think everything is about you. Let me finish this email. And by the way, I'm mad at you. You've been in my pantry again and my side of the office. Things were so much simpler when you did lists in your head. You do realise I can't find anything when you re-arrange things?"

"I was bored. You weren't here to play with."

"You mean man-handle."

"True." He let his hand move up her leg again.

"Not funny, Nico. I have a good mind to banish you to the spare room when we get home tonight." Lia smacked his hand away again.

"No, you won't," he replied sliding his hand up her thigh again. This time he dipped one long finger and smiled smugly at what he found. Withdrawing the slender digit, he sucked it clean.

"You are insatiable and this fixation questionable. Come on or we'll be late." Lia pressed Enter. The computer went back to displaying photos. The one of Laura before Lucy's birth struck a chord. Lia stored the thought away for later and shut the computer down.

Next morning reality hit her hard. The red dress, waisted, had been uncomfortable. She moved closer to the mirror, sliding her dressing gown off her slim shoulders. Lia couldn't see anything out of the ordinary. *Both Gina and Cinzia commenting didn't have to mean something, did it?* Close to panic, she recalled how the smell and taste of coffee didn't sit right lately. *Should I go to the pharmacy*? Without conscious thought, she found herself walking over to the phone, and dialling through to Greg.

Two days later after Greg had rung with the more thorough blood test results, Lia stood in front of that same mirror, berating her stupidity. *That night in Sydney when he'd first arrived.* She glared at her reflection. Three months! *Not a single sick day in all that time.* She hadn't worried about not having a period. They'd been erratic since the car accident.

Nico hadn't commented. Then again, he had filed the details of her cycle and knew it to be irregular, and these days often spent a couple of days away up north, doing work for Andrea. She sat on the bed, tapping her fingers on the white silk. Lia grabbed a handful of fabric and tugged, smoothed it back in place and reached for her phone.

"Silvia," she said, "I need you to do me a favour." These days she and Silvia knew each other well, no preamble necessary.

"Of course, what is it?"

"I need you to make me an appointment to see Marco. As soon as possible. And Silvia, I need you to make it clear he say nothing to Nico about it until he sees me. Nothing."

"Okay but..."

"I will explain, not now though. Today with the appointment if you can, Silvia. It's important."

"Let me check his schedule. I may be able to juggle an appointment for this afternoon. I'll ring you straight back."

"Good. That's good." She hung up. Greg's courier, with a letter and copies of her test results, would arrive shortly, giving her time for a shower and to consider Nico's feelings when he found out. The sinking feeling in her tummy had her shaking her head. This would not be easy on anyone, least of all Marco who would take the brunt of Nico's reactions. Yet, what else could she do, she asked herself.

Four hours later she sat with an unhappy Marco in his surgery.

"I need you to explain it to me again in simple language." She bit down on her lip hard enough to hurt. She licked the metallic tang of blood away.

"Look what can I say? I would have preferred this not happen. Lia, you have one kidney. Your body has had its share of problems. The situation is not ideal, but if we watch the blood pressure and I keep you on a tight schedule of visits, we can do this. Regardless, Nico will go crazy. When it comes to you, he becomes the monkey shit."

"Marco, you mean ape-shit, he goes ape-shit." Lia laughed despite the seriousness of the conversation.

"Monkeys or apes Lia, it's the same thing. He won't accept this; he won't believe you didn't know. To be honest I'm struggling too with how you could have missed something like this."

"Marco, give me a break. I haven't gained weight and I haven't been sick. No other signs, nothing...and Marco, it would not have made a difference. I want the baby."

"Yes. Well, I want you to see Giuseppe again. He knows his job and he knows you. He can keep his eye on the kidney. I want you in my office at the slightest twinge, do you hear me?"

"Yes, yes I do. Marco, can you talk to him?"

"Lia, I love you, but you have to tell him, not someone else. I will talk to him later and try and get him to understand that it won't be a repeat of last time."

He sighed. Rising from his desk, he walked around to where Lia sat and enfolded her hands in his.

"Marco..." She stared down at her feet.

He shook his head and squeezed her fingers. "Lia, I can say those words to him, but he knows just like we do - I can't promise they'll be true. You're fit and so strong-willed, and I will do my best to make sure things go well but I can't promise you or him that things won't go wrong. He'll want you to get rid of this child. He's not rational where you're concerned.

"Marco."

"He's right, Lia."

Reaching up she patted the soft hand on her shoulder, acknowledging Silvia words. "I know." Lia sighed as she stood. She gave Marco a quick nod and picked up her bag. "Let me know about appointments," she said and walked out.

~

The confrontation with Nico had come and gone, an emotional minefield exactly as Marco had predicted. Consequently, Nico had been sleeping at the office for a full week. Lia thought it time to end his childish behaviour. She'd organised with Ivana for Nico to be client free. Heartily sick of his black moods, Ivana had been eager to help. To her credit she didn't question Nico spending his nights at the office. Neither had Gina. Lia could imagine the conversations Gina and Ivana had been having over the last few days. *How much had the dynamic duo deduced?*

Ivana greeted Lia warmly. Wearing a flowing skirt, black boots and a fitted long-sleeved black top, Ivana looked professional and approachable. It bolstered Lia's waning confidence, more so when Ivana enveloped her in an embrace.

"Angelia, he's in a most unpleasant frame of mind."

"Is that code for being an arsehole?"

"You could say that. Is there something I can do to help?"

"It's complicated…." She stopped speaking as her body heated. Nico hugged the doorway to his office.

"Well, this is interesting! What do you want?" The belligerent tone, hardly an auspicious beginning to negotiations.

"I missed you," Lia replied sweetly.

He scowled. "Enough to have come to your senses. Organised the termination?" Nico ignored Ivana's shocked gasp, completely unconcerned at the quick departure it elicited.

"Fuck you!" Not a great opening line if she wanted to reason with him, though his behaviour did make reasoning unlikely. "You had no right to say that in front of Ivana, no right at all. You've upset her and confused her when this is about you and me. You're such an arse, such a spoilt bloody brat, so fuck you. Fuck your whole attitude."

Lia watched the arrogant lift of his eyebrows. She leapt in before he could speak. "I talk, you listen."

"You think so?" He folded his arms across his chest, the tension in every line of his body not dampening his smouldering sex appeal. Today it annoyed her.

"Shut up and grow up in that order. I'm not changing my mind on this. You have two choices."

"Really," he interrupted, sounding casual, sure of himself. "You come here and think you can dictate terms?"

Nico's sanctimonious attitude pushed all her buttons. She walked up to him and shoved at his chest with both hands. He grabbed them. Nico drew her close, powerful, and overwhelming. Lia's heart accelerated. He hated their being apart as much as she did. Lia leaned, her body swaying towards him automatically. Catching herself, she stepped back from his physical pull.

"Am I making you nervous?"

"It seems to me, it might be the other way around, if that bulge in your pants is anything to go by," Lia replied, choosing to convert his innuendo to her advantage.

"I'm not the one who stepped back."

"You have two options, two. Choose carefully." Holding up two fingers, she ignored the sullen, incensed face. "You can come home and accept the situation, or you can keep sulking. I know the risks. Marco and I have got them under control. I want to share this with you. If you choose not to come home, I will never forgive you. I will walk away. You will lose me. Not the way that insane imagination has pictured it happening, but you will lose me. Listen and listen well. I intend to have her. It's too late, in any case."

He recoiled. Her use of the word *her*, infuriated him. It gave the baby credence, reinforcing the reality this child had for Lia, outweighing Nico, his thoughts, and their life together. "Not if it's a health risk."

"I am having her."

"I don't matter in this?"

His continued belligerence saddened Lia. "No, you don't because you are not being rational. In your right mind you'd never ask me to have an abortion. For fuck's sake, you know that's true."

He retreated, turned his back. She exhaled loudly, frustrated yet needing to acknowledge his fractured state of mind. "Nico, it will be okay."

"You can't know for certain. You forget you have a child that needs his mother. Maybe I need his mother."

She heard his fear, and her heart broke for him. "Nico. Look at me."

He turned. His beautiful face contorted into a mask of mixed emotion where anger and hurt battled to dominate. Lia couldn't afford to show weakness.

"Believe me," she told him, "I haven't forgotten."

"Then how can you risk what we have?"

"Whatever this is between us...it's worth everything." A hand circled her belly. "Do you remember me asking you why you have to win every time...a few days before we left Australia?" She waited. With his memory, he probably knew the exact minute of the day. When he chose not to reply, she continued. "Sometimes Nico, winning and losing are the same thing. It all depends on your point of view. Don't win this one and you'll come out on top. And you know how much you like being on top."

"What's your point, Lia?"

"Winning. Think about it." Walking away, giving him time to think made her sick. It had to be done.

Reaching the doorway, she faced him. "If you choose to come home then it has to be in every sense of the word. You had better be prepared to make up for this week of hell you have put both of us through. Gina and Lucio have Antonio. The first time I want it hard and fast. The second is negotiable. And so you know, understand I mean what I say, I won't be wearing any underwear, like now." Lia hoped the fierce look of urgent desire to possess and consume her, the last thing she saw as she left, would soon have him home where he belonged.

~

As he heard the lift signal its arrival and the door open to swallow her, he picked up the file he'd been working on and threw it across the room. He used his fist to sweep his desk clean, enjoying the sound of broken glass. Nico didn't know what he hated most: her for making him feel so helpless, or her for being right. Either way he hated her as much as it was possible to hate the air you breathe. He couldn't let her do this alone, and he wasn't finished with her, never would be. Fuck, he hated his inability to explain this continuing consuming desire for her.

Five nights away from her had been torture. He felt a terrible urge to crush her into submission. In their sexual relationship, the balance of power sat perfectly in his corner. When it came to everyday living, he hated her ability to stand firm. Like now, choosing the unborn, unknown child above what they had between them. It enraged him whilst conversely forcing him to admire her steely and independent thinking. How could he crush what drew him and held him prisoner? He wondered if some would consider him a monster for the way he felt about his own child. Of course, they would, Nico decided. Footsteps sounded in the outer office. Ivana had returned. Nico pressed the intercom. She would clean up and not ask questions no matter how curious. She knew better.

~

He let himself in. Ravenous, the aromas filling the air made him salivate. Food this last week hadn't been a priority. She didn't move from her position at the sink. Other than turning the tap off, Lia held perfectly still. He had to decide the first move.

"How can you be so sure things will go well?"

She leaned back into his warmth. "I was unlucky last time. This time is different. I know it."

"I've missed you. *Senza di te, mi manca il sole.*"

Without you, there is no sun. Her smile at his words reflected in the window, small but enough to ease the ache in his chest. "Why is it we never speak in Italian? It's so damn sexy." She rubbed her head under his chin in a soft, soothing motion.

"In the beginning it was a way to make you feel you didn't belong here. Now, I suspect it's because hearing you say *fuck me* in your language is so much sexier than saying it in mine." He licked and nibbled at the corner of her ear; she shivered deliciously for him.

"Well, in that case why don't you stop talking?"

"That's right. You had specific instructions as to what should happen. I'm worried about this addiction to my body. I'm not sure it's healthy or seemly in a respectable married pregnant woman." He slid one hand down the fabric of her dress and then underneath. "No underwear."

"I did tell you."

Nico's answer was to swing her into his arms and carry her to their bedroom.

She laughed as he dragged the hem of her dress up to her waist. Here with her, he knew exactly what to do. Her slickness housed the erection that had plagued him since she had left his office. Her arms housed his being.

Lia dug her nails into his back, tightening her hold by locking her legs around his waist. Her hands tightened as she tugged herself away to look at him. "Do you know how much I love this, you and me?" Slowly, she eased one hand into his hair and pulled hard enough to hurt but not enough to stop his thrusts, the thrusts she met with equal abandon. "It won't be enough, nothing will be, if you keep trying to force me into doing what you think is right."

"Lia." Her name came out muffled. Two thrusts and he exploded, sending her into convulsions. He lost his hold on reality with her. Some food would revive him and then they had the whole night. There were toys he had been obsessing over this past week that fit his mood nicely, and in this, he had confidence he could persuade her to agree with him.

Chapter 46

She moaned. Eyelashes fluttered, desperate to lift open. "Nico?"

"I'm here." He said, squeezing the hand he held.

"Did I fall asleep again? It's dark outside. The baby, where is she?"

"Hush." He brought the hand he held to his mouth. "Everything is fine, she's in the nursery. You needed the rest. Apparently, not sleeping for two nights can do that." She had the grace to blush, he noted. Lia had managed to create a ruckus in the labour ward, if only momentarily.

"I remember holding her, feeding her. I handed her to you and then I had to close my eyes. Oh, Marco lost the plot, didn't he?"

"I thought, Marco thought...for that brief second..." Nico's eyelids chose the opposite of her and drifted down to hide his thoughts.

"I'm sorry. The pains were so slight, and I knew you'd be back the next day."

"Lia, did you honestly believe you could orchestrate her birth to suit you?"

"I knew the importance of the conference. I didn't want to make a fuss. It honestly didn't seem that bad. And then I got scared Nico. I...I... We hadn't discussed you coming in with me. I knew how you felt about it, but I knew I couldn't do it without you. I couldn't have the conversation on the phone. I thought if I could wait till you got back maybe we could...I don't know. I was stupid."

"Your blood pressure agreed."

"Don't be mad at me."

"Lia," he tried to keep the censure out of his voice. She slid her teeth over the plump bottom lip and his heart melted. "You're right. We should have discussed things, and over the phone would not have been a good idea. This getting here at the last-minute precipitated things. I couldn't let you go in without me. Did your devious little mind plan it?"

Lia gave a small nervous laugh. "What, you think I've picked up your predilection for control? I'm not sure living with you works that way, at least not with labour."

"I wouldn't put it past you." At her pout he grinned, then quickly re-arranged his features to a serious note. "I was here. I wouldn't have missed it for the world."

"Really?"

"Really. She's beautiful. Just don't get smug because it all went the way you said it would. Go back to sleep. You're exhausted." He settled back into the armchair at her bedside, keeping hold of her hand.

"You need to go home. You look as tired as I feel, and it was messy. Your mind needs to deal with that."

"Well," he quipped, "my tongue and tender bits may never recover from the trauma. They certainly were privy to more than they needed to know. It may take some time to forget. Five weeks I think, should cover it. Less if we're lucky."

"Nico," she squealed his name. "That's gross and kind of sweet at the same time."

"Exactly."

She poked what he considered her delicious little tongue at him and giggled. "You know, you weren't exactly a pretty sight after the vasectomy, and I didn't complain."

'True, but somehow it's not the same thing. Now, go to sleep. All this talk of body parts is making me horny."

"You sound like Robert."

"Horny and Robert aren't exactly words I want to hear in the same conversation from my wife."

"Go home! And I hope you were kidding about the horny."

"No to the first thing and yes to the other. I can sleep in the chair. I don't want to leave you yet." The last bit came out sharp, his anger darting through despite his best intentions. He rose to his feet and strode to the window, afraid to share his emotions. For a brief instance, Nico had thought fate cruel enough to repeat the past without his having a chance to tell her so much. He didn't know how to, was afraid to.

"Nico! I'm so sorry," she whispered.

Returning to her bedside he placed his hand against her cheek. She breathed him in, the familiar gesture melting some of the ice in his heart. "Don't worry about anything except getting well and coming home." He bent to kiss her mouth. "You'll need your strength to handle Marco. He may never forgive you for scaring him."

"Poor Marco! I heard some of the things he said. He's had a rough trot with us."

"Rough trot. An Australianism?"

"Maybe. I'm not sure."

"He was wonderful. It gave me a whole new perspective."

"Yes. He was." She gave a small yawn, tired but needing to speak. "Nico...I had to have her."

"I know."

"Do you? You have some convoluted perception I chose the baby over us. She is us, part of you and me. I had to give that a chance."

"I know that. I comprehended the moment she was born, the look on your face. You need to understand, I would choose you every time, including over them." His jaw felt ready to snap but he had to speak up, to say the words. "You though, you can survive without me."

"No, it's not like that."

"This isn't the time and place to discuss it," he said quietly.

"Yes, it is." Lia tugged at his arms to bring him closer, to bring his hand back to the cheek he'd abandoned, wanting desperately for him to see and hear her level of commitment. He went by logic. Things had a sequence of events. She needed to think in those terms in order for him to fully comprehend her logic.

"Lia..."

"Nico, listen to me. The first pregnancy, an accident because neither one of us stopped to think, right? Nico, we then did the same thing again. I think it means something. Neither one of us is a careless person. I think...we, all of this, is meant to be. It would be wrong to go against it."

"I'd rather have you. I don't care if that makes me a bad person or that it undermines the meaning of fatherhood. I can't breathe without you. It doesn't mean I don't love them."

"I know, Nico, I know. I know you love them. I know this," she said softly, gently as if he were a difficult child, "the same way I know...you love me. The problem has been you didn't want to know it."

"You see so much, know so much."

"I know."

"Shut up, Lia."

"You're lucky that doesn't offend me." She gave a pout but couldn't prevent a tear escaping.

He wiped it away, his fingers trailing a path down the smoothness of her skin. Nico loved the contrast of dark hair and alabaster white. "Lia?"

At his tone she cocked her head to one side, considering him with a steadfast look. Her beautiful big brown eyes stared straight through him and widened with insight. He saw the exact moment she comprehended what he wanted to ask.

"You're not sure how this can last, are you? You don't think it can?"

"Honestly? Realistically? I don't know," Nico said, not bothering to hide his relief at her asking *the question,* at having her say *the words* out loud. "All I know is the strength of what I feel frightens me. But I can't live without you. I don't have the luxury of deciding anymore."

"Nico, it's been going on since I was seven years old. For me, it's already been a long time." Her eyes narrowed, pensive, distant. "You didn't hesitate to pick me up that day. You did wrinkle your aristocratic nose at the smell. You ran a bath for me, found me some clothes, combed my hair."

"You looked like an abandoned kitten." He stroked that same hair as he spoke. "You were such a pest, following me everywhere. I couldn't deny you, despite Marco's teasing. The adoration was hard to resist, still is."

"Shut up, Nico."

He grinned then his face tightened, his tone serious. "That awful day...I wanted to hate you so much. If we hadn't come back early because of you...I don't know. And then, you pre-empted everything by deciding to take the blame. I couldn't let you believe that. It wasn't right for such a little thing to carry such a heavy burden."

"I took the first steps to loving you that day. I think I've been on a voyage to fall the rest of the way ever since." She touched his cheek in wonder. "You are my harbour."

"You were such an annoying child. You're still as aggravating, and it's possible I may be psychologically scarred for life. Not to mention looking dishevelled has become the normal around you." Long fingers tore through his hair while the other hand brushed off imaginary spots of dust.

"Stop it." She gave him an exasperated look and pinched him. He huffed in protest but met her gaze squarely.

"What now?" He looked down at their entwined hands and back up into her face. "Happy ever after?"

"Why don't we choose that option and see where it takes us?"

"Go back to sleep," he whispered. "I'll sit here until you do."

She moved herself further over in the bed. Taking the hint, he took off his shoes and jacket to lie down beside her. A private room offered many privileges, he thought, sliding his arms around her, his chin resting on her shoulder, loving the way they fit. She'd need another butterfly tattoo, a pink one for their daughter to sit beside the tiny blue one representing their son.

"Come back early," she whispered back.

"Dream about butterflies, don't...."

"Chase them," she replied softly. "I know. You told me that during labour."

"Jesus Lia, bringing up butterflies wasn't your finest moment."

"I wanted to tell you how pretty they were, so many of them every time I closed my eyes. I think Mama sent them."

"Yes, well if you want butterflies, I will take you to the butterfly garden but until then, can we not discuss them. Go to sleep."

"Not yet but soon. She's beautiful, isn't she? All that hair and those eyes, beautiful."

"Yes, Marissa is very beautiful."

"Nico!" Lia went still, her indrawn breath, the only sound in the room.

He could imagine the look on her face, the emotion at his words. No, he thought, not just imagine. He could feel what she felt. *Soul kissed.* The expression Marco had used so long ago now made perfect sense.

His fingers itched to take hold of the delicate chin and look into her eyes. He wouldn't survive that amount of emotion.

Loving such a complicated man would never be an easy feat. She smiled in the dark, tightened her hold on the hand she had over his, her body pliant against his, and kept silent.

The words *'I love you'* could be said in many ways. Calling their baby Marissa, he hoped qualified for the moment. The rest would come. Nico closed his eyes.

The end

Coming soon

Please stay with me for a brief introduction to Lexi and Ricardo, characters taking centre stage in Book 2, **Unexpected Passion** and to Julieann and James in Book 3, **Unexpected Celebrations.** These are only brief teasers, but I hope they are enough to have you come back and see me. I am hoping for a Christmas 2021 release or at the very least Valentine's Day 2022 for **Passion** and June 2022 for **Celebrations**.

Like **Unexpected Obsession**, these novels will be stand-alone. However, Lia and Nico 's continuing story will weave through it. I love continuity and my characters are all great friends who eventually become family. Sometimes families are more than bloodlines.

Unexpected Passion: Love can happen at any age as Lexi in Unexpected Passion finds out, but does it have a bumpy road and a happy ending? Have a look at what she's up against from her first meeting from her point of view and his.

--it was her holiday and she wanted to be comfortable...and screw just about everyone else she knew.

--God knows what she will turn up in considering what she wore travelling. A track suit, a navy-blue track suit with sports shoes, really?

--He didn't say anything. Payback for the length of time it took her to answer his simple question, perhaps, Lexi wondered. *Damn it, why wasn't he saying something. "Bloody shrivelled penis head," said her inside voice.* "Ricardo, what a pleasure to meet you." Said Lexi in her best outside voice

--You...stupid...demented, idiotic woman.

--You're not what I want. You're too emotional.

--Each time his lips parted a little more, his breath asked, demanded her acquiesce. When he finally surged fully, arms, mouth, body, Lexi couldn't deny him the passion, or the power to submerge every ounce of her common sense.

Unexpected Celebrations: They fell in love in kindergarten. Distance changed everything. They reconnected but life got in the way. Can it be third time lucky thanks to some unexpected matchmaking, or will Julie let the past and her insecurities, get in the way of real love? Have a look at my notes and see what you think.

--Taking a deep breath, Julieann reminded herself she would do anything for Lexi. If the part she would play put her in a precarious position she would handle it, or so she told herself. *Bloody Lia is an unstoppable force and not above manipulation.* Part of her wanted someone to take control. She couldn't do it for herself. Her fear, stronger than her desires would always win.

--Lia takes one situation, and an awesome one at that, and manages to create just the scenario I have been praying for. Bless her little heart. Julieann won't be happy when she figures it out if she hasn't already. --Too bad. This is one-time perseverance will win the day and the girl. Jules, I'm coming for you.

--Ten minutes later Nico walked back out to find no coffee and his wife crying in another man's embrace. "What the fuck is going on? What did you do to Lia?"

From the Author

If you have read this far then you have finished reading my freshly edited copy of **Unexpected Obsession**, the first book in my **Unexpected Love** series. Thank you so much. It's been a long journey of rewrites as I learn a craft bent on making unreasonable demands on my time and energy. I first published this in 2016 and I had so much yet to learn. The second book in the series **Unexpected Passion** is almost ready, but I wanted a better version of this first book before my Lexi joins the fictional world I have created.

Have I given you a better version? I hope so but I can only know what you tell me. I can only improve by your feedback. With your reviews I can improve my skills so that I can give you the best experience possible. Would you please consider leaving a review?

Just a few brief words and a rating left at Amazon and Goodreads (a wonderful free website connecting readers and writers) can truly make a difference. It guarantees me feedback so I can improve and financial solvency so I can keep going in this writing journey.

Rather than have a newsletter I have chosen to keep my blog and will post my book news at the bottom of my blogs under the *News* section. I love blogging and try to introduce new writers and books and all sorts of things that may interest you so please sign up to my Amorina Rose's blog at my official website: www.brstrickland.com

Feel free to contact me at: barb@brstrickland.com or follow me at:
Amazon.com
Goodreads
Facebook
Twitter
Pinterest
Instagram

Barbara Strickland
October 2021

About the author

I'm an Aussie with an Italian heritage. The warmth and beauty of both cultures has always inspired me, and I thought mixing it all together and adding a few other cultures in my books would be fun. I grew up in a multi-cultural environment with a dream to speak as many languages as possible, travel till there was no more to be seen, and own a dog and cat and have space for them both. I have a degree in teaching, three children and some amazing grandchildren and love reading, reading and more reading. Pretty boring? I promise the steamy scenes in my novel will make you reconsider.

Books

Unexpected Obsession (Unexpected - Book 1) Print and eBook

Coming early 2022

Unexpected Passion (Unexpected Love - Book 2)

Coming late 2022

Unexpected Celebrations (Unexpected Love – Book 3)

TBA

Unexpected Desire (Unexpected Love - Book 4)

Unexpected Summer Heat (Unexpected Love - Book 5)

Unexpected Outcomes (Unexpected Love – Book 6)

Green Mists (a science fiction romance)

The Narrow Hallway

Memories of the Heart (memoirs with a twist)

Lance finds Home (a children's book)

Other Books: Poetry (Both in eBooks and print copies)

Emotions in Eruption (A Journey in Prose)

Emotions in Evolution (A Journey in Prose)

Emotions in Existence (A Journey in Prose)

The Emotions Anthology Box Set